SUPERNATURAL
DETECTIVES

2

SUPERNATURAL DETECTIVES

2

AYLMER VANCE

Alice and Claude Askew

THE METHODS OF MORRIS KLAW

Sax Rohmer

COACHWHIP PUBLICATIONS

Landisville, Pennsylvania

Supernatural Detectives 2: Aylmer Vance / Morris Klaw
Copyright © 2011 Coachwhip Publications
No claims made on public domain material.

The Aylmer Vance stories were written by Alice and Claude Askew, and first
    published in *The Weekly Tale-Teller* in 1914.
The Morris Klaw stories were written by Sax Rohmer, and first published
    1913-1914.

ISBN 1-61646-092-X
ISBN-13 978-1-61646-092-1

Front cover: Lunar Eclipse © Shane Partridge

CoachwhipBooks.com

AYLMER VANCE

The Methods of Morris Klaw

Aylmer Vance

THE INVADER

"What a wonderful moonlight night!" The words broke slowly from Aylmer Vance's lips, then he turned and looked at me strangely.

We were fellow-guests at the same little inn in Surrey, and we had just made our way out of the hot, stuffy parlour into a cool and perfumed garden.

"Does the moonlight ever affect you?" Vance asked. "Does a night like this fill you with vague longings? Do you yearn to discover the secret of the universe—to know more than is good for man to know—perhaps to peer into the future?"

I nodded.

"Yes," I answered slowly, then I turned to my companion. "You have made a pretty deep study of spiritual phenomena, haven't you, Vance? I wish you would tell me something about the various experiences that have befallen you during the years you have been investigating on behalf of the 'Ghost Circle'."

Vance shook his head. "No, no," he answered hurriedly. "You wouldn't really be interested, Dexter. You are a level-headed barrister, my friend. You don't believe in spooks."

"You're wrong there," I retorted. "The subject interests me profoundly, and tonight is just the night for a ghost story. There's a white, witching moon in the heavens—the pine trees look weird in the distance—and hark how the wind is sighing amongst their branches!"

Aylmer Vance smiled. He was a curious-looking man, tall and lean in build, with a pale but distinctly interesting face. His eyes were a bright blue, very sharp and keen, and he had long thin hands. There was a certain hardness about him—a chill austerity—but his voice, in strange contrast to his manner, was rich and flexible, and I had already fallen under the spell of his arresting personality.

We had first met at a dinner party in London about two months ago—a men's dinner—and I had been very interested in Aylmer Vance at the time. He had been pointed out to me as a ghost-seer. I had been told that ghost-hunting was his cult. And now, as luck would have it, we had tumbled across each other again, for we were both staying at the same little inn in Surrey. I had come down that day for some pike fishing, but I could not make out what had induced Aylmer Vance to spend a week at the Magpie Inn. But there he was, anyway.

We had recognised each other, dined by mutual consent at the same little round table, and now as we stood in the garden smoking our cigarettes I hoped that our acquaintance would end by developing into a friendship—a real friendship. But I had been told that Vance rarely made friends—that he lived a very solitary and self-contained life. He was quite well-off, and owned an old Georgian house situated somewhere in Essex, but he was not often in England. He was a great traveller—a born wanderer—and, needless to say, a bachelor.

"If you're really interested I don't mind telling you about three or four strange experiences that have befallen me during the years I have devoted to the investigation of spiritual phenomena."

Aylmer Vance threw away his cigarette as he spoke. A queer look came over his face.

"I have certainly had some amazing adventures," he continued. "I have come across all sorts and conditions of men. I have been the means of detecting several instances of fraud and imposition on the part of so-called 'mediums'—also of proving that natural causes are often responsible for the 'haunting' that is supposed to go on in various houses. But I must admit that I have been absolutely baffled once or twice—unable to account for what I have seen with my own eyes, heard with my own ears."

Vance paused and put a long thin hand upon my arm.

"Let us go and sit in the summer-house at the end of the garden, and I will tell you what happened about six years ago to two dear friends of mine—Annie Sinclair and her husband—for never have I been more impressed than by the Sinclair tragedy. In fact, it was the Sinclair affair that first induced me to take an interest in psychical research. The whole episode was so wrapped in mystery that even now I cannot explain it to myself. I am still in the dark as to what actually occurred."

A curious, very intent note stole in Aylmer Vance's voice as he said the last words. A faraway look came into his eyes.

"Yes, I will tell you what happened to the Sinclairs," he repeated. "My story will certainly prove to you, if it proves nothing else, how dangerous it is to meddle with forces of which we know little."

Still keeping his hand on my shoulder, he led me in the direction of the summer-house, which stood just at the bottom of the garden, and I remember how pungent the scent of the pines was—how overpoweringly pungent—and the wind made a queer rustling and sobbing amongst the branches of the pine trees—a low, monotonous moaning.

We settled ourselves down in the summer-house and I lit a cigarette. The moonlight was particularly brilliant that evening, I remember. It illuminated the whole garden. But the pine woods looked strangely blurred and black in the distance, and I felt rather eerie. Still I wished my companion would begin his story. I was sure it would be worth listening to.

"George Sinclair was my greatest friend when we were up at Oxford together," Vance began, "and after we left Magdalen we kept up our friendship, seeing each other constantly. Then I went abroad for two or three years. When I came back to England George had a great piece of news for me. He had just got engaged to be married to a Scotch girl. Her name was Annie Riddell.

"I went up to Scotland for the wedding. In fact, I was George's best man, and I'm bound to confess that I envied him his bride, for Annie looked a young goddess on her wedding day. She was tall and fair—rather a large woman, with a beautiful placid face and very sweet blue eyes; there was immense repose about her. George was just the opposite—very restless and excitable, dark, thin, and rather undersized; but they were crazily in love with each other, these two—as much in love as any man and woman could be, I think, and when I went to stay with them about six months later at George's place down in Wiltshire it was really delightful—in these days of matrimonial discontent—to see how fond a man and his wife could be of each other; not but what Annie gave away a little too much to George, I thought. She hardly appeared to have a will of her own—whatever he said was her law; but then George, for his part, was absolutely devoted to Annie. He thought her the most beautiful and perfect creature on God's earth—he worshipped her openly all day long, and Annie accepted her husband's homage with a bland serenity. If she hadn't been so beautiful I expect I should have thought her a dull woman, for she certainly lacked ideas, but she was so good to look at that one really hardly wanted to maintain a long conversation with her; you could stare at Annie for hours just as you could stare at a beautiful picture, and with the same pleasure."

Vance paused for a minute. He seemed to be looking right into the pine wood, then he suddenly turned to me with one of his quick movements.

"Yes, they were intensely happy, those two, for the first three or four years of their married life—extraordinarily happy—but they began to be a bit disappointed by-and-by when no babies came—not that it made any difference to their love for each other. Their mutual sorrow knit them more closely together, if anything; but George, having no children to interest himself in, took it into his head to go in for occult research.

"The subject had always fascinated him, even from his boyhood, and then one day, as ill-luck would have it, George's attention was directed to the fact that he had a barrow on his property, by an archaeological friend of his who happened to be staying with the Sinclairs at Grey Towers. You know what I mean by a barrow, don't you?—one of those old British burial places of which there are still a few to be found in England.

"Well, George, egged on by his friend, started to dig up the barrow, and his efforts were rewarded, for he found two heavy gold armlets in it, and you cannot imagine how excited George got over this find. He had a theory that these armlets had belonged to some Druid priestess, and he took them to a medium, who spun him no end of a yarn about the woman who had once worn them; but she wasn't a priestess at all, the medium declared; she was a British princess, a very beautiful but jealous, black-hearted woman who had had a strange love affair and had been murdered by her lover.

"George drank in this yarn eagerly, and then what must the silly fool of a medium do but tell him that he possessed occult powers himself, and that Annie—who, needless to say, had always accompanied George on his visits to the medium—beautiful, quiet, meditative Annie, would make a very fine trance subject.

"Of course George, on hearing this, determined to exert his gifts, and Annie, who had always been like wax in his hands since the day of their marriage, went off obligingly enough into trances whenever he wanted her to. I don't think she was at all interested herself in occult subjects—at least not at the start, though she pretended to take an interest in them for George's sake, but she soon got frightened. She realised, being a sensible woman, that a certain amount of danger must always attend occult studies.

"Besides, she didn't like to feel—at least so she told me one day—that the spirits of dead men and dead women were talking through her to George, for Annie honestly believed that when she went off into one of her queer trances, she really became the vehicle of communication between the quick and the dead. She never doubted her own powers in that respect, but she was afraid of them.

"The whole thing began to prey on her after a time—to get upon her nerves, but George couldn't see this—or wouldn't see it. Evening after evening he insisted on putting Annie into a trance—he was never tired of experimenting with her. He didn't seem to realise that these experiments might have a disastrous effect upon his wife's health—that it might shatter Annie's entire system. He believed that in time the secrets of the other world would be revealed through her instrumentality—that a link would at last be established between the spirit world and our world."

Vance paused. He threw away his cigarette—he drew a deep breath.

"Mark you, I don't blame George very much. He was an explorer into realms unknown, and, just like any other explorer, he was ready to sacrifice even his nearest and dearest, and I believe Annie's trances were quite genuine. I don't think for one instant she could have invented the things she said; besides, she wasn't that sort of woman—neither was she an hysterical subject."

"So you think these trances were genuine?" I remarked.

"I do," Vance replied. He bent forward and frowned and, frowned; I thought how pale his face looked in the moonlight—how ghastly white. I noticed how tightly his hands were clenched; it was evident that the relating of this tale caused him deep emotion. "I must own that I became profoundly interested myself in Annie's strange trances after a time, especially when the spirit of the British princess to whom the gold armlets found in the barrow had originally belonged began to take possession of Annie when she went off into her trances and talk through her mouth—and a mighty lot the princess had to say, too—queer, strange talk.

"She told us that she regretted most passionately that she was dead—that she longed to be alive again, walking the earth. She admitted that she was one of those restless, tormented spirits who, in psychical parlance, are known as 'earth-bound spirits'—that all her desires were material, and she told George with brazen effrontery later on that she had fallen in love with him and that she would like to remain in possession of his wife's body—in fact, to take Annie's place in his life, and her language was plain and unvarnished, I can assure you—distinctly primitive. It gave me quite a shock to hear such words proceeding from Annie's lips, unconscious though she was, poor girl, of what the spirit who possessed her body for the time being was saying."

Vance stirred in his seat—his lips twitched. He looked paler than I had thought it possible for a man to be.

"After the second or third séance, absorbing and interesting though they were, I got a bit uneasy in my mind. The whole thing struck me as horrible—repulsive, this dead woman invoking George in the most passionate language and having the audacity to suggest that she should try and keep Annie's gentle spirit out of its own tenement—continue to inhabit Annie's body. I said as much to George. I told him that I thought the séances had better stop, but he wouldn't listen to me; he was far too interested—far too keen on continuing his experiments.

"A fortnight later Annie spoke to him herself, however, and declined to go into any more trances. She declared that it had been a difficult matter to eject the princess's spirit after the last séance— that quite a fight had taken place between her own soul and the dead woman's soul, and that she was unwilling to run the risk of such a conflict again.

"'I assure you, George, I feel quite frightened,' Annie exclaimed, 'I am convinced that the princess wants to get possession of me. She'd like to live again in my body, and she's so strong—she's so frightfully strong—that it's difficult to drive her away after the trance is over—when I want to wake up—when you tell me to wake up.'

"George laughed at this. He thought Annie was talking very foolishly, but he was seriously annoyed with her all the same for wanting to stop the séances—he insisted that they should continue—he was absolutely determined to proceed with his investigations.

"Well, Annie held out for a longtime, but she gave way in the end. She was the sweetest woman on earth, I think, and though she made no secret of the fact that she simply loathed being put into a trance, George only laughed at her and finally got her to sit again, but Annie kept saying she would only sit once more. I don't know whether George believed that she would stick to her word, but anyway he asked me to go down to Grey Towers to be present at this last séance, but I couldn't go, so those two were just left to themselves and George's devil tricks."

Vance rose abruptly to his feet. He looked very lean and haggard; the Sinclair tragedy seemed to have become his tragedy as
well.

"Even now, after all these years, Dexter, I turn sick when I think
of what happened down at Grey Towers. You see, I heard all about
it afterwards—from George."

Vance walked to the summer-house door. His thin face worked
painfully. He kept clenching and unclenching his hands.

"They sat on a Saturday night that is what George told me, for
I had the whole story later on from his lips. He put Annie into a
trance at once—Annie very nervous and unwilling—and after a bit
the British woman came and took possession of her as usual. To
make the connecting link as strong as he could, George had insisted that Annie should wear the gold bracelets dug up from the
barrow, and so with these heavy links upon her arms, these relics
from a barbarous past, Annie sat in her husband's study, a passive
agent to what happened; but she repeated before the séance began
what she had already said before. She told George that this would
be the last time she would ever allow him to put her into a trance—
that the coming back into her body was so difficult. She said just
before she went off that she really would not sit again—that he
mustn't ask her to, and that speech may have precipitated matters, of course, for I bet you the British woman knew that Annie
meant what she said, and so she was aware that she would never
again have the chance of speaking through Annie's lips—clothing
her naked soul in Annie's body, and she determined to pit her
strength against Annie's—to fight for what she wanted."

"But what happened?" I interrupted eagerly. "Did Mrs. Sinclair
find some difficulty in getting out of her trance? Did her heart fail
suddenly—did she die that night?"

"I wish she had—I wish to God she had," Vance answered bitterly. "But worse—far worse—befell Annie. The British she-devil
having taken complete possession of Annie's body absolutely refused to budge, for when George endeavoured to wake Annie up
from her trance another woman—a passionate, primitive woman—

stared at him out of his wife's eyes, and he knew that what Annie had feared had come to pass. A new tenant had taken up its habitation in her body—a tenant who refused to quit. There, Dexter, can you imagine a more grim and terrible situation; can you?

Vance turned to me and put a hand upon my arm. I could feel how his fingers shook.

"I don't suppose you believe my story—it sounds pretty incredible—I don't think I believe it myself; but George swore to me that he knew Annie's gentle loving spirit couldn't get back into her body—that the British woman wouldn't turn out. Why, he declared that Annie's face changed before his eyes—that a devilish expression came into it, and to add to the sickening horror of the whole scene, the woman who called herself his wife began to make violent love to him—fierce, unrestrained love, and he had to suffer her hot, burning kisses; he couldn't tear himself away from her arms, and presently the woman demanded food and drink and ate ravenously, and then she began to croon and sing to herself, and George swore that he seemed to hear people singing outside the house, answering her—the low murmur of innumerable voices. It was just like a nightmare—an awful nightmare.

"It was hours that night before the woman fell asleep, and she gripped George's hand in her sleep—she held on to him as if she would never let him go, and when she woke up at dawn she began to sing to herself, some queer outlandish chant, and she sang as she brushed her hair, the wonderful pale gold hair that had always been one of Annie's greatest charms, and George, lying in bed, shivered, and lay there shivering and shaking, watching a beautiful woman combing her beautiful hair, but afraid of her—*afraid.*"

Vance hesitated, then he gave a queer hoarse laugh.

"I know what you're thinking. You are telling yourself that in all probability Annie Sinclair had got into a queer mental condition, thanks to all the séances that her husband had been insisting on, and that would account for her changed looks and manner—the singular way she was behaving—and no doubt George was feeling a bit queer and shaky himself—as nervous as a cat—frightened of his crazy wife, the wife who was apparently going off her head. That's the rational view to take of the situation isn't it—the most feasible view?"

"I don't altogether agree with you," I retorted. "We know that there have been several authenticated cases of demoniacal possessions." I hesitated, then added, not looking at Vance as I addressed him, "Did you see Mrs. Sinclair after the—the séance?"

"Yes, I went straight down to Grey Towers on the receipt of an urgent telegram from George, and I felt when I met Annie as though I was meeting a stranger—and a strange woman who was always on her guard, but I dared not admit as much to George. I pretended that there was nothing amiss. Good Lord, man, what else could I do? But I was conscious all the time that some evil spirit had taken up its habitation in Annie's beautiful body—a wicked, baneful spirit—and the leer in Annie's eyes made me feel sick—I could hardly bear to look at her, and such a cruel smile played about her lips. She watched George just as a cat watches a mouse, and her hands were never still—those dreadful restless hands of hers. She walked with a stride, not as Annie used to walk, and her clothes seemed to hang on her awkwardly—Annie's clothes."

Vance sat down again on the seat by my side. He was breathing hard; I could see that little beads of perspiration had broken out on his forehead, and he shivered, for all that it was such a hot evening.

"Wasn't it horrible, Dexter?" he whispered hoarsely. "Wasn't it horrible? You see, George and I were absolutely certain that Annie's body had been possessed by a she-devil, and we knew that Annie's soul—her sweet, gentle, loving soul—was trying its hardest to get back to its earthly habitation, only the intruder wouldn't go, and we both knew that she was trying to come back to us and that she just couldn't; and we were aware—tragically aware—that as so often happens in this world, evil was conquering goodness. But the awful reflection, from George's point of view, was that he had deliberately played into evil's hands—that he himself had brought this terrible thing to pass—that it was *his* work—*his*."

"Good Lord—how ghastly for the poor chap!" I muttered the words low, half under my breath. Listening to Vance it was impossible to disbelieve the story he was telling me—he spoke with such extraordinary conviction; then I leaned forward eagerly. "Go on, Vance what was the end of it all?"

"The end." Vance drew a deep breath. "Well, it wasn't a pretty end, Dexter." He rose to his feet again; he looked absolutely livid in the moonlight. "I stayed at Grey Towers for about a week—I simply couldn't have borne to remain there another day, for that creature—that thing who inhabited Annie's body—was beginning to show herself in her true colours. It was a barbaric woman whom George had for a wife now—a woman who loved cruelty for cruelty's sake. Why, she half killed George's dog one day because the poor brute wouldn't come to her when she called it—and can you wonder? She beat the dog with a stick till George got hold of her by the wrists and dragged her off to her own room, and I don't know what passed between them there—I don't even like to think of it, but I honestly believe that George beat her—beat her as she had beaten the dog, for when she came down she looked cowed. But she killed a bird the next day—Annie's pet canary—walked up to the cage, took the bird out and wrung its neck deliberately, and all because its singing annoyed her. Can you wonder that I came away from Grey Towers that afternoon?—And yet perhaps I ought to have stayed for George's sake—for Annie's."

Vance folded his arms. He drew another deep, half-sobbing breath.

"I heard from George a fortnight later. He told me that things were going from bad to worse—that the woman—for that was how he referred to her—had ridden Annie's favourite mare pretty well to death—that the servants had all given notice at Grey Towers, explaining that they couldn't understand the strange change that had come over their mistress—her ugly ways.

"Then George went on to say in his letter that he intended to put the woman into a trance that night and try and eject the evil spirit out of Annie's body, but I knew, even as I read George's letter—

something seemed to tell me—that the woman would never consent to be put into a trance. She would be too clever for that—too
cunning. And I was right, for two days later I got another letter
from George—a letter in which he explained that the woman refused to sit.

"She was becoming wilder and more barbaric than ever, he
added. A curious atmosphere seemed to hang over Grey Towers—
an atmosphere of evil—and he could bear strange sounds at night.
The whole house seemed to be full of mutterings and rumblings.
There had been a terrible thunderstorm the day before, and the
storm seemed to have broken directly over Grey Towers, and the
woman had stood by the window laughing at the storm. He had
been obliged to send his two dogs away, they kept up such an
incessant howling; and he was left with hardly a servant in the
house. The neighbours seemed to realise that something strange
was happening and stopped calling. He felt forsaken by God and
man."

Vance paused.

"I ought to have gone straight back to Grey Towers on receipt
of that letter, Dexter—hurried to my poor friend at once—but I
didn't—I just didn't. I wrote to George, however, a long letter, and
I suggested that it mightn't be a bad thing if he called in a certain
famous psychic investigator to his aid, who might be able to exor-
cise the evil spirit that had taken up its habitation in Annie's body.
But George wouldn't do this. Perhaps he was shy of making his
story public. Perhaps he hoped to conquer by himself.

"What he did was to remove himself and the woman from Grey
Towers. He rented a little cottage at Dartmoor and he and the
woman went down there by themselves, and then I suppose the
fight began—the long fight between George and the woman—for
you may be certain that day after day—night after night—he tried
his level best to throw her into a trance. But the woman refused to
let herself go—to be conquered—and you can imagine, can you not,
Annie's spirit hovering vaguely in the background—a silent witness of what was going on—an anguished witness.

"They could keep no servants at the cottage. A village woman came in in the morning and did the cleaning and what simple cooking was required. And so the days passed—the long sultry midsummer days—and George ceased to write to me. He left me in the dark as to what was going on."

Vance sank down on his seat again. He covered his face with his hands—those long, thin nervous hands of his.

"I couldn't stand George's silence, not knowing what was happening, and at last I determined to go down to Dartmoor. I wrote to George announcing I was coming, and asked if he could either put me up at the cottage or take a room for me in the village. But George wired back to me and told me not to come.

> YOU CAN DO NO GOOD. (so the telegram ran) No
> ONE CAN DO US ANY GOOD. LEAVE US ALONE, PLEASE.

"So I left them alone. I—I left them alone."

A long silence fell, a silence I dared not break. I could hear the wind shaking and rustling the branches of the pine trees, keeping up a dull moaning. I could smell the sharp pungent scent of the pines.

The moon suddenly went in behind a cloud, and Aylmer Vance and I were alone in the darkness, and I was glad that the moon had hid her face. I did not want to look at Vance at that moment, and I felt sure that he did not want to look at me.

"You wish to hear the end of the story, Dexter?"

"Yes, I do."

"Well, two days after I got that telegram from George I was sitting in the smoking-room of my club, when I suddenly heard some newsboys running down the street, and they were shouting out at the top of their shrill cockney vices: ''Orrible murder at Dartmoor—'orrible murder at Dartmoor', and I knew at once what had happened.

"I went out and bought a paper and I read that a gentleman—a Mr. George Sinclair, who had recently rented a small cottage on

Dartmoor—had murdered his wife the night before—had stuck a knife into her heart as they sat alone in their little cottage parlour, and had blown out his brains a few hours later—shot himself just when the dawn was breaking.

"The romantic part of the murder from the journalistic point of view consisted in the fact that the murderer, after killing his victim, had carried the dead woman's body up to their bedroom, dressed the corpse in a rich white satin gown, combed out her long fair hair, lit any amount of candles, and arranged them round the bed, and had then gone out into the little garden and picked nearly every flower, strewing these flowers over the dead woman, piling them in great scented masses at her feet; and there was no motive for the crime—so the newspapers informed their readers. Oh, they made capital enough, did those newspaper johnnies, out of the Sinclair mystery, I can assure you. They fairly revelled in it for days. And they didn't know—not a clever chap amongst them—that I could have told them the true history of the crime if I had chosen to unlock my lips. But I didn't.

"I went straight down to Dartmoor, however, and I said goodbye to George and I said goodbye to Annie. Lovely and pleasant they had been in their lives till that devil woman came between them, and in their deaths they were not divided.

"They were buried on the same day. The jury, of course, brought in a verdict of 'temporary insanity' in George's case. I wish they could have slept in the same grave, but popular sentiment forbade that. The murderer and his victim couldn't lie together; for the public didn't know that it was not his wife whom George Sinclair had stabbed through the breast on a warm midsummer night—that it was a strange woman, a woman who belonged to the Stone Age."

Vance paused, then gave another of his odd, mirthless laughs. He let his hands drip from his face.

"Queer yarn, mine, isn't it, Dexter—a bit hard to swallow? I don't ask you to believe it—to credit it. George Sinclair and myself may both have been the victims of a terrible delusion. The constant sitting at séances may have effected a deterioration in Annie's character, which we wrongly attributed to demoniacal possession, or of course overwrought nerves would account for the hysterical rages into which she threw herself at times. It is quite on the cards that the Sinclair affair was no case of demoniacal possession. But it was a tragedy for all that, wasn't it—a ghastly tragedy?"

"The most ghastly tragedy," I repeated. The moon came out at that moment, and as I looked at Aylmer Vance our eyes met. I bent forward and laid an impulsive hand upon his arm. "You do believe, don't you?" I whispered hoarsely. "You do believe that the dead woman's spirit—the spirit of the British woman—had got hold of Annie Sinclair's body? You feel as I feel—that George did right when he killed the woman whom the world believed to be Annie Sinclair?"

"I don't know—I can't say," Vance answered. "But I am certain of one thing—that George Sinclair and his wife would be alive to-day if George had not persuaded Annie to go in for those ghastly sittings—if he had left that barrow undisturbed—for it does not do to meddle with the burial places of the primitive dead. It's an unwise proceeding to have anything to do with an earth-bound soul—a soul whose desires are all of the earth, earthy. And Annie knew this, mark you, and felt it. She was wiser in her generation than George, but just because she was sweet and gentle—"

He paused, and did not finish his sentence. But he drew his hand hurriedly across his eyes, and I realised—the knowledge suddenly came to me—that in his own quiet, reserved way Aylmer Vance had loved his friend's wife, the woman who belonged heart and soul to her husband.

We walked out of the summer-house. The pine woods looked as dark and mysterious as ever. I was conscious that Nature guarded innumerable secrets from man—secrets which she was loth to give up.

My grasp tightened on Vance's arm.

"Vance," I whispered, "have you ever seen a ghost with your own eyes—a visitant from the other world?"

"Have I?" Vance smiled—a curious smile. "I will tell you about a little ghost whom I once had the pleasure of meeting, tomorrow night if you feel inclined to stay on at the inn and have another day's pike fishing. Yes, I will tell you where I met Lady Green-Sleeves. And there's nothing tragic about this story, Dexter. It was merely a singular experience—a romantic episode."

THE STRANGER

I reminded Aylmer Vance of his promise to tell me about the little ghost whom he called Lady Green-Sleeves next evening, for, needless to state, I had stayed on at the Magpie Inn for another day's pike fishing; in fact, I had determined to spend a week in Surrey, for I had found out from Vance that he would not be taking his departure before the end of the week, and I wanted to remain as long as he did—to see as much of my new friend as possible.

I had been thinking of the strange story Aylmer Vance had told me the previous evening—the tale of the Sinclair tragedy. The horror of it had got hold of me—haunted me all day long—and now, as we sat in the little parlour of the quaint, old-fashioned inn, I wondered what other weird experiences Vance had gone through.

It was a wet night; no moon lit up the skies this evening, and heavy rain was falling—drenching rain. The weather had suddenly turned much colder—so damp and chilly that our worthy landlady had lit a fire, and I confess that the sight of that crackling fire pleased me. Besides, the parlour smelt rather musty; a fire in the room would do all the good in the world.

Vance drew up a big armchair to the hearth when we entered the parlour after dinner. He held out his hands to the cheerful blaze, a slow smile playing about his thin lips.

"I call this very comfortable," he exclaimed. "Very comfortable indeed. We will send for a bottle of port presently. We will drink

old wine and we will crack old jokes. We will forget that it is rain-
ing and that the wind is howling outside."

"And you will tell me all about Lady Green-Sleeves?" I interrupted. "We will drink a toast to her—a toast to her sweet memory
for I am sure that she was gentle and young and fair."

"Lady Green-Sleeves was small and dark, a little, eager, twinkling flame; but I am not going to tell you about her tonight. We
will leave that for another evening—a warm, star-lit evening. I think
I will tell you Daphne Darrell's story—Daphne Darrell's."

He moved his chair closer to mine—he gazed right into the heart
of the glowing fire. His very voice had changed—it was charged
with a regretful tenderness.

"Yes, I will tell you Daphne Darrell's story tonight, and if it is a
fine evening tomorrow, you shall hear all about little Lady Green-
Sleeves—the dainty ghost I met face to face. I don't mind telling
you my tales, Dexter, for you've a spark of romance in your heart.
You're a dreamer as well as a shrewd barrister; but I wonder what
you will make of Daphne Darrell's story? Anyway, the poetry of it
will appeal to you—it must."

He bent forward. The firelight flickered over his pale, thin face;
he laughed softly to himself.

"The great elemental forces, Dexter—why do we no longer believe in them—the old gods and goddesses—the lost faiths? Either
we are much wiser than our forefathers, or our forefathers were
much wiser than us. But that's a question for the gods to decide—
they who know."

Vance paused—one of those long pauses to which I was getting
accustomed—then he suddenly started and looked up at me.

"I was going to tell you about Daphne Darrell. I happened to
be her guardian. She was the posthumous child of a cousin of mine,
a young fellow who met his death under very tragic circumstances
about six months after his marriage. He and his wife were pioneers
of the open-air movement. They were immensely rich folk, but they
liked to jog about the country in a big caravan during the summer,
and live a sort of gipsy life.

"It was whilst they were on one of these caravan expeditions that the great tragedy happened. Robert Darrell, bathing in the Thames one morning, was suddenly seized with cramp and drowned before his wife's eyes. Poor Lucy Darrell was prostrate with grief at first, for she was absolutely devoted to her husband, but she kept up as bravely as she could for the sake of her unborn child. Nothing would induce her to go back to Darrell Court, however—my cousins had a fine place in Hampshire, I must tell you. She continued her nomad life all that summer, and the baby was actually born in the caravan, the caravan pitched for the night in Savernake Forest.

"Poor Lucy died within a few days of her child's birth, and perhaps it was just as well, for she was a heartbroken woman; but it seemed a little rough on Daphne—for the child, I must explain, was christened Daphne at her mother's request—to have lost both her parents in her infancy. However, an old aunt came forward—one of those dear, sweet, maiden ladies who are always ready to step into the breach in moments of difficulty, and Miss Jane Darrell volunteered to look after her little niece and make her home at Darrell Court. It was a bit of a sacrifice, I can tell you, for the old lady had a charming house in London and a big circle of friends.

"She was a delightful old gentlewoman was Miss Jane, and it was a great pleasure to me to run down to Darrell Court whenever I found myself in England. It interested me greatly to watch my little ward in the various stages of her evolution. She was a very interesting child, strikingly original in her thoughts and ways, but she was the terror of her nurse and governess, for Daphne would never take the least trouble to learn her lessons, and it made her ill to be kept indoors. She would have liked to spend all her time in the woods and the stately park that fenced Darrell Court from the world. She hated indoor life, and Miss Jane gave way to Daphne in everything. She spoilt her niece shamefully; the consequence was that Daphne grew up lovely, but quite uneducated—a wild, woodland creature."

"Was she very lovely?" I leaned back in my chair as I spoke. It was pleasant to sit in this warm, cosy little parlour and listen to the rain pelting outside, and the melancholy howling of the wind—interesting to watch Aylmer Vance as he talked, very interesting.

"Lovely—was Daphne Darrell lovely?" Vance laughed. "Why, at eighteen she was the most beautiful creature that ever trod the earth! She was tall and slim as a young pine tree, with the most wonderful dark blue eyes and any amount of fair hair. Her face was pure Greek; she had a forehead—a brow—that Clytie herself might have envied. She was flawless—perfect; she reminded one of a nymph, so there was some reason for the pride Miss Jane took in her niece. There was no one like Daphne in her eyes, and I can assure you that Miss Jane's opinion was shared by a good many people; for what did it matter if Daphne had never learnt her dates, if her spelling was atrocious, her knowledge of history nil, her French accent hopeless? She made other women in a room look dim when she walked in; she was the living incarnation of youth and strength. She had a clear, beautiful voice, that was not unlike the sound of rippling waters, and her laugh—why, woodland nymphs must have laughed like that when the world was young; our girls have lost the trick of it nowadays.

"She was very fond of me; a curious rapport prevailed between us—a strange comradeship; in fact, years ago—when Daphne was a child of eight or nine—she confided a great secret to me—a secret she had shrunk from telling anyone else, even Miss Jane. She whispered it into my ear one afternoon as we walked up and down the long green terrace walk—the terrace that stretched out in front of Darrell Court. She explained that she was in the habit of meeting someone in the woods—a tall youth, as far as I could make out—and playing with him.

"'I hide behind the bushes, and he runs after me,' Daphne explained; 'but he never catches me—I never let him. He is so tall and graceful, and so strong.'

"'You mustn't play with strangers, Daphne,' I remarked; 'with strange young men. Is this youth a village boy?'

"Daphne shook her head. To this day I can remember the curious smile that played about her lips—the wise smile.

"'A village boy—oh, no!' she answered. 'And yet he is not a stranger; I have known him—'

"She paused, and, did not finish the sentence. A strange look came into her deep blue eyes—a look that puzzled and vaguely alarmed me.

"She would never tell me any more about the youth, except once, when I had taken her up to London to see the Academy. I remember her standing entranced in front of a statue by one of our rising young artists—a statue of the god Apollo.

"'Do you like this statue, Daphne?' I queried.

"The child—for Daphne was little more than a child—turned to me with shining eyes and flaming cheeks.

"'Like it?' she cried. 'Why of course I do; it's so like him.' She paused and laughed—shy, rather conscious laughter. 'I mean like the stranger I meet in the woods sometimes—the stranger I play hide-and-seek with.'

"'You mustn't be so fanciful, Daphne,' I remember saying. 'Of course, this is only a game of make-believe; you don't really meet anyone in the woods.'

"'No, I suppose not,' Daphne admitted. She spoke with a singular reluctance, and we did not refer to the subject again; but three years later, on Daphne's seventeenth birthday, she bought a small marble copy of the famous Apollo Belvedere statue, and put it on a small table in her bedroom, and there was always a vase standing in front of the statue; and the curious thing was that Daphne never put flowers in this vase, but only grass—the freshest, greenest, and juiciest grass she could find.

"By the time Daphne was nineteen there was hardly a young man in Hampshire who was not in love with her, but her choice finally fell on Anthony Halbert. Anthony's father and mother, Sir George and Lady Melton, were devoted to Daphne. She had known the family all her life, for the two estates joined; also Miss Jane was very much in favour of the marriage, for she was an old friend of Tony's mother.

"Besides, Miss Jane felt—at least, so she confided to me after-wards—that it would be a very good thing if Daphne had a husband to look after her, for she was getting just a little out of hand. She did unconventional things that worried Miss Jane—worried her exceedingly. She would go off to the woods for whole days at a time, quite oblivious of the social engagements which her aunt had made for her—the garden-parties and tennis-parties which would have appealed to most young girls—the local race meetings.

"Daphne also insisted, during the spring and summer months, on sleeping out of doors. She had a hammock slung between the boughs of two high cedars on the lawn, and nothing would content her but she must sleep in this hammock. Notwithstanding all Miss Jane's entreaties, she absolutely refused to wear corsets—not that that mattered in the very least—her firm young figure needed no artificial support. Also, she had a marked aversion to wearing hats—it was difficult to persuade her ever to put one on; and she loved to take off her shoes and stockings and wade through long wet grass. She would throw herself down with a cry of the purest physical enjoyment amongst bracken; she loved to lie for hours on the lawn in the sunshine, hardly moving a finger—just sleeking her body in the hot sun-rays.

"Of course, these traits in Daphne's character were partly hereditary, but, all the same, Miss Jane was uncommonly glad when young Tony Halbert got Daphne's promise to marry him. She felt as if a great load had been taken off her shoulders—as if she had been relieved from an immense responsibility, for to look after Daphne the child was quite a different matter to looking after Daphne the woman; and the poor old lady realised this—realised it keenly."

Vance paused and drew a deep breath, then he stroked his chin meditatively with his left hand. His eyes looked very dreamy and reflectful.

"Daphne wrote to me herself to announce her engagement. I had just returned to England from Egypt; I had been spending a fine time in Egypt, exploring some old temples, and I remember being profoundly struck by Daphne's letter, and dismayed.

I am engaged to be married to Tony Halbert, dear guardian—so the note began, as well as I can remember—and I am sure you will approve of my choice. Tony is absolutely devoted to me, and so are his people, and I am very, very fond of him; also, I think in many ways it would be a good thing for me to marry and settle down, as Aunt Jane puts it.

Come and stay with us as soon as you can, guardy dear; and please give me away at my wedding. We are going to be married quite soon—in about six weeks' time.

Daphne

P.S. You are a dreadfully clever man, guardy, and you investigate, don't you, for the Ghost Circle? So will you please tell me what people ought to do when they see visions—visions in broad daylight? Ought they to regard themselves as mentally afflicted, or believe that their eyes, for some purpose, have been opened? Do you think this world only belongs to the living, or do you believe that the past still has some hold on it—some claim? And have we lived before, or are we just ourselves?

"I answered Daphne's letter in person. I do not mind confessing to you, Dexter, that it worried me—that I felt distinctly uneasy, but when I arrived at Darrell Court I was quite reassured.

"Daphne was playing tennis with her fiancé, and she looked splendidly healthy, exceedingly happy, not at all the sort of girl to indulge in delusions. She threw down her racquet directly she caught sight of me, and ran across the lawn to meet me, Tony following her. She seemed in wonderful spirits, and she could talk of nothing else but her forthcoming wedding. She told me, all in a breath, where she and Tony were going for their honeymoon—what beautiful presents friends were sending them—how there was to be a presentation from the tenantry in a day or two's time, and Daphne was especially eloquent about the dance that was to be given at Darrell Court the night before the wedding.

"'I am having the dance the night before,' she exclaimed, 'because I think it's such a silly thing to have the dance after the wedding, when the bride and bridegroom have gone. Besides, Tony and I both love dancing. There's to be a big ballroom built out on the lawn, and we are having the Blue Hungarian Band, and it's sure to be a lovely midsummer night. I hope you will enjoy the dance, guardy—I think we must open it together.'

"I laughed and shook my head.

"'No, Daphne,' I answered. 'I think it will be Tony's place to lead you out. Now, if that young man of yours can spare you to me for a few minutes, I think we will take a turn together, for your old guardian has all sorts of questions to ask you.'

"Tony surrendered Daphne to me at once. He was a tall, good-looking young fellow, with an honest face and a pair of good, brown eyes. He was close on six feet in height, a very muscular young Englishman—a sweetheart to be proud of.

"I led Daphne into the rose garden. It was a quaint, old-fashioned little garden, sheltered by high yew hedges, and roses bloomed there in great masses—the air was heavy with their fragrance. There was a marble seat in one corner of the rose garden, and Daphne and I sat down. She was all in white, I remember, and, as usual, she wore no hat; her hair shone in the sunlight gold. Her beautiful throat was bare, and she wore no rings on her hands; she had refused—so I learnt afterwards—to wear an engagement ring.

"'You are quite happy, Daphne, are you not?' I began. 'I don't think you could possibly be engaged to a nicer young fellow. I have always liked Tony Halbert, and I have never heard anything but good of him; in fact, your guardian highly approves of the match you are making—he considers it a most suitable one.'

"Daphne looked at me queerly.

"'That's how I feel myself, guardy—that I am doing a very sensible thing in marrying Tony, for I could never marry anyone who was nicer—in fact, half so nice; but—' She paused. Colour suddenly flooded her face, warm colour. She turned to me nervously, a little shyly. 'Did you think me mad when I wrote that postscript to my letter, guardy—quite mad?'

"I shook my head.

"'No, Daphne,' I answered, 'but I felt a little puzzled by that postscript. What does it mean, my dear, tell me frankly, what does it mean?'

"'I don't know myself.' She shook her head. 'Except that I fancy I must suffer from hallucinations at times—ridiculous hallucinations. Do you remember when I was quite a little girl, guardy, how I told you one day about the beautiful stranger whom I said I used to meet in the woods and play hide and seek with behind the trees and bushes? Well, I expect you thought I was romancing, telling stories, but I wasn't. I really used to meet that stranger, and—and I meet him still.'

"'My dear Daphne!' I looked at my ward sternly. 'You really mustn't say such things to me—such absurd things.'

"'But it's the truth, guardy. I do meet someone in the woods. I have never spoken to him, nor has he spoken to me; I have never even touched his hand, and I always call him the stranger to myself, except when I call him the—the god.'

"She lowered her voice to a faint whisper. An extraordinary look had come into her eyes—a look that frightened me.

"'He's glorious—so glorious that I cannot believe him to be mortal man. He frightens me a little now, though he never frightened me when I was a child. He is as bright as a flame is bright, his shining flesh gleams like marble through the green bushes. His eyes draw me—compel me, and yet they are fierce eyes—very fierce.'

"She checked herself abruptly.

"'Tell me that it is all nonsense, guardy—that it is only an hallucination of mine. That I shall forget all about my stranger—my god—once Tony has got me in his own safe keeping.'

"'Of course it is all nonsense, Daphne,' I replied. 'You fancied that you met this—this stranger when you were a child, and you have kept up the fancy all your life, and it's become a sort of delusion with you—an unhealthy delusion. But, as you truly say, once you are married to Tony you will put all this nonsense out of your head; you will have to.'

"'Yes, I shall have to.' She gave a quiet little nod, then she crept closer to me on the seat. 'Guardy, I must tell you something else. I had better confess straight out that though I am awfully fond of Tony I am not the least bit in love with him. It's the stranger I love; why, I should die with sheer delight if he kissed me, I think, but he is only a dream, I suppose, a dream.'

"I took Daphne by one of her cold hands. I looked straight into her eyes.

"'Child, madness lies in such dreams,' I cried. 'Do you realise that?—Madness. You must forget all about this stranger—you must put him out of your life, out of your thoughts; but with Tony to help you, my dear, you will soon succeed in conquering this hallucination. Thank God you are going to be married, Daphne, and that the wedding is fixed to take place soon.'"

Aylmer Vance rose from his chair, and began to walk up and down the room His long arms hung down by his side, his face looked thinner and paler than ever.

"Just listen to the rain, how it beats against the windows. Does my story interest you, Dexter?"

"Distinctly. Please go on—don't stop at such an exciting moment. What did Miss Darrell say in answer to your speech?"

"Very little, nor did she appear at all disposed to continue the conversation. She merely gave me a faint, shadowy smile; and Tony turned up a few minutes later and carried her back to the tennis court to finish the game I had interrupted. They ran off together, laughing like two children, but I thought Daphne looked very distrait during dinner. She hardly ate or drank anything, and she kept staring vaguely through the open window—gazing in the direction of the wise green woods. She wanted to go out for a walk after dinner, to roam with Tony in the grounds, but Miss Jane asked her to sing to us instead—I must hear how wonderfully Daphne's voice had improved, the old lady said. But Daphne wouldn't sing, and she grew more and more restless as the evening wore on. She even seemed in a hurry to get rid of Tony; certainly she did not press him to stay when he finally rose to depart, nor were their *adieux* very prolonged.

"'You are not going to sleep out of doors again this evening, are you, darling?' Miss Jane asked, rather anxiously, as she kissed Daphne good night a few minutes later. 'I can hardly bear to think of you in the darkness—your hammock swinging from those big cedar trees.'

"'Why, it's lovely out of doors, Aunt Jane,' Daphne answered. 'I couldn't sleep indoors—I really couldn't—on such a hot night as this, and I'm not a bit frightened. Why should I be frightened? Do you think someone will steal out of the woods and carry me away— some stranger?'

"She laughed and left the room laughing. Miss Jane and I looked at each other anxiously.

"'Isn't she a queer girl?' Miss Jane exclaimed. 'Oh, I shall be thankful, Mr. Vance, when Daphne is safely married to dear Tony.'

"'And I shall be thankful too,' I answered, and I meant what I said."

Vance walked back to his chair again. The fire was beginning to burn down; he put some more coals on, and I noticed that his hands were shaking a little.

"Well, you want to hear the rest of my yarn, I supposed, Dexter? I left Darrell Court next morning. I had only been able to arrange to come down for the night—I had a lot of business to attend to, you see, having so recently returned to England. But I promised Daphne that I would come back the day before the wedding in order to be present at her dance, and I gave her a word of warning as we said goodbye.

"'Don't think any more of that dream of yours, Daphne—that silly delusion. Forget it, my dear—keep your thoughts fixed on Tony.'

"Daphne smiled and nodded her head.

"'That's all right, guardy,' she answered. 'You can trust me to be quite sensible in the future.'

"She waved her hand to me gaily enough as I drove away, and how was I to guess that even then her thoughts were turning to the stranger in the forest—that she was deceiving all of us, and perhaps herself?

"I returned to Darrell Court for the dance, as I had arranged to do. I found the house packed with young people; four of the brides-maids were staying there and several of the groomsmen. The sound of wedding bells was in the air, a happy excitement prevailed, and Daphne herself seemed the gayest of the gay, not that I saw much of her; she seemed to be always surrounded by a bevy of girls—pretty girls, who chattered at the top of their voices.

"She sought me out of her own free will just before dinner, how-ever. I had dressed early, and had gone down to the study, feeling a little out of things, for the young people were having it all their own way in the drawing-room; they were dancing there already.

"'Guardy, I want to speak to you.' Daphne spoke in low, rather hesitating tones, then she shut the study door behind her and walked up to me. She looked more beautiful than I had ever seen her. She was dressed all in white, as became tomorrow's bride, and her gown clung tightly to her glorious young figure. She wore no jewels beyond a fillet of pearls in her hair; but the expression in her face troubled me—there was such a yearning look in her eyes—such a strange look.

"'What's the matter, Daphne?' I asked. 'My dear, you are not unhappy, are you?'

"'I am very unhappy, guardy.' She bowed her head; two big tears rolled down her cheeks. 'I don't love Tony, I shall never love Tony, and I am going to marry him tomorrow; and he will take me away from all that I care for most—from my freedom, my solitude, my woods. I shall never be able to spend long days by myself in the future, alone with the wild things. I shall have to become domesti-cated; I shall be a wife—perhaps later on a mother.'

"She paused, then added, speaking very quickly and nervously:

"'I ought never to have become engaged, I see that now. I ought always to have belonged to myself. I oughtn't to have been afraid of my dreams, my fancies, and anxious to have them dispelled, for what can Tony give me in exchange—what can he give me?' She threw back her head—she gazed at me defiantly.

"'Tony can give you love,' I answered steadily. 'He can give you reality.'

"'I want neither.' She laughed, queer broken laughter. 'I want, guardy, what I shall never find—what I never can find now.'

"She swayed from foot to foot, such a slim young figure, then she suddenly sank on her knees and raised her white arms high above her head.

"'Oh, my dreams—my beautiful dreams,' she moaned, 'my lost dreams! Have I got to say goodbye to them forever tonight, and goodbye to the stranger, goodbye to the lover who has never kissed me, who never will kiss me, but whose kisses I desire above all things, whose love I crave for?'

"She trembled violently. I remember putting my hand upon her shoulder and feeling how her flesh quivered. I also recollect that I shook Daphne—shook her fiercely.

"'Child, don't talk so madly,' I cried. 'You forget yourself you don't know what you are saying. You are overtired, you are hysterical tonight—you must be hysterical.'

"Daphne swayed slowly to her feet, then a film seemed to gather over her eyes. She laughed, soft, broken laughter.

"'Yes, that's what's the matter with me, guardy,' she murmured. 'I am hysterical—overwrought. I have been trying on clothes all this last week without ceasing, and there's been so much to see to with regard to the wedding. I must pull myself together now. I shall be all right for the dance tonight, and quite all right tomorrow; and of course I don't want to fail Tony at the last minute—I wouldn't do that for anything. Think how Tony loves me, and what a dear he is!'

"She ran out of the room before I could say another word, and joined her guests in the drawing-room, and I got no opportunity of talking to her during dinner.

"Directly after dinner the entire house-party made their way in gay procession to the huge marquee that had been built out on the lawn and turned into a temporary ballroom. The band struck up a waltz as we entered. Tony caught Daphne round her waist and spun her into the middle of the floor, and in a few minutes the whole house-party was dancing, and Daphne's laugh rang out gaily as Tony waltzed her round. It was hard to believe that I had seen her on her knees in the study only an hour before, indulging in passionate invocation.

"Guests began to arrive. Miss Jane insisted on introducing me to various ladies, with whom I was in duty bound to dance, but at last I managed to sneak off by myself to enjoy a quiet cigarette on the terrace. It was a stiflingly hot evening, and I had rather a bad headache. I fancied there was a storm about; once or twice I thought I heard the distant rumble of thunder, but I hoped the storm would not come on before morning. Still there were not so many stars out as there had been an hour ago.

"I lit my cigarette, and proceeded to stroll up and down the terrace. Suddenly I caught sight of Daphne's figure in the distance, stealing out of the ballroom, and she was alone, much to my amazement; she had evidently deserted her partner. She ran like a hare across the lawn—ran straight in the direction of the woods that slope to the right of Darrell Court; I determined to follow at a safe distance, and see for myself what would happen in those woods— and I did see."

A curious change came over Aylmer Vance's voice as he said the last words. His whole body appeared to stiffen as he sat in his chair. A strange thrill ran through me; I sat up erect in my chair, too.

"Daphne gained the wood without noticing that I was following her. She ran at a breathless pace, as if she was in the greatest hurry, and when we entered that dark wood, Dexter, I was distinctly conscious of the sound of music—the music of the flute. I told myself at once—for I hope I am a sensible man—that of course it was merely the echo of the dance music that I was listening to, and I suppose that's what it was."

Vance hesitated, and bit his lips.

"I hardly know how to describe to you what happened next. I don't want you to think me a lunatic, but it seemed to me as though the wood was full of people, and yet I could see no one actually; but every now and then I caught glimpses of the white arms of girls. I could hear what sounded like soft girlish laughter, and once a long tress of hair seemed to be blown right across my face; I could have sworn to this at the time, but perhaps it was only my fancy. Maybe it was merely some dark bough I brushed against—some soft, sweet-scented bough, for everything was so vague, Dexter, so hopelessly indefinite, and yet, if I can make you understand, so real."

Vance half-closed his eyes. He was talking in very slow, measured tones; I strained my ears to catch every word.

"Daphne ran on right into the heart of the wood. It was getting very dark overhead. I was certain that the storm would break quite Soon, the thunderstorm I had been anticipating. The angry rumbles of distant thunder had grown much louder lately, but the strange thing was I never once thought of calling to Daphne to come back with me to the house, or of warning her that a storm was approaching. Perhaps I was no more myself that night than she was—maybe we were both fey, but I was conscious as I followed her through the wood that there were strange powers abroad that evening—strange forces. I felt curiously excited—oddly stirred. A longing to say goodbye to civilisation and to conventionality came over me. I yearned for greater freedom than I had ever known—for a more intimate knowledge of nature. I felt it would be delightful to cast my clothes from me and bathe in the dew-moistened grass. I forgot that I was a staid and respectable man of forty; all the feelings of youth came back—the sublime intoxication of youth."

Vance's head dropped forward on his breast. His eyes were completely closed.

"Well, Dexter, I must make an end of my story, or I shall weary you to death. Daphne suddenly fell down on her knees, just as she had done in the study, and she held up her white arms and seemed to cry to someone to come to her—a long, passionate, half-inarticulate cry, and it was the cry of a woman calling to her beloved, summoning him to her, and as I am a living man, Dexter, something—someone—came in answer to Daphne's cry. He—for it was a man—seemed to shoot down from the branches of a high fir tree, and he was white and shining and nude. A fierce brightness seemed to diffuse from him, and he carried a bow in his hand—he was the archer."

Vance raised his head as he said the last words, opened his eyes, and stared me in the face.

"I am not asking you to believe me, Dexter—I know that my tale sounds too incredible—but I tell you when I saw this flash of light descending, as it were, upon Daphne, I covered my face with my hands, and fell to the ground myself, for what right had I, a mere man, to spy upon this meeting of a maid and an immortal? Yes, I crouched abashed to the ground, and as I did so a great thunderclap seemed to shake the earth to its foundations—such a thunderclap."

Vance bent forward in his chair and put a hand upon my arm.

"There's very little more to tell you now," he whispered. "There was no wedding at Darrell Court the next day, for the tragic reason that the bride had been struck by lightning the night before. We don't believe, you and I, being wise, sensible, practical men, that it was a lover's kiss that killed her—a lover's burning kiss; and yet the lightning had hardly scarred her sweet body, though it had struck her dead."

"What a horrible—what a ghastly tragedy!" I interrupted. A cold shiver ran through my spine as I spoke, but Aylmer Vance shook his head.

"You're making a mistake, my dear friend. There was nothing really tragic about Daphne Darrell's death. It was the fate she would have chosen, I have no doubt, if she had been given her choice, for remember—if we are to believe her own story—she was not the least in love with Tony Halbert; and think what a loveless marriage would have meant to a girl of Daphne's temperament! She met her dream and her death at the same time. Besides, have you forgotten, Dexter, that 'those whom the gods love die young'?"

I made no answer, but as I watched Aylmer Vance kneel down in front of the fire to warm his hands, I ventured to ask him a question.

"Do you believe that the old gods are dead, Vance?—do you really believe that?"

Vance smiled—a strange inscrutable smile.

"They are dead to some," he answered, "but they are alive to others."

LADY GREEN-SLEEVES

"As you're not fishing—this being the Sabbath Day—would you like to walk as far as the pine woods with me, Dexter, and I'll tell you the story of Lady Green-Sleeves—that is, if you're not getting bored with my yarns?"

Aylmer Vance smiled, his quiet, wise smile, as he addressed me. He had just wandered into the quaint old-fashioned garden of the Magpie Inn, and had found me lounging in a basket chair—basking in the sunshine, for the rainy night had been followed by a glorious morning, and, needless to say, I sprang to my feet at once, for the two queer tales that Vance had already told me had made me very curious to hear about Lady Green-Sleeves, and I said as much to my friend.

"So you're quite ready to wander to the pine woods with me, and you'd like to be told about my little ghost—the daintiest ghost a man could ever have the pleasure of meeting. There's nothing dreadful or tragic in this tale—'tis sheer romance; you'll enjoy it, Dexter—you'll enjoy it."

Vance slipped his arm familiarly through mine, then he laughed softly.

"You're such a surprising person, Dexter. Who, to look at you, would imagine for one instant that you are a dreamer of dreams—a firm believer in spooks? You are such a typical barrister, as far as appearances go; yet here I am pouring out all my adventures to you—every uncanny adventure I have ever had—for you do believe in my stories. There's nothing of the sniffing sceptic about you; that's why I am able to talk so freely—to open out my heart."

"I couldn't fail to believe your stories," I answered slowly; "no one could who watched your face whilst you are relating them—heard your voice; and now I am impatient—most impatient—to hear all about Lady Green-Sleeves."

"Wait till we reach the pine woods. I'll throw myself down on a bed of pine needles, close my eyes, and you shall have the whole story as it occurred. It may tax your credulity more than the other tales, though; it's so dreamy and so unexplainable."

Vance lowered his voice. I could feel the nervous trembling of his thin, sensitive fingers as he clutched my arm, and I was more than ever conscious of the strange sympathy that existed between us. I knew—something seemed to tell me—that we were going to be friends, firm friends, for the rest of our lives, and I hoped that Vance would ask me to be his companion during some of his future expeditions to haunted houses.

It took us about ten minutes to walk to the woods. The spicy scent of the pines filled the air; hot sunshine poured down upon a world that was literally a riot of green this morning, and I felt—I could not help feeling—how good it was to be alive. I said as much to Vance, and he laughed; I confess I was extremely puzzled by his laughter at times, but I understood why he had laughed after he told me his story—I understood quite well.

Vance threw himself down on a great heap of pine needles, just as he had said he would—a soft, scented heap, and I made myself a similar couch. We both lay luxuriating in the brilliant sunshine for a minute or two, then Vance bent towards me. His face looked much softer than I had ever seen it, a vague smile played about his mouth.

"Now I will tell you all about my Lady Green-Sleeves. I met her about twelve years ago, and the evening we spent together stands out with startling distinctness in my memory—such a rose-scented evening."

"The evening you spent together?" I raised myself on my elbow and stared hard at Vance, wondering if I had heard aright. "Why, did Lady Green-Sleeves' ghost pay the world such a long visit as all that? I thought ghosts only appeared for a few seconds and then vanished?"

Vance nodded his head.

"So did I; but I was wrong, it appeared—quite wrong; and now, with your leave, my good friend, I will continue my narrative."

Vance paused. He had thrown himself down on his back. He was gazing straight up into a dazzlingly blue sky, and I knew he saw far more than I could see—that he was conjuring up the ghost of a little dead and gone lady—recalling a romantic episode.

"Well, Dexter, I must commence my story by explaining to you that I had not the least idea that my Lady Green-Sleeves was a ghost till she had made me her pretty curtsy and departed. I took her for a masquerader first of all—a dainty rogue of a masquerader; for, you see, I met her at a fancy dress ball, a big dance given by some very rich people in Yorkshire—a dance to which I had been taken by friends."

Vance closed his eyes. His voice sounded very rich and musical; the dreamy smile still played about his lips.

"How well I remember that night, Dexter. It was a cold December evening, and we had to drive over nine miles to Arden Hall, for that was the name of the house where the dance was taking place. I felt very cross at being taken to the ball; I was not particularly fond of dancing, and I hated—as so many men do—the bother of having to go to it in fancy dress. I wore a Georgian suit; the coat was of plum-coloured satin, I recollect, with a white brocade waistcoat sprigged with silver, and my hostess had been pleased to compliment me on my appearance—I was ten years younger than I am now."

Aylmer Vance paused. Looking at him as he lay on the ground, it was not difficult to guess that with his long, well-knit limbs he would cut a fine figure in Georgian costume, and that a white peruke would prove very becoming. There was certainly an old-world dignity about him, a polished refinement.

"Continue your story!" I exclaimed. "I want to hear when you first caught sight of Lady Green-Sleeves. Your plum-coloured coat was very beautiful, I expect; but let us get to the lady."

"I caught sight of her the moment I entered the hall. There was a great balcony running round it, and she was bending over the oak balcony gazing down into the hall below, watching the guests arrive, so I imagined she must be one of the house-party. Our eyes met, and I can tell you, Dexter, a thrill ran through me; my heart suddenly began beating wildly. I made up my mind I'd contrive to get introduced to Lady Green-Sleeves that evening, for that was the name I gave her to myself—Lady Green-Sleeves."

Vance raised himself suddenly to a sitting position. His eyes were wide open now, but he did not look at me; he gazed straight ahead, and I knew who he was gazing at, for his smile deepened; he had forgotten me for the moment—he had conjured up a memory.

"Was Lady Green-Sleeves very pretty?"

I put the question rather diffidently. I hated to arouse Vance from his reverie, yet I longed to hear the rest of the story.

"Pretty! That's a poor word to describe Lady Green-Sleeves. She was adorable; but I think it was her daintiness that most appealed to me—her delicious daintiness. She had a sweet face, a roguish smile; her eyes were as violet and velvety as purple pansies. Her brown curls, innocent of powder, clustered becomingly about a pure low forehead, peeping from under a lace hood, a hood fastened under Lady Green-Sleeves' soft little chin with a rosebud. She was very young—barely seventeen, I thought—a sweet child, who would blossom presently into a delightful woman; and I suddenly found myself wishing that I was a few years younger—more of an age with this brown-haired beauty."

Vance played idly with a handful of fir cones; a longing look had come over his face; then he sighed heavily.

"I hardly know how to describe what Lady Green-Sleeves had on. Her dress struck me as being distinctly fantastic, but I suppose it belonged to the Georgian period, like my own. Her hooped petticoat was of fine creamy silk, and over this petticoat she wore a sort of looped-up green mantle, with long wide sleeves. As far as I can recollect, her bodice was of the same creamy stuff as her petticoat, fastened in front with a green lace. She wore a small bunch

of pink roses at her breast, and her green mantle was looped up
with a slightly bigger bunch of the same roses.

"Her shoes—such tiny little shoes to fit such tiny little feet—
had high red heels, and she wore dainty white silk mittens on her
small, exquisitely-shaped hands. Oh! I tell you there wasn't another girl at the dance to match Lady Green-Sleeves for looks; I
knew that directly I caught sight of her bending over the wide balustrade. Besides, there was something about her that set her apart
from all other women a delicate, ineffable charm, a distinctive daintiness, a curious elusiveness. The extraordinary thing was—at least,
I thought it extraordinary first of all—that no one else seemed to
see her bending over the balcony rail, for I remember turning to
one of the other men of the party and asking him if he knew who
Lady Green-Sleeves was, but he shook his head and looked at me
queerly.

"'I don't see anyone on the balcony,' he said, peering up. 'It's
quite deserted.' And as he spoke Lady Green-Sleeves disappeared.

"I couldn't make out what in the world had become of her, how
she had managed to flit away so quickly; but I caught sight of her
about a quarter of an hour later standing alone and partnerless in
a corner of the ballroom. The band was playing 'The Choristers'
Waltz', playing it well, and I thought what a shame it was that such
a bewitching little lady should not be dancing—I couldn't think
what all the men were about. I expect my partner, a plump, unat-
tractive girl, dressed as a Swiss peasant, found me uncommonly
dull and distrait during the rest of our waltz—I kept watching Lady
Green-Sleeves, I remember. Presently I lost sight of her; she disappeared just as suddenly as she had vanished from the balcony,
and I couldn't for the life of me imagine what had become of her. I
determined to ask my hostess for an introduction to Lady Green-
Sleeves, however; so after I had sat out with my Swiss girl, given
her an ice, and handed her over thankfully to her next partner, I made
my way up to Mrs. Latham—for that was my hostess's name—and
asked her if she would very kindly introduce me to the girl who
was wearing a green silk mantle, a creamy silk petticoat, and a little
white lace cap, and who did not appear to be dancing very much.

"Mrs. Latham looked distinctly puzzled.

"'I am awfully sorry, Mr. Vance,' she answered, 'but I don't seem to know the girl whom you want to be introduced to, or to recognise her from your description. It's very stupid of me, I know, but so many people have brought friends with them tonight, that perhaps I have not noticed the lady who is wearing a green silk mantle. If you can only find her, I will introduce you to her at once, with the greatest pleasure.'

"I gazed helplessly round the ballroom, and as I did so I suddenly caught sight of Lady Green-Sleeves. She was standing by the raised dais on which the band were playing; she was still alone and unattended.

"'There she is!' I cried, turning to Mrs. Latham. 'There's Lady Green-Sleeves by the dais.'

"Mrs. Latham looked straight across the room at Lady Green-Sleeves. As she did so her eyes opened—opened wide.

"'How extraordinary!' she exclaimed. 'To think that I never caught sight of that girl before—noticed her! Why, she ought to be the belle of the ball; and she's paid us such a pretty compliment, Mr. Vance; she has copied the dress of one of our ancestresses—copied it exactly. The portrait hangs in the long gallery, and now I come to think of it, she's strikingly like poor Mistress Latham's portrait—yes, there really is an extraordinary resemblance.'

"Mrs. Latham rose from her chair. She was a tall, dignified woman—one of those slow, quiet women whom it is impossible to hurry. I wished she would hasten her pace as she made her leisurely way round the ballroom towards the bandstand—I was so afraid that Lady Green-Sleeves would disappear again; and my fears were not ill-founded. We had to wait for a second to allow a couple who were dancing to pass us, and during that brief second lady Green Sleeves had disappeared. When we reached the bandstand she had gone.

"Mrs. Latham looked at me in a puzzled sort of way. 'Dear me, Mr. Vance, how very annoying,' she remarked, 'and how singular.' I could see she looked vaguely troubled—a little bewildered.

"'It's all right, Mrs. Latham,' I assured her. 'Don't you worry about me. I will contrive to get introduced to Lady Green-Sleeves somehow, even if I have to introduce myself, for after all it's a fancy dress ball; we are none of us ourselves tonight, our staid, decorous, conventional selves.'

"Mrs. Latham hesitated, then she suddenly put a hand upon my arm.

"'If you do get introduced to Lady Green-Sleeves, if you do manage to speak to her, I wish you would bring her round to me, Mr. Vance; I should like to compliment her upon her dress.'

"'I shall be delighted,' I answered.

"Some other guest came up at that moment and claimed Mrs. Latham's attention, and so set me free to go searching for Lady Green-Sleeves, but it was a long search. She was not to be found in any of the rooms given over to the sitting-out couples, neither could I discover her in the refreshment-room. When the music sounded for the next dance she did not come back to the ballroom; just as I was giving up heart, I caught sight of her bending over the gallery balustrade again. She looked a little tired, I thought, vaguely disappointed, and she was still alone."

Aylmer Vance paused, then he suddenly turned to me.

"You can imagine how fast I ran up those wide oak stairs, can you not, Dexter? I suppose you have been in love in your time; and I don't mind confessing to you that this was a case of love at first sight on my part. I had absolutely lost my head over Lady Green-Sleeves. I might have been a callow youth of eighteen instead of a man of thirty, and my heart beat like a boy's heart—it did indeed—when Lady Green-Sleeves suddenly turned her head and looked at me when I reached the gallery; and then, without waiting for me to speak, she dropped me a formal curtsy, the most graceful, dipping, sweeping curtsy that you could imagine; she seemed to touch the floor and then to rise again in a vast billow of silk, and her voice, when she addressed me, was extraordinarily soft and sweet.

"'Your servant, sir.'

"That was all she said, but the pretty conceit of the words pleased me; here was a masquerader who was clearly acting up to her part.

"I made my very best bow.

"'Will you accord me the pleasure of a dance, madam?' I requested. 'I have my hostess's permission to introduce myself to you. My name is Aylmer Vance.'

"'I should be delighted for you to lead me out in a dance, Mr. Vance,' the little lady answered, 'but unfortunately I know none of these modern dances; they are after my time.'

"A faint note of regret tinged Lady Green-Sleeves' voice as she spoke. The corners of her mouth drooped a little.

"'Oh! You know how to dance the waltz, madam,' I protested. 'It is true that it is a dance that does not accord with our costume, but still—'

"I bowed, and offered my arm, but she declined it with a faint shake of her head.

"'I am afraid I could not venture on that dance, sir. The very music to which the dancers revolve has an unfamiliar sound to me, and yet it is tuneful music—very tuneful.'

"'May I have the honour of taking you in to supper? I believe supper is to be served at twelve o'clock, and it is a quarter to twelve now.'

"'I never take supper, sir.' Lady Green-Sleeves folded her little hands together, the little hands that I longed to hold in my own; then she suddenly looked at me from under her long lashes, her face dimpled into smiles. 'You will think me vastly uncivil. I declined your invitation to dance with you and to have supper, but I'll tell you what I will do, sir; I will take you into my own parlour, and we will sit and converse there together till midnight strikes.'

"'I should like nothing better,' I answered; but as I said the words I felt puzzled—distinctly puzzled, for my hostess had told me that she did not know who the girl in the green mantle was, and yet Lady Green-Sleeves must be staying here—she must be one of the house-party. It was all rather mysterious, to say the least of it.

"'I will take you to my parlour at once. To confess the truth, I shall not be sorry to rest there a few minutes. I find this gay scene a little confusing, and the music is very strident.'

"Lady Green-Sleeves glanced slowly about her. She appeared to be trying to remember something, then her brow suddenly cleared.

"'Ah! I recollect; this is the way to the oak parlour.'

"She led me along a balcony, stopping in front of a closed door. She gazed at me silently, as though asking me to open the door.

"I obeyed that glance. I turned the handle and held the door open. Lady Green-Sleeves gave a happy little cry when she found herself in the parlour; her eyes roved round the queer little three-cornered room, a soft smile played on her lips.

"'My own parlour—I bid you welcome to it.'

"She sat down on a big chair. She folded her small mittened hands in her lap; she glanced about the room with eager interest.

"'Hardly anything has been changed; the parlour is very much as I left it. The curtains have been altered, and my spinet has gone. The old mirror still hangs over the mantelpiece, however; 'tis over a hundred and fifty years since that glass reflected my face.'

"I laughed—this was pretty fooling, then I gazed round the oak-panelled room in my turn. It was full of quaint old furniture; there was a beautiful apple-green tea set in a high china cupboard, a big bowl full of sweet-scented purple violets stood on a gate-leg table; the air was quite heavy with the perfume of the flowers—oppressively heavy.

"'It is so strange to come back again.'

"Lady Green-Sleeves spoke in soft, reflectful tones. She seemed to have forgotten me for the moment and to be talking to herself.

"'Where have you been?' I asked. 'Abroad?'

"She started and smiled—a faint, curious smile.

"'Very far away, and I found it difficult to come back—exceedingly difficult; but, indeed, I wanted to see what the world is like nowadays. I protest it has greatly changed.' She gave an airy wave of her little hands. 'I was so young when my time came—barely seventeen; an' 'twas hard to say farewell to this world. I would gladly have remained here longer. I was the toast of the country, and my worshipful parents made my days one long delight; but I fell into a decline suddenly.'

"'Am I to understand that I am conversing with a ghost?'

"I put the question laughingly to Lady Green-Sleeves, never doubting that the pretty little masquerader, as I took her to be, would laugh back; but instead of laughing she gazed at me reproachfully.

"'Why, indeed, sir, I thought you knew that. Oh! 'twas a foolish thought of mine to return to my old home tonight. This world belongs to another generation than mine, and I feel I am a stranger in my father's house—a flitting guest.'

"She paused. A tear trembled on one of her long eyelashes.

"'I do not understand modern ways. Everything is unfamiliar to me—strange; and the glamour has departed. Once it would have pleased me vastly to dance till the dawn stole into the ballroom, but it would be no such great pleasure now; I have tasted deeper joys, known far more exquisite pleasures.'

"She spoke with intense gravity, intense simplicity, but I still thought that Lady Green-Sleeves was playing a part. I could not believe that it was really an apparition from another world who was addressing me; but I knew one thing—I knew that I had lost my heart to the girl in the green silk mantle—lost it irretrievably.

"'Dear Lady Green-Sleeves!' I threw myself on my knees at her feet. 'Now that you have come back to this world, won't you stay here—consent to remain in it? Will you be angry with me when I tell you that I have dared to fall in love with you?'

"'What! You have fallen in love with me?' She clasped her little hands tightly together; she gave the low, delighted laugh of an innocent coquette. 'Oh, la! Sir, what a romance! But indeed'—her laugh was suddenly followed by a sigh, a short, sweet sigh— 'I may not listen to lovers' vows; it would not be right, it would not be fair to you. My time for love is over. I told you, did I not, that I died when I was barely seventeen?'

"'Oh! Lady Green-Sleeves, Lady Green-Sleeves, don't tease me any longer by pretending to be a ghost. Don't you realise that I am speaking to you seriously—that I am in earnest? I tell you that I love you—that I have fallen in love at first sight, and I want to know your name; I want to be allowed to call you and see you, to woo you, to win you.'

"She rose to her feet, her silk skirts rustling heavily, the laces fluttering at her breast, but she was not angry with me—oh, no, she was not angry.

"'Sir, believe me, I am very sorry that I have got to leave you. I wish that we had met a hundred and fifty years ago, that we could have danced together, for indeed, sir, none of the suitors who wooed me in the past took my fancy as greatly as you have done, and yet they were brave gentlemen in their day—brave gentlemen.'

"She paused a second. She fixed her big blue eyes upon me. Her voice was like the sweetest and most exquisite music, but it seemed to come from a long way off.

"'This may not be farewell, sir. It is quite likely that in the future we shall meet again, but not in this world—oh, no, not in this world—indeed, it is more than likely.' She hesitated. 'Shall we say "*Au revoir*" instead of "Goodbye"?'

"She swept me another of her long sweeping curtsies, and I realised that she was on the eve of taking her departure. I begged her passionately to stay with me, but she shook her head.

"'Indeed, sir, you must not ask that of me. I had a foolish fancy to come back to this world, as I told you. I remembered it as such a brave place, but now that I have returned—now that I can contrast it with another land that I know—why, I would not remain here if I could.' She gave a gentle little wave of her hands. 'I wish I could make you see the truth as plainly as I see it, sir. This world lacks reality, and the men and women who inhabit it are but as changing shadows; here today, they will be gone tomorrow. There is nothing in this world that endures except—except love.'

"She looked at me straight in the eyes as she said the last words. I remember that I opened my arms, and would have drawn her into my embrace, only she stepped back.

"'No, sir—no!' she rebuked me. 'Your lips may not touch mine any more than my lips may touch yours. Now I am going back from whence I came.'

"'Where are you going?' I cried passionately. 'Do you prefer the grave to my arms, Lady Green-Sleeves—to my love?'

"She shook her head.

"'The grave—what have I to do with the grave? I said farewell to my mortal body over a hundred years ago; I have merely clothed

myself in my old semblance to come here. I am a spirit—an immortal spirit—and it is not to the grave I am returning, but life—
life!'

"She smiled. There was such wisdom in her smile, such infinite knowledge; and then, before my eyes, she slowly faded away—
vanished. I found myself alone in the oak parlour, most tragically,
most sombrely alone. I could hear the violins playing wild gipsy
music in the ballroom, I could hear the rhythmical swing of the
dancers' feet, and 'tip-tap' down the passage sounded like the click
of little red-heeled shoes; but I knew—something seemed to tell
me—that even if I went out on to the balcony I should not see her.
I realised that no one on this earth would ever catch a glimpse of
Lady Green-Sleeves again; her home was in a better country."

Aylmer Vance paused. He put up his hands to his eyes and he
sighed—sighed heavily.

"Ah, me—it might have been! Still, it's no use to cherish foolish fancies, is it, Dexter—to dream day and night about a little
sweet-eyed ghost—a little lady who will never revisit this dusty old
world again. It's better to be practical and sensible—and to forget."

I looked at him very gravely.

"You will never be able to forget her," I said slowly, "to really
forget Lady Green-Sleeves; and you will meet her one day, Vance—
you know you will."

"How can I tell?" He shrugged his shoulders. "It may all have
been hallucination on my part; and yet Mrs. Latham saw Lady
Green-Sleeves too—or thought she did; but, of course, I may have
conveyed the impression to her—it may only have been a case of
thought transference. Still, for me Lady Green-Sleeves exists—will
always exist."

He rose slowly to his feet. He stretched himself, and stood up—
a tall, lean figure in the sunshine.

"She said 'Au revoir'—not 'Goodbye', mark you; I like to remember that—that she only said 'Au revoir.'"

THE FIRE UNQUENCHABLE

One night Aylmer Vance handed me a book of poems in manuscript, and asked me to read it.

We had spent a quiet day fishing, wandering to quite a considerable distance from the inn, and sport had occupied us to the complete exclusion of any other subject whatever. Perhaps, in a sense, it was a healthy return to the normal.

It was as we bade each other good night that he handed me the book, producing it from one of his pockets. It was roughly bound in brown paper—merely a number of closely-written sheets fastened together—and there was no kind of title page nor any suggestion as to the name of the author. The verses were all inscribed by hand, and the writing was obviously feminine, neat and precise. That was my impression from the first casual glance.

"I don't know if you are like me," Vance remarked, "and care to read when you are in bed. Anyhow, I'd like you to glance through these poems—for I think you will allow they are poems in the strict sense of the word—and let me know in the morning what sort of impression you get from them."

Vance spoke carelessly, but some instinct warned me that he had an ulterior motive in wishing me to peruse the book, and so I decided that I would read it from end to end even if I kept awake all night to do so.

We bade each other good night, and I made my way to my bedroom—a charming room, criss-crossed with old oak beams and possessing low lattice windows, just the sort of thing that one would expect in such an inn as the Magpie, which had stood just as it was for quite four hundred years. The only trace of modernity it possesses is the electric light, but this has been so artfully introduced that somehow it does not seem to strike a discordant note.

I threw one of the windows open and gazed out. It was a sultry night, characterised by alternate phases of light and darkness, as the moon either rode clear of scudding clouds or was obscured by them.

The western horizon was black and threatening. The atmosphere struck me as electric, and I thought it more than likely that a storm was gathering.

I took the book and got into bed, propping myself up comfortably against the pillows, and prepared to give my undivided attention to the subject in hand.

I don't profess to be a judge of poetry—or, indeed, of any kind of literature. Hard legal documents are more in my line. However, I hadn't read many of the stanzas in that book before I was quite convinced that this was the real thing—genuine poetry, as Vance had said.

There was something about it very difficult to describe. If it makes my meaning clear, I would say that the writer had a curious faculty of drawing quite ordinary things—say a flower, or a tree, or a human personality—in such a way that one saw that flower, or that tree, or that person, not with one's natural living eyes, but with the eyes of the spirit. One derived a curious sense of being outside one's self and of looking down upon the world from some other sphere, a sphere of infinite vastness and mystery.

But there is no need to dilate upon this subject any further, for the poems of Ewan Trail are now known to the world; they have met with the recognition that they deserve, and the curious feature which I have noticed has been commented upon over and over again.

I believe, however, that I am now giving the real story of these poems to the world for the first time.

I read steadily for an hour or more, and the sense of fatigue which had oppressed me when I went to bed, seemed to have departed altogether; My brain became unusually active and alert—indeed, it had to be so, for the handwriting that I was perusing was not always quite easy to decipher. There were curious breaks here and there, followed by blank spaces—as if inspiration had failed—and sometimes I noticed an exactly contrary effect—that is to say, the words ran into each other as if the writer had been so absorbed that the pen had not been lifted from the paper.

I must not forget to mention that before starting to read seriously, I glanced at the last page, and gathered that the manuscript was incomplete—a break had come in the middle of a poem, and there were some curious marks as if there had been an attempt to write further, but the pen had only straggled away across the page, leaving a series of indecipherable lines and curves.

Gradually, as I read, I became conscious of a remarkable sensation which, absorbed as I was, I had not noticed as soon as I might otherwise have done. It was that the atmosphere of my room had become almost insufferably hot. I found my forehead wet with perspiration. It was a dry heat, quite distinct from the warmth of the night—just as if I had a hot fire burning in my room.

I closed my eyes, though, as I have said, I didn't feel in the least bit sleepy, and tried to think it out. My whole body was tingling, the blood in my veins seemed to run like liquid fire. It occurred to me that I ought to get out of bed to investigate—perhaps the inn itself was burning—but when I tried to move I simply couldn't do so—I was like a man poisoned with curare—my senses were keenly alert, but I had lost all power over my limbs. I tried to continue reading, but there was a purple haze before my eyes—it rolled up so that all was dark and then dissipated, allowing me to see the written page of the book I was still holding—but this only for a moment, as the darkness quickly supervened again. I was reminded of the moon in its struggle to penetrate the clouds.

I lay there propped up against my pillows as if I were in a trance, and soon the purple haze before my eyes seemed to envelop everything so that I could not distinguish a single object in the room.

Yet I knew that my eyes were wide open; it was just as if I was staring into illimitable space.

And first it was nothing but a deep purple void, and then, after a little while, I was conscious of shafts of fire shooting across that void—long streaks of light, like falling stars or meteors, only the word "falling" is hardly correct, for they passed in all directions; and there were many that flew upwards like rockets, and these seemed to coalesce with those that fell, forming a glowing mass that would remain stationary for a moment or two, growing brighter and brighter until the glare was so overpowering that my eyes were unable to support it. Then the purple mantle would roll up again and darkness supervene.

And presently—it seemed so astonishingly natural to me, just as if what was happening was the rational sequence of all that had gone before—the mist gradually dispersed again—or rather, I should say, it lifted like a series of diaphanous curtains rising one after another—so that the scene behind was at first little more than a blur, giving merely a suggestion of shapes which became clearer and clearer as each curtain went up, so that at last, instead of my own room being revealed to me, which was what I had expected, my queer many-cornered room, with its dimity-covered furniture and its lattice windows and white-washed walls, all lit up by the incongruous glare of the electric light, I found myself gazing into another room altogether—a room that was absolutely unknown to me and which had no light in it save that of a red-shaded lamp.

There was an old-fashioned four-post bedstead to one side, and the bed was not, nor had been, occupied, for the sheets, turned back, were quite smooth and unruffled. The room was panelled in dark oak, and directly facing me was a large window which stood wide open, so that through it I could see the sky—or, rather, I could see an expanse of inky blackness which quivered at frequent intervals, as if it were rent by summer lightning. And somehow I felt that the heat in that room was as intolerable as it was in my own.

And through the window, in the glow of the lightning, I could clearly distinguish the swaying heads of pine trees, trees that must have been growing close up to the house, and so real was my vision that I could hear the very rustling of the wind in the branches, a queer, gentle soughing which seemed to fall upon my ears like the refrain of a long-forgotten song; and the scent of the pine was in my nostrils, too—that deep aromatic perfume always intensified when there is a storm in the air.

There was a small table drawn up by the window, and at that table sat a woman. She was writing by the light of the shaded lamp; her back was turned to me, and she was leaning forward, deeply engrossed in her work. There was a small clock on a bracket close by—I remember it particularly, for the sound of its ticking was like that of a pulsing human heart. The woman glanced at it now and again, but did not slacken in her work. She wrote on feverishly, and it seemed to me that there was something curious about the way she held her pen. Her fingers appeared to exert no pressure upon it, they merely followed its course—it was much more as if the pen, merely maintained in an upright position by her hand, was writing of its own accord.

The woman was slender, and delicately made, and she was dressed in black, and she had a wonderful aureole of golden hair which positively glowed when the lightning illuminated it. I felt that she must be wonderfully beautiful, and I was possessed of an acute longing to see her face. And presently this wish was gratified, for, uttering a low cry which fell distinctly upon my ears, she dropped her pen, pushed back her chair, and turned. It was just as if she had heard some sound behind her, and I can hardly describe the eager, expectant look upon the face that, for a moment, was turned to me.

It was, as I had guessed, a face of exceptional beauty. The woman was quite young, little more than a girl, but she seemed to have lost, if I may express it so, the natural glamour and health of youth—it was the face of one who had passed through terrible stress of soul, if not of body—a violent spiritual stress, which had caused the delicately-rounded cheeks to lose their contour, the warm colour to fade, the exquisitely-moulded lips to become bloodless, and the eyes hollow and weary. And yet those eyes! I shall carry the impression of them till I go to my own grave, for if the rest of the face was like the face of a spirit from another world, those eyes shone with the very agony of life. I don't know why I have used the word "agony" in this connection, but it is the one that most accurately expresses my meaning—I can only repeat that the woman's eyes blazed with life—a life that was equivalent to exquisite pain.

The desire, the intense eager longing for something unattainable, for something beyond the ken of humanity—that is what I read in the sombre flame of those eyes; and I knew instinctively that when she turned it was in the hope, the wild, frantic desire, that the thing she longed for might be granted to her.

But it seemed that her desire, for the moment at least, was to go ungratified, for nothing happened, and with an expression of unutterable despair she stepped to the window, and, with arms extended, seemed to be invoking the night. And as she stood there, her arms lifted above her head, there came a flash of vivid lightning, so vivid that for a moment my eyes were dazzled and the vision was blotted out.

It lasted only the briefest second, I can swear to that, yet, when sight was restored to me, the woman was no longer alone. A man was with her—a tall, lean man, whose face was as white as her own, and whose hair was black as hers was golden. He wore some sort of cloak, and it glistened as though rain had fallen upon it; but whence he had come or how he had entered the room, I could not guess.

He clasped the woman in his arms, enveloping her, as it were, with his cloak. For a moment, however, I caught sight of her face, and if her eyes had glowed before, they were burning now as if with living fire. And I knew that her wish was gratified—that the impossible had become possible—that *He* had come. And so they stood, and no word passed between them, for had either spoken I should have been aware of it.

I was as conscious, for instance, of the low rumble of the thunder as I was of the lightning which played about them so that they seemed to stand enveloped in flame. And I could hear the ticking of the clock also.

And after a while the man, still holding the woman closely to him, stooped over the table and picked up the pen and wrote, apparently completing a sentence which the woman had left unfinished. And when this was done he laid the pen down, and instinctively I knew that there was finality in what he did and that the pen would be needed no more.

And then, over the completed manuscript, the lips of the man and woman met and hung together, and so, slowly, she clinging to him and covered by his cloak, they made their way to the door. I saw it open to allow them to pass out and then close gently behind them.

The clock struck the hour of two. The lamp burned on steadily, throwing its glare upon the completed page; then there came another blinding flash of lightning, and, with it, the vision passed.

The transition was so sudden that at first I could hardly, realise that I was in my own familiar room at the Magpie Inn. I rubbed my eyes, for I felt dazed and not sure that I was fully awake. And, indeed, my experiences of the night were not yet over, for, looking towards the window, I was conscious of a curious glare, which was not that of lightning, for this, so vivid in my dream, was here but a feeble reflection of a distant storm.

But a still more pressing sensation demanded my attention. I became conscious of a sense of tingling pain in my left arm, which was lying across the open book upon my knees. "Pain" is, perhaps, hardly the right word—my arm felt more as if it had been severely scorched by the sun; and this, I argued at first, was quite possible, since I had had my coat off and shirt sleeves turned up while fishing this afternoon.

Only, if this were so, why should it be only my left arm that was affected? I examined it and found it red from wrist to elbow, and on the underside only, while upon my right arm there was no trace of scorching whatever.

It was curious and inexplicable, as, too, was the heat in the room which had now become almost stifling. I sprang out of bed—for I had recovered the use of my limbs by now—closed the book and laid it aside, and then stepped quickly across to the open window. It was necessary to find some explanation for that persistent glow in the sky. I had a momentary fear that the inn might be on fire.

But the cause was soon quite clear. There was a fire, but it could not be less than twenty miles away—perhaps more than that. I ascribed it at once to one of those conflagrations of forest and common land, unfortunately only too frequent in some parts of Surrey. I have seen acres of wood and heather made black and desolate by their ravages.

And so this fire did not in the least explain the heat of my room. Could it be only a mental impression? I asked myself that question as I reached my hand out of the window and then stretched out my head as far as it would go. But the night air was pleasantly cool and refreshing. The heat was undoubtedly within. And so, puzzled and wondering, but overcome with fatigue, I went back to bed, switched off the light, and was soon sleeping profoundly.

In spite of my strange experiences of the night, I was up and about quite early—soon after seven, for it was at that hour that I usually had breakfast with my friend, Aylmer Vance. I found him in the comfortable parlour of the inn, and he was already half way through his morning meal, which was usually a light one.

He smiled and nodded as I took my place at his table and laid the paper-bound book down beside him.

"Well?" he inquired, lifting his eyebrows a little, and, I think, scanning my face rather curiously.

"They're wonderful poems," I said. "The author of them—I don't know if it is a man or a woman—should make a big reputation."

Having regard to my vision of the night, I had come to the conclusion that the author was a woman; I was surprised, therefore, when Vance replied:

"The author is a man—Ewan Trail—and if he makes a reputation, as I am sure he will, it will be a posthumous one. For he died only a few months ago, a bitterly disappointed man. He died tragically.

"Presently you shall hear the story. But first I want you to tell me any impressions you may have received while reading the poems. Don't be afraid of mentioning anything, however slight—I have a reason for asking you."

So I had guessed correctly that Vance wished to put me to the test, and I wondered, as I had been wondering ever since I got up that morning, if my vision of the night and the heat and the other incidents had any real significance. I felt more than a little agitated, for this was my first experience of anything in the remotest degree concerned with the occult.

I had been doing justice to an excellent dish of eggs and bacon, but now I laid down my knife and fork.

"I don't know if you will call it an impression," I faltered, "but the most remarkable sensation I experienced last night was one of intense heat. I know the weather was hot and that there was a storm, but it wasn't like the natural heat of the atmosphere—"

"More like that of a fire?" Vance interrupted.

I nodded. "Yes; that of an intensely hot fire. My forehead was bathed with perspiration; and look here, Vance"—I lifted my arm and pulled up my sleeve— "how do you account for this? I thought of sunburn, but it's only the one arm, and on the underside of it."

"Curious," he muttered, "very interesting. In what position did you hold your arm last night?"

"It was resting upon the book," I replied, casting a side glance at that apparently innocent object, which still lay upon the table where I had placed it. "And I had a sort of a vision," I resumed in a low, almost awestruck tone, "while I was sitting propped up in bed with my arm upon the book. It may have been a dream, just an ordinary dream—but I've never had such a dream before."

"Tell me about it." Vance leaned forward, his elbows upon the table, his chin supported by his hands. His keen eyes were fixed upon me; he appeared intensely interested.

I told him of my vision, omitting not the smallest detail. It had impressed itself so vividly upon my mind that I forgot nothing. Vance sat quite still, not interrupting me once.

"This is most deeply interesting, Dexter," he said when I had concluded; "and what is more, it goes to show that you—you yourself—are possessed of powers which probably you have never dreamed of." His lips parted in a slight smile. "I suppose, a few

days ago, you would have been consumed with amusement if anyone had suggested that you, a hard-headed man of the law, had it
in you to be a clairvoyant, a medium—and yet such is undoubtedly
the case, and it was because I suspected it that I gave you those
poems to read. And now I know this, Dexter, I hope that we may
do good work together, you and I—work for the furtherance of
human knowledge in the little-known paths of what we now call
the super-physical, but which may prove to be the normal and
natural after all."

He extended his long slim hand to me across the table, and I
took it, not without a certain trepidation and bewilderment, for all
this was so astonishingly new to me, so absolutely unexpected. It
was true that I had never realised the latent gifts of which, apparently, I was possessed. And the wonder of it all was great upon me.

"You think," I faltered, "that my dream—my vision—had actual
significance?"

"I have no doubt about it," was the reply. "You were most certainly in telepathic rapport last night with someone with whom I
am acquainted. What the vision actually portends it is difficult to
say. I have my fears, but we shall know the truth quite soon—this
very morning."

I drew a deep breath and accepted my destiny. Luckily, being
of independent means, my profession had never meant more to
me than the occupation which every man should have. And now I
had found a fresh occupation—one to which I could give myself up
with earnest devotion. From that day forth I was a disciple of
Aylmer Vance.

"There is one fact that I should mention," I said, when he had
smilingly agreed that we should in future make common cause,
"and that is that there really was a fire last night. I saw it from my
window, and I think it had not long broken out; but it was spreading rapidly—a forest fire, I am practically certain. But it was a long
way off—quite twenty miles, I calculated—and so, of course, it is
absurd to think that I could have felt the heat of it."

Vance rose to his feet as I spoke. A look of agitation had come
into his face.

"A forest fire?" he questioned. "Tell me in what direction it was."

"My room faces the north-west."

He made a rapid mental calculation. "To the north-west, and about twenty miles away. Dexter"—he spoke hurriedly— "we mustn't delay. This may be of deep importance."

He rang the bell, and when the servant came gave instructions that his car should be brought round at once. Then he turned to me.

"Williams shall drive us," he said. Williams was his chauffeur. "That will leave me free to tell you all there is to be told as we go along. Will you be ready to start in a few minutes?"

Barely a quarter of an hour later we were on our way to some destination with which I was still unacquainted. Vance's car was a Darracq, light and swift. He usually drove it himself, but on this occasion he had delegated that duty to his man. It was in order that he might tell me a story, and here, more or less in his words, is the story he told.

"Early in the spring of this year I was invited by a man with whom I had a slight acquaintance—a Mr. Tyrrell—to spend a few days with him at his country house and investigate certain curious happenings. The house is named 'Cheswold Lodge', and it is situated near the little village of Hillinghurst, which is at the foot of the south slope of the Hog's Back. It is there we are going.

"I had travelled down by train to Guildford, where Tyrrell met me with his car, and he told me about the trouble as we drove to his house—just as I am telling it to you now. He had only been in residence at Cheswold Lodge—he and his wife and their two little girls—for about a month, and curious things had happened almost at once.

"In a sense, he had bought the house out of charity. A tragedy had happened there the preceding winter, and people were inclined to look upon it askance. It is an old house—as you will see—and it had belonged for generations to the family of the Trails, the last representative of which was Ewan Trail, who is the author of the poems which you have just read.

"Now Ewan was a rather extraordinary individual—the 'mad poet' he used to be called in the neighbourhood. He was a tall, lean fellow, with a face that was almost mediaeval in character, very black hair, and a complexion that was as olive as that of a southerner. I expect he had foreign blood in him somewhere."

Here I ventured on an interruption. I could scarcely help myself. "Was it he whom I saw last night?" I asked in an awed whisper.

"You shall judge for yourself as I proceed," responded Vance. Then he took up his story again. "Ewan Trail was so much of a poet that he could not get on with ordinary people, and he was really quite incapable of managing his own affairs. He had started life with good prospects and a fair fortune, but somehow he contrived to fritter practically everything away. His one absorbing idea was that his poems should be given to the world—that the genius which he knew he possessed should not be overlooked, should not go down with him unrecognised to the grave.

"And he knew that he had not very long to live. He was endowed with a fine appreciation of the beauty of life, and yet the spirit from which he had derived his inspiration was housed in a weak and diseased body, although that, too, had a certain beauty of its own.

"About a year ago he married, and took his wife to live with him at Cheswold Lodge. She adored him passionately—indeed, the passion was mutual—but it was essentially a passion of the spirit. For Leila Trail, like her husband, held but a poor tenure upon life. She was very young and very beautiful, and many of Trail's finest poems are addressed to her.

"Well, disaster fell upon them quite soon after their marriage. Ewan Trail lost practically all his money; but this, at the time, seemed to be of but small account to him, for he believed that he had only to publish his poems and that all the world would be at his feet. It was not for himself, however, that he cared so much— he did not mind poverty, if you understand me—but it was for his poetry, that those verses of his, those rhapsodies of emotion, the passionate expression of his soul, should live when he was dust. The fire that was in him, that was, in fact, consuming him, must have its vent.

"And then began a series of the most bitter disappointments. For, strange as it may seem to you who have read his poems, there wasn't a publisher in London who would take the risk of producing them. Poetry, they said, was a drug upon the market and, except in the case of one or two famous names, not worth looking at. Who would purchase a book of verses by Ewan Trail, whose name had never been heard of? If he chose, he might, of course, be his own publisher. But here a fatal difficulty arose—Trail had no money, absolutely no money, that he might expend in such a way. His creditors were already pressing him on every side.

"And so, like Chatterton before him, and others whom one may think of even at a quite recent date, Trail, who was barely twenty-five years of age, took his own life. He shot himself in a little summer house situated in the midst of the pine wood which reached almost up to the very walls of Cheswold Lodge, and which stretches out thence for the best part of a mile towards the south until it merges in open common land.

"Poor Leila was left destitute. The house and everything it contained would have been sold up had not my friend Tyrrell, who was acquainted with her family, come to the rescue. He purchased the house as it stood, and he invited Leila to remain with him as governess to his two little girls. She is there now, Dexter—at least, she was there yesterday. But now I'm not so sure—I'm not so sure."

Vance paused in his story, and the pause was impressive. We were nearing our destination by now, for, straight ahead of us, I recognised the long unbroken ridge of the Hog's Back. We were following a road that undulated across open country, and the air was fragrant with the scent of heather.

Presently Vance resumed. "Having told me all this about the former owner of his house, Tyrrell proceeded to recount his troubles since he had entered into occupation. They were of a curious character, and new to me, in spite of all my experience.

"The danger with which he had to contend was, in a sense, a material one—the danger of fire.

"There had been several outbreaks in the house itself, all of which were wholly inexplicable. Two or three had occurred in the bedroom which Trail and his wife had occupied, and which Leila had been allowed to retain for her own use. Once it was curtains in front of the window, another time the curtains of the bed, and then again fire had been discovered springing up mysteriously from underneath an easy chair which had been a particular favourite of the dead poet's. Luckily, all these outbreaks were discovered in time to prevent any serious damage being done.

"In other parts of the house, too, the same thing had occurred, and especially in Trail's study, which Tyrrell, who was also a literary man by profession, had now adapted to his own purpose.

"'Do you know, Vance,' so Tyrrell said to me, 'there was one occasion at least when I actually saw the fire break out, and there was no possible cause for it, no suggestion of carelessness on my part or upon that of anyone else. I'd been sitting up late to finish an article that I was writing, and everyone had gone to bed. There was a fire burning in the grate, for it was early in the year, and the nights were cold. The only other light in the room was from a couple of lamps, one of which was on the table where I was working, a shaded reading-lamp; and the other, a tall standard, was at some distance away. I'm not a smoker, so there can be no suggestion of a dropped match or anything of that sort. Well, the room seemed to me to get hotter and hotter—and it wasn't at all the first time that I had noticed the peculiar heat, for one experienced it all over the house—nearly every member of my family had noticed it as well, and so had the servants—and by degrees this heat became so intolerable that I got up to throw open the window. And then well, I'm not a superstitious man, and I've never in my life before had anything to do with the superphysical—the queerest sensation you can imagine went through me, and I felt a conviction that I wasn't alone in the room. I'd had the same sort of feeling on other occasions—the involuntary glance over, one's shoulder to assure one's self that there was no one there—I expect you know what I mean. But upon this occasion I felt positively sure, and when I looked towards the chair upon which I had been sitting, I give you my word that a cold shudder went through me, for though I couldn't distinguish anything—anything definite, that is to say—I somehow knew in my inner conscience that the chair was occupied. And then, almost immediately afterwards, I smelt fire, and I saw smoke issuing from a drawer of the table, a drawer in which I kept my papers and which, no doubt, had served the same purpose for my predecessor. Of course, I hadn't the smallest difficulty in putting the fire out, and no material damage was done. But I cite this as an example of the sort of thing that is happening, and which is so in-explicable—and dangerous—for who can say that one day we may not be caught off our guard and have the whole place burnt down over our heads?'

"Tyrrell spoke the last words very seriously, and I had to agree with him that the danger was one not to be ignored.

"But it wasn't only in the house that these outbreaks of fire occurred. They were far more frequent in the pine wood which I have already mentioned—yet it wasn't at all the time of year when one would expect such conflagrations. Mr. Tyrrell assured me that there were dozens of places in the wood where charred traces could be seen of the beginning of such fires—just as if the gipsies had been encamped there—that was the expression he used—only it was known that there had been no gipsies at that time in the neighbourhood.

"And now people were beginning to talk about it, and all sorts of stories were going round. It was said that lights were seen in the wood, like moving lanterns, and sometimes the appearances were much more erratic—someone had spoken of shooting stars, or of fireworks let off among the trees. Someone else had a yarn about a ball of fire hovering over the tree-tops and then bursting. Anyhow, the whole place had acquired a bad name."

Here Vance paused again and then proceeded, with as much detail as time allowed, to narrate the investigations he had made into the phenomena and the conclusion to which he had arrived.

"I did not at first associate the dead poet with the mischief," he admitted. "I thought of a fire elemental, but quickly had to exclude that supposition. I soon assured myself, for instance, that the fires were not kindled in any spirit of mischief."

"What, then?" I inquired. I admit I was puzzled.

"I want you to draw your own conclusions," said Vance, "from what I tell you. And understand that in these matters one cannot, one must not, dare to speak with certainty. Our knowledge is too vague, too indefinite."

"You made some important discovery?"

"I made a discovery that at least indicated to me how I should act. It resulted from a careful examination of the wood, which, by the way, was regularly patrolled during the daytime—they wouldn't stay at flight—by a number of boy scouts whom Tyrrell had engaged to put out any fires which they might come across. One of these boys, a particularly intelligent one, reported to me that on two or three occasions he had found pieces of burning paper in different parts of the wood, and that these, if let alone, would no doubt have given rise to more serious outbreaks. Well, at last I myself found one of these pieces of burning paper, and having extinguished it, I noticed that it bore traces of handwriting, which Leila Trail, on being consulted, recognised and was able to account for.

"She burst into a passion of tears. 'I can tell you,' she cried, 'how that paper came to be in the wood. When Ewan's work came back to him from the publishers—when he lost all hope—he destroyed all his typewritten copies—he threw them into the fire here in the house—but his own original manuscript—the words that he had written down as they came hot from his brain—that he carried about on his own person.' She lowered her voice, speaking in a tone that was charged with the deepest pain. 'It was on the day that he killed himself. He was more than half distracted—I tried to pacify him, but he would not listen to me. He threw me roughly away from him—he who loved me so devotedly—and he ran off into the wood, ran wildly towards the summer-house. And I followed him as best I was able, but I could not catch him up. It was night, and there was only a dim moon, but I saw him, as he ran, tearing the manuscript of his poems into fragments and scattering them about him to the right and to the left. He destroyed everything—everything. I caught my foot in the root of a tree and fell, and I hurt myself and could not move. I lay there, crying and moaning;

and I heard the report of the pistol when he shot himself, and could do nothing to prevent it—nothing.'

"She broke off, sobbing as if her heart would break. I must tell you, Dexter, that I had already taken particular notice of Leila Trail, and that I had recognised the deep spirituality of her nature.

"Well, I got as many of these fragments of paper together as I could collect, and studied them. With the help of Leila, I even succeeded in reconstructing a complete poem, and though I don't profess to be an expert, I realised the worth of the thing. In any case, I came to a decided conclusion, and determined upon a course of action.

"It was Leila Trail who was to help me, and I couldn't possibly have had a better subject to deal with. As I have told you, there were times when she seemed far more spiritual than human.

"By my instruction, she sat at a table in her bedroom with the window open, and I put paper before her and a pen in her hand, and I told her to concentrate her thoughts upon her husband, to let her mind be a blank upon all other subjects. And she was wonderfully responsive; she understood what I wanted of her almost without any explanation at all.

"'If only he would come back to me,' she sighed. 'If only I could see him again! I love him so—I love him so!'

"You understand what I wanted of her, Dexter? You are beginning to see light, are you not? The unfortunate poet, Ewan Trail, had destroyed all his manuscript—there was no longer any possibility of giving to the world those burning and impassioned words of his. And who can say that the fire of inspiration dies with the death of the body? Who can say that, released from fleshly bonds, it does not continue to burn with a zest and ardour that we poor humans are totally unable to appreciate? I don't know; we can't really explain these things; and I myself, today, can only be said to have faintly touched the border line of understanding.

"At any rate, Dexter, you understand the supposition upon which I decided to act. If those lost poems could be regained—if, eventually, they could be given to the world—was it not possible that these pent-up fires would find their desired outlet? The fire unquenchable—the fire of inspiration—it was with that, I argued, that I had to deal.

"I have said that Leila Trail was responsive. She had never before tried her hand at automatic writing, and so it was a day or two before actual results were achieved. But when they once began it was astonishing—astonishing—to watch the rate with which her pen would fly across the paper. You have seen the result for yourself, for the book you were reading last night was written, every word of it, by Leila Trail under the inspiration of her dead husband. Through her he has sent his message to the world, and unless I'm very much mistaken, when those poems see the light of publicity—as they will do, for I myself shall have them published—the fire that emanates from the restless spirit of Ewan Trail, the checked flame of inspiration, will be drawn to its natural channel, where it may burn for ever, a power for good, unquenched and unquenchable in the minds and hearts of men."

I drew a deep breath. "Then what I saw last night—" I ventured.

"We shall know the significance of your vision very shortly now," he replied gravely. "For the moment all that I feel sure of is that Ewan Trail has imparted his last message, and that he is content. You noticed, of course, that the book I gave you is incomplete. I was waiting only for the conclusion of the last poem—and I think we have that now."

Suddenly he stood up in the car and pointed. "Look, Dexter, look!" he exclaimed.

I looked and saw a blackened track of land where the fire had passed. The flames were not yet fully extinguished, and there were men at work tearing up the heather to prevent their further encroachment.

"You were right, Dexter," muttered Vance; "you saw truly. The whole wood has been destroyed. And look, Dexter, there is the house. Thank heaven, that seems to have been spared."

Presently the car drove up to the door of Cheswold Lodge, a long, low, old-fashioned building of many gables. Mr. Tyrrell arrived almost at the same time as ourselves—he had been assisting his men with their work in the burning wood. His face, I noticed, was very grave, and he hardly waited to be introduced to me, so anxious did he seem to impart some important intelligence to my friend. And instinctively I knew what that intelligence must be.

"You may speak without reserve, Tyrrell," said Vance. "Mr. Dexter is fully acquainted with all the circumstances of the case."

And so Mr. Tyrrell told his story. Leila Trail was dead. She had been found lying in the same summer-house where her husband had met his death, and there was no sign of injury upon the body, and she looked very happy, happier far than she had done in life. The fire had swept round the summer-house, which stood in a clear space, and had left it absolutely untouched.

What was the cause of the fire? No doubt the storm—a tree struck by lightning. So the neighbourhood decided, and there was no reason to doubt the verdict.

A little later we went together to the bedroom where Leila had been sitting overnight with her work. I recognised it at once, for every detail was as I had seen it in my vision. The lamp, extinguished now, stood on the table, and beneath it was the paper upon which she had been writing. The pen lay there where it was dropped, and the small clock upon the bracket had stopped at the hour of two.

"Look, Dexter," said Vance simply. He pointed to the written page.

Beneath the completed poem one word had been added, and it was in quite a different handwriting to that of Leila Trail—a firm masculine handwriting. The word was "Finis."

And yet, perhaps, for him and for her the finish meant the real beginning.

THE VAMPIRE

Aylmer Vance had rooms in Dover Street, Piccadilly, and now that I had decided to follow in his footsteps and to accept him as my instructor in matters psychic, I found it convenient to lodge in the same house. Aylmer, and I quickly became close friends, and he showed me how to develop that faculty of clairvoyance which I had possessed without being aware of it. And I may say at once that this particular faculty of mine proved of service on several important occasions.

At the same time I made myself useful to Vance in other ways, not the least of which was that of acting as recorder of his many strange adventures. For himself, he never cared much about publicity, and it was some time before I could persuade him, in the interests of science, to allow me to give any detailed account of his experiences to the world.

The incidents which I will now relate occurred very soon after we had taken up our residence together, and while I was still, so to speak, a novice.

It was about ten o'clock in the morning that a visitor was announced. He sent up a card which bore upon it the name of Paul Davenant.

The name was familiar to me, and I wondered if this could be the same Mr. Davenant who was so well known for his polo playing and for his success as an amateur rider, especially over the hurdles? He was a young man of wealth and position, and I recollected that

he had married, about a year ago, a girl who was reckoned the greatest beauty of the season. All the illustrated papers had given their
portraits at the time, and I remember thinking what a remarkably
handsome couple they made.

Mr. Davenant was ushered in, and at first I was uncertain as to
whether this could be the individual whom I had in mind, so wan
and pale and ill did he appear. A finely-built, upstanding man at
the time of his marriage, he had now acquired a languid droop of
the shoulders and a shuffling gait, while his face, especially about
the lips, was bloodless to an alarming degree.

And yet it was the same man, for behind all this I could
recognise the shadow of the good looks that had once distinguished
Paul Davenant.

He took the chair which Aylmer offered him—after the usual
preliminary civilities had been exchanged—and then glanced
doubtfully in my direction. "I wish to consult you privately, Mr.
Vance," he said. "The matter is of considerable importance to myself, and, if I may say so, of a somewhat delicate nature."

Of course I rose immediately to withdraw from the room, but
Vance laid his hand upon my arm.

"If the matter is connected with research in my particular line,
Mr. Davenant," he said, "if there is any investigation you wish me
to take up on your, behalf, I shall be glad if you will include Mr.
Dexter in your confidence. Mr. Dexter assists me in my work. But,
of course—"

"Oh, no," interrupted the other, "if that is the case, pray let
Mr. Dexter remain. I think," he added, glancing at me with a
friendly smile, "that you are an Oxford man, are you not, Mr. Dexter? It was before my time, but I have heard of your name in connection with the river. You rowed at Henley, unless I am very much
mistaken."

I admitted the fact, with a pleasurable sensation of pride. I was
very keen upon rowing in those days, and a man's prowess at school
and college always remains dear to his heart.

After this we quickly became on friendly terms, and Paul
Davenant proceeded to take Aylmer and myself into his confidence.

He began by calling attention to his personal appearance. "You would hardly recognise me for the same man I was a year ago," he said. "I've been losing flesh steadily for the last six months. I came up from Scotland about a week ago, to consult a London doctor. I've seen two—in fact they've held a sort of consultation over me—but the result, I may say, is far from satisfactory. They don't seem to know what is really the matter with me."

"Anaemia—heart," suggested Vance. He was scrutinising his visitor keenly, and yet without any particular appearance of doing so. "I believe it not infrequently happens that you athletes overdo yourselves—put too much strain upon the heart—"

"My heart is quite sound," responded Davenant. "Physically it is in perfect condition. The trouble seems to be that it hasn't enough blood to pump into my veins. The doctors wanted to know if I had met with an accident involving a great loss of blood—but I haven't. I've had no accident at all, and as for anaemia, well I don't seem to show the ordinary symptoms of it. The inexplicable thing is that I've lost blood without knowing it, and apparently this has been going on for some time, for I've been getting steadily worse. It was almost imperceptible at first—not a sudden collapse, you understand, but a gradual failure of health."

"I wonder," remarked Vance slowly, "what induced you to consult me? For you know, of course, the direction in which I pursue my investigations. May I ask if you have reason to consider that your state of health is due to some cause which we may describe as superphysical?"

A slight colour came to Davenant's cheeks.

"There are curious circumstances," he said, in a low and earnest tone of voice. "I've been turning them over in my mind, trying to see light through them. I daresay it's all the sheerest folly—and I must tell you that I'm not in the least a superstitious sort of man. I don't mean to say that I'm absolutely incredulous, but I've never given thought to such things—I've led too active a life. But, as I have said, there are curious circumstances about my case, and that is why I decided upon consulting you."

"Will you tell me everything without reserve?" said Vance. I could see that he was interested. He was sitting up in his chair, his feet supported on a stool, his elbows on his knees, his chin in his hands—a favourite attitude of his. "Have you," he suggested slowly, "any mark upon your body, anything that you might associate, however remotely, with your present weakness and ill-health?"

"It's a curious thing that you should ask me that question," returned Davenant, "because I have got a curious mark, a sort of scar, that I can't account for. But I showed it to the doctors, and they assured me that it could have nothing whatever to do with my condition. In any case, if it had, it was something altogether outside their experience. I think they imagined it to be nothing more than a birthmark, a sort of mole, for they asked me if I'd had it all my life. But that I can swear I haven't. I only noticed it for the first time about six months ago, when my health began to fail. But you can see for yourself."

He loosened his collar and bared his throat. Vance rose and made a careful scrutiny of the suspicious mark. It was situated a very little to the left of the central line, just above the clavicle, and, as Vance pointed out, directly over the big vessels of the throat. My friend called to me so that I might examine it, too. Whatever the opinion of the doctors may have been, Aylmer was obviously deeply interested.

And yet there was very little to show. The skin was quite intact, and there was no sign of inflammation. There were two red marks, about an inch apart, each of which was inclined to be crescent in shape. They were more visible than they might otherwise have been owing to the peculiar whiteness of Davenant's skin.

"It can't be anything of importance," said Davenant, with a slightly uneasy laugh. "I'm inclined to think the marks are dying away."

"Have you ever noticed them more inflamed than they are at present?" inquired Vance. "If so, was it at any special time?"

Davenant reflected. "Yes," he replied slowly, "there have been times, usually, I think perhaps invariably, when I wake up in the morning, that I've noticed them larger and more angry looking.

And I've felt a slight sensation of pain—a tingling—oh, very slight, and I've never worried about it. Only now you suggest it to my mind, I believe that those same mornings I have felt particularly tired and done up—a sensation of lassitude absolutely unusual to me. And once, Mr. Vance, I remember quite distinctly that there was a stain of blood close to the mark I didn't think anything of it at the time, and just wiped it away."

"I see." Aylmer Vance resumed his seat and invited his visitor to do the same. "And now," he resumed, "you said, Mr. Davenant, that there are certain peculiar circumstances you wish to acquaint me with. Will you do so?"

And so Davenant readjusted his collar and proceeded to tell his story. I will tell it as far as I can, without any reference to the occasional interruptions of Vance and myself.

Paul Davenant, as I have said, was a man of wealth and position, and so, in every sense of the word, he was a suitable husband for Miss Jessica MacThane, the young lady who eventually became his wife. Before coming to the incidents attending his loss of health, he had a great deal to recount about Miss MacThane and her family history.

She was of Scottish descent, and although she had certain characteristic features of her race, she was not really Scotch in appearance. Hers was the beauty of the far South rather than that of the Highlands from which she had her origin. Names are not always suited to their owners, and Miss MacThane's was peculiarly inappropriate. She had, in fact, been christened Jessica in a sort of pathetic effort to counteract her obvious departure from normal type. There was a reason for this which we were soon to learn.

Miss MacThane was especially, remarkable for her wonderful red hair, hair such as one hardly ever sees outside Italy—not the Celtic red—and it was so long that it reached to her feet, and it had an extraordinary gloss upon it, so that it seemed almost to have individual life of its own. Then she had just the complexion that one would expect with such hair, the purest ivory white, and not in the least marred by freckles, as is so often the case with red-haired girls. Her beauty was derived from an ancestress who had been brought to Scotland from some foreign shore—no one knew exactly whence.

Davenant fell in love with her almost at once, and he had every reason to believe, in spite of her many admirers, that his love was returned. At this time he knew very little about her personal history. He was aware only that she was very wealthy in her own right, an orphan, and the last representative of a race that had once been famous in the annals of history—or rather infamous, for the MacThanes had distinguished themselves more by cruelty and lust of blood than by deeds of chivalry. A clan of turbulent robbers in the past, they had helped to add many a blood-stained page to the history of their country.

Jessica had lived with her father, who owned a house in London, until his death when she was about fifteen years of age. Her mother had died in Scotland when Jessica was still a tiny child. Mr. MacThane had been so affected by his wife's death that, with his little daughter, he had abandoned his Scotch estate altogether— or so it was believed—leaving it to the management of a bailiff— though, indeed, there was but little work for the bailiff to do, since there were practically no tenants left. Blackwick Castle had borne for many years a most unenviable reputation.

After the death of her father, Miss MacThane had gone to live with a certain Mrs. Meredith, who was a connection of her mother's—on her father's side she had not a single relation left. Jessica was absolutely the last of a clan once so extensive that intermarriage had been a tradition of the family, but which for the last two hundred years had been gradually dwindling to extinction.

Mrs. Meredith took Jessica into Society—which would never have been her privilege had Mr. MacThane lived, for he was a moody, self-absorbed man, and prematurely old—one who seemed worn down by the weight of a great grief.

Well, I have said that Paul Davenant quickly fell in love with Jessica, and it was not long before he proposed for her hand. To his great surprise, for he had good reason to believe that she cared for him, he met with a refusal; nor would she give any explanation, though she burst into a flood of pitiful tears.

Bewildered and bitterly disappointed, he consulted Mrs. Meredith, with whom he happened to be on friendly terms, and from her he learnt that Jessica had already had several proposals, all from quite desirable men, but that one after another had been rejected.

Paul consoled himself with the reflection that perhaps Jessica did not love them, whereas he was quite sure that she cared for himself. Under these circumstances he determined to try again.

He did so, and with better result. Jessica admitted her love, but at the same time she repeated that she could not marry him. Love and marriage were not for her. Then, to his utter amaze, she declared that she had been born under a curse—a curse which sooner or later was bound to show itself in her, and which, more-over, must react cruelly, perhaps fatally, upon anyone with whom she linked her life. How could she allow a man she loved to take such a risk? Above all, since the evil was hereditary, there was one point upon which she had quite made up her mind: no child should ever call her mother—she must be the last of her race indeed.

Of course, Davenant was amazed, and inclined to think that Jessica had got some absurd idea into her head which a little rea-soning on his part would dispel. There was only one other possible explanation. Was it lunacy she was afraid of?

But Jessica shook her head; She did not know of any lunacy in her family. The ill was deeper, more subtle than that. And then she told him all that she knew.

The curse—she made use of that word for want of a better— was attached to the ancient race from which she had her origin. Her father had suffered from it, and his father and grandfather before him. All three had taken to themselves young wives who had died mysteriously, of some wasting disease, within a few years. Had they observed the ancient family tradition of intermarriage this might possibly not have happened, but in their case; since the family was so near extinction, this had not been possible.

For the curse—or whatever it was—did not kill those who bore the name of MacThane. It only rendered them a danger to others. It was as if they absorbed from the blood-soaked walls of their fatal castle a deadly taint which reacted terribly upon those with whom they were brought into contact, especially their nearest and dearest.

"Do you know what my father said we have it in us to become?" said Jessica with a shudder. "He used the word vampires. Paul, think of it—vampires—preying upon the life-blood of others."

And then, when Davenant was inclined to laugh, she checked him. "No," she cried out, "it is not impossible. Think. We are a decadent race. From the earliest times our history has been marked by bloodshed and cruelty. The walls of Blackwick Castle are impregnated with evil—every stone could tell its tale of violence, pain, lust, and murder. What can one expect of those who have spent their lifetime between its walls?"

"But you have not done so," exclaimed Paul. "You have been spared that, Jessica. You were taken away after your mother died, and you have no recollection of Blackwick Castle, none at all. And you need never set foot in it again."

"I'm afraid the evil is in my blood," she replied sadly, "although I am unconscious of it now. And as for not returning to Blackwick— I'm not sure that I can help myself. At least, that is what my father warned me of. He said that there is something there, some compelling force, that will call me to it in spite of myself. But, oh, I don't know—I don't know, and that is what makes it so difficult. If I could only believe that all this is nothing but an idle superstition, I might be happy again, for I have it in me to enjoy life, and I'm young, very young; but my father told me these things when he was on his death-bed." She added the last words in a low, awe-stricken tone.

Paul pressed her to tell him all that she knew, and eventually she revealed another fragment of family history which seemed to have some bearing upon the case. It dealt with her own astonishing likeness to that ancestress of a couple of hundred years ago, whose existence seemed to have presaged the gradual downfall of the clan of the MacThanes.

A certain Robert MacThane, departing from the traditions of his family, which demanded that he should not marry outside his clan, brought home a wife from foreign shores, a woman of wonderful beauty, who was possessed of glowing masses of red hair and a complexion of ivory whiteness—such as had more or less distinguished since then every female of the race born in the direct line.

It was not long before this woman came to be regarded in the neighbourhood as a witch. Queer stories were circulated abroad as to her doings, and the reputation of Blackwick Castle became worse than ever before.

And then one day she disappeared. Robert MacThane had been absent upon some business for twenty-four hours, and it was upon his return that he found her gone. The neighbourhood was searched, but without avail, and then Robert, who was a violent man and who had adored his foreign wife, called together certain of his tenants whom he suspected, rightly or wrongly, of foul play, and had them murdered in cold blood. Murder was easy in those days, yet such an outcry was raised that Robert had to take flight, leaving his two children in the care of their nurse, and for a long while Blackwick Castle was without a master.

But its evil reputation persisted. It was said that Zaida, the witch, though dead, still made her presence felt. Many children of the tenantry and young people of the neighbourhood sickened and died—possibly of quite natural causes; but this did not prevent a mantle of terror settling upon the countryside, for it was said that Zaida had been seen—a pale woman clad in white—flitting about the cottages at night, and where she passed sickness and death were sure to supervene.

And from that time the fortune of the family gradually declined. Heir succeeded heir, but no sooner was he installed at Blackwick Castle than his nature, whatever it may previously have been, seemed to undergo a change. It was as if he absorbed into himself all the weight of evil that had stained his family name—as if he did, indeed, become a vampire, bringing blight upon any not directly connected with his own house.

And so, by degrees, Blackwick was deserted of its tenantry. The land around it was left uncultivated—the farms stood empty. This had persisted to the present day, for the superstitious peasantry still told their tales of the mysterious white woman who hovered about the neighbourhood, and whose appearance betokened death—and possibly worse than death.

And yet it seemed that the last representatives of the Mac-Thanes could not desert their ancestral home. Riches they had, sufficient to live happily upon elsewhere, but, drawn by some power they could not contend against, they had preferred to spend their lives in the solitude of the now half-ruined castle, shunned by their neighbours, feared and execrated by the few tenants that still clung to their soil.

So it had been with Jessica's grandfather and great-grandfather. Each of them had married a young wife, and in each case their love story had been all too brief. The vampire spirit was still abroad, expressing itself—or so it seemed—through the living representatives of bygone generations of evil, and young blood had been demanded at the sacrifice.

And to them had succeeded Jessica's father. He had not profited by their example, but had followed directly in their footsteps. And the same fate had befallen the wife whom he passionately adored. She had died of pernicious anaemia—so the doctors said—but he had regarded himself as her murderer.

But, unlike his predecessors, he had torn himself away from Blackwick—and this for the sake of his child. Unknown to her, however, he had returned year after year, for there were times when the passionate longing for the gloomy, mysterious halls and corridors of the old castle, for the wild stretches of moorland, and the dark pine woods, would come upon him too strongly to be resisted. And so he knew that for his daughter, as for himself, there was no escape, and he warned her, when the relief of death was at last granted to him, of what her fate must be.

This was the tale that Jessica told the man who wished to make her his wife, and he made light of it, as such a man would, regarding it all as foolish superstition, the delusion of a mind over-wrought. And at last—perhaps it was not very difficult, for she loved him with all her heart and soul—he succeeded in inducing Jessica to think as he did, to banish morbid ideas, as he called them, from her brain, and to consent to marry him at an early date.

"I'll take any risk you like," he declared. "I'll even go and live at Blackwick if you should desire it. To think of you, my lovely Jessica, a vampire! Why, I never heard such nonsense in my life."

"Father said I'm very like Zaida, the witch," she protested, but he silenced her with a kiss.

And so they were married and spent their honeymoon abroad, and in the autumn Paul accepted an invitation to a house party in Scotland for the grouse shooting, a sport to which he was absolutely devoted, and Jessica agreed with him that there was no reason why he should forego his pleasure.

Perhaps it was an unwise thing to do, to venture to Scotland, but by this time the young couple, more deeply in love with each other than ever, had got quite over their fears. Jessica was redolent with health and spirits, and more than once she declared that if they should be anywhere in the neighbourhood of Blackwick she would like to see the old castle out of curiosity, and just to show how absolutely she had got over the foolish terrors that used to assail her.

This seemed to Paul to be quite a wise plan, and so one day, since they were actually staying at no great distance, they motored over to Blackwick, and finding the bailiff, got him to show them over the castle.

It was a great castellated pile, grey with age, and in places falling into ruin. It stood on a steep hillside, with the rock of which it seemed to form part, and on one side of it there was a precipitous drop to a mountain stream a hundred feet below. The robber Mac-Thanes of the old days could not have desired a better stronghold.

At the back, climbing up the mountain side, were dark pine woods, from which, here and there, rugged crags protruded, and these were fantastically shaped, some like gigantic and misshapen human forms, which stood up as if they mounted guard over the castle and the narrow gorge, by which alone it could be approached.

This gorge was always full of weird, uncanny sound. It might have been a storehouse for the wind, which, even on calm days, rushed up and down as if seeking an escape, and it moaned among the pines and whistled in the crags and shouted derisive laughter as it was tossed from side to side of the rocky heights. It was like the plaint of lost souls—that is the expression Davenant made use of—the plaint of lost souls.

The road, little more than a track now, passed through this gorge, and then, after skirting a small but deep lake, which hardly knew the light of the sun, so shut in was it by overhanging trees, climbed the hill to the castle.

And the castle! Davenant used but a few words to describe it, yet somehow I could see the gloomy edifice in my mind's eye, and something of the lurking horror that it contained communicated itself to my brain. Perhaps my clairvoyant sense assisted me, for when he spoke of them I seemed already acquainted with the great stone halls, the long corridors, gloomy and cold even on the brightest and warmest of days; the dark, oak-panelled rooms, and the broad central staircase up which one of the early MacThanes had once led a dozen men on horseback in pursuit of a stag which had taken refuge within the precincts of the castle. There was the keep, too, its walls so thick that the ravages of time had made no impression upon them, and beneath the keep were dungeons which could tell terrible tales of ancient wrong and lingering pain.

Well, Mr. and Mrs. Davenant visited as much as the bailiff could show them of this ill-omened edifice, and Paul, for his part, thought pleasantly of his own Derbyshire home, the fine Georgian mansion, replete with every modern comfort, where he proposed to settle with his wife. And so he received something of a shock when, as they drove away, she slipped her hand into his and whispered: "Paul, you promised, didn't you, that you would refuse me nothing?"

She had been strangely silent till she spoke these words. Paul, slightly apprehensive, assured her that she only had to ask—but the speech did not come from his heart, for he guessed vaguely what she desired.

She wanted to go and live at the castle—oh, only for a little while, for she was sure she would soon tire of it. But the bailiff had told her that there were papers, documents, which she ought to examine, since the property was now hers—and, besides, she was interested in this home of her ancestors, and wanted to explore it more thoroughly. Oh, no, she wasn't in the least influenced by the old superstition—that wasn't the attraction—she had quite got over those silly ideas. Paul had cured her, and since he himself was so convinced that they were without foundation he ought not to mind granting her her whim.

This was a plausible argument, not easy to controvert. In the end Paul yielded, though it was not without a struggle. He suggested amendments. Let him at least have the place done up for her—that would take time; or let them postpone their visit till next year—in the summer—not move in just as the winter was upon them.

But Jessica did not want to delay longer than she could help, and she hated the idea of redecoration. Why, it would spoil the illusion of the old place, and, besides, it would be a waste of money since she only wished to remain there for a week or two. The Derbyshire house was not quite ready yet; they must allow time for the paper to dry on the walls.

And so, a week later, when their stay with their friends was concluded, they went to Blackwick, the bailiff having engaged a few raw servants and generally made things as comfortable for them as possible. Paul was worried and apprehensive, but he could not admit this to his wife after having so loudly proclaimed his theories on the subject of superstition.

They had been married three months at this time—nine had passed since then, and they had never left Blackwick for more than a few hours—till now Paul had come to London—alone.

"Over and over again," he declared, "my wife has begged me to go. With tears in her eyes, almost upon her knees, she has entreated me to leave her, but I have steadily refused unless she will accompany me. But that is the trouble, Mr. Vance, she cannot; there is something, some mysterious horror, that holds her there as surely as if she were bound with fetters. It holds her more strongly even than it held her father—we found out that he used to spend six

months at least of every year at Blackwick—months when he pretended that he was travelling abroad. You see the spell—or whatever the accursed thing may be—never really relaxed its grip of him."

"Did you never attempt to take your wife away?" asked Vance.

"Yes, several times; but it was hopeless. She would become so
ill as soon as we were beyond the limit of the estate that I invariably had to take her back. Once we got as far as Dorekirk—that is
the nearest town, you know—and I thought I should be successful
if only I could get through the night. But she escaped me; she
climbed out of a window—she meant to go back on foot, at night,
all those long miles. Then I have had doctors down; but it is I who
wanted the doctors, not she. They have ordered me away, but I
have refused to obey them till now."

"Is your wife changed at all—physically?" interrupted Vance.

Davenant reflected. "Changed," he said, "yes, but so subtly that
I hardly know how to describe it. She is more beautiful than ever—
and yet it isn't the same beauty, if you can understand me. I have
spoken of her white complexion, well, one is more than ever conscious of it now, because her lips have become so red—they are
almost like a splash of blood upon her face. And the upper one has
a peculiar curve that I don't think it had before, and when she
laughs she doesn't smile—do you know what I mean? Then her
hair—it has lost its wonderful gloss. Of course, I know she is fret-
ting about me; but that is so peculiar, too, for at times, as I have
told you, she will implore me to go and leave her, and then, perhaps only a few minutes later, she will wreathe her arms round my
neck and say she cannot live without me. And I feel that there is a
struggle going on within her, that she is only yielding slowly to the
horrible influence—whatever it is—that she is herself when she begs
me to go. But when she entreats me to stay—and it is then that her
fascination is most intense—oh, I can't help remembering what she
told me before we were married, and that word"—he lowered his
voice— "the word 'vampire'—"

He passed his hand over his brow that was wet with perspiration. "But that's absurd, ridiculous," he muttered; "these fantastic

beliefs have been exploded years ago. We live in the twentieth century."

A pause ensued, then Vance said quietly, "Mr. Davenant, since you have taken me into your confidence, since you have found doctors of no avail, will you let me try to help you? I think I may be of some use—if it is not already too late. Should you agree, Mr. Dexter and I will accompany you, as you have suggested, to Blackwick Castle as early as possible—by tonight's mail North. Under ordinary circumstances, I should tell you, as you value your life, not to return—"

Davenant shook his head. "That is advice which I should never take," he declared. "I had already decided, under any circumstances, to travel North tonight. I am glad that you both will accompany me."

And so it was decided. We settled to meet at the station, and presently Paul Davenant took his departure. Any other details that remained to be told he would put us in possession of during the course of the journey.

"A curious and most interesting case," remarked Vance when we were alone. "What do you make of it, Dexter?"

"I suppose," I replied cautiously, "that there is such a thing as vampirism even in these days of advanced civilisation? I can understand the evil influence that a very old person may have upon a young one if they happen to be in constant intercourse—the worn-out tissue sapping healthy vitality for their own support. And there are certain people—I could think of several myself—who seem to depress one and undermine one's energies, quite unconsciously of course, but one feels somehow that vitality has passed from oneself to them. And in this case, when the force is centuries old, expressing itself, in some mysterious way, through Davenant's wife, is it not feasible to believe that he may be physically affected by it, even though the whole thing is sheerly mental?"

"You think, then," demanded Vance, "that it is sheerly mental? Tell me, if that is so, how do you account for the marks on Davenant's throat?"

This was a question to which I found no reply, and though I pressed him for his views, Vance would not commit himself further just then.

Of our long journey to Scotland I need say nothing. We did not reach Blackwick Castle till late in the afternoon of the following day. The place was just as I had conceived it—as I have already described it. And a sense of gloom settled upon me as our car jolted us over the rough road that led through the Gorge of the Winds—a gloom that deepened when we penetrated into the vast cold hall of the castle.

Mrs. Davenant, who had been informed by telegram of our arrival, received us cordially. She knew nothing of our actual mission, regarding us merely as friends of her husband's. She was most solicitous on his behalf, but there was something strained about her tone, and it made me feel vaguely uneasy. The impression that I got was that the woman was impelled to everything that she said or did by some force outside herself—but, of course, this was a conclusion that the circumstances I was aware of might easily have conduced to. In every other respect she was charming, and she had an extraordinary fascination of appearance and manner that made me readily understand the force of a remark made by Davenant during our journey.

"I want to live for Jessica's sake. Get her away from Blackwick, Vance, and I feel that all will be well. I'd go through hell to have her restored to me—as she was."

And now that I have seen Mrs. Davenant I realised what he meant by those last words. Her fascination was stronger than ever, but it was not a natural fascination—not that of a normal woman, such as she had been. It was the fascination of a Circe, of a witch, of an enchantress—and as such was irresistible.

We had strong proof of the evil within her soon after our arrival. It was a test that Vance had quietly prepared. Davenant had mentioned that no flowers grew at Blackwick, and Vance declared that we must take some with us as a present for the lady of the house. He purchased a bouquet of pure white roses at the little town where we left the train, for the motor-car had been sent to meet us.

Soon after our arrival he presented these to Mrs. Davenant. She took them, it seemed to me nervously, and hardly had her hand touched them before they fell to pieces, in a shower of crumpled petals, to the floor.

"We must act at once," said Vance to me when we were descending to dinner that night. "There must be no delay."

"What are you afraid of?" I whispered.

"Davenant has been absent a week," he replied grimly. "He is stronger than when he went away, but not strong enough to survive the loss of more blood. He must be protected. There is danger tonight."

"You mean from his wife?" I shuddered at the ghastliness of the suggestion.

"That is what time will show." Vance turned to me and added a few words with intense earnestness. "Mrs. Davenant, Dexter, is at present hovering between two conditions. The evil thing has not yet completely mastered her—you remember what Davenant said, how she would beg him to go away and at the next moment entreat him to stay? She has made a struggle, but she is gradually succumbing, and this last week, spent here alone, has strengthened the evil. And that is what I have got to fight, Dexter—it is to be a contest of will, a contest that will go on silently till one or the other obtains the mastery. If you watch you may see. Should a change show itself in Mrs. Davenant you will know that I have won."

Thus I knew the direction in which my friend proposed to act. It was to be a war of his will against the mysterious power that had laid its curse upon the house of MacThane. Mrs. Davenant must be released from the fatal charm that held her.

And I, knowing what was going on, was able to watch and understand. I realised that the silent contest had begun even while we sat at dinner. Mrs. Davenant ate practically nothing and seemed ill at ease; she fidgeted in her chair, talked a great deal, and laughed—it was the laugh without a smile, as Davenant had described it. And as soon as she was able she withdrew.

Later, as we sat in the drawing-room, I could still feel the clash of wills. The air in the room felt electric and heavy, charged with tremendous but invisible forces. And outside, round the castle, the wind whistled and shrieked and moaned—it was as if all the dead and gone MacThanes, a grim army, had collected to fight the battle of their race.

And all this while we four in the drawing-room were sitting and talking the ordinary commonplaces of after-dinner conversation! That was the extraordinary part of it—Paul Davenant suspected nothing, and I, who knew, had to play my part. But I hardly took my eyes from Jessica's face. When would the change come, or was it, indeed, too late?

At last Davenant rose and remarked that he was tired and would go to bed. There was no need for Jessica to hurry. He would sleep that night in his dressing-room, and did not want to be disturbed.

And it was at that moment, as his lips met hers in a good night kiss, as she wreathed her enchantress arms about him, careless of our presence, her eyes gleaming hungrily, that the change came.

It came with a fierce and threatening shriek of wind, and a rattling of the casement, as if the horde of ghosts without was about to break in upon us. A long, quivering sigh escaped from Jessica's lips, her arms fell from her husband's shoulders, and she drew back, swaying a little from side to side.

"Paul," she cried, and somehow the whole timbre of her voice was changed, "what a wretch I've been to bring you back to Blackwick, ill as you are! But we'll go away, dear; yes, I'll go, too. Oh, will you take me away—take me away tomorrow?" She spoke with an intense earnestness—unconscious all the time of what had been happening to her. Long shudders were convulsing her frame. "I don't know why I've wanted to stay here," she kept repeating. "I hate the place, really—it's evil—evil."

Having heard these words I exulted, for surely Vance's success was assured. But I was soon to learn that the danger was not yet past.

Husband and wife separated, each going to their own room. I noticed the grateful, if mystified, glance that Davenant threw at

Vance, vaguely aware, as he must have been, that my friend was somehow responsible for what had happened. It was settled that plans for departure were to be discussed on the morrow.

"I have succeeded," Vance said hurriedly, when we were alone, "but the change may be transitory. I must keep watch tonight. Go you to bed, Dexter, there is nothing that you can do."

I obeyed—though I would sooner have kept watch, too—watch against a danger of which I had no understanding. I went to my room, a gloomy and sparsely furnished apartment, but I knew that it was quite impossible for me to think of sleeping. And so, dressed as I was, I went and sat by the open window, for now the wind that had raged round the castle had died down to a low moaning in the pine trees—a whimpering of time-worn agony.

And it was as I sat thus that I became aware of a white figure that stole out from the castle by a door I could not see, and, with hands clasped, ran swiftly across the terrace to the wood. I had but a momentary glance, but I felt convinced that the figure was that of Jessica Davenant.

And instinctively I knew that some great danger was imminent. It was, I think, the suggestion of despair conveyed by those clasped hands. At any rate, I did not hesitate. My window was some height from the ground, but the wall below was ivy-clad and afforded good foot-hold. The descent was quite easy. I achieved it, and was just in time to take up the pursuit in the right direction, which was into the thickness of the wood that clung to the slope of the hill.

I shall never forget that wild chase. There was just sufficient room to enable me to follow the rough path, which, luckily, since I had now lost sight of my quarry, was the only possible way that she could have taken; there were no intersecting tracks, and the wood was too thick on either side to permit of deviation.

And the wood seemed full of dreadful sound—moaning and wailing and hideous laughter. The wind, of course, and the screaming of night birds—once I felt the fluttering of wings in close proximity to my face. But I could not rid myself of the thought that I, in turn, was being pursued, that the forces of hell were combined against me.

The path came to an abrupt end on the border of the sombre lake that I have already mentioned. And now I realised that I was indeed only just in time, for before me, plunging knee-deep in the water, I recognised the white-clad figure of the woman I had been pursuing. Hearing my footsteps, she turned her head, and then threw up her arms and screamed. Her red hair fell in heavy masses about her shoulders, and her face, as I saw it that moment, was hardly human for. the agony of remorse that it depicted.

"Go!" she screamed. "For God's sake let me die!"

But I was by her side almost as she spoke. She struggled with me—sought vainly to tear herself from my clasp—implored me, with panting breath, to let her drown.

"It's the only way to save him!" she gasped. "Don't you understand that I am a thing accursed? For it is I—I—who have sapped his lifeblood! I know it now, the truth has been revealed to me to-night! I am a vampire, without hope in this world or the next, so for his sake—for the sake of his unborn child—let me die—let me die!"

Was ever so terrible an appeal made? Yet what could I do? Gently I overcame her resistance and drew her back to shore. By the time I reached it she was lying a dead weight upon my arm. I laid her down upon a mossy bank, and, kneeling by her side, gazed into her face.

And then I knew that I had done well. For the face I looked upon was not that of Jessica the vampire, as I had seen it that afternoon, it was the face of Jessica, the woman whom Paul Davenant had loved.

And later Aylmer Vance had his tale to tell.

"I waited," he said, "until I knew that Davenant was asleep, and then I stole into his room to watch by his bedside. And presently she came, as I guessed she would, the vampire, the accursed thing that has preyed upon the souls of her kin, making them like to herself when they too have passed into Shadowland, and gathering sustenance for her horrid task from the blood of those who are alien to her race. Paul's body and Jessica's soul—it is for one and the other, Dexter, that we have fought."

"You mean," I hesitated, "Zaida, the witch!"

"Even so," he agreed. "Here is the evil spirit that has fallen like a blight upon the house of MacThane. But now I think she may be exorcised for ever."

"Tell me."

"She came to Paul Davenant last night, as she must have done before, in the guise of his wife. You know that Jessica bears a strong resemblance to her ancestress. He opened his arms, but she was foiled of her prey, for I had taken my precautions; I had placed That upon Davenant's breast while he slept which robbed the vampire of her power of ill. She sped wailing from the room—a shadow—she who a minute before had looked at him with Jessica's eyes and spoken to him with Jessica's voice. Her red lips were Jessica's lips, and they were close to his when his eyes opened and he saw her as she was—a hideous phantom of the corruption of the ages. And so the spell was removed, and she fled away to the place whence she had come—"

He paused. "And now?" I inquired.

"Blackwick Castle must be razed to the ground," he replied. "That is the only way. Every stone of it, every brick, must be ground to powder and burnt with fire, for therein is the cause of all the evil. Davenant has consented."

"And Mrs. Davenant?"

"I think," Vance answered cautiously, "that all may be well with her. The curse will be removed with the destruction of the castle. She has not—thanks to you—perished under its influence. She was less guilty than she imagined—herself preyed upon rather than preying. But can't you understand her remorse when she realised, as she was bound to realise, the part she had played? And the knowledge of the child to come—its fatal inheritance—"

"I understand," I muttered with a shudder. And then, under my breath, I whispered, "Thank God!"

THE BOY OF BLACKSTOCK

HAVE INTERESTING CASE ON HAND. IF NOTHING BET-
TER TO DO, JOIN ME TOMORROW, HEDSTONE, ESSEX.

Such was the wording of a telegram which I received (at the little French watering-place where I happened to be staying) from Aylmer Vance, whom I imagined to be somewhere in Syria, busy with the exploration of certain ancient ruins.

It was autumn, and I, for my part, was getting tired of a rather purposeless Continental ramble, so I hailed Vance's telegram with joy. I cabled back that I was coming at once, caught a night boat from Dieppe, spent an hour or two in London, and arrived at Hedstone Grange, my friend's house in Essex, in time for lunch.

He would not say a word about the "case," however, until we had disposed of that meal and were lazily indulging in dessert. For himself he ate very little but fruit and vegetables at any time.

"Syria will keep till later on," he observed then. "I had decided to go, and ran down to Hedstone to get a few things together. And then I received a visit from a certain gentleman, and—well, it promised to be interesting, so I sent you that cable."

He interrupted my expression of pleasure that he had done so by asking a question. "Do you know the meaning of the term 'Poultergeist,' Dexter?" he inquired.

I had heard the expression. "Isn't it a German word that expresses a sort of mischievous ghost?" I replied. "An elemental spirit that pulls furniture about, rings bells, smashes crockery, and makes itself generally obnoxious? Is that the kind of thing that we've to deal with this time?"

Aylmer smiled. "Perhaps," he responded with his usual caution. "But there are circumstances about this 'Poultergeist'—if the term is at all relevant—that lifts it above the common. The ghost of Blackstock Priory—where we are invited to go tomorrow—is really a family spectre, and it bears a name that is traditional—the Mischievous Boy of Blackstock—you may have heard of it, for the old legend is quite well-known. It belongs to the Rystone family. Lord Rystone owns Blackstock Priory to this day, though the possession was once very bitterly disputed."

"I've an idea that I've heard the story," I put in here, "but I should like you to refresh my memory."

"The tradition goes back to the Stuart times," resumed Vance, "and, of course, there is a tragedy connected with it. The Lord Rystone of that day happened to have a very beautiful young wife of whom he was immensely proud, and at the same time, inordinately jealous—probably with good reason, for she appears to have been as frivolous as she was beautiful. Anyhow, the story goes that one day he surprised his wife, under compromising conditions, in the company of a certain handsome young fellow named Gregory Laidlaw, who was the son of the very man who disputed Lord Rystone's title to the property of Blackstock. Well, the husband's jealousy and wrath got the better of him, and he murdered them both upon the spot—murdered them in cold blood just where he had found them, in a certain room at Blackstock Priory which, at that time, was his wife's boudoir. He then reported what he had done, and, in the result, was acquitted—or received no punishment worth speaking about.

"But he wasn't let off so easily by his victim, Gregory Laidlaw. Lord Rystone continued to live at Blackstock, which, by the way, is in Essex, and at no great distance from here, but his life was made a burden for him. The 'Mischievous Boy' soon began his pranks. I take it that the term 'Boy' has been applied to Gregory Laidlaw, or, rather, to Gregory Laidlaw's ghost, more on account of the monkey-tricks that he perpetrated than because of his actual age—

according to the story, he must have been at least twenty-three or twenty-four when he was murdered. Anyway, he gave Lord Rystone no peace, never making himself actually visible, but playing most ridiculous pranks at inopportune times—throwing open doors, wailing and laughing about the corridors, pealing the bells, and often frightening people out of their wits by touching them with his cold, clammy hands.

"Well, this went on for months and months, until one day Lord Rystone did actually see his enemy. Something—heaven knows what—took him to the room where the tragedy had been enacted— he said he obeyed an impulse that he couldn't resist—and there he saw both his victims, and Gregory, his hand upon his heart and a derisive smile upon his lips, bowed to him three times. A few days later Lord Rystone died.

"After that, Master Gregory played no more pranks unless his room—the scene of his murder—was interfered with—which it was by several subsequent Lord Rystones. People who were given that room to sleep in were frightened out of their wits—their bedclothes were pulled off them or they were jerked about in the most uncomfortable fashion—but the Boy himself was not seen. He appeared only once to each Lord Rystone in succession—and that was as a foreteller of death.

"At last the Rystones became sick of their ancestral ghost, and let the Priory on a ninety-nine years' lease to the then representative of the Laidlaw family, which was really as it should be, for the Laidlaws were the first owners of the property which they had been unfairly jostled out of. They were Essex people, which the Rystones were not, and had always been popular in the country. As soon as Mr. Laidlaw came into possession he had the haunted room shut up, and from that day on nothing whatever was heard of the 'Mischievous Boy.'"

Aylmer Vance paused and carefully peeled the skin from an apple to which he had just helped himself. Having consumed the fruit, he resumed: "The lease granted to the Laidlaws has now expired, and the present Lord Rystone, who appears to be a man of obstinate and cantankerous temper, has refused to renew it. He has, in fact, elected to go and live at Blackstock himself."

"And the 'Mischievous Boy' has broken out again," I hazarded, "and is giving him a warm time of it?"

"That is so." Aylmer smiled his slow smile. "Lord Rystone refuses, however, to believe that there is any truth in the old tradition, and maintains that he is being made the victim of a conspiracy. He suspects some agent of his late tenant's to be at the bottom of the whole thing—for the Laidlaws want to get back to Blackstock, and the people of the neighbourhood want nothing so much as to see them reinstated. In spite of this belief, he has come to me, which proves that there is some latent superstition about him, though he won't admit it."

"Or, of course," I ventured, "there may be some other natural cause for what is going on. I know that this sort of thing is usually associated with a human subject—some hysterical individual affected, perhaps, by the old tradition. Doesn't the 'Poultergeist' usually act through a human medium? You have told me of such cases. There was Halton Manor, for instance. Do you know anything of Lord Rystone's family?"

Vance nodded appreciatively. He liked me to show an intelligent interest in his cases.

"I know very little further at present," he responded. "Lord Rystone was not very communicative. It appears that he has been in residence at Blackstock for about a month, and I imagine that there is no one in the family except himself, his wife, his two boys, and their tutor. The boys are his sons by his first wife, for you may remember that it is only a couple of years since he married for the second time. His wife is ever so much younger than himself, and she was, I believe, the daughter of a clergyman, quite a poor man, who is now the vicar of Blackstock. These, things I know from hearsay—local gossip. I've met the vicar—his name is Gaynor—the Revd. Alison Gaynor—at some county function. An able man, from all accounts, and one who is ambitious for higher things. Of course, he obtained his present living through the influence of his son-in-law.

But, for the moment, all this is outside the question. The point we have to solve is whether the manifestations at Blackstock are of human or superhuman origin—and we'll get to work tomorrow. I've mentioned that I propose to bring a friend with me, so you are expected."

The next day, accordingly, we proceeded by car to Blackstock Priory, which is situated to the north-east of the county, a lonely and rather uninviting spot not far away from the sea.

We arrived in the course of the afternoon, and we found the whole household, together with one or two visitors, in the garden, partaking of tea under a huge oak that was still leafy in spite of its great age.

Lord Rystone came forward to receive us, and I was formally introduced.

The man's appearance did not impress me favourably. I could readily understand why Vance had described him as an obstinate, pigheaded man. He had a square jaw and an ugly mouth that had a way of twisting sarcastically when he spoke. One could imagine him capable of saying most unpleasant things upon the slightest provocation. He had black hair and black bushy eyebrows which came close together over the bridge of his nose. I put him down as being about fifty years of age, perhaps a little more.

His voice was loud and raucous.

"Glad to know you, Mr. Dexter," he said, "and I hope you and Mr. Vance will find means to put an end to this infernal nuisance that I've got to submit to in this house. Of course, I don't believe for a moment that it's anything to do with spooks, and the story of the Mischievous Boy is nothing but a silly superstition. No, sir, I don't believe in spooks, and I can tell you straight away that I suspect my servants. There are people about the place who have a spite against me and who want nothing better than to turn me out. They think they can frighten me away, but that's where they are mistaken. I'm not the kind of man to give in when I've made up my mind about a thing."

It wasn't the time to argue the point, so I merely made some commonplace observation, after which I was introduced to the rest of the company.

Naturally, my interest at that moment was centred upon Lady Rystone.

She was charmingly pretty after a delicate Dresden china sort of style. She could not have been much over twenty, very fair and with tiny little hands and feet. She had eyes and lips that seemed made for love and laughter, and pretty dimples in her cheeks; but looking at her closely, one felt painfully that all these charming attributes were gradually fading, and that it would not be long before the piquante little face became pinched and fretful.

It was obvious, even to the casual observer, that she was not happy.

What on earth had induced her to marry Lord Rystone? That was the first thought that shot into my brain upon seeing her. Then I remembered that she was the daughter of a poor clergyman, and that probably family interests had been the chief factor in the case.

I felt sorry for her, for certainly she must be paying heavily for her sacrifice.

Lord Rystone's two sons, boys of twelve and fourteen years of age, were present with their tutor, whose name was James Felton. The boys were dark-haired, heavy-jowled young cubs, who had never been to school in their lives, and whose manners were atrocious.

Nor did I like the appearance of the tutor. He, too, seemed to have absorbed some of the prevailing gloom. He was a good-looking young man, but he had a discontented mouth and eyes that seemed to me shifty and untrustworthy.

The rest of the party consisted of the vicar, Lady Rystone's father, who seemed pleased to renew his acquaintance with Vance. He was a handsome man with intelligent, well-cut features; but somehow he looked no happier than the rest, and I fancied that he often glanced uneasily at his daughter. Besides him there were a couple of callers, a dull man and his even duller wife; they left soon after we arrived.

After their departure, conversation turned on the supposed haunting, and Lord Rystone repeated the story of the "Mischievous Boy," the story with which I was already acquainted.

"There's never been a hint of a ghost at the Priory for the last hundred years," he said. "And looking up the records, the last allusion I can find to the 'Boy's' appearance is when he appeared to my great grandfather some time in the nineteenth century, just before he died. That, of course, was years before the Priory was leased to the Laidlaws. The superstition is, you must understand, that the 'Boy' only shows himself when one of our family is going to die—otherwise he is never visible; nor does he get up to his tricks unless the room in which he and his lady love were murdered is interfered with. That's the yarn they tell."

"And you have opened up that room?" inquired Vance, who had settled himself comfortably in a deck chair.

"Yes; and why not, I should like to know?" retorted Lord Rystone with some asperity. "It's one of the finest rooms in the house, and situated in a part of the building where it can't be easily dispensed with. It's ridiculous that it should be shut up for ever on account of an old wives' tale. I'm furnishing it as a bedroom, and eventually I shall sleep there myself."

He spoke the last words defiantly.

"You have the courage of your opinions," replied Vance quietly. "But if you desire peace, might it not be just as well to try the effect of closing the room again—as an experiment?"

"No," was the abrupt and rather surly response. "I've told you that I don't believe there's anything supernormal in the whole business. It's all a got up job by someone who wants me to leave the place altogether. If you can prove to me the contrary, Mr. Vance, then I'll shut up the room—but not until then."

While this conversation was in progress, a conversation in which I took no part, I was watching the faces of the rest of the company, and I could not help imagining that the tutor, Mr. Felton, kept his dark eyes fixed upon the face of Lady Rystone, and that she was uncomfortably aware of the fact. And I imagined that there was something malignant in his regard—almost a threat—and that he wished to convey the fact to her.

The moment, however, that he noticed that I was looking at him, he turned his attention to his pupils, to whom he made some half-laughing remark.

As for the two boys, they seemed to take the whole thing in the light of a joke, and I could see them giggling together, although they were evidently in some awe of their father.

They were ill-conditioned and badly brought up youngsters, and it naturally occurred to me that they might have something to do with the manifestations—if these really had a human origin.

Anyway, I decided to keep my eyes upon them.

"May I ask," inquired Vance, addressing our host, "if you opened up the haunted room as soon as you came into residence at the Priory?"

Lord Rystone shook his head.

"No," he replied, "it wasn't till a fortnight later."

"And did you have any trouble during the first fortnight?"

The answer, rather grudgingly delivered, was again in the negative.

"But it was only after I'd been here a fortnight," added his lordship, "that the neighbourhood began to show me that I wasn't wanted. I'd taken on some of the old servants, keepers and others, who had been in the employ of my predecessors. They were a lazy lot, and I told them so—the Laidlaws have always been notorious fools in their treatment of their people—and I suppose the fellows didn't like the new administration. Anyway, they all gave notice in a body, and it was after that that the trouble began."

"I see."

Aylmer sat back in his chair pensively, and for a little while after that took no part in the general conversation.

One of the boys—the eldest—was recounting how he had been told that morning that one of the servants, happening to pass the door of the haunted room rather late the night before, had heard curious sounds from within, and being braver than most of his fellows, had ventured very gingerly to open the door.

It was not quite dark within, because the moon was shining, and the room, as yet only half-furnished, had not been provided with curtains, and the man declared that he caught sight of what he imagined to be two dim figures standing in the moonlight apparently clasped in each other's arms.

He was not, however, able to swear positively to anything, because before he had had time to open the door wide, it was torn from his hand and then slammed violently in his face.

Lord Rystone frowned heavily. Incredulous though he professed to be, he was palpably worried at this suggestion of the actual appearance of the "Boy"—an appearance reputed to bode him ill.

"Who told you this absurd story, Paul?" he asked gruffly.

"It was Lomax, the under-footman," responded the boy readily.

"Very well, go and tell Lomax that I want to speak to him at once. We may as well question him here in your presence, Mr. Vance."

Lord Rystone addressed the last words to my friend, who quietly nodded his acquiescence.

And so Paul ran off, evidently delighted with his mission, and a few minutes later returned with the under-footman who, in our presence, confirmed in every respect the story which we had just heard, adding one or two details of his own.

He had imagined that he heard voices in the room, low whisperings, and it was that which had at first attracted his attention, knowing, as he did, that the room was not yet in use, and that, in any case, nobody was likely to be there at that hour of the night.

He told his story gravely, palpably convinced of the truth of every word he said. He seemed to me a well-spoken, dependable sort of young man, and I felt genuinely sorry for him when Lord Rystone, unable to shake his story in any particular, lost his temper, addressed him roughly, and told him that he was a coward and a fool.

"Why on earth didn't you open the door again after it had been slammed in your face?" shouted the angry earl. "I suppose you were too frightened to do so, eh?"

"I did try," responded the young man, flushing to his hair, "but it was no use. The door was locked."

"Well, that's a proof that you are telling a lie," was the fierce retort, "for there's been no key fitted to the lock yet." He turned to Vance and myself. "The room had been walled up," he explained, "and after I had it opened up, we found an unlocked door without a key; and as I haven't got a new one yet, how was it possible that the door could be locked? The fellow's a palpable liar."

The natural consequence of this repeated assertion was that the footman gave notice upon the spot—and I may say that I thoroughly sympathised with him under the circumstances.

Lord Rystone fumed with rage. He swore violently without the smallest regard to the presence of his wife and children.

"It's a conspiracy," he declared, "and they are all in it; but I'll get even with them yet."

Soon after this we went into the house, and Vance and I were left to ourselves till dinner time.

During this interview I took the opportunity of mentioning to him the curious expression which I had seen upon the tutor's face and the significant glance which he had cast at Lady Rystone.

"I don't like the look, of that fellow," I said, "but, of course, it may only have been my imagination. Have you formed any opinion so far?"

"It's much too early yet to form any opinion," was my friend's reply. He smiled a little. "You ought to know by now, Dexter," he said, "that I never jump to conclusions."

At dinner that evening we were introduced to yet another member of the household—Mrs. Mellish, who acted as companion to the young countess. She was an elderly and austere woman who did not in the least add to the gaiety of the company.

And it was while we were at dinner that we were treated to our first manifestation of the mischievous influence that was at work in the house.

There came a tremendous crash all of a sudden in the hall without, and on running to the door we discovered the butler standing in the midst of a debris of broken plates and dishes and other paraphernalia that he had been carrying to the dining-room upon a tray.

He was white and trembling, and he had cut his hand a little.

Lord Rystone's cheeks grew florid with rage, and he began to bluster. He had never known such gross carelessness in his life, he declared. What on earth had the man done to drop the tray?

The butler stooped and picked up something from the floor, where it lay among the fragments of broken china.

"That's what did it, your lordship," he said nervously, holding up for our inspection a heavy flint stone. "It fell down from overhead right into the middle of my tray. I couldn't help dropping the things, no one could have."

The hall was large and square, and a gallery ran round three sides of it. It would have been quite easy, I reflected, for anyone concealed up there to drop the stone as the butler passed below. But the incident made one thing practically certain: if anyone of the house party was responsible for the trouble, there must undoubtedly be a confederate as well.

For we had all, including the two boys, been assembled at the dinner table.

The boys rushed off upstairs, and for the next few minutes, while their father blustered, we could hear them careering up and down the gallery and opening every available door in their pursuit of the ghost. But their efforts were quite futile, and presently they returned, excited and looking upon the whole thing as excellent sport.

I was soon to find out that they behaved in exactly the same way after every manifestation of which they were witness.

The butler was still quaking, partly with fear and partly with wrath at the way his explanation had been received.

"I can't stand it any longer," he muttered, stanching the blood from a small cut upon his hand. He looked almost as if he were about to faint. "I'm sorry, my lord, but I should like to leave—to-morrow; if you will allow me."

"Yes, go, and the devil take you," roared his lordship furiously, after which we all returned to the dining-room and continued our interrupted meal as best we could.

Nothing further occurred till about an hour later, when we were assembled in the drawing-room, except the two boys, who had been sent off to bed.

The first intimation we had of the return of the poltergeist—if poltergeist it was—was the sudden opening of the drawing-room

door. It was flung violently back, so violently as nearly to throw it
off its hinges, and at the same moment I distinctly heard the sound
of a chuckling laugh.

Yet, once again, when we rushed out into the hall, it was to
find no trace of any living soul.

Almost immediately afterwards, however, and while we were
still standing there literally gaping at each other, a series of bells
began to ring, apparently from somewhere in the servants' quarters.

Poor Lady Rystone was nearly in tears—to all appearance terribly afraid.

"Oh, Kelsey," she entreated her husband, "what's the use of
going on like this? Why won't you shut up the haunted room again,
or, better still, why won't you leave this horrid place altogether?"

"I dare say you'd like me to take you away, wouldn't you?" he
retorted in a tone that to me sounded quite unnecessarily brutal.
"But I've had enough of London, and so have you, for some time to
come. And as for shutting up the haunted room, I am damned if I
do. I'll get to the bottom of this infernal conspiracy first."

There was something terrifying in the frown he bestowed upon
his wife, and Lady Rystone seemed to shrink under it—her lips
quivered pitifully, and she shook in every limb. I felt more sorry
for her than ever, and deeply incensed against the man for his sheer
brutality. I was puzzled, too, for at the same moment I was again
conscious of that queer, menacing look in the tutor's eyes as he
watched the scene. There was something horribly exultant about
it—I think that is the word that most nearly expresses my meaning.

Well, we had no more alarms that night, and the next day Vance
and I set about making a thorough exploration of the Priory, which,
I don't think I have mentioned, was a low-built, rambling edifice
with walls of considerable thickness.

I suspected secret chambers and passages, and, indeed, several of these were known and pointed out to us by Lord Rystone.
For the most part, however, they had been blocked up so efficiently
as to render them impossible as hiding-places.

We examined the haunted room.

It was a large, low apartment upon the first floor. After its use as a boudoir by the murdered Lady Rystone, it had been used as a bedroom, and then dismantled because of the hauntings. It was at present unfurnished save for a few old-fashioned chairs and a sofa. It had a painted ceiling, and its walls were hung with faded tapestry. There were one or two curtained recesses which added to the eerie aspect of the room.

"With your permission, Lord Rystone," said Vane, "I will pass the night in this room. You need not worry about the bed. I shall be quite comfortable in one of the chairs."

Permission was granted, and then, very naturally, I asked Vance to allow me to share his vigil. But to my surprise, and a little to my mortification, he refused.

He laid his hand in a friendly manner upon my shoulder.

"Don't be vexed, Dexter," he said. "I have my reasons. Believe me, it is for the best."

He would not give his reasons, and I knew him well enough by now to appreciate that argument was useless, so I was forced to accept the inevitable.

Well, I had thought out all manner of plans for trapping the "ghost," if the "ghost" should prove to be human—thread entanglements over the bell-wires, and that sort of thing—but Vance would have none of them.

"Wait till tomorrow," he said. "I shall know better then how to act." I could not induce him to tell me his suspicions, yet I knew they were already forming in his mind.

At dinner that night there was another unpleasant scene—not due this time to ghostly phenomena.

Lord Rystone came in palpably in a bad temper. He attacked his wife almost before a particle of food had passed his lips.

"Your father's been to see me privately this afternoon, Elsa. Do you know why?"

It was his tone rather than what he said that implied wrath. She looked up—eagerly, I thought.

"No, Kelsey; what was it?"

"He's giving up his living—the living he begged me for and which I gave him. He's quite independent of me now, if you please. They want him in a large London parish, and I suppose we shall hear of him being made a bishop next. And not a word of gratitude. A wretched, penniless curate whom I set on his feet because I happened to take a fancy to his daughter! He fawned about my neck as long as there was anything to be got out of me, but now I may go hang."

He muttered other things which were only half audible, luckily.

I watched Lady Rystone and wondered at the joy which I read in her eyes—joy which her disconcerted air at this public outbreak could not quite conceal.

She made no retort, carefully avoiding to say a word which might still further incense her husband, and as soon as possible turned the conversation into a safer channel. But I think that Vance, like myself, noticed her flushed cheeks and eager expression.

We had very little in the way of phenomena that evening, and at ten o'clock we parted for the night. Vance went to the haunted room, and I saw him no more till the morning.

He came to me quite early—before I was up—and sat on the edge of my bed.

"Dexter," he said gravely, "we have got to give up this job; it isn't in our line. I wish we could leave today, but there are people asked to meet us at dinner. However, tomorrow—"

I sat up in bed in my surprise.

"Vance," I exclaimed, "have you solved the mystery?"

He inclined his head. His face was more than usually serious. "Yes," he said.

"Won't you tell me?"

"When we get home—not now. There's still some work that I must do—and it is no pleasant task. But this I want to ask you—don't trouble me with questions till we are clear of Blackstock Priory."

I promised that I would not; but, needless to say, I was puzzled to a degree. However, as fate would have it, the day did not pass without my making a discovery on my own account.

It happened in the course of the afternoon.

Vance had gone out on some errand with which he had not acquainted me, and I was amusing myself with a book in the garden. It was a hot day, and I had found a comfortable nook, screened by trees, close to a little glade, where there was a marble seat—probably a trophy carried off from some ancient Italian palace.

I must have dropped off to sleep, for I can only remember starting up at the sound of voices in the glade—from which I was completely hidden.

A woman was speaking—I recognised the voice of Lady Rystone. "You are an unutterable blackguard"—that is what I heard her say—"a loathsome blackmailer! But you daren't do what you threaten."

"Why not?"

The answer came in the suave, unpleasing voice of Felton, the tutor.

"Because, however much you might hurt me, my husband would thrash you as you deserve."

"That may be." The man gave an ugly laugh. "Nevertheless, my lady, I refuse to abate one jot of my demand. A thousand pounds—and I know that you've got the money—that you've been saving up for contingencies—pawning your jewels. You could give me that sum without hurting yourself. Come, be sensible." His voice had a persuasive note in it now. "I don't want to hurt you, but I'm hard up—desperate. Like yourself, I want to get away from this accursed place and from those two unlicked cubs I'm supposed to look after. And I can only do it by putting pressure upon you—now that I've found you out. Think of the scandal, my lady, if it became known that the 'Mischievous Boy of Blackstock'"—he laughed again— "is no other than your lover, in order to avoid whom your husband took you away from London, because he had begun to have his suspicions? Supposing Lord Rystone knew—as I know—that this man can get in and out of the Priory as he pleases by means of a secret passage opening into the so-called haunted room? That as long as the haunted room was shut off, you were both quite happy, since you, my lady, had secret access to it as well; but when it was opened up, your trysting place was no longer safe, so you had to

have recourse to the old superstition in order to frighten his lordship into walling it off again—or, better still, to compel him to leave
the Priory altogether. Supposing all this were known, what then?"

My horror at hearing this cold-blooded revelation may be imagined. I hated to think that, all unwittingly, I had been an eaves-
dropper; but from the first it was impossible for me to reveal myself—it might only have made matters worse—and I could not steal
away without betraying my presence.

So this was the pitiful explanation of the mystery—this was what
Vance, too, had found out and refused to tell me!

I could understand his reluctance now!

It was all I could do to restrain myself from springing out of
my hiding-place and laying violent hands upon the vile blackmailer—every nerve in my body tingled with the desire to pay him
in different coin to what he demanded—but I kept myself in con-
trol.

And of the rest of that abominable interview I need record no
more than this: Felton accorded his victim a period of twenty-four
hours in which to make up her mind. Unless he received his pound
of flesh upon the following day, he would unfailingly betray Lady
Rystone to her husband.

I waited impatiently for Vance's return, and when, late that
afternoon, we met, I told him everything.

He was deeply concerned, for of this trouble threatening Lady
Rystone he was quite unaware.

"Twenty-four hours' grace," he muttered. "This is serious, Dexter, very serious. For I can foresee what will happen. Lady Rystone
and her lover—for it's true about the lover, unfortunately true—
will act at once—tonight, instead of waiting till tomorrow, as they
proposed."

He wrinkled up his brows in deep thought. I did not understand what he meant, so after a few minutes he proceeded to enlighten me.

He told me of his experiences the night before.

"I had my suspicions," he said. "You see, I had had a chat with
Gaynor in the garden the day we arrived. The vicar confided to me

that his daughter was unhappy—that she was being treated like a prisoner—always watched except when she was in the house—that unpleasant woman, Mrs. Mellish, you know. She was too fond of gaiety, and there was a man who was fond of her—a man named Frank Prescot. Anyway, Lord Rystone became jealous and carried her off to Blackstock. And Mr. Gaynor blamed himself bitterly. You see, it was on his account that his daughter married—in order that he might get the living and the benefits.

"Well, these things made me suspicious—and I formed my own conclusions, too, by studying Lady Rystone's face. I arranged to spend a night in the haunted room. I found a secret passage—as I had expected to. It leads to a ruined chapel just outside the big wall, and it communicates with another room in the house—an empty one—as well as with the haunted room. So, you see, while the latter was shut up, two people could meet there practically with impunity. It was less safe afterwards, as we know from the experience of Lomax, the under-footman. It is evident, in that case, that the lovers had secured the key, and were able to save themselves by using it.

"And later that night I saw them. Yes, Dexter, the lovers met and never dreamed that they were watched from behind one of those curtained recesses. No one knew that I was spending a night in the haunted room, so they had no suspicions.

"They were only together a few minutes, and it was to plan an elopement—not for tonight, because there were preparations to be made, but for tomorrow. Lady Rystone considered herself free at last. She had borne all the indignities that her husband heaped upon her because her father has been dependent upon Lord Rystone, but now—you noticed her hardly-concealed joy at dinner when she heard that Gaynor had secured his independence?—she was free to do as she liked, so she declared, and her husband had long ago forfeited, by his brutality, all right to her love. It appears he had struck her over and over again.

"And so everything was settled between them. Tomorrow night they would fly together and brave the world. But now, Dexter, I foresee that they will change their plans—that they will go to-night."

I admitted the force of this reasoning.

"What is to be done?" I asked.

"I saw Gaynor this afternoon," resumed Vance, "and told him everything. His sympathies are wholly with his daughter, but he naturally wishes to save her from taking a false step. We had arranged that he should come tomorrow morning and take her away. Rystone cannot keep her in the Priory by force. And now—well, there is nothing for it but for me to return to the vicarage and warn Gaynor of what has happened. He must act at once, dinner-party or no dinner-party. He must come to the Priory this very evening, see Lady Rystone, and persuade her to go away with him. That is the only practical course."

And this was the plan upon which we decided. Vance set off at once, and he did not return till near the dinner hour. But he had failed in his mission, for the vicar was away from home, and all efforts to find him had proved unavailing.

That hateful dinner-party—how well I remember it! The whole company seemed to be on tenterhooks, and when about ten o'clock Lady Rystone pleaded a bad headache, Vance and I glanced meaningly but helplessly at each other.

Luckily, the guests departed soon after that, and we men—with the exception of the tutor, who had pleaded some excuse—retired to Lord Rystone's study to smoke.

Half an hour later there came a horrible interruption. The door flung open, and Felton, excited and dishevelled, rushed in.

"I've come to warn you, my lord," he cried. He gazed at us defiantly. "I consider it my duty to do so. Your wife has introduced her lover into your house. It is he who is the author of the disturbances—which have only been contrived in order that they may continue a guilty intrigue without interruption. They are now—"

I was boiling over with rage.

"This man is a vile blackmailer," I began, but Lord Rystone silenced me with a gesture. He had risen, and his face was congested with suppressed rage.

"Go on, Felton," he said hoarsely. "Where are they now?"

"In the haunted room—if you hurry you will find them there together. They are eloping—tonight." He gnashed his teeth with the wrath of a blackmailer foiled.

Lord Rystone did not speak another word. He jerked open a door of his desk, extracted something which he held under his hand, and then, without a glance at any of us, made for the door.

He was across the hall and mounting the stairs before we had time to realise the full horror of the situation.

"Quick—he's got a revolver!" cried Vance.

He set off in pursuit, followed by myself and then by the tutor, who had turned deathly white and staggered as he went.

But Lord Rystone was fleeter than any of us. He had thrown open the door of the haunted room before any of us could come up with him. I heard him mutter a hoarse cry—then he lifted his hand and fired—the shot echoed horribly down the corridor.

The next moment Lord Rystone repeated his cry—but this time it was a scream of fear. He fired again wildly, and then, throwing up his arms, staggered back. Vance caught him as he fell.

And I—for a brief moment I was able to see through the open door into the haunted room. And I was dimly conscious of a figure—that of a young man clad in garments of a bygone day, who stood smiling and bowing towards Lord Rystone, his hand upon his heart.

The "Mischievous Boy of Blackstock" had fulfilled his destiny.

Lord Rystone died a few days later—of a stroke of apoplexy, so the doctors declared.

And it was not many weeks later that Lady Rystone was quietly married.

THE INDISSOLUBLE BOND

I have probably already made clear in these records that it was to the elucidation of certain abstruse and little known branches of psychology that my friend, Aylmer Vance, mainly directed his activities. The incidents which I will now narrate illustrate the limitation of human power—even such as his—in the face of forces which as yet we hardly realise—which are, in fact, barely conceivable to our finite intelligence.

In the course of the summer we had met in London a charming family named Verriker—Colonel Verriker, his wife, son, and daughter. It is with the latter that my story has mainly to do.

She was a charming girl, twenty-two or three years of age, and she had soft dreamy eyes, which hinted at a spirituality in contradiction to more superficial appearances. For she seemed in every sense of the word a thoroughly normal girl.

She was keen on active exercise, and did not care much for books. She was an excellent horsewoman, and rode every morning in the Row, getting up early for that purpose. She excelled at tennis and golf, and could even handle a gun—or so I was assured—without losing anything of her natural femininity. I mention these things to show that she was about the last person in the world whom one would expect to find developing attributes out of the ordinary run.

For the rest, she had a slim and lithe figure, was above the medium height, and had fine masses of chestnut hair. She was of a type that most men would admire, because of her splendid vitality and undisguised joy of life.

We struck up rather a friendship with the Verrikers that summer, and were sorry that they had to leave London before the season was actually over, returning to their own residence, which was at Sandminster—I will call it so, as it is very necessary in this case that no true names should be revealed.

The colonel was an important personage in the parochial affairs of the little cathedral town, and he could never be away for very long at a time. Before parting, however, he exacted a promise from us that we should come to stay with him later in the year.

One day Vance showed me a letter which he had received from Colonel Verriker. It contained an invitation to both of us to run down to Sandminster as soon as ever we could spare the time.

"It is not only the pleasure of your company that we desire," so the colonel wrote, "though that, of course, is the first consideration. The fact is, my wife and I are a little troubled about our daughter Beryl, and there are certain features in the case which make me think that you, better than most men—having regard to your deep knowledge of matters psychical—may be able to advise us. For my part, I must candidly admit that I am old-fashioned, and know practically nothing about these things. Girls get delusions into their heads at times, and, as a rule, they mean very little—but it's queer in the case of Beryl, who isn't in the least of an hysterical type. However, you shall judge for yourself, and the sooner we see you, the happier we shall be."

As it happened, we were very busy just then—an important investigation that we could not possibly abandon—and so it was not till a full fortnight later that we were able to accept Colonel Verriker's invitation.

We reached Sandminster one afternoon early in the week. It is a charming old-world town, and the cathedral—not a large one—is famed for its beauty of architecture and for its picturesque surroundings. It stands in an open space, reached by narrow roads between high walls from the town side, while on the other there is open country. The Verrikers owned a large modern house within five minutes' walk of the cathedral.

We were most cordially received by Colonel and Mrs. Verriker and by Beryl, who looked to me quite unchanged and in the best of health. Her brother was away, we were told, staying with some friends in Scotland.

It was not till the ladies had retired, after we had spent a pleasant evening together, that the colonel referred to the subject of his letter. He began by repeating what he had already said—that, for his own part, he did not think there was anything to worry about—it was his wife who was nervous.

"I fancy that my opinion was wholly justified," he remarked. "And I feel almost guilty for having troubled you at all. For since I wrote to you—and that's more than a fortnight ago—Beryl has been quite herself, she hasn't had a single attack. Yes, I really feel as if I owe you an apology."

He spoke as if he were half ashamed of troubling us with the story at all.

"Miss Beryl seems to me to be in excellent health and spirits," commented Vance, "so let us hope that your surmise is correct. However, if you would like to confide in us—"

He spoke encouragingly; it was very evident that the colonel wished to unburden his soul.

"Well, it's like this," was the answer. "There were times when an extraordinary change seemed to come over Beryl's appearance and demeanour. It usually happened quite suddenly and unexpectedly, generally in the late afternoon, but I've seen it at all manner of times. One could imagine that she was listening for something, listening intently, and there was a tense, half-frightened look upon her face which, I assure you, was quite alarming. And then after a few minutes she would make some excuse, usually of a headache, and go off to her own room. If she happened to be anywhere outside at the time she would go straight home. After about an hour she would usually show up again—looking terribly pale, but in other respects quite herself. Of course, her mother and I questioned her, and we have had the doctor to see her, but he finds nothing amiss, and I expect he's right; but that curious listening attitude worried us, and then there was something else—"

He paused.

"Yes?" prompted Vance, who was listening with sympathetic interest, sitting in his favourite attitude, his elbows on his knees, his chin resting in his hands.

"Well," continued the colonel, "after the thing had happened several times, my wife went to see Beryl in her room, bringing her something to relieve her headache. The door was locked, and when she knocked no one answered. Beryl's room, I must tell you, has a flight of steps leading down to the garden. Not being able to get in by the door, Mrs. Verriker went round by the window. Well, the girl wasn't there, and she hadn't been lying down upon the bed—she had gone straight out again—"

"Did you ask her where she went?"

"Yes. And she had an answer ready. The air did her headache good. That may, of course, be true, but it's curious, for why did she wish to deceive us? And I'm sure it's always been the case, that she goes somewhere, and does not want to admit to us where she goes."

"You haven't tried to follow her?"

The colonel shook his head.

"No. You see, we only arrived at a definite conclusion on the subject just before I wrote to you, and nothing has happened since. I'm hoping nothing more will happen. And I shouldn't have troubled you at all, but we were really getting alarmed. You can't imagine how strange she looks when the attack—I suppose I must call it an attack—gets hold of her."

"At those moments," queried Vance, "does she seem to be acting of her own volition? Do you think she is aware of what she does?"

Colonel Verriker pondered.

"She doesn't seem to lose the sense of her own individuality," he answered. "But at the same time she seems to be responding to some force outside herself—if I may put it so."

"And you say that your daughter gives you no explanation of all this, no explanation at all?"

Our host shook his head.

"She makes light of it to us," he replied. "Says that there is nothing the matter except for her headaches. However, as I've told you, she's been quite free from these attacks for the last fortnight, so let's hope there's nothing in it after all."

I could see from Vance's expression that he did not hold this view. Also he continued to put questions.

"Tell me, colonel," he said, "have you any sort of suspicion in your own mind? Don't be afraid of telling me, however slight the point may actually seem to you. Is there, for instance, any love affair?"

"Nothing that could cause her any trouble of this sort," responded the colonel. "And that's a very puzzling feature of the case. Beryl has been engaged for the last four months—it happened while we were in London—to an altogether desirable young man, a Mr. Geoffrey Beynion, who had just passed very creditably into the Foreign Office, and who is destined for the Indian Civil. They have decided to get married this winter. Geoffrey's at St Petersburg at present, because he's making a special study of Russian."

"And you are sure your daughter is as fond of her fiancé as ever? For if she repented of her engagement—"

"No, I am certain it isn't that," was the response, "for I've questioned her very seriously on the subject. She assures me that she loves Geoffrey devotedly, and would like to hasten on the marriage if she were not afraid of interfering with his studies. In fact, it seemed to me that it was in her marriage that she looked for safety."

"And have you noticed anything else?"

"Well"—there was a certain hesitation in the colonel's speech—"it hardly seems worth mentioning, and yet perhaps I had better do so. Beryl has always been fond of music, and she used to love nothing better than to play the organ in the Minster whenever she got the chance. After our return from London we found that they'd got a new organist, and we attended a recital which he gave one evening. The man's playing seemed to impress my girl tremendously, and eventually she got him to give her a few lessons. It was soon after this that the trouble began, and somehow—I hardly know why—I always associate that curious listening attitude of hers with

her attraction for the organ. It was just such an attitude that I noticed on the evening when we attended the recital."

Colonel Verriker paused.

"And this man, the organist—" prompted Vance.

"It's ridiculous, perfectly ridiculous—unthinkable—to imagine
him as any sort of factor in the case," asserted Verriker with decision. "He's an impossible creature, the merest shadow of a man.
Oh, no, he's out of the question; he's absolutely out of the question."

Vance did not argue the point, and as there was nothing more
that Colonel Verriker could tell us, it was eventually agreed that
we should just wait and watch, while hoping that his surmise was
correct, and that the trouble, whatever it might be, was really at
an end.

And at first it seemed as if this was going to be the case, for
two or three days passed pleasantly without any manifestation of
unrest upon the part of Beryl.

We watched her closely, and she gave us every opportunity of
doing so, for she was constantly in our company, acting as a charming cicerone in showing us the various sights of the neighbourhood.
We spent a certain amount of time in the Minster, too, for there
were some beautiful old brasses there of great archaeological interest, in the study of which Vance was deeply interested.

On the day of our visit to the Minster, Vance questioned Miss
Verriker, in an apparently unconcerned manner, on the subject of
the organ. I watched her keenly as she made answer, and her embarrassment, although she tried to hide it, was obvious. She told
us that the organist, Mr. Cuthbert Ford, had been laid up for the
last fortnight, and that he was the most wonderful player that they
had ever had at Sandminster.

As we left the church Vance whispered to me: "The organist
has been ill a fortnight—and it is a fortnight since Miss Verriker
has had an attack. Do you draw any deduction, Dexter?"

His tone was ominous.

It was on the fourth day after our arrival that something happened. Several young people had been asked in the afternoon to

tennis and croquet, and Beryl apparently enjoyed herself as much as anybody.

It must have been after six o'clock, and many of the guests had departed, while the few that remained were resting in basket chairs on the lawn, chatting pleasantly together.

I was quite close to Beryl, and was probably the first to notice the change come over her.

For some minutes she was very silent, sitting back in her chair. It was her racquet falling off her knees that attracted my attention to her; I noticed then that she was sitting up, that her cheeks had become pale, and that there was a look of intense eagerness upon her face.

Her eyes shone brightly, her lips were a little parted, and her fingers, lying in her lap, kept up a persistent tattoo. There was a marked straining forward of the neck, and an unmistakable suggestion in her whole attitude of listening—listening for something that was audible to her ears alone.

I spoke to her, but, for the moment, she took no notice of me, and I seized the opportunity of beckoning to Vance, who, luckily, was not far away.

He came at once, and it was just as he approached that Miss Verriker rose to her feet, without any alteration of the strained and listening attitude, and, turning to me, remarked in a tone of voice that was natural enough to deceive me if I had not been prepared for it: "I'm sorry, Mr. Dexter, but I've got a violent headache just come on. It's the sun, I expect, and I've really been rather energetic this afternoon. I must go and lie down a bit, and then I shall be all right again. You'll excuse me, I know. I'm not going to say a word to anybody, as I don't want to worry them."

Her father and mother were engaged just then with some guests in another part of the grounds, and were therefore unaware of what was happening.

The girl hardly waited for my reply, but moved away, and Vance and I watched her disappearing in the direction of the house. When she was out of sight Vance laid his hand upon my arm. "Come, Dexter," he said, "there's work for us to do—for you especially."

With which he led me away and into the house where, presumably, Miss Verriker had already gone.

"You wish to follow her?" I whispered. "If so, we'd better wait somewhere outside. She goes to her room first, at least so the colonel says, locks the door so that people should think she's still there, and then makes her way out by the window."

"No, we are not going to follow her—at any rate, not in the flesh; but you shall do so, Dexter, in the spirit."

I knew what he meant. He was going to make use of my clairvoyant power.

I nodded without further remark, and together we went to my room, where I allowed him to put me to sleep as he had done on many other occasions.

In my hand I held a glove belonging to Miss Verriker, which she had dropped in her hasty departure, and which Vance had picked up and brought to the house with him.

Well, it was not long before my vision began to develop itself, a vision more vivid than any I have ever experienced. I will try to relate exactly what I saw and what I heard—for in these trances I am as keenly susceptible to sound as to sight.

That the exact words which I record were actually spoken I cannot assert—but I had the impression of them, most definite and unmistakable.

I found myself gazing into a narrow, dark room, so dark that it was some time before I realised from the array of tall painted pipes that it was the organ loft of the Minster.

But by degrees I began to see more clearly. The last long beams of the sun, now near its setting, shimmered through the diamond-shaped pane and rested upon a pair of hands which were dreamily hovering over the keyboard.

So thin and white were these hands that I almost imagined them transparent, perforated by the rays, and I remember that it seemed to me for a moment that it must be a spirit and not a man who was seated there at the organ.

Yet this was not so, for the face, as soon as I could discern it more clearly, was palpably of human flesh and blood. But how thin and sunken! The cheekbones stood out in painful prominence, and the eyes glittered from deep sockets cruelly black-rimmed. So this must be Cuthbert Ford, the man of whom Colonel Verriker had spoken to us.

He was sitting there playing the organ, making strange and weird music, the sound of which reached my ears distinctly, though it was all of the substance of a dream.

It was the strangest music that I have ever listened to, unlike that of any composer, living or dead, and I knew instinctively that the player must love the instrument he played upon so passionately as to give his very soul to it.

I felt that he himself, sitting alone in the narrow loft with the twilight creeping about him, with the great church holy in its emptiness, had become bereft of feeling, devoid of emotion, while the organ, to him, was a sentient being.

The man had developed his spirit at the expense of his body, and his spirit sang in harmony with the music of the organ—merged in it—was it.

I listened, overwhelmed with emotion such as I had never felt before. The organ breathed softly of dead hopes and strange desires—the unknown and unknowable.

To have understood would have meant the solution of the mystery of the soul of man—and I knew that it was best not to understand.

Suddenly there came a step upon the narrow wooden staircase that led to the organ loft. The sound appeared to disturb the player, and instantly the tone of his music changed.

The church resounded with the conventional strains of Beethoven.

The door opened, and Beryl Verriker entered. She was clad in the light afternoon frock which she had been wearing for the tennis party. She was intensely pale.

She stool a while silent by his side while he continued to play the familiar sonata. Then she touched his arm.

"Why do you play that now?" she said. "It is Beethoven, not you." He stopped and turned to her.

"Well?" he inquired.

"You called me, Cuthbert," she murmured. Her voice trembled, and I knew that she was shuddering from head to foot.

"You heard me?" he said. His voice sounded hoarse and unsympathetic, as ugly and as unpleasing as the man's whole personality.

"You heard me," he repeated, "and you were bound to obey. When soul speaks to soul, Beryl, the flesh is powerless to resist."

"I know it too well." Her voice was full of shuddering awe. She seated herself on the bench beside him. "You are murdering my body, and it's wicked, it's cruel." She buried her face in her hands. "For I want to live, I want to live!"

He made no answer for a few moments, but his eyes, those eyes in which all the life of him seemed to be concentrated, blazed upon her out of their hollow sockets.

"How do I hurt you?" he said at last, and there was a deep irony in his tone. "I've spoken no word to you of love, and I know, as well as you know yourself, that every nerve of your body revolts from me. But over your soul, Beryl, I have a right, since I have the power to command it. And if, through the harmony of the organ, I can speak to you of the beauty of the soul, freed from the hampering prison of its vile earthly body, of spiritual love undreamed of in this hollow world, of things beyond the comprehension of human sense, then I am doing what your soul must be grateful for— I am fulfilling destiny—but leading you to the achievement of the inevitable."

He caught her hands in his, those gaunt bony hands, and I saw her tremble at his touch.

"Our souls belong to each other, Beryl," he said. "They have belonged to each other through the long dark ages of the past, they will be in harmony through the infinite aeons of futurity. You are mine—shall I prove it to you?"

As he spoke his hands left hers and once more began to press the notes of the organ. Again that strange, weird harmony sprang into being—a call of spirit to spirit—and I could see that Beryl's eyes were closing dreamingly; then suddenly, with a violent struggle, she seemed to recover herself. In her turn she seized the man's hands and dragged them from the keyboard.

Then, panting, she closed the lid.

"Stop playing that music! Stop, I say!" she cried passionately. "Things must not go on as they are. You have bewitched me. I don't understand myself. But it must cease. I say it must cease!"

He looked at her, and all the vitality of his poor body leaped to his eyes.

"You have given me your soul, Beryl," he said. "You would not take it away—now? But you cannot—it is beyond your power."

"I have not given it," she panted. "You have tried to steal it from me, thief that you are! But, still, my soul is my own!"

"So speaks the body," he replied, with a shrug of his humped shoulders. "What does it know of the desires of the soul?"

"I hate you with my body and with my soul!" she gasped. "I loathe and abhor you."

"You are wrong," he replied callously; "and I've only to touch the organ"—he seemed about to raise the lid.

"No," she murmured despairingly. "Spare me, Cuthbert, I'm not strong enough to resist you. I know it. But I'm going to plead with you for mercy. Listen! I am young, and the world is very sweet to me. I want to live, to enjoy my life. It is only a few short years, after all, in comparison with the eternity of which you have spoken. I want warm, human love, Cuthbert, and I know nothing—understand, nothing—of the love of the spirit. I have never told you, have I, that I'm engaged to be married, and that I love the man who will be my husband? I want to give myself to him body and soul—"

"You cannot give the latter," he interrupted grimly.

"I can, if you will let me," she pleaded. "Release me from this bondage; it is bad for us both—unnatural, wicked. It will kill me."

"And is not that a consummation to be desired?" he cried fiercely. "To pass from this hateful existence of pain and misery and vain hopes to the freedom of spiritual happiness?"

"I do not want to die. I love, and love is life."

"Sordid lusts of the flesh!" he retorted contemptuously. "I tell you that your spirit is mine, and shall be mine through all eternity. It is fate, and you cannot struggle against it."

He paused, and for a few moments there was silence in the organ loft. I could hear the girl's quiet sobbing and the hard breathing of the man as he sat huddled up by her side.

At last he spoke, and again the tone of biting irony was evident in his words.

"What matter a year or two, when we have eternity before us? It shall be as you desire. You ask for freedom in this life. You crave for the gratification of the flesh. Go, then—while I live I shall call upon my fellow soul no more."

She sprang to her feet with joy.

"You promise me this—oh! you do promise it?" she cried. "Thank God! Thank God! Then I am free!"

"Remember," he continued, with unaltered expression, "I said, 'while I live.' Look at me."

She looked, and then sank down upon the bench with a shuddering cry. For she read death in every line of his face.

For a short space neither spoke.

At last he gently raised the lid of the keyboard.

"Listen!" he said. "I will play you no more of my own music—while I live—but this you may hear."

Then slowly, solemnly, across the oppressive silence of the Minster rang out the dirge of Chopin's funeral March, played, surely, as it had never been played before.

"Herein is death," said Cuthbert Ford, without looking at the cowering girl; and the dissolution of the body, the grave, the worm, were told in every note he touched.

"And herein is life eternal."

The melody poured forth its appeal. Surely the organ spoke! Spirit voices called to spirit, telling of life that mocked the finality of earth. The world's passion, the world's pain, its petty hopes and fears, what were they to this? Come all ye that rejoice, come all ye that are weary, for here is your reward. O Death, where is thy sting; O Grave, where is thy victory?

It was as I followed thus the plaint of the organ, as the wonderful melody seemed to sink into my very being, destroying consciousness of all else, that I awoke—awoke to find myself in my own room, with Aylmer Vance bending over me a little anxiously.

For the last few minutes he had been trying to arouse me, but in vain. Never before had I been in so deep a sleep, never before had I had so intensely vivid a dream.

As soon as I was sufficiently recovered I told him all that I had seen and heard.

"What do you make of it?" I inquired eagerly, when I had finished—for there was no doubt in my mind that my vision had been a true representation of what had actually happened.

"It seems to me," I went on, "that this horrible creature, this perversion of a man, has made use of his wonderful gift of music to work upon some latent emotion in the girl's nature; he has palpably no influence over her except through the organ, and knowing this, it is by means of the organ he compels her to his will. If we can get him away, see that he is removed from Sandminster altogether, then the horrible, corrupting influence will be got rid of, and Miss Verriker should be restored to her normal senses. There is nothing she desires more ardently for herself, poor girl."

But Aylmer's face remained very grave, and he did not seem disposed to fall in easily with the sanguine view which I had expressed.

Yet he was ready to agree that what I proposed was the only course that could be adopted.

Beryl came in to dinner that evening, and professed to be feeling ever so much better for her supposed rest.

She must have possessed a tremendous amount of self-restraint, for she gave no sign, in face or manner, of the strain which she had undergone.

But she left us early, and withdrew to her own room.

Over our cigars, later on, I related my vision to the colonel, who, although he did not say so in so many words, was rather disposed to regard it as a vision, and nothing more.

He was a man who had never in his life been brought face to face with anything outside the normal, and the idea of soul appealing to soul struck him, I have no doubt, as incongruous and impossible.

He accepted, however, our evidence as to the danger of Cuthbert Ford.

"I can see how it is," he muttered. "The fellow's got a wonderful gift of music, there's no doubt about that, and my girl has always been readily influenced by that sort of thing. I can remember, when she was a child, how she would stand and listen for hours together when her uncle, my brother, who was a fine pianist, would consent to play for her. And I've seen her, in later years, sobbing behind a handkerchief when I've taken her, at her request, to classical concerts, which, for my part, I found intensely boring. That's how the fellow's got hold of her, and I don't for a moment believe she can hear his music when it is inaudible to others. I expect she knows his habits, guesses when he will be playing. We may thank our lucky stars that he's such a parody of a man—had he been different, there might have been danger for her, real danger."

Vance acquiesced, and I could see that he was glad the colonel should take this view—a view which seemed to be justified; or, in any case, it was evident that the organist was keeping his promise, for during the rest of our stay which was prolonged to quite a fortnight, nothing further occurred to mar the harmony of the household.

Cuthbert Ford was got rid of without any difficulty—indeed, he left Sandminster of his own accord, after Vance had secretly paid him a visit. But my friend returned from that visit with an expression upon his face that was by no means reassuring; he evidently anticipated some danger which I could only vaguely guess at.

And he begged Colonel Verriker to hurry on his daughter's marriage.

"The strength of a new affinity," he said to me, "that is the only hope. But is such an affinity possible? Dexter, I don't know—I don't know. And we—how utterly powerless we are!"

We returned to London, and though I did not forget my strange experience at Sandminster, I found my time fully occupied by other interesting experiences which cropped up as time went on.

Vance mentioned to me now and again that he had heard from Colonel Verriker, and that everything was going well, that Miss Verriker was in the best of health, that her fiancé had returned to England, and that the marriage had been arranged to take place early in November.

And so the months passed, and eventually we received our invitation to the wedding. We were to go down and spend a week with the Verrikers, who proposed to have a full house for the occasion.

Vance appeared to be much relieved that the day of the ceremony was so close at hand. He repeated that he regarded this as the only safeguard for Beryl Verriker. She was in no danger, or so he maintained, as long as Cuthbert Ford lived and kept his promise; but Ford was a man with the seal of death upon his brow—and then—what then?

"A new and stronger affinity," Vance repeated. "I have no hope but that."

And so, when the time came, we went to Sandminster, and found great preparations for the wedding going on, Colonel and Mrs. Verriker happy and pleased with themselves, Beryl the picture of health and brightness, and Geoffrey Beynion, who was staying with some relations in the neighbourhood, and whom we now met for the first time, as fine a specimen of young English manhood as one could desire to see.

The wedding was to take place of the fifth day after our arrival, and on the third there was to be a big ball, at which all the best people in the county were to be present.

Of that ball, which duly took place, I need say nothing beyond this: that Beryl Verriker was easily the belle of it, and that she met with the admiration that she deserved.

The function was in every sense of the word a success, and there seemed to be not the smallest suggestion of cloud upon an horizon fair with promise for the future happiness of the young couple.

Upon the day following the ball, Miss Verriker, accompanied by Vance and myself, went for a spin in a new motor which her brother had just purchased, and which he drove himself.

We were on our way home, and were chatting and laughing together, while Vance, sitting in the front next to young Verriker, was turned towards us relating some amusing experience of the dance the night before, when, suddenly glancing at the girl's face, I realised that she was not listening to us, but that she was staring straight in front of her with a strained, unnatural look in her eyes.

I know that a cold shudder ran down my spine. I laid my hand upon hers with some idea in my mind of arousing her, and calling her back to herself, and the moment I touched her—strange as it may appear, I can swear to its truth—I seemed to hear, just as she must be hearing, the strain of a distant organ, the swelling of that weird, unnatural melody that I had once listened to in a dream.

The touch of my hand, however, had the effect of rousing her. I realised that she was struggling to conceal from us that there was anything wrong.

She spoke quite quietly, leaning forward and addressing her brother.

"Will you stop the car, Jim, and let me get out? I've just remembered that there are one or two shops I want to go to—a few things that I really must buy. No, I don't want you men to be with me, and we are quite close to so I can walk that little way back. You go straight on and have your tea—I'll have mine as soon as I get in."

Verriker obeyed—he was always obedient to his sister's smallest request, and he did not suspect that there was anything amiss. Beryl descended from the car, and then, as we seemed to hesitate, said, with a suggestion of impatience:

"That's right, drive on, Jim, I shall be home quite soon."

She had alighted at the corner of one of those narrow streets close to the Minster; our way home lay straight on. Vance and I exchanged troubled glances, but I left it to him to take the initiative—I did not dare to suggest any course of action myself.

Jim, I knew, had never been told of his sister's troubles.

Vance spoke not a word, and in another five minutes, or less, the car pulled up at the house, and we all descended; then, making some hurried excuse, Vance drew me aside.

His face was grave in the extreme, and his lips were set in a straight line.

"There's no time to be lost, Dexter," he said. "We must go to the church—we must follow her."

It took us only a few minutes to reach the church, and we spoke not a word to each other upon the way. The great edifice appeared to be quite empty, and not a sound was to be heard. We turned our steps straight to the organ loft, and I had to strike a match as we mounted the narrow stairs, for the sun had already set, and it was quite dark in the narrow, confined space of the loft.

The organist, as we had expected, was there. He was seated upon the narrow bench, and his hands rested upon the keyboard, but his head and shoulders had fallen forward upon them, and he lay thus still, immobile, dead.

In the farther corner crouched Beryl Verriker, her hands clasped over her eyes, her whole body quivering and shaking.

It needed but an instant to take in the scene, then the match fell from my hand and we were plunged into darkness.

It was with difficulty that we got Miss Verriker home; she was half-fainting, and in an emotional, hysterical condition.

We placed her under the care of her mother, and, as soon as we were able, confided to the colonel everything that had happened.

And his answer was: "Thank God the fellow's dead, so there's no further danger to be anticipated."

I could see Vance smile grimly when he heard these words, but he uttered no protest, for what was the use of explaining to the good, simple-minded man that the real danger had only just come into being?

Upon inquiries being made we learnt that Cuthbert Ford had returned to Sandminster early that morning; he had been seen about the town, but no one knew whence he had come, or what business had brought him back. But for us it was easy to conjecture that, knowing the imminence of death, he had elected to die beside his beloved organ.

His body was removed to the mortuary to await the necessary inquest.

The next day Beryl Verriker, as her father confidently predicted, seemed to be better. She had recovered her composure, but, watching her closely, I knew that she was not ignorant of her danger. And I remembered how Cuthbert Ford had threatened her—how he had declared that her immunity was only to last until his death— not after.

There was a suggestion of postponing the wedding for a few days, but she would have none of this, seeming to desire nothing so much as to give herself up to her future husband's care; only she stipulated that the full choral service which had been arranged for should be completely abandoned, and that the organ should on no account be played, not even for the traditional Wedding March.

"I couldn't stand it," she shuddered; and, indeed, under the circumstances of the tragic death, her decision seemed only right and proper.

And so the fateful time arrived. The Minster was filled with a gaily-dressed crowd. The bridegroom paced nervously up and down in his allotted place.

People smiled at his anxious face, deeming it due to mere personal nervousness.

The hum of carefully-modulated voices filled the church. The news that the service was not to be choral had gone abroad, and the people who had come from a distance were asking the reason. I heard the explanation given by a well-informed gentleman sitting just in front of me, who whispered it to his friends.

"It's because that extraordinary creature, Cuthbert Ford, who used to be organist here, was found dead in the organ loft only yesterday. It was a bit of a tragedy—awkward thing to happen in the church, you know. The organ has not been touched since. I suppose they decided not to do so till the poor fellow is buried."

Suddenly a murmur from pew to pew: "The bride is coming!"

Beryl passed up the aisle leaning on her father's arm. "Why, what is the matter with her?" Surprised comment followed her as she advanced. "She is the very spectre of herself. Surely she isn't marrying a man she does not love?"

The guests farther removed from the aisle craned their necks to see.

Beryl, looking neither to right nor left, passed on, and stood impassive by the side of the bridegroom. So she remained through the service which followed, considerately cut as short as possible.

It was over, they were made man and wife, and the register was signed. A little colour stole into Beryl's pale cheeks as she emerged from the vestry, and she looked up and smiled at her husband.

She was smiling, too, as they came abreast of the altar and took up their position at the head of the procession.

"Why, she looks happy, after all!" murmured somebody close beside me. "What a pity it is that there is no one here to play the Wedding March!"

The first steps down the aisle were taken, and then, suddenly, the solemn silence of the great church was rudely broken.

Surely the strangest, most incongruous sound that ever greeted a wedding party!

Loud and resonant through the vaulted aisles of the church rolled forth the thunder of the first bars of Chopin's Funeral March. The first bars only, but they were sufficient to express the presence of death.

Scarcely a second, it seemed, the sound had been there clear in the ears of all; but even as every member of that assembly tried to grasp the meaning of it, straining ears to the utmost, they found themselves listening, not to sound, but to a speaking silence.

Women turned pale and sank back in their seats; men muttered beneath their breath. Could the senses of all have been deceived?

The bridegroom clutched his wife's arm and hurried on; anything to escape from the church.

She staggered rather than walked, and soon he was supporting almost her whole weight. So the broken procession approached the west door, in the gallery above which was placed the great organ.

Then, gently at first, but clear to the hearing of all, the swell of the organ rose again; but this time it was the melody of the Grand March, speaking of life and spiritual love, that was vaguely suggested to the hearer, and every note of it was a passionate appeal.

How passionate, how intense, none knew, perhaps, but the bride, for she alone understood.

To all others it came as a shock, an insult, an abomination; to her it was a summons.

She stood rigid, her arms extended to the organ. Then, as the melody—no earthly melody, as it seemed now—rose to its full cadence, and died away in a quivering sigh, she fell to her knees.

"The call—the call!" she murmured; and as her husband raised her in his strong arms and bore her out, he heard her whisper gently: "I come!"

It was rumoured afterwards that someone had gained access to the organ loft and played an evil practical joke. It is also possible for people to die from sudden fright.

Thus do we humans slur over what we cannot understand. For me, it was the sense of our utter impotence that appalled.

"Why had this evil thing to be?" I demanded of Vance.

There was some measure of comfort in his reply.

"We do not know that it was really an evil thing. Is it not possible that, in our ignorance, we appraise far too highly these poor bodies of ours? What do we know of our souls and of the laws that govern spiritual existence? May it not be that for some inscrutable reason it was necessary that those two souls should be brought together—that it was the appointed time for their union? And though the man's body was warped and hideous—though his mind may have been as ugly as his body—who shall judge of the soul panting for freedom? Not you or I, Dexter." He placed his hand affectionately upon my arm. "The laws of this world are not the laws of the hereafter. Some day the truth will be revealed."

THE FEAR

One morning in late summer Aylmer Vance, after glancing through his correspondence, remarked that there was a gentleman coming to see us that day who would probably have something interesting to communicate.

"His name is Robert Balliston, and he's by way of being a millionaire," explained Vance. "A self-made man, so I understand. He's had a letter of introduction to me through some mutual friends, and he appears to be in great trouble about a house which he has recently taken on a long lease."

"Have you any idea what form the trouble takes?" I inquired.

Vance shook his head. "No," he responded, "I haven't been told anything about it yet. But I understand it's so serious that Mr. Balliston and his family have had to turn out after being in residence barely a month. No doubt we shall hear all about it when he comes."

In the course of the morning Mr. Balliston put in his appearance. Somehow I think I could have guessed at once that he was a man who had made a lot of money by his own endeavours—he was so exactly the type one would expect. Coarse, but withal kindly-faced; thin hair—still dark—that scarcely hid his shining scalp; overdressed; rotund of figure as of pocket-book—we have all met his like many a time. His loud voice filled the room.

"Mr. Vance," he said, "you are a man whose name is well-known to me, though, upon my word, I never expected to meet you in your professional capacity."

Vance and I exchanged a glance, for there is nothing that my friend dislikes more than to be described as a "professional." He is a dilettante in every sense of the word, and has never in his life undertaken a research except for the sheer love of the thing. But it was impossible to be in the least offended with Mr. Balliston.

"You are, sir, I believe, an authority on ghosts," resumed the latter. He spoke the last word in a tone of depreciation almost comic.

Level-headed Robert Balliston and ghosts!—the conjunction of ideas seemed quite ridiculous.

"On what you call ghosts," corrected Vance gently, "perhaps I am."

"I don't call 'em anything, sir," snapped the millionaire. "I don't believe in 'em, there aren't any such things. I've been told so all my life, and my father was a businessman like myself. Yet a funny thing has happened to me, and as it seems to be in your line I got my friends, the Whittakers, to give me an introduction. And I needn't say that I'm pleased to make your acquaintance as well as that of Mr. Dexter."

Of course we acknowledged the compliment, and then Aylmer Vance proceeded to inquire the source of the trouble.

"Well, it's this," was the reply. "How would you like it, Mr. Vance, if you had leased a house—spent a great deal of money on it, too—and then had to leave it in a hurry, without any particular prospects of going back? Pleasant, isn't it? One may be well off, but there are limits."

"Was it a new house?"

"New? No, old as they make 'em. Dates back to I don't know what period. Never was good at that sort of thing myself. Moated grange kind of place, you know. It was my wife's idea. She said when we had made enough we should take a big house and become county people. I heard of Camplin Castle from an agent, who said that it was just what we wanted—Lord of the Manor, good style of neighbour, and the rest of it. It's in Hampshire, near the borders of the Forest, not far from the sea. A fine, imposing place I found it, but out of repair. It hadn't been occupied for quite a time, as the price was so stiff. That put me on my mettle, I suppose, and I closed the bargain. Well, it took more repairing than I thought, and I spent quite a lot of money on it before we moved in. That's not a month ago, and here we are." He spread out his hands with a despondent gesture.

Vance regarded our visitor critically.

"A man like you wouldn't give in easily," he observed. "Now what was it that drove you away, Mr. Balliston?"

"That's just what beats me," cried the other. "I don't know. We've seen nothing, heard nothing—at least, not in the ordinary sense of the word. Every room is as comfortable as money can make it. But we couldn't stay in the castle, and the only explanation I can give is that we were frightened away."

"And what frightened you?"

"Don't I say I haven't an idea? Every one of us in turn got seized with an unaccountable sense of fear. It's very difficult to explain, and all I know is that it's there, and that you can't fight against it. The feeling you get is of an invisible presence that is itself suffering from fear, a fear that is imparted to you. The thing, whatever it may be, radiates fear, if I may put it so."

"And is this fear confined to one place, or to any particular time?"

"No, that's just the worst of it. If it were, we could avoid the place, for the castle's so big that I shouldn't in the least mind shutting up any particular room. But it happens at all manner of times and anywhere."

"You say that you have all felt it. How many are you in family, Mr. Balliston?"

"My wife and myself and our four children, two girls and two boys, ranging in age from twelve to eighteen. Our youngest child got it first—she's a girl of twelve, and we put her and her sister into two rooms communicating with each other. It was the very first night after we moved in. Gertrude—that's the eldest girl—heard her little sister sobbing, and when she went to find out what was the matter the child told her that she couldn't sleep, she was too frightened. She couldn't say what she was frightened of, and

Gertrude laughed at her and told her not to be a little goose. But the child wouldn't stop crying, and so, to soothe her, Gertrude got into bed with her. And then she felt it too. She said it was awful. She snatched up little Myra and carried her to the other room, and there they both lay, shivering and trembling with the recollection of it, till the morning, when they told us what had happened."

"And did anyone else ever sleep in that room?"

"Yes, we tried it one after another, at least, my two sons and I did, and we found it just as they had said. So we decided not to occupy that room any more, as there seemed to be something queer about it, and it would have been all right if things had not developed in another direction."

"You got the same impression in other parts of the house?"

"Yes. A day or two later my wife had hysterics in the drawing-room; she said that she felt certain there was something going to happen to her, and it was a long time before she came round. Then one of the servants pitched down the stairs and hurt herself badly. It was rather late, and she was going up to bed. She said that there was something following her, and she knew it meant mischief. And so it went on, everybody was affected, and sometimes it caught several of us together. The sensation never lasted long, but it always made one feel as if one couldn't get through it alive. And so that's why we've left Camplin Castle, Mr. Vance, and that's why I've come to consult you."

Vance reflected for a few moments, then he inquired:

"Do you know anything of the history of Camplin Castle, Mr. Balliston?"

"Very little. It didn't interest me, you understand. And we hadn't time to get to know any of the neighbours."

"But you must of course, be acquainted with the name of the owner?"

"Yes. Camplin has belonged for hundreds of years to the Oswald family—the last of them died about a dozen years ago. He was never married, and there is no heir in the direct line. The present owner is a nephew and he is too poor to live in the place himself—at least, that's what the agent told me."

"And didn't you try to get any more information from the agent?"

"Catch him giving me any!" was the somewhat scornful response. "The man had done his deal and pocketed his commission. He wasn't likely to tell me anything against the place, and quite right, too, from a business point of view."

Vance put a few more leading questions, and then informed Mr. Balliston that he and I would go down to Camplin Castle the next day.

"I suppose there is someone on the premises to look after us?" he inquired.

"Yes, there's the lodge-keeper and his wife. I couldn't get any of the other servants to remain. I'll wire to Smith to expect you." With a sudden burst of confidence Mr. Balliston added: "For heaven's sake, Mr. Vance, find out the cause of the mystery. I tell you I was so frightened that the hair stood up on my head!"

I was trying to picture Mr. Balliston's thin hair taking on this peculiar disposition as he took his leave.

The next day we travelled down to Camplin Castle, which we found to be situated several miles from the nearest station.

Mr. Balliston had arranged for a motor car to be placed at our disposal for as long as we cared to stay. It was to be garaged at the village close by.

The sun was setting when we reached the gates of the park, which were opened for us by a somewhat surly and reticent lodge-keeper. He mounted the box by the side of our chauffeur, after informing us that his wife was at the castle making preparations for our reception.

Neither of them slept at the house, which we were to have quite to ourselves.

We passed down a fine avenue of elms, and presently, on either side, appeared great stretches of well-kept lawns and carefully-planted flower beds—every indication of the expenditure of much money.

A sweep of the road brought us to the house, which was a huge grey pile of varied architecture. Yet the whole effect was one of symmetry. In the centre appeared a timeworn, ivy-covered tower, round which the rest of the edifice had sprung up.

A neat, comfortable-looking woman admitted us to a vast hall, and thence to a dining-room, where the table was laid for dinner.

Vance spoke a few words of compliment on the arrangements that had been made for our comfort.

"You will look after us, I suppose, during our stay?" he remarked to Mrs. Smith.

"Oh, yes, sir, as long as I don't have to remain at night," was the response. "I don't mind it so much otherwise."

"It?" queried Vance, looking at her keenly.

"Yes, sir, the Fear. One never knows when it may come. I felt it this afternoon, but it passed quickly. At night, oh, it's terrible at night. I think Smith has taken your bags to your rooms," she added hurriedly, as if to change the subject.

At this moment Smith reappeared, evidently anxious to take his departure. His more self-possessed wife conducted us upstairs to two large adjoining rooms on the first floor.

"It was Mr. Balliston's instructions, gentlemen, that these rooms should be prepared for you tonight. This one that we are now in"—she seemed to be looking over her shoulder with an expression of tremulous nervousness— "is the one in which nobody has been able to sleep. It's a long time now since it has been occupied at all."

"Do you know anything of the story of this house, Mrs. Smith?" inquired Vance.

"No, sir. We are London people. Mr. Balliston brought us down."

"But the village folk, don't they talk?"

"Well, sir," was the answer, given in a faltering tone, "of course we have heard all manner of stories, Smith and I, but there isn't one of them that really explains the Fear. You see, nobody had ever heard of it before Mr. Balliston took the Castle. The house had stood empty ever since old Mr. Luke Oswald died, and he only used to occupy a few rooms in the south wing. He was a queer old gentleman, they say, and lived quite by himself except for one servant, and he wouldn't ever see any company, so that people got to calling him a miser and whatnot. The old servant, whose name was Somers—John Somers—died soon after his master, but his grandson is living in the village—he is a builder by trade, and I should think he could tell you more than anyone else about the Oswald family, if you cared to go and have a chat with him."

"I certainly shall make a point of doing so," replied Vance, "and thank you very much, Mrs. Smith, for the information."

With which he dismissed the good woman, who bustled away evidently pleased at being able to take her departure from the dreaded room.

I think I have said that our rooms had a communicating door between them—they were the ones originally occupied by Robert Balliston's two daughters.

The "haunted room"—I will define it as such—was the smaller, and I imagine that the larger one—which I was to occupy—may have once been a boudoir. It was a bright, cheerful room, with windows looking out upon the front. Both apartments were quite modern in appearance, and had no suggestion of ghostly influence about them. They had evidently been quite recently furnished and decorated with good taste and the expenditure of plenty of money.

It struck me that the only antique piece of furniture was the bed in the smaller room, and this was of handsomely carved oak, surmounted by a high canopy.

I commenced unpacking my portmanteau, talking to Vance all the time through the open door. I could not see him, but could hear him moving about.

"We must certainly go to the village tomorrow and make some inquiries of this man Somers," he was saying. "I want to know—"

Suddenly he ceased speaking, and I thought I heard a sound like a stifled gasp, and then there came a deep silence.

I was seated by my dressing-table. I was about to turn and ask what was the matter when suddenly a cold breath seemed to pass across my face and I became riveted where I sat; I could not have looked round to save my life, though I felt that there was something there just behind me.

I could not utter a sound, my tongue seemed to cleave to a dry palate. I knew that I was trembling, filled with a sensation, a terrible pervading fear of impending death, a feeling that long fingers were about to grip me by the neck from behind and squeeze the life out of me. If not now, immediately, I knew that it must come soon, that a death, swift and cruel and terrible, awaited me.

I grasped the arms of the chair, and during that ghastly second a very eternity seemed to pass over me.

At last relief came. I felt the cold breath upon my face once more, and the next moment I was able to turn my head. Aylmer Vance stood in the doorway between our rooms.

I put my hand to my forehead and found the hair wringing wet. "So you've had a turn, too?" asked Vance with a quiet smile. "It isn't pleasant, is it?"

I vowed that it was anything but pleasant. I think I swore lustily. "What does it mean?" I inquired.

"That's what we've got to find out," he replied, looking at me with some anxiety. "Whatever it is it seems to have passed from my room to yours—as if it follows the course of some invisible being—a being that is afraid, horribly afraid, and that is able to impart its fear to anyone who comes in its way. It's a ghastly kind of experience, Dexter, and it will no doubt be worse at night. Are you prepared to go through with it?"

I grasped his hand and said I was. But I must admit that I was anything but happy in my mind.

Mrs. Smith looked at us curiously when we appeared for dinner, but made no remark The meal over, she took her departure, promising to be round early in the morning to give us our breakfast.

After dinner we sat and smoked for a while, and then, as the night was oppressively hot, we made our way to the garden.

It was really delightful to escape for a short time from the evil influence which seemed to pervade the house—even in the absence of the actual overwhelming terror. One felt—one knew—that something horribly, abominably cruel must have been enacted within the walls of the Castle, and that, however long ago it may have been, the impression had never been eradicated.

The night air was deliciously cool and balmy with scented air. It was rather dark, though the sky was rich with stars. Our walk was not objectless. Vance wanted to explore the house on the outside and at night.

Twice we made the circle of it. There were broad terraces to most of the wings, but at the back, beneath the tower, there was only a narrow strip of lawn flanked by a shrubbery.

There were a few windows in the tower, but quite high up there seemed to be a circular apartment with several windows, and one of these stood wide open. And while we were looking up at it the Fear overtook us once more, although, on this occasion, it was only of a very transitory nature and disappeared altogether as soon as we were able to leave the spot.

When, a few minutes later, we mustered up courage to return, there was no recurrence of the ghastly feeling, but as we stood there, waiting for it, Vance suddenly placed his hand upon my shoulder, and pointing up to the tower exclaimed:

"Look there, Dexter. Do you notice anything strange?"

I looked and realised at once that the window, which had stood open only a few minutes ago, was now closed—yet, as we knew, the house was absolutely untenanted.

"What is the time, Dexter?" asked Vance in a tone that, for him, was almost excited. "I think it is of importance."

I struck a match and looked at my watch. It was then half-past eleven.

We returned to the house after this experience, and I knew that I was glad of a stiff peg of whisky and soda—for it wasn't as if the terrors of the night were at an end.

There was still the haunted room to be faced.

But Vance would not allow me to share this room with him as I offered to do. My nerves were already sufficiently on edge, he declared, and though I protested, I must admit that I allowed myself to be easily persuaded. I insisted, however, that the communicating door between the two rooms should be left open so that I might be summoned, if necessary, at any moment.

And so we retired for the night, though, as far as I was concerned, it was not to sleep. I lay tossing about in my bed, expecting at every moment to hear Vance's call, and at last, unable to bear the strain any longer, I got up and went into his room to see how he was faring.

To my surprise, I found him sleeping calmly and peacefully. He had a shaded light burning beside the bed, and he did not stir when I approached. It was evident that the Fear had not assailed him, for I was quite sure he could not have slept through it if it had.

I tiptoed back to my room, and lay down again, and soon afterwards, my mind relieved, I got off to sleep, and did not open my eyes until I was aroused by the sun shining in at the window.

Vance was already up and dressing, and when he heard me astir he called out to know how I had slept.

"I've had a remarkably good night myself," he said cheerfully. "Not a sign of the Fear or of anything else."

"And yet other people have been unable to sleep in that room!" I exclaimed wonderingly. "How do you account for that, Vance?" He shrugged his shoulders.

"I can't account for it—yet," he replied. "We must wait and see what happens tonight. I've got a theory, but I'll keep it to myself at present."

"Well, I claim my turn to sleep there tonight," I declared, for in the sunlight my courage was completely restored. "Perhaps my faculty of seeing visions may be of service in solving the mystery."

We found that Mrs. Smith had provided us with an excellent breakfast, and though I am sure she wanted to question us, she did not venture to do so directly, nor did Vance or I show ourselves responsive to her hints.

We spent the morning exploring the Castle, and, as may be expected, it was to the tower that we first turned our attention.

We mounted to the circular room near the summit by means of a winding staircase to which access was obtained from the portrait gallery.

The room had been furnished, evidently by Mr. Balliston, in semi-oriental fashion, and the walls, of great age, were hung with tapestry. Somehow the impression of modernity jarred. We soon localised the window which we had seen open the night before. It was now closely shut. It was large and heavy, and we found that it was only with difficulty and by our united efforts, that we could raise the sash. Looking out, we saw beneath the little shrubbery where we had received the impression of fear.

There was nothing, however, by which the mystery might be elucidated, and we could only decide to make a further investigation when night came on.

In the afternoon we made our way to the village and inquired for Mr. Somers, the builder.

Unfortunately, he was absent for the day, so all we could do was to leave a message making an appointment for the next morning. We made certain other inquiries, but learnt little more than we already knew.

With the exception of Mr. Somers, no one in the village—at least no one that we could find—had been inside the Castle while it stood empty. Stories had, of course, got abroad, but they were indefinite, and did not touch upon the Fear. Mr. Somers's father and grandfather had both been reticent men, while the builder himself was apparently loath to admit that there was anything wrong. In fact, he made light of what had become common talk.

We returned to the Castle towards six o'clock, and were again caught by the Fear in our rooms at the same time as the night before. All that we could determine was that it certainly passed from the smaller to the larger room and then went out to the passage. We felt it quite distinctly just outside the door.

After that we proceeded to the tower room and made sure that all the windows were firmly closed.

We dined, attended by Mrs. Smith, as on the night before, but we retired early to our bedrooms, for Vance wished to put his theory to the test. He explained his undisturbed sleep of last night by the possibility that the Fear, which everyone had experienced who slept in that room, came on earlier—before he went to bed—and that consequently he had missed it.

"Mr. Balliston did not say that anyone spent the whole night in that room," he remarked.

It was decided that I should occupy the "haunted room." I lay down accordingly, practically fully dressed, on the outside of the bed, and Vance sat up in the other room, with the light full on, reading a book. It was then about half-past ten.

And half an hour later the Fear assailed me.

I have already described the sensation, so I need not repeat it, except to say that tonight it seemed increased a hundredfold.

I lay perfectly rigid, fully conscious of Vance's propinquity in the next room, but voiceless, absolutely unable to call out to him for assistance. My forehead was wringing wet with perspiration, and all my being was strung up with expectation—the expectation of something imminent, something ghastly, something inevitable.

And then, of a sudden, though there was nothing to be seen, absolutely nothing, I received the impression that the bed upon which I lay was already occupied—that someone else was lying there, someone who trembled and shook and sobbed so that the whole structure seemed to quiver beneath me.

I reached out my hand, but it encountered nothing, and yet I knew—I *knew*.

I cannot say how long I lay thus. It seemed to me an eternity—it may in reality have been a quarter of an hour. And the most awful part of it was the sense of helplessness, and the fact that instead of passing off as it had done on the other occasions, the Fear seemed to be increasing, to be growing momentarily more intense. Every successive moment was charged with acuter agony. Something was going to happen, and it was going to be now—now, at once.

I found myself sitting up upon the bed, straining my ears to listen for the approach of the danger. Perhaps my power of visualising things added to the intensity of the emotion, for I knew that I myself underwent every tiny detail of the agony that was endured by someone who had occupied that bed in years long gone by, and whose presence I vaguely felt by my side.

And as I sat thus it seemed to me that certain sounds fell upon my ears, and yet I cannot assert that they existed except through some impression mysteriously imparted to my brain.

Had there been any reality about them they were certainly loud enough to have disturbed Vance, who sat in his room quietly reading on, totally unconscious of the torture that I was enduring.

I thought I heard the furtive opening and closing of a door below and then a stealthy step upon the stair drawing nearer and nearer, and it seemed to me, as I listened, that I gave vent to a wild scream of terror—and yet I know now that not a sound escaped my lips.

Like all other impressions of those ghastly moments, the scream was a suggested product of my own brain—just as was the feeble crying of a child that I heard at the same moment, the frightened wail of an infant disturbed in its sleep.

And now I could hear laboured breathing in the passage outside, and the next moment it was at the door.

I felt a strange tingling at the roots of my hair, and the sudden recollection flashed through my brain of what Mr. Balliston had said: "I assure you it made my hair stand on end!"

A suggestion that had amused me at the moment, but now I understood it—if Mr. Balliston had gone through one tithe of what I was enduring.

I gazed with horror-riveted eyes at the door, and presently it seemed that the handle moved as if it were being slowly turned; then I was vaguely conscious of another shriek, louder by far than the first, and this was followed, to my acutely sharpened perception, by a sound as if someone had sprung from the bed by my side and was pattering across the floor with bare feet in the direction of the room occupied by Vance.

And all the while I could hear the whimpering of the child, carried, as it seemed, by the owner of the running feet, into the adjoining room.

The next moment the spell was broken—the terror had passed from me, and I lay there, panting and gasping, struggling to recover my shattered senses.

I had regained the use of my limbs, and blindly, wildly, following some impulse which I could not for the moment account for, I sprang from the bed and rushed into my friend's room.

Vance was sitting immobile in his chair, and the book which he had been reading had dropped to the floor. His face was drawn and troubled, and his eyes were intently fixed upon the door leading into the passage.

And I knew that the Fear was upon him, that it had passed from my room to his.

"It's there at the door," he whispered. "Do you feel it too, Dexter? It's there at the door."

I felt it afresh. I knew that someone was struggling to open the door from the inside, to turn a key which appeared to resist the nerveless, frightened fingers.

And there was the whimpering of the child too.

And then it passed away. Vance sprang to his feet, and we stood gazing at each other for one distracted moment.

Then, like myself, a few moments before, he seemed to pull himself together.

"Dexter," he muttered hoarsely, "we must follow."

Without pausing for my reply he made for the door, tore it open, and together we rushed out into the darkness of the passage.

Luckily he had his electric lamp with him, otherwise we should never have found our way along those little-known corridors and staircases, enveloped as they were in complete obscurity.

And it must be remembered that we were not following anything that we could actually see or hear—we were following the thread of terror that by some inconceivable means was imparted to our brains.

On we went, and we knew that we were following something that was following something else—a wild, cruel chase in which the pursued, in a very agony of terror, sought vainly for some means of escape.

And so, across the picture gallery, we came to the tower, and eventually to the room at its summit.

A breath of night air blew in upon my forehead. The window stood wide open, and it was there that the Fear reached its climax, though to the normal sense perfect stillness reigned—the whole room seemed to me full of horrid sound.

Vance and I were rooted to the spot where we stood while some abominable tragedy, only dimly guessed at, was played out to its culmination.

And then the window slid softly down, and all was over.

And it was well that it was so, for it seemed to me that another moment of such strain would have sent me mad. I looked at Vance and noticed the great beads of perspiration upon his forehead, the ghastly pallor of his face, the quivering of his hands and his shoulders—he had felt the terror no less than I.

"It's all over," he muttered; "it's gone!"

"Thanks God for that!" I panted in reply. "Let's get away, Vance, for fear that it may recur. I—I couldn't stand it any more."

"It won't recur tonight," he replied, trying to force a smile. "But let's go down to the dining-room, Dexter, and have some brandy and a smoke. That will steady our nerves."

I was very glad to act upon this suggestion, and a stiff dose of brandy soon put me to rights again.

And then I told Vance of all I had gone through in the earlier part of the night; how I had lain there upon the bed, unable to call out to him, while the Fear gradually possessed me.

"What do you make of it?" I inquired.

He shrugged his shoulders and remarked that at present we could do little but conjecture.

"It's to be hoped that tomorrow may bring light," he continued; "that is, if we can persuade Mr. Somers to speak."

We spent an hour, however, discussing our own theories, which, as it turned out, were not very far from the truth, and eventually we went back to bed, where our sleep was undisturbed for the rest of the night.

The next day we sought out Mr. Somers, whom we found to be a young man of rather taciturn disposition; nevertheless, he eventually yielded to the charm of Aylmer Vance's manner, and consented to tell us all he knew, after exacting a promise that, for his own family reputation, the story should not be published abroad.

"But, indeed, gentlemen," he said, "if you can do anything to stop the horror—to clear Camplin Castle of its ghosts—I shall be grateful to you, and glad I have spoken. You see, my grandfather—but I'd better tell you the story."

And so, sitting there in the little shop parlour to which he had led us, we listened to the story of Camplin Castle, or, rather, to the portion of it that was of interest to us at that moment.

Camplin Castle had belonged to the Oswald family for centuries. For years and years it was handed down from father to son, and nothing had occurred to break the succession till about the middle of the nineteenth century, when the then owner of the estate, Jasper Oswald, quarrelled with his eldest son, Luke, who was a wild young fellow and had contrived to offend his father deeply. Luke ran away from home before he was twenty-one, and at last a report was received that he was dead.

So, on the death of Jasper, the younger brother, Philip succeeded to the estate.

Philip had a beautiful wife, whose name was Elen, and a child, of whom they were both inordinately fond—a little boy of two. He was a passionate, ambitious man, was Philip, imbued with the violent temper that was characteristic of the Oswalds.

But Luke, the elder son, was not really dead, and soon after Philip and his family were installed at the castle he returned to claim his own from his brother. They would not recognise him, said that he was an impostor, and when he took his case to the Law Courts he lost it. He could not wholly prove his identity at the time, and it was suggested that Philip was able to suborn evidence against him.

Well, Luke came up to the house and saw his brother after the case was over. Philip sat in the dining-room with his wife and child, and made the servants throw Luke out.

Then Luke turned and cursed him, swore that he would kill them all, and that he would not do it at once, but, as they had made him suffer, so should they suffer, too. The torture of Fear, fear of impending death, the knowledge that it might fall upon them at any moment, was to be their fate.

And they read in his face that he meant what he said.

From that day they knew no rest; the fear of death was constantly upon them. And so it was that fear, a fear which was drawn out for the best part of twelve months or more, that impregnated the walls of Camplin Castle, had reigned there ever since.

"And did Luke Oswald kill his brother?" inquired Vance. The builder shrugged his shoulders.

"Philip Oswald died mysteriously about six months after the termination of the law case. He was found drowned in a pond, and it was assumed that he was killed by poachers, with whom he was constantly coming into conflict. But the murderer was never found."

"And the wife and child?"

"Luke did not spare them, either. You see, it was not only revenge that he wanted. He wished to recover the estate for himself and his possible heirs. But nobody knows exactly what happened. Another six months went by, and then it was reported that Elen Oswald had gone mad, and that, in a fit of frenzy, she had thrown her child from a window in the tower, killing it at once. She was carried off to an asylum, where she died soon after. And then, some years later, Luke Oswald was able to bring evidence to show that he was indeed the rightful heir to Camplin Castle, and so he took possession and moved in, and it seemed at first as if he was going to live in luxury and in great style.

"But everything went wrong with him. He got engaged to a beautiful girl, but she died a few days before the wedding. And so he never married, and there was no child to succeed him, no Oswald to be lord of the manor after his death. And then, no one could say why, but people shunned him; there was something in his appearance that set them against him—he was hard and cruel to his tenants, who loathed him, and would not work for him, so that his land went to waste. And by degrees health forsook him, too, and he would go about, worn and old before his time, with the appearance of a haunted man.

"No servants would stay with him at the castle—none, at least, except my old grandfather, who had been there in Philip's time, too, and who was a queer type of man, sullen and morose, and who was not afraid of God or devil. They shut up the best part of the castle, and lived in a few rooms only, seeing no one and wanting to see no one—a pair of recluses.

"And so, twelve years ago, Luke Oswald died, and the mystery of his life remained a mystery to the world outside. Camplin Castle passed into the hands of the next-of-kin, who was a distant cousin, a man who had no interests in the estate, and who bore another name. He came to Hampshire to view his new property, stayed there a few days, and then placed it in the hands of the house agents, took his departure, and has not been seen again in the neighbourhood."

"You think that he had his experience of the Fear," suggested Vance, "and made the best of a bad bargain by attempting to let his property?"

"He gave out that he was too poor a man to live at the castle," was the guarded reply, "and I know nothing of what happened while he was actually in possession. My grandfather remained as caretaker until his death the following year, and it was upon his deathbed that he told my father things that my father only told me when he, in turn, was dying, begging me to keep the secret for our honour's sake."

"And you can tell us this secret?" asked Vance gently.

The young man flushed.

"Let it be a hint," he said. "My grandfather, while in Mr. Philip's service—and after his death, too—was in the pay of Mr. Luke. He connived at that year of terror. It was with his help that Luke obtained access to the castle whenever he wished. And"—he lowered his eyes— "I do not think that the unfortunate woman threw her child from the window. Oh! do you wonder," he added, with some display of emotion, "that Camplin Castle is not habitable today, that it reeks with horror from cellar to attic?

"My advice to Mr. Balliston," he concluded, "would be to raze the whole place to the ground, and to build a new house upon the site. Short of that, I don't see what he can do."

"I'm inclined to think that our friend the builder's advice is good," remarked Vance to me, after this interesting interview. "So long as bricks and mortar, and the atmosphere itself, are retentive, as we know them to be, there is little, Dexter, that you or I, or anyone else, can do to be of assistance.

"And that's the worst of this hobby of ours," he added, with a suggestion of sadness in his voice; "for people come to us, as Mr. Balliston did, begging for our assistance, and thinking that by some strange mysterious power we can lay the ghosts, or what they are pleased to call the ghosts. But that's just what we can't do; we can only prove what has been proved hundreds of times before, that there are more things in heaven and earth than the human philosophy of the present day can understand.

"And again and again I find the same advice recurring—the advice which Somers has given us—the advice of one who has not had the experience of years such as I have had, but which is quite as good as any that I can give—destroy. And that, too, is the advice that applies to Camplin Castle."

THE METHODS
OF MORRIS KLAW

CASE OF THE TRAGEDIES IN THE GREEK ROOM

I

When did Moris Klaw first appear in London? It is a question which I am asked sometimes and to which I reply, "To the best of my knowledge, shortly before the commencement of the strange happenings at the Menzies Museum."

What I know of him I have gathered from various sources; and in these papers, which represent an attempt to justify the methods of one frequently accused of being an insane theorist, I propose to recount all the facts which have come to my knowledge. In some few of the cases I was personally though slightly concerned; but regard me merely as the historian and on no account as the principal or even minor character in the story. My friendship with Martin Coram led, then, to my first meeting with Moris Klaw—a meeting which resulted in my becoming his biographer, inadequate though my information unfortunately remains.

It was some three months after the appointment of Coram to the curatorship of the Menzies Museum that the first of a series of singular occurrences took place there.

This occurrence befell one night in August, and the matter was brought to my ears by Coram himself on the following morning. I had, in fact, just taken my seat at the breakfast table, when he walked in unexpectedly and sank into an armchair. His dark, clean-shaven face looked more gaunt than usual and I saw, as he lighted the cigarette which I proffered, that his hand shook nervously.

"There's trouble at the Museum!" he said, abruptly. "I want you to run around."

I looked at him for a moment without replying, and, knowing the responsibility of his position, feared that he referred to a theft from the collection.

"Something gone?" I asked.

"No; worse!" was his reply.

"What do you mean, Coram?"

He threw the cigarette, unsmoked, into the hearth. "You know Conway?" he said; "Conway, the night attendant? Well—he's dead!

I stood up from the table, my breakfast forgotten, and stared incredulously. "Do you mean that he died in the night?" I inquired.

"Yes. Done for, poor devil!"

"What! murdered?"

"Without a doubt, Searles! He's had his neck broken!"

I waited for no further explanations, but, hastily dressing, accompanied Coram to the Museum. It consists, I should mention, of four long, rectangular rooms, the windows of two overlooking South Grafton Square, those of the third giving upon the court that leads to the curator's private entrance, and the fourth adjoining an enclosed garden attached to the building. This fourth room is on the ground floor and is entered through the hall from the Square, the other three, containing the principal and more valuable exhibits, are upon the first floor and are reached by a flight of stairs from the hall. The remainder of the building is occupied by an office and the curator's private apartments, and is completely shut off from that portion open to the public, the only communicating door—an iron one—being kept locked.

The room described in the catalogue as the "Greek Room" proved to be the scene of the tragedy. This room is one of the two overlooking the Square and contains some of the finest items of the collection. The Museum is not open to the public until ten o'clock, and I found, upon arriving there, that the only occupants of the Greek Room were the commissionaire on duty, two constables, a plain-clothes officer and an inspector—that is, if I except the body of poor Conway.

He had not been touched, but lay as he was found by Beale, the commissionaire who took charge of the upper rooms during the day, and, indeed, it was patent that he was beyond medical aid. In fact, the position of his body was so extraordinary as almost to defy description.

There are three windows in the Greek Room, with wall cases between, and, in the gap corresponding to the east window and just by the door opening into the next room, is a chair for the attendant. Conway lay downward on the polished floor with his limbs partly under this chair and his clenched fists thrust straight out before him. His head, turned partially to one side, was doubled underneath his breast in a most dreadful manner, indisputably pointing to a broken neck, and his commissionaire's cap lay some distance away, under a table supporting a heavy case of vases.

So much was revealed at a glance, and I immediately turned blankly to Coram.

"What do you make of it?" he said.

I shook my head in silence. I could scarce grasp the reality of the thing; indeed, I was still staring at the huddled figure when the doctor arrived. At his request we laid the dead man flat upon the floor to facilitate an examination, and we then saw that he was greatly cut and bruised about the head and face, and that his features were distorted in a most extraordinary manner, almost as though he had been suffocated.

The doctor did not fail to notice this expression. "Made a hard fight of it!" he said. "He must have been in the last stages of exhaustion when his neck was broken!"

"My dear fellow!" cried Coram, somewhat irritably, "what do you mean when you say that he made a hard fight? There could not possibly have been any one else in these rooms last night!"

"Excuse me, sir!" said the inspector, "but there certainly was something going on here. Have you seen the glass case in the next room?"

"Glass case?" muttered Coram, running his hand distractedly through his thick black hair. "No; what of a glass case?"

"In here, sir," explained the inspector, leading the way into the adjoining apartment.

At his words, we all followed, and found that he referred to the glass front of a wall case containing statuettes and images of Egyptian deities. The centre pane of this was smashed into fragments, the broken glass strewing the floor and the shelves inside the case.

"That looks like a struggle, sir, doesn't it?" said the inspector.

"Heaven help us! What does it mean?" groaned poor Coram. "Who could possibly have gained access to the building in the night, or, having done so, have quitted it again, when all the doors remained locked?"

"That we must try and find out!" replied the inspector. "Meanwhile, here are his keys. They lay on the floor in a corner of the Greek Room."

Coram took them, mechanically. "Beale," he said to the commissionaire, "see if any of the cases are unlocked."

The man proceeded to go around the rooms. He had progressed no farther than the Greek Room when he made a discovery. "Here's the top of this unfastened, sir!" he suddenly cried, excitedly.

We hurriedly joined him, to find that he stood before a marble pedestal surmounted by a thick glass case containing what Coram had frequently assured me was the gem of the collection—the Athenean Harp.

It was alleged to be of very ancient Greek workmanship, and was constructed of fine gold inlaid with jewels. It represented two reclining female figures, their arms thrown above their heads, their hands meeting; and the strings, several of which were still intact, were of incredibly fine gold wire. The instrument was said to have belonged to a Temple of Pallas in an extremely remote age, and at the time it was brought to light much controversy had waged concerning its claims to authenticity, several connoisseurs proclaiming it the work of a famous goldsmith of mediaeval Florence, and nothing but a clever forgery. However, Greek or Florentine, amazingly ancient or comparatively modern, it was a beautiful piece of workmanship and of very great intrinsic value, apart from its artistic worth and unique character.

"I thought so!" said the plain-clothes man. "A clever museum thief!"

Coram sighed wearily. "My good fellow," he replied, "can you explain, by any earthly hypothesis, how a man could get into these apartments and leave them again during the night?"

"Regarding that, sir," remarked the detective, "there are a few questions I should like to ask you. In the first place, at what time does the Museum close?"

"At six o'clock in the summer."

"What do you do when the last visitor has gone?"

"Having locked the outside door, Beale, here, thoroughly examines every room to make certain that no one remains concealed. He next locks the communicating doors and comes down into the hall. It was then his custom to hand me the keys. I gave them into poor Conway's keeping when he came on duty at half-past six, and every hour he went through the Museum, relocking all the doors behind him."

"I understand that there is a tell-tale watch in each room?"

"Yes. That in the Greek Room registers 4 A. M., so that it was about then that he met his death. He had evidently opened the door communicating with the next room—that containing the broken glass case; but he did not touch the detector and the door was found open this morning."

"Someone must have lain concealed there and sprung upon him as he entered."

"Impossible! There is no other means of entrance or exit. The three windows are iron-barred and they have not been tampered with. Moreover, the watch shows that he was there at three o'clock, and nothing larger than a mouse could find shelter in the place; there is nowhere a man could hide."

"Then the murderer followed him into the Greek Room."

"Might I venture to point out that, had he done so, he would have been there this morning when Beale arrived? The door of the Greek Room was locked and the keys were found inside upon the floor!"

"The thief might have had a duplicate set."

"Quite impossible; but, granting the impossible, how did he get in, since the hall door was bolted and barred?"

"We must assume that he succeeded in concealing himself before the Museum was closed."

"The assumption is not permissible, in view of the fact that Beale and I both examined the rooms last night prior to handing the keys to Conway. However, again granting the impossible, how did he get out?"

The Scotland Yard man removed his hat and mopped his forehead with his handkerchief. "I must say, sir, it is a very strange thing," he said; "but how about the iron door here?"

"It leads to my own apartments. I, alone, hold a key. It was locked."

A brief examination served to show that exit from any of the barred windows was impossible.

"Well, sir," said the detective, "if the man had keys he could have come down into the hall and the lower room."

"Step down and look," was Coram's invitation.

The windows of the room on the ground floor were also heavily protected, and it was easy to see that none of them had been opened.

"Upon my word," exclaimed the inspector, "it's uncanny! He couldn't have gone out by the hall door, because you say it was bolted and barred on the inside."

"It was," replied Coram.

"One moment, sir," interrupted the plain-clothes man. "If that was so, how did you get in this morning?"

"It was Beale's custom," said Coram, "to come around by the private entrance to my apartments. We then entered the Museum together by the iron door into the Greek Room and relieved Conway of the keys. There are several little matters to be attended to in the morning before admitting the public, and the other door is never unlocked before ten o'clock."

"Did you lock the door behind you when you came through this morning?"

"Immediately on finding poor Conway."

"Could any one have come through this door in the night, provided he had a duplicate key?"

"No. There is a bolt on the private side."

"And you were in your rooms all last night?"

"From twelve o'clock, yes."

The police looked at one another silently; then the inspector gave an embarrassed laugh. "Frankly, sir," he said, "I'm completely puzzled!"

We passed upstairs again and Coram turned to the doctor. "Anything else to report about poor Conway?" he asked.

"His face is all cut by the broken glass and he seems to have had a desperate struggle, although, curiously enough, his body bears no other marks of violence. The direct cause of death was, of course, a broken neck."

"And how should you think he came by it?"

"I should say that he was hurled upon the floor by an opponent possessing more than ordinary strength!"

Thus the physician, and was about to depart when there came a knocking upon the iron door.

"It is Hilda," said Coram, slipping the key in the lock— "my daughter," he added, turning to the detective.

II

The heavy door swinging open, there entered Hilda Coram, a slim, classical figure, with the regular features of her father and the pale gold hair of her dead mother. She looked unwell, and stared about her apprehensively.

"Good morning, Mr. Searles," she greeted me. "Is it not dreadful about poor Conway!"—and then glanced at Coram. I saw that she held a card in her hand. "Father, there is such a singular old man asking to see you."

She handed the card to Coram, who in turn passed it to me. It was that of Douglas Glade of the *Daily Cable*, and had written upon it in Glade's hand the words, "To introduce Mr. Moris Klaw."

"I suppose it is all right if Mr. Glade vouches for him," said Coram. "But does anybody here know Moris Klaw?"

"I do," replied the Scotland Yard man, smiling shortly. "He's an antique dealer or something of the kind; got a ramshackle old place by Wapping Old Stairs—sort of a cross between Jamrach's and a rag shop. He's lately been hanging about the Central Criminal Court a lot. Seems to fancy his luck as an amateur investigator. He's certainly smart," he added, grudgingly, "but cranky."

"Ask Mr. Klaw to come through, Hilda," said Coram.

Shortly afterward entered a strange figure. It was that of a tall man who stooped, so that his apparent height was diminished—a very old man who carried his many years lightly, or a younger man prematurely aged; none could say which. His skin had the hue of dirty vellum, and his hair, his shaggy brows, his scanty beard were so toneless as to defy classification in terms of colour. He wore an archaic brown bowler, smart, gold-rimmed pince-nez, and a black silk muffler. A long, caped black cloak completely enveloped the stooping figure; from beneath its mud-spattered edge peeped long-toed continental boots.

He removed his hat.

"Good morning, Mr. Coram," he said. His voice reminded me of the distant rumbling of empty casks; his accent was wholly indescribable. "Good morning" (to the detective), "Mr. Grimsby. Good morning, Mr. Searles. Your friend, Mr. Glade, tells me I shall find you here. Good morning, Inspector. To Miss Coram I already have said good morning."

From the lining of the flat-topped hat he took out one of those small cylindrical scent sprays and played its contents upon his high, bald brow. An odour of verbena filled the air. He replaced the spray in the hat, the hat upon his scantily thatched crown.

"There is here a smell of dead men!" he explained.

I turned aside to hide my smiles, so grotesque was my first impression of the amazing individual known as Moris Klaw.

"Mr. Coram," he continued, "I am an old fool who sometimes has wise dreams. Crime has been the hobby of a busy life. I have seen crime upon the Gold Coast, where the black fever it danced in the air above the murdered one like a lingering soul, and I have seen blood flow in Arctic Lapland, where it was frozen up into red ice almost before it left the veins. Have I your permit to see if I can help?"

All of us, the police included, were strangely impressed now.

"Certainly," said Coram; "will you step this way?"

Moris Klaw bent over the dead man.

"You have moved him!" he said, sharply.

It was explained that this had been for the purpose of a medical examination. He nodded absently. With the aid of a large magnifying glass he was scrutinizing poor Conway. He examined his hair, his eyes, his hands, his fingernails. He rubbed long, flexible fingers upon the floor beside the body—and sniffed at the dust.

"Someone so kindly will tell me all about it," he said, turning out the dead man's pockets.

Coram briefly recounted much of the foregoing, and replied to the oddly chosen questions which from time to time Moris Klaw put to him. Throughout the duologue, the singular old man conducted a detailed search of every square inch, I think, of the Greek Room. Before the case containing the harp he stood, peering.

"It is here that the trouble centres," he muttered. "What do I know of such a Grecian instrument? Let me think."

He threw back his head, closing his eyes.

"Such valuable curios," he rumbled, "have histories—and the crimes they occasion operate in cycles." He waved his hand in a slow circle. "If I but knew the history of this harp! Mr. Coram!"

He glanced toward my friend.

"Thoughts are things, Mr. Coram. If I might spend a night here upon the very spot of floor where the poor Conway fell—I could from the surrounding atmosphere (it is a sensitive plate) recover a picture of the thing in his mind"—indicating Conway— "at the last!"

The Scotland Yard man blew down his nose.

"You snort, my friend," said Moris Klaw, turning upon him. "You would snort less if you had waked screaming, out in the desert; screaming out with fear of the dripping beaks of the vultures—the last dreadful fear which the mind had known of him who had died of thirst upon that haunted spot!"

The words and the manner of their delivery thrilled us all.

"What is it," continued the weird old man, "but the odic force, the ether—say it how you please—which carries the wireless message, the lightning? It is a huge, subtile, sensitive plate. Inspiration, what you call bad luck and good luck—all are but reflections from it. The supreme thought preceding death is imprinted on the surrounding atmosphere like a photograph. I have trained this"—he tapped his brow— "to reproduce those photographs! May I sleep here to-night, Mr. Coram?"

Somewhere beneath the ramshackle exterior we had caught a glimpse of a man of power. From behind the thick pebbles momentarily had shone out the light of a tremendous and original mind.

"I should be most glad of your assistance," answered my friend.

"No police must be here to-night," rumbled Moris Klaw. "No heavy-footed constables, filling the room with thoughts of large cooks and small Basses, must fog my negative!"

"Can that be arranged?" asked Coram of the inspector.

"The men on duty can remain in the hall, if you wish it, sir."

"Good!" rumbled Moris Klaw.

He moistened his brow with verbena, bowed uncouthly, and shuffled from the Greek Room.

III

Moris Klaw reappeared in the evening, accompanied by a strikingly beautiful brunette.

The change of face upon the part of Mr. Grimsby of New Scotland Yard was singular.

"My daughter—Isis," explained Moris Klaw. "She assists to develop my negatives."

Grimsby became all attention. Leaving two men on duty in the hall, Moris Klaw, his daughter, Grimsby, Coram, and I went up to the Greek Room. Its darkness was relieved by a single lamp.

"I've had the stones in the Athenean Harp examined by a lapidary," said Coram. "It occurred to me that they might have been removed and paste substituted. It was not so, however."

"No," rumbled Klaw. "I thought of that, too. No visitors have been admitted here during the day?"

"The Greek Room has been closed."

"It is well, Mr. Coram. Let no one disturb me until my daughter comes in the morning."

Isis Klaw placed a red silk cushion upon the spot where the dead man had lain.

"Some pillows and a blanket, Mr. Klaw?" suggested the suddenly attentive Mr. Grimsby.

"I thank you, no," was the reply. "They would be saturated with alien impressions. My cushion it is odically sterilized! The 'etheric storm' created by Conway's last mental emotion reaches my brain unpolluted. Good-night, gentlemen. Good-night, Isis!"

We withdrew, leaving Moris Klaw to his ghostly vigil.

"I suppose Mr. Klaw is quite trustworthy?" whispered Coram to the detective.

"Oh, undoubtedly!" was the reply. "In any case, he can do no harm. My men will be on duty downstairs here all night."

"Do you speak of my father, Mr. Grimsby?" came a soft, thrilling voice.

Grimsby turned, and met the flashing black eyes of Isis Klaw.

"I was assuring Mr. Coram," he answered, readily, "that Mr. Klaw's methods have several times proved successful!"

"Several times!" she cried, scornfully. "What! has he ever failed?"

Her accent was certainly French, I determined; her voice, her entire person, as certainly charming—to which the detective's manner bore witness.

"I'm afraid I'm not familiar with all his cases, miss," he said. "Can I call you a cab?"

"I thank you, no." She rewarded him with a dazzling smile. "Good-night."

Coram opened the doors of the Museum, and she passed out. Leaving the men on duty in the hall, Coram and I shortly afterward also quitted the Museum by the main entrance, in order to avoid disturbing Moris Klaw by using the curator's private door.

To my friend's study Hilda Coram brought us coffee. She was unnaturally pale, and her eyes were feverishly bright. I concluded that the tragedy was responsible.

"Perhaps, to an extent," said Coram; "but she is studying music and, I fear, overworking in order to pass a stiff exam."

Coram and I surveyed the Greek Room problem from every conceivable standpoint, but were unable to surmise how the thief had entered, how left, and why he had fled without his booty.

"I don't mind confessing," said Coram, "that I am very ill at ease. We haven't the remotest idea how the murderer got into the Greek Room or how he got out again. Bolts and bars, it is evident, do not prevail against him, so that we may expect a repetition of the dreadful business at any time!"

"What precautions do you propose to take?"

"Well, there will be a couple of police on duty in the Museum for the next week or so, but, after that, we shall have to rely upon a night watchman. The funds only allow of the appointment of four attendants: three for day and one for night duty."

"Do you think you'll find any difficulty in getting a man?"

"No," replied Coram. "I know of a steady man who will come as soon as we are ready for him."

I slept but little that night, and was early afoot and around to the Museum. Isis Klaw was there before me, carrying the red cushion, and her father was deep in conversation with Coram.

Detective-Inspector Grimsby approached me.

"I see you're looking at the cushion, sir!" he said, smilingly. "But it's not a 'plant.' He's not an up-to-date cracksman. Nothing's missing!"

"You need not assure me of that," I replied. "I do not doubt Mr. Klaw's honesty of purpose."

"Wait till you hear his mad theory, though!" he said, with a glance aside at the girl.

"Mr. Coram," Moris Klaw was saying, in his odd, rumbling tones, "my psychic photograph is of a woman! A woman dressed all in white!"

Grimsby coughed—then flushed as he caught the eye of Isis.

"Poor Conway's mind," continued Klaw, "is filled with such a picture when he breathes his last—great wonder he has for the white woman and great fear for the Athenean Harp, which she carries!"

"Which she carries!" cried Coram.

"Some woman took the harp from its case a few minutes before Conway died!" affirmed Moris Klaw. "I have much research to make now, and with aid from Isis shall develop my negative! Yesterday I learnt from the constable who was on night duty at the corner of the Square that a heavy pantechnicon van went driving round at four o'clock. It was shortly after four o'clock that the tragedy occurred. The driver was unaware that there was no way out, you understand. Is it important? I cannot say. It often is such points that matter. We must, however, waste no time. Until you hear from me again you will lay dry plaster of Paris all around the stand of the Athenean Harp each night. Good morning, gentlemen!"

His arm linked in his daughter's, he left the Museum.

IV

For some weeks after this mysterious affair, all went well at the Menzies Museum. The new night watchman, a big Scot, by name John Macalister, seemed to have fallen thoroughly into his duties, and everything was proceeding smoothly. No clue concerning the previous outrage had come to light, the police being clearly at a loss. From Moris Klaw we heard not a word. But Macalister did not appear to suffer from nervousness, saying that he was quite big enough to look after himself.

Poor Macalister! His bulk did not save him from a dreadful fate. He was found, one fine morning, lying flat on his back in the Greek Room—*dead!*

As in the case of Conway, the place showed unmistakable signs of a furious struggle. The attendant's chair had been dashed upon the floor with such violence as to break three of the legs; a bust of Pallas, that had occupied a corner position upon a marble pedestal, was found to be hurled down; and the top of the case which usually contained the Athenean Harp had been unlocked, and the priceless antique lay close by, upon the floor!

The cause of death, in Macalister's case, was heart failure, an unsuspected weakness of that organ being brought to light at the inquest; but, according to the medical testimony, deceased must have undergone unnaturally violent exertions to bring about death. In other respects, the circumstances of the two cases were almost identical. The door of the Greek Room was locked upon the inside and the keys were found on the floor. From the detector watches in the other rooms it was evident that his death must have taken place about three o'clock. Nothing was missing, and the jewels in the harp had not been tampered with.

But, most amazing circumstance of all, imprinted upon the dry plaster of Paris which, in accordance with the instructions of the mysteriously absent Moris Klaw, had nightly been placed around the case containing the harp, *were the marks of little bare feet!*

A message sent, through the willing agency of Inspector Grimsby, to the Wapping abode of the old Curio dealer, resulted in the discovery that Moris Klaw was abroad. His daughter, however, reported having received a letter from her father which contained the words—

"Let Mr. Coram keep the key of the case containing the Athenean Harp under his pillow at night."

"What does she mean?" asked Coram. "That I am to detach that particular key from the bunch or place them all beneath my pillow?"

Grimsby shrugged his shoulders.

"I'm simply telling you what she told me, sir."

"I should suspect the man to be an impostor," said Coram, "if it were not for the extraordinary confirmation of his theory furnished by the footprints. They certainly looked like those of a woman!"

Remembering how Moris Klaw had acted, I sought out the constable who had been on duty at the corner of South Grafton Square on the night of the second tragedy. From him I elicited a fact which, though insignificant in itself, was, when associated with another circumstance, certainty singular.

A Pickford traction engine, drawing two heavy wagons, had been driven round the Square at 3 A. M., the driver thinking that he could get out on the other side.

That was practically all I learned from the constable, but it served to set me thinking. Was it merely a coincidence that, at almost the exact hour of the previous tragedy, a heavy pantechnicon had passed the Museum?

"It's not once in six months," the man assured me, "that any vehicle but a tradesman's cart goes round the Square. You see, it doesn't lead anywhere, but this Pickford chap he was rattling by before I could stop him, and though I shouted he couldn't hear me, the engine making such a noise, so I just let him drive round and find out for himself."

I now come to the event which concluded this extraordinary case, and, that it may be clearly understood, I must explain the positions which we took up during the nights of the following week; for Coram had asked me to take a night watch, with himself, Grimsby, and Beale, in the Museum.

Beale, the commissionaire, remained in the hall and lower room—it was catalogued as the "Bronze Room"—Coram patrolled the room at the top of the stairs, Grimsby the next, or Greek, Room, and I the Egyptian Room. None of the doors was locked, and Grimsby, by his own special request, held the keys of the cases in the Greek Room.

We commenced our vigil on the Saturday, and I, for one, found it a lugubrious business. One electric lamp was usually left burning in each apartment throughout the night, and I sat as near to that in the Egyptian Room as possible and endeavoured to distract my thoughts with a bundle of papers with which I had provided myself.

In the next room I could hear Grimsby walking about incessantly, and, at regular intervals, the scratching of a match as he lighted a cigar. He was an inveterate cheroot smoker.

Our first night's watching, then, was productive of no result, and the five that followed were equally monotonous.

Upon Grimsby's suggestion we observed great secrecy in the matter of these dispositions. Even Coram's small household was kept in ignorance of this midnight watching. Grimsby, following out some theory of his own, now determined to dispense altogether with light in the Greek Room. Friday was intensely hot, and occasional fitful breezes brought with them banks of black thundercloud, which, however, did not break; and, up to the time that we assumed our posts at the Museum, no rain had fallen. At about twelve o'clock I looked out into South Grafton Square and saw that the sky was entirely obscured by a heavy mass of inky cloud, ominous of a gathering storm.

Returning to my chair beneath the electric lamp, I took up a work of Mark Twain's, which I had brought as a likely antidote to melancholy or nervousness. As I commenced to read, for the twentieth time, "The Jumping Frog," I heard the scratch of Grimsby's match in the next room and knew that he had lighted his fifth cigar.

It must have been about one o'clock when the rain came. I heard the big drops on the glass roof, followed by the steady pouring of the deluge. For perhaps five minutes it rained steadily, and then ceased as abruptly as it had begun. Above the noise of the water rushing down the metal gutters, I distinctly detected the sound of Grimsby striking another match. Then, with a mighty crash, came the thunder.

Directly above the Museum it seemed as though the very heavens had burst, and the glass roof rattled as if a shower of stones had fallen, the thunderous report echoing and reverberating hollowly through the building.

As the lightning flashed with dazzling brilliance, I started from my chair and stood, breathless, with every sense on the alert; for, strangely intermingling with the patter of the rain that now commenced to fall again, came a low wailing, like nothing so much as the voice of a patient succumbing to an anaesthetic. There was something indefinably sweet, but indescribably weird, in the low and mysterious music.

Not knowing from whence it proceeded, I stood undetermined what to do; but, just as the thunder boomed again, I heard a wild cry—undoubtedly proceeding from the Greek Room! Springing to the door, I threw it open.

All was in darkness, but, as I entered, a vivid flash of lightning illuminated the place.

I saw a sight which I can never forget. Grimsby lay flat upon the floor by the farther door. But, dreadful as that spectacle was, it scarce engaged my attention; nor did I waste a second glance upon the Athenean Harp, which lay close beside its empty case.

For the figure of a woman, draped in flimsy white, was passing across the Greek Room!

Grim fear took me by the throat, since I could not doubt that what I saw was a supernatural manifestation. Darkness followed. I heard a loud wailing cry and a sound as of a fall.

Then Coram came running through the Greek Room.

Trembling violently, I joined him; and together we stood looking down at Grimsby.

"Good God!" whispered Coram; "this is awful. It cannot be the work of mortal hands! Poor Grimsby is dead!"

"Did you—see—the woman?" I muttered. I will confess it: my courage had completely deserted me.

He shook his head; but as Beale came running to join us, glanced fearfully into the shadows of the Greek Room. The storm seemed to have passed, and, as we three frightened men stood around Grimsby's recumbent body, we could almost hear the beating of each other's hearts.

Suddenly, giving a great start, Coram clutched my arm. "Listen!" he said. "What's that?"

I held my breath and listened. "It's the thunder in the distance," said Beale.

"You are wrong," I answered. "It is someone knocking at the hall entrance! There goes the bell, now!"

Coram gave a sigh of relief. "Heavens!" he said; "I've no nerves left! Come on and see who it is."

The three of us, keeping very close together, passed quickly through the Greek Room and down into the hall. As the ringing continued, Coram unbolted the door—and there, on the steps, stood Moris Klaw!

Some vague idea of his mission flashed through my mind. "You are too late!" I cried. "Grimsby has gone!"

I saw a look of something like anger pass over his large pale features, and then he had darted past us and vanished up the stairs.

V

Having rebolted the door, we rejoined Moris Klaw in the Greek Room. He was kneeling beside Grimsby in the dim light—and Grimsby, his face ghastly pale, was sitting up and drinking from a flask!

"I am in time!" said Moris Klaw. "He has only fainted!"

"It was the ghost!" whispered the Scotland Yard man. "My God! I'm prepared for anything human—but when the lightning came and I saw that white thing—playing the harp—"

Coram turned aside and was about to pick up the harp, which lay upon the floor near, when—

"Ah!" cried Moris Klaw, "do not touch it! It is death!"

Coram started back as though he had been stung as Grimsby very unsteadily got upon his feet.

"Turn up lights," directed Moris Klaw, "and I will show you!"

The curator went out to the switchboard and the Greek Room became brightly illuminated. The ramshackle figure of Moris Klaw seemed to be in vested with triumphant majesty. Behind the pebbles his eyes gleamed.

"Observe," he said, "I raise the harp from the floor." He did so. "And I live. For why? Because I do not take hold upon it in a natural manner—*by the top!* I take it by the side! Conway and Macalister took hold upon it at the top; and where are they—Conway and Macalister?"

"Mr. Klaw," said Coram, "I cannot doubt that this black business is all clear to your very unusual intelligence; but to me it is a profound mystery. I have, myself, in the past, taken up the harp in the way you describe as fatal, and without injury—"

"But not immediately after it had been played upon!" interrupted Moris Klaw.

"Played upon! I have never attempted to play upon it!"

"Even had you done so you might yet have escaped, provided you *set it down* before touching the top part! Note, please!"

He ran his long white fingers over the golden strings. Instantly there stole upon my ears that weird, wailing music which had heralded the strange happenings of the night!

"And now," continued our mentor, "whilst I who am cunning hold it where the ladies' gold feet join, observe the top—where the hand would in ordinary rest in holding it."

We gathered around him.

"A *needle-point*," he rumbled, impressively, "protruding! The player touches it not! But who takes it from the hand of the player *dies!* By placing the harp again upon its base the point again retires! Shall I say what is upon that point, to drive a man mad like a dog with rabies, to stay potent for generations? I cannot. It is a secret buried with the ugly body of Caesar Borgia!"

"Caesar Borgia!" we cried in chorus.

"Ah!" rumbled Moris Klaw, "your Athenean Harp was indeed made by Paduano Zelloni, the Florentine! It is a clever forge! I have been in Rome until yesterday. You are surprised? I am sorry, for the poor Macalister died. Having perfected, with the aid of Isis, my mind photograph of the lady who plays the harp, I go to Rome to perfect the story of the harp. For why? At my house I have records, but incomplete, useless. In Rome I have a friend, of so old a family, and once so wicked, I shall not name it!

"He has recourse to the great Vatican Library—to the annals of his race. There he finds me an account of such a harp. In those priceless parchments it is called 'a Greek lyre of gold.' It is described. I am convinced. I am sure!

"Once the beautiful Lucrece Borgia play upon this harp. To one who is distasteful to her she says: 'Replace for me my harp.' He does so. He is a dead man! God! what cleverness!

"Where has it lain for generations before your Sir Menzies find it? No man knows. But it has still its virtues! How did the poor Menzies die? Throw himself from his room window, I recently learn. This harp certainly was in his room. Conway, after dashing, mad, about the place, springs head downward from the attendant's chair. Macalister dies in exhaustion and convulsions!"

A silence; when—

"What caused the harp to play?" asked Coram.

Moris Klaw looked hard at him. Then a thrill of new horror ran through my veins. A low moan came from somewhere hard by! Coram turned in a flash!

"Why, my private door is open!" he whispered.

"Where do you keep your private keys?" rumbled Klaw.

"In my study." Coram was staring at the open door, but seemed afraid to approach it. "We have been using the attendant's keys at night. My own are on my study mantelpiece now."

"I think not," continued the thick voice. "Your daughter has them!"

"My daughter!" cried Coram, and sprang to the open door. "Heavens! Hilda! Hilda!"

"She is somnambulistic!" whispered Moris Klaw in my ear. "When certain unusual sounds—such as heavy vehicles at night—reach her in her sleep (ah! how little we know of the phenomenon of sleep!), she arises, and, in common with many sleepwalkers, always acts the same. Something, in the case of Miss Hilda, attracts her to the golden harp—"

"She is studying music!"

"She must rest from it. Her brain is overwrought! She unlocks the case and strikes the cords of the harp, relocking the door, replacing the keys—I before have known such cases—then retires as she came. Who takes the harp from her hands, or raises it, if she has laid it down upon its side, dies! These dead attendants were brave fellows both, for, hearing the music, they came running, saw how the matter was, and did not waken the sleeping player. Conway was poisoned as he returned the harp to its case; Macalister, as he took it up from where it lay. Something to-night awoke her ere she could relock the door. The fright of so awaking made her to swoon."

Coram's kindly voice and the sound of a girl sobbing affrightedly reached us.

"It was my yell of fear, Mr. Klaw!" said Grimsby, shamefacedly. "She looked like a ghost!"

"I understand," rumbled Moris Klaw, soothingly. "As I see her in my sleep she is very awesome! I will show you the picture Isis has made from my etheric photograph. I saw it, finished, earlier to-night. It confirmed me that the Miss Hilda with the harp in her hand was poor Conway's last thought in life!"

"Mr. Klaw," said Grimsby, earnestly, "you are a very remarkable man!"

"Yes?" he rumbled, and gingerly placed in its case the "Greek lyre of gold" which Paduano Zelloni had wrought for Cesar Borgia.

From the brown hat he took out his scent spray and squirted verbena upon his heated forehead "That harp," he explained, "it smells of dead men!"

CASE OF THE POTSHERD OF ANUBIS

In examining the mass of material which I have collated respecting Moris Klaw, several outstanding facts strike me as being worthy of some special notice.

For instance, an unusual number of the cases in which he was concerned centred about curios and relics of various kinds. His personal tastes (he was, I think, primarily, an antiquarian) may have led him to examine such cases in preference to others. Then again, no two of his acquaintances agree upon the point of Moris Klaw's actual identity and personality. He was a master of disguise; and the grand secret of his life was one which he jealously guarded from all.

But was the Moris Klaw who kept the curio shop in Wapping the real Moris Klaw? And to what extent did he believe in those psychical phenomena upon which professedly his methods were based? As particularly bearing upon this phase of the matter, I have selected, for narration here, the story of the potsherd.

Since the Boswell, in records of this kind, has often appeared, to my mind, to overshadow the Johnson, I have decided to present this episode in the words of Mr. J. E. Wilson Clifford, electrical engineer, of Copthall House, Copthall Avenue, E. C., to whom I am indebted for a full and careful account. I do not think I could improve upon his paper, and my own views might unduly intrude upon the story; therefore, with your permission, I will vacate the rostrum in favour of Mr. Clifford, for whom I solicit your attention.

MR. CLIFFORD'S STORY OF THE EGYPTIAN POTSHERD

I

During the autumn of 19—, I was sharing a pleasant set of rooms with Mark Lesty, who was shortly taking up an appointment at a London hospital, and it was, I think, about the middle of that month that the extraordinary affair of Halesowen and his Egyptian potsherd came under our notice.

Our rooms (they were in a southwest suburb) overlooked a fine expanse of Common. Halesowen rented a flat commanding a similar prospect; and, at the time of which I write, he had but recently returned from a protracted visit to Egypt.

Halesowen was a tall, fair man, clean-shaven, very fresh coloured, and wearing his hair cropped close to his head. He was well travelled and no mean antiquary. He lived entirely by himself; and Lesty and I frequently spent the evening at his place, which was a veritable museum of curiosities. I distinctly recall the first time that he showed us his latest acquisitions.

Both the windows were wide open and the awning fluttered in the slight breeze. Dusk was just descending, and we sat looking out over the Common and puffing silently at our briars. We had been examining the relics that Halesowen had brought back from the land of the Pharaohs, the one, I remember, which had most impressed me, tyro that I was, being the mummy of a sacred cat from Bubastis.

"It wouldn't have been worth bringing back only for the wrapping," Halesowen assured me. "This, now, is really unique."

The object referred to was a broken pot or vase, upon which he pointed out a number of hieroglyphics and a figure with the head of a jackal. "A potsherd inscribed with the figure of Anubis," he explained. "Very valuable."

"Why?" Lesty inquired, in his lazy way.

"Well," Halesowen replied, "the characters of the inscription are of a kind entirely unfamiliar to me. I believe them to be a sort of secret writing, possibly peculiar to some brotherhood. I am risking expert opinion, although, in every sense, I stole the thing!"

"How's that?" I asked.

"Well, Professor Sheraton—you'll see his name on a row of cases in the B. M.—excavated it. But it's a moral certainty he didn't intend to advise the authorities of his find. He was going to smuggle it out of Egypt into his private collection. I had marked the spot where he found it for inquiries of my own. This dishonest old fossil—"

Lesty laughed.

"Oh! my own motives weren't above suspicion! But, anyway, the Professor anticipated me. Accordingly, I employed one Ali, a distinguished member of a family of thieves, to visit the learned gentleman's tent! Cutting the story—there's the pot!"

"Here! I say!" drawled Lesty. "You'll come to a bad end, young fellow!"

"The position is a peculiar one," replied Halesowen, smiling. "Neither of us had any legal claim to the sherd—whilst we were upon Egyptian territory. Therefore, even if the Professor learnt that I had the thing—and he may suspect—he couldn't prosecute me!"

"Devilish high-handed!" commented Lesty.

"Yes. But remember we were well off the map—miles away from Cook's route. The possession of this potsherd ought to make a man's reputation—any man who knows a bit about the subject. Curiously enough, a third party had had his eye upon the place where this much-sought sherd was found. And in some mysterious fashion he tumbled to the fact that it had fallen into my hands. He made a sort of veiled offer of a hundred pounds for it. I refused, but ran across him again, a week or so later, in Cairo, and he raised his price to two hundred."

"That's strange," I said. "Who was he?"

"Called himself Zeda—Dr. Louis Zeda. He quite lost his temper when I declined to sell, and I've not set eyes on him since."

He relocked the fragment in his cabinet, and we lapsed into silence, to sit gazing meditatively across the Common, picturesque in the dim autumn twilight.

"By the way, Halesowen," I said, "I see that the flat next door, same floor as this, is to let."

"That's so," he replied. "Why don't you men take it?"

"We'll think about it," yawned Lesty, stretching his long limbs. "Might look over it in the morning."

The following day we viewed the vacant flat, but found, upon inquiry of the agent, that it had already been let. However, as our own rooms suited us very well, we were not greatly concerned. Just as we finished dinner the same evening, Halesowen came in, and, without preamble, plunged into a surprising tale of uncanny happenings at his place.

"Take it slow," said Lesty. "You say it was after we came away?"

"About an hour after," replied Halesowen. "I had brought out the potsherd, and had it in the wooden stand on the table before me. I was copying the hieroglyphics, which are unusual, and had my reading lamp burning only, the rest of the room being consequently in shadow. I was sitting with my back to the windows, facing the door, so no one could possibly have entered the room unseen by me. It was as I bent down to scrutinize a badly defaced character that I felt a queer sensation stealing over me, as though someone were standing close behind my chair, watching me!"

"Very common," explained Lesty; "merely nerves."

"Yes, I know; but not what followed. The sensation became so pronounced that I stood up. No one was in the room. I determined to take a stroll, concluding that the fresh air would clear these uncanny cobwebs out of my brain. Accordingly, I extinguished the lamp and went out. I was just putting my cap on when something prompted me to return and lock up the potsherd."

He fixed his eyes upon us with an expression of doubt.

"There was someone, or something, in the room!"

"What do you mean?" asked Lesty, incredulously.

"I quite distinctly saw a hand and bare white arm pass away from the table—and vanish! It was dark in the room, remember; but I could see the arm well enough. I switched on the reading lamp. Not a thing was to be seen. There was no one in the room and no one but myself in the flat, for I searched it thoroughly!"

Some moments of silence followed this remarkable story, and I sat watching Lesty, who, in turn, was regarding Halesowen with the stolid, vacant stare which sometimes served to conceal the working of his keen brain.

"Pity you didn't let us know sooner," he said, rising slowly to his feet. "This is interesting."

II

Halesowen's nerves evidently had been shaken by the inexplicable incident. As the three of us strode across the corner of the Common, he informed us that the new tenant of the adjoining flat had moved in. "I have been away all day," he said; "but the stuff was bundled in some time during the afternoon."

We proceeded upstairs and into the cosy room which had been the scene of the remarkable occurrence related. As it was growing dark, Halesowen turned on the electric light, and, indicating a chair by the writing table, explained that it was there he had been seated at the time.

"Did you have the windows open?" asked Lesty.

"Yes," was the reply. "I left the chairs and the awning out, too, as it was a fine night; in fact, you can see that they still remain practically as you left them."

"When you returned, and saw, or thought you saw, the hand and arm—you would have to pass around to this side of the table in order to reach the lamp?"

"Yes."

Apparently Lesty was about to make some observation, when an interruption occurred in the form of a ringing on the door bell, followed by a discreet fandango on the knocker.

"Who the deuce have we here!" muttered Halesowen. "I saw no one go in below."

As our host passed through the lighted room and into the hall, my friend and I both leant forward in our chairs, the better to hear what should pass; nor were we kept long in suspense, for, as we heard the outer door opened, an odd, rumbling voice came, with a queer accent:

"Ah, my dear Mr. Halesowen, it is indeed an intrusion of me! But when I find how we are neighbours I cannot resist to make the call and renew a so pleasant acquaintance!"

"Doctor Zeda!" we heard Halesowen exclaim, with little cordiality.

"Ever your devoted servant!" replied the courteous foreigner.

I glanced at Lesty, and we rose together and stepped through the open window in time to see a truly remarkable personage enter.

This was a large-framed man, with snow-white hair cut close to his skull, French fashion. He had a high and very wrinkled brow and wore gold-rimmed pince-nez. Jet-black and heavy eyebrows were his, and his waxed moustache, his neat imperial, were likewise of the hue of coal. His complexion was pallid; and in his well-cut frock coat, with a loose black tie overhanging his vest, he made a striking picture, standing bowing profoundly in the doorway.

Halesowen rapidly muttered the usual formalities; in fact, I remember mentally contrasting our friend's unceremonious manners with the courtly deportment of Doctor Zeda.

The latter explained that he had taken the adjacent flat, only learning, that evening, whom he had for a neighbour, and, despite the lateness of the hour, he said, he could not resist the desire to see Halesowen, of whose company in Egypt he retained such pleasant memories. Allowing for his effusiveness, there was nothing one could take exception to in his behaviour, and I rather wondered at the brusque responses of our usually polite host.

When, after a brief chat, the foreign gentleman rose to take his leave, he extended an invitation to all of us to lunch with him on the following day. "My place is in somewhat disorder," he said, smiling, "but you are Bohemian, like myself, and will not care!"

Though I half expected that Halesowen would decline, he did not do so; I, therefore, also accepted, as did Lesty. Whereupon, Zeda departed.

Halesowen, returning to the chair which he had vacated to usher out his visitor, lighted a cigarette, regarded it for a moment, meditatively, and then frankly expressed his doubts.

"He's been watching me!" he said; "and when he saw the next flat vacant he jumped at the chance."

"My dear chap," I retorted, "he must be very keen on securing your potsherd if he is prepared to take and furnish a flat next door to you simply with a view to keeping an eye on it!"

"You have no idea how anxious he is," he assured me. "If you had seen his face, in Cairo, when I flatly declined to sell, you would be better able to understand."

"Why not sell, then?"

"I'm dashed if I do!" said Halesowen, stubbornly.

On the following day we lunched with Doctor Zeda and were surprised at the orderly state of his establishment. Everything, from floor to ceiling, was in its proper place.

"It hasn't taken you long to get things straight," commented Lesty.

"Ah, no," replied the other. "These big firms, they do it all in a day if you insist—and I insist, see?"

I thoroughly enjoyed my visit, for he proved an excellent host, and I think even Lesty grew less suspicious of him. During the weeks that followed, the doctor came several times to our rooms, and we frequently met at Halesowen's. The latter, who boldly had submitted photographs and drawings of the sherd to the British Museum, experienced no repetition of the mysterious phenomenon already described. Then, about seven o'clock one morning, when the mists hung low over the Common in promise of a hot day, a boy came for Lesty and myself with news of a fresh development. He was a lad who did odd jobs for Halesowen, and he brought word of an attempted burglary, together with a request that we should go over without delay.

Our curiosity keenly aroused, we were soon with our friend, and found him seated in the familiar room, before a large cabinet, with double glass doors, which, as was clearly evident, had been hastily ransacked. Other cases in which he kept various curios were also opened, and the place was in general disorder.

"What's gone?" asked Lesty, quickly.

"Nothing!" was the answer. "The potsherd is in the safe, and the safe is in my bedroom—or perhaps something might have gone!"

"You lock it up at night, then? I thought you kept it in the cabinet."

"Only during the day. It goes in the safe, with one or two other trifles, at night; but *everybody* doesn't know that!"

We looked at one another, silently; but the name that was on all our lips remained unspoken—for we were startled by a loud knocking and ringing at the door. Carter opening it, into the room ran Doctor Zeda!

"Oh, my dear friends!" he cried, in his hoarse, rumbling voice, "there has been to my flat a midnight robber! He has turned completely upside-down all my collections!"

Lesty coughed loudly; but, as I turned my head to look at him, his face was quite expressionless. Halesowen seemed stricken dumb by surprise; whilst, for my own part, as I watched the foreigner staring about the disordered room, and noted the growing look of bewilderment creeping over his pallid countenance, I was compelled to admit to myself that here was either a consummate actor or a man of whom we hastily had formed a most unwarrantable opinion.

"But, my friend—my good Halesowen," he exclaimed, with widely opened eyes and extended palms, "what is it that I see? You are as disordered as myself!"

Halesowen nodded. "The burglar gave me a call, too!" he said, grimly.

"My dear sir!" gasped Zeda, seizing the speaker's arm, "tell me quickly—you have lost nothing?"

Halesowen glanced at him rather hard. "No," he answered.

"Ah! what a relief! I feared," rumbled the doctor. "But perhaps you wonder for what it is they came?"

"I can guess!"

"You need no longer to guess; I will tell you. It is for your fragment of the sacred vase, and to me they come for mine!"

We were even more astonished by this assertion than we had been by the doctor's first. "Your fragment!" said Halesowen, slowly, with his eyes fixed on Zeda; "to what fragment do you refer?"

"To that which, together with your potsherd, makes up the complete vase! But you doubt?" he suggested, shrugging his shoulders. "Wait but a moment and I will prove!"

He moved from the room; his gait had a mincing awkwardness, quite indescribable; and we heard his retreating, heavy footsteps as he passed downstairs. Then we stood and gaped at one another. "His confounded ingenuity," rapped Halesowen, "has completely tied my hands."

Being interrupted, at this moment, by the reentrance of the gentleman in question, further discussion of the subject was precluded. Zeda carried a small iron box which he placed carefully upon the table and unlocked. A second box of polished ebony was revealed within, and this, being unlocked in turn, was proved to contain, reposing in a nest of blue velvet, a fragment of antique pottery. Taking the fragment in his hand, the doctor begged that the potsherd be produced.

Halesowen, after a momentary hesitation, retired from the room, to return almost immediately with the broken vase in its wooden frame. Doctor Zeda, placing the portion which he held in his hand against that in the frame, but not so closely as to bring the parts in contact, turned to us with a triumphant smile. "They correspond, gentlemen, to a smallest fraction!" he declared; which, indeed, was perfectly true.

"And now," continued Zeda, evidently gratified by the surprise which we could not conceal, "I will relate to you a story. I do not ask that you shall credit it; I only say that I have given up my life to such studies, and that I am willing, as matters have so arrived, that you shall join me to prove false or true what I think of the potsherd of Anubis."

"Good!" said Lesty, and settled himself to listen, an example that was followed by Halesowen and myself. Zeda paused for a moment, evidently to collect his ideas, a pause upon which my stolid friend placed a dubious interpretation, for he cleared his throat, significantly.

III

"The date is no matter," said Doctor Zeda, "but there was at Gizeh, to the north of the Sphinx, a temple dedicated to Isis, but wherein the worship was different. We only know of this shrine by the monuments, but they prove it to have been—eh, Mr. Halesowen?"

Halesowen nodded.

"Here, then, the gods of the dead were adored—but the worship of Anubis took precedence, and was conducted at a shrine apart. Here, locked within three-and-thirty doors, having each its separate janitor who held the key, reposed a sacred symbol—a symbol, my friends, upon which was based the occult knowledge of the initiated; a symbol more precious than the lives of a hundred-hundred warriors—for so it is written!"

"I have never met with the inscription!" said Halesowen, drily.

Doctor Zeda smiled.

"You never are likely to meet it!" he responded. "Your Belzoni and Lepsius, your Birch, Renouf, Brugsch and Petrie, is a mere unseeing vandal, blinded to the great truth—to the ultimate secret that Egypt holds for him who has eyes to see and a brain to realize!"

The mysterious foreign gentleman looked about him with a sort of challenge in his glance; then he quietly resumed his story.

"At the change of the moon in the sacred month, Methori, a maiden selected from a noble house for her beauty and purity, and for a whole year dedicated to the service of the gods, held in her hands the sacred thing—held it aloft that the initiated might worship, until the first white beam lit up the receptacle, when all bowed down their heads and chanted the 'Hymn of the Souls Who Are Passing.' Then was it locked again within the three-and-thirty doors, there to remain for another year. None saw the symbol itself but the high priest, who looked upon it when he was so ordained—for any other that gazed upon it died! It was contained in a holy vase!"

He paused impressively. We had all fallen under the peculiar fascination of the speaker's personality; we felt as though he spoke of matters wherein he had had personal concern. I could almost believe him to have witnessed the strange rites that he told of with such conviction.

"In a year so long ago," he softly resumed, his voice now a kind of jagged whisper, "that to speak of its date were to convey nothing to you, the high-born virgin on whom the exalted office was conferred closed upon her unhappy soul the gates of paradise for ages unnumbered; called down upon her head the curse of the high priest and the anger of the most high gods; was rejected of Set himself!

"She let fall from her hands the sacred vase, and the holy symbol was lost to the children of earth for evermore! Lost was the key to the book of wisdom; closed was that book to man for all time!"

"Go on!" said Halesowen, harshly, for Zeda had paused again.

"You do not grasp?" asked the doctor. "Well, then, know that the sentence was 'Until the parts of this vase be made whole again.' Five fragments there were: a large one, which is your potsherd, and four smaller. The four smaller, after twenty years of untiring search, I have recovered and joined together. What if we now make whole that which was broken? May I not, by the exercise of such poor shreds of the lost wisdom as I have gathered up, summon before me that wandering spirit ere it return again to plead for rest at the judgment seat of Amenti?"

When I say that the man's words proved electrical, I do not exaggerate the effect which this astounding proposition had upon us. Halesowen was fairly startled out of his chair, and stood with his eyes fixed on the other in a fascinated gaze.

Zeda, entirely returning to his customary urbanity, shrugged and smiled. "You believe my story?"

Lesty was the first to recover himself, and his reply was characteristic. "Can't say I do," he drawled, frankly. "I don't say that you may not, though," he added.

"Then do you not owe it to assist in proving my words? A little séance? You are sceptical, quite? Very well; I try to show you. If I fail, then it is unfortunate, but—I bow to an inevitable!"

We looked at each other, interrogatively, and then Halesowen answered, "All right. It's a queer yarn, but we leave the matter entirely in your hands."

The doctor bowed. "Shall we say to-night to begin?" he said, tentatively.

"By all means."

The doctor expressed himself delighted, and, carefully relocking the fragment of the vase in its double case, he was about to depart, when a point occurred to me.

"Might I ask whom you suspect of the attempted burglary?" I said.

He turned, in the door, and fixed a strange glance upon me. "There are others," he replied, "who seek as I seek, and who do not scruple to gain their ends how they may. Of them we shall beware, my friends, for we know they design upon us!"

With that and a low bow he retired.

Little of interest occurred during the day, until about four in the afternoon, when Halesowen aroused us out of a lazy doze to show a letter just received from the British Museum.

It was in reply to one asking why he had received no acknowledgment of the photographs and drawings submitted; and it informed him that no such photographs and drawings had come to hand!

We usually took tea in the afternoon, and Halesowen joined us on this occasion, whilst, at about five o'clock, Doctor Zeda also looked in. He remained until it began to grow dusk, when we all went over to Halesowen's to arrange the first "sitting"—for so the doctor referred to the projected séance. Retiring, for a few minutes, to his own establishment, Zeda returned with the iron box and explained what he proposed to do.

"Around this small table we sit, as at séance," he said; "but no medium—only the potsherd. With these flexible bands I will attach, temporarily, the parts, and stand the vase in Mr. Halesowen's frame, here by the window—so. Beside it we will place the lamp, shaded thus—so that a dim light is upon it. We can just see from where we sit in the dark. We will now wait until it is more dusk."

Accordingly, we went out on to the balcony and smoked for an hour, Zeda polluting the clean air with the fumes of the long, black cigars he affected. They had an appearance as of dried twigs and an odour so wholly original as to defy simile. Between eight and nine o'clock he expressed himself satisfied with the light—or, rather, lack of it—and we all gathered around the table in the gloom, spreading our hands as he directed. For close upon an hour we sat in tense silence, the room seeming to be very hot. A slight breeze off the Common had wafted the fumes of Zeda's cigar in through the open windows, which he had afterward closed, and the reek filled the air as with something palpable and nauseous. I was growing very weary of the business, and Lesty, despite the doctor's warning against disturbing the silence, had begun to cough and fidget irritably, when the rumbling foreign voice came, so unexpectedly as to startle us all: "It is useless to-night; something is not propitious. Turn up the lights."

From the celerity with which Halesowen complied, I divined that he, too, had been growing impatient.

"There is some not suitable condition," said Zeda, relocking his portion of the vase in its case. "To-morrow we shall make some changes in the order."

He seemed not at all disappointed, being apparently as confident as ever in the ultimate success of the séances. One of the windows, he suggested, should be left open on the following evening during our sitting; and this we were only too glad to agree upon, since it would possibly serve to clear the atmosphere, somewhat, of the odour emanating from the doctor's cigars. Several other points he also mentioned as being conceivably responsible for our initial failure—such as our positions around the table, and the relative distance of the potsherd. "We shall see to-morrow," were his last words as he left us.

"A perfect monument of mendacity!" muttered Lesty, as we heard the retiring footsteps of our foreign friend on the gravel below; "and I think his accent is assumed. I don't know why we even seem to credit such an incredible fable."

"I don't know, either," said Halesowen, reflectively. "But he certainly possesses the missing part of the vase, and if he does not believe the story himself, what earthly object can he hope to serve by these séances?"

"Give it up!" replied Lesty, promptly; and that, I think, rather aptly expressed the mental attitude of all three.

We saw nothing of Zeda throughout the following day, but he duly put in an appearance in the evening, and placed us around the table again, but in different order. One of the French windows was left open, and the potsherd, with the lamp beside it, placed somewhat to the left.

After persevering for about forty minutes, we were rewarded by a rather conventional phenomenon. The table rocked and gave forth cracking sounds. There was no other manifestation, and, at about half past ten, the doctor again terminated the séance.

"Excellent!" said Zeda, enthusiastically, "excellent! We were *en rapport*, and within the circle there was power. To-morrow we shall triumph, my friends, but there is again an alteration that occurs to me. You, Mr. Clifford, shall sit next to Mr. Lesty on the left, Mr. Halesowen shall be upon his right, and I, facing Mr. Lesty between. Also, there is too much light from the lamps in the road. It is good, I think, to have open the windows, but this Japanese Screen will keep out that too much light and shelter the vase. To-morrow we will observe these things."

This, then, concluded our second sitting, and brings me to the final episode of that affair which, strange enough in its several developments, was stranger still in its denouement.

IV

Zeda, on the following day, entertained us to luncheon in town, followed by an afternoon concert, for which he had procured seats, being interested, or professing to be, in a certain fiddler who figured largely in the programme. We had arranged that Halesowen and the doctor should dine with us in the evening, before we went to the former's flat for the séance, and we accordingly returned direct to our rooms and chatted over the doings of the day until dinner was served. Zeda surpassed himself in brilliant conversation. He must, I remember thinking, have led a strange and eventful life.

At about nine o'clock, we walked over, in the dark, to our friend's flat, where we had to grope for and light an oil lamp which he had, Zeda declaring that something in the atmosphere was propitious and that the electric light would tend to disturb these favourable conditions. He seemed to be strung to high tension, perhaps with expectancy, but was not so preoccupied as to forget his black cigars, one of which he lighted as he was about to go out for the iron box. He borrowed my matches for the purpose and forgot to return them.

It was, perhaps, a quarter to ten before Zeda had matters arranged to his satisfaction, and so dark, by reason of the tall Japanese screen which stood before the open windows, that I could see neither Zeda, on my left, nor Lesty, who sat on my right. Halesowen was a dim silhouette against the patch of light cast by the oil reading lamp beside the vase, which stood the whole length of the room away. I was conscious of a suppressed excitement, which I am sure was shared by my companions.

I heard a distant clock striking the half hour, and then the three quarters; but still nothing had occurred. A motor car drove around from the road and stopped somewhere at the outer end of the drive. I wondered, idly, if it were that of the surgeon who lived at Number 10. After that, everything was very quiet, and I was expecting to hear the hour strike, and straining my ears to catch the sound of the first chime, when the rocking and cracking of the table began. This was much more violent than hitherto, and Zeda's gruff tones came softly: "Whatever shall happen, do not remove your hands from the table!"

He ceased speaking, and the rocking motions, together with the rapping and cracking that had sounded from all about us, also ceased, with disconcerting suddenness. A silence fell, so short in duration as to be scarcely appreciable; for it was almost instantly broken by an unexpected sound.

It was a woman's voice, very low and clear, and it seemed to mutter something in a weird, rising cadence, with a high note at the end of every third bar or so, and this over and over again—an eerie thing, vaguely like a Gregorian chant.

"Triumph!" whispered Zeda. "The 'Hymn of the Souls Who Are Passing.'"

His speech seemed to disturb the singer, but only for a moment. The Hymn was continued.

This singular performance was proving too much for my nerves; at each recurrence of the quiet, clear note on the fourth beat of the third bar, a cold shudder ran down my spine. Then, as the very monotony of the thing was beginning to grow appalling, I suddenly became aware of a slim, white figure standing beside the vase!

The chant stopped, and I could hear nothing but the nervous breathing of my companions. Seated as they were, I doubted whether Halesowen or Lesty, could see this apparition, but I was facing directly toward her—for it was a woman. I could see every line of her figure—the curves of her throat and arms and shoulders, the dull, metallic gleaming of her clustering hair. As she extended her hand toward the light, I distinctly saw the large green stone set in a ring on her index finger. She must be very beautiful, I thought, and I was peering through the gloom in a vain endeavour to see her more clearly, when there came a disconcerting crash—and utter darkness! The table whereat we were seated was overturned, and I found myself capsized from my chair!

"Hold him!" yelled the voice of Lesty. "Hold him, Halesowen—Clifford!"

A door banged loudly.

"Confound it! I'm on the floor!"—from Halesowen.

I shouted for someone to turn up the light, at the same time scrambling through the gloom with that intent. After severely damaging my shins against the intervening furniture, I found the switch. It would not work!

"It's cut off!" I cried. "Strike a match, somebody."

"Haven't got any!" said Lesty.

"Zeda has mine!" responded Halesowen. "Open the door."

"Locked!" was Lesty's next report.

"Break it down!" shouted Halesowen, hurling aside the Japanese screen. *"The potsherd is gone!"*

Lesty applied his shoulder to the oak—once—twice—thrice. Then all together we attacked it, and it flew open with a splintering crash.

"Round to his flat!" panted Halesowen, running downstairs.

Out on to the drive we sprinted, into the next entrance and up to the first landing. Knocking and ringing proved ineffectual, and the door was too strong to be burst open. We stood in dismayed silence, staring at one another.

"Off your balcony, on to his and through the French window!" said Lesty, suddenly; so back we all ran again.

I had never before realized how easy it was to get from one balcony to another, until I saw Lesty swing himself across. Halesowen and I followed in a trice, and we all blundered into the dark room through the open window and made for the electric switch beside the mantelpiece. We turned on the light. The room was unfurnished!

"Good Lord!" breathed Halesowen, hurrying into the next.

That, too, was quite bare, as were all the rest! The outer door was locked.

"While we were fooling at that concert, he had every scrap of stuff removed!" I said. "He probably had the lot on hire from a big furnishing firm—curios and all. I remember noticing that his curiosities were of a very ordinary character, considering his extensive travels and the nature of his studies."

"No doubt whatever," agreed Lesty. "His burglary proved a failure (and, I think, must have been interrupted), though I am compelled to admire the neat manner in which he handled the very delicate situation that resulted. His more recent and elaborate device has turned out all that could be desired— from Zeda's point of view!"

"But how has he got away?" said Halesowen, in bewilderment.

"Motor waiting at the corner," replied Lesty, promptly. "Heard it come up. When the reading lamp was capsized, and whoever had crept from his balcony to yours and in behind the screen had returned the same way—with the vase!—Zeda overturned the table and pushed you two men backward in your chairs. Then, before I could reach him, he bolted out and locked the door after him. For, having lulled my suspicions by two practically uneventful séances, he cunningly placed himself nearest to the door and me farthest away. He probably removed the key when he went out for the box and placed it outside in the lock when he returned. His accomplice had run straight through Zeda's flat and out to the waiting car, and there he joined her. They may be thirty miles away by now!"

Being unable to open the door, we perforce returned to Halesowen's balcony by the same way that we had come, our friend bewailing his lost potsherd and exclaiming: "The cunning, cunning scamp!"

"I knew he had some deep game in hand," said Lesty; "but I hadn't bargained for this move. Of course, I had noticed the dodge of borrowing all our matches, but I didn't grasp its importance until too late. It never occurred to me that he'd disconnected the electric light (which he probably did sometime in the night, by the way). I was a fool not to realize it, too, when he insisted on our using only the oil lamp. Then, again, I was slow not to go straight through the window and into Zeda's flat that way. It is just possible I might have caught the lady songster if I had done that in the first place. The possibility, however, had not been overlooked, since she took the precaution to lock the door after her."

"A clever rogue!" I declared. "But wasn't the first attempt—for I suppose we must classify the mysterious arm under that head—more than a trifle indiscreet?"

"No doubt," agreed Lesty. "But we didn't know, then, that Zeda was in London, and the flat was still unfurnished. Also, they may have thought Halesowen was in bed; or the woman (whom he has so cleverly kept out of sight) may have exceeded her instructions in attempting to touch the potsherd while any one remained in the room."

"But," said Halesowen, slowly, "we don't know that there was any woman!"

"Eh?" queried Lesty.

"Did you see her?"

"I did. She was lovely, very lovely—for a woman!"

Lesty stared curiously. "You surprise me," he commented, drily.

"Zeda was a strange man," pursued the other, "and there were certainly things occurred as we sat round that table that need a lot of explaining."

"Very ordinary three-and-six-a-head phenomena!" was the reply. "Merely a blind."

"Then what was the reason of his burning desire to secure my potsherd, if not to complete the vase?"

"Do you mean to tell me," asked Lesty, "that you are going to credit that story about the priestess—*now*, after he has shown his hand? Do you wish to suggest that he was aided by a spirit?"

"Then why was he so keen to get the thing?" persisted Halesowen.

Lesty looked at him, looked at me, shrugged his shoulders and began to load his pipe. Having done so, he sat smoking and staring at the brilliant moon.

"Well?" inquired our host.

"Give it up!" admitted Lesty.

CONCLUSION OF MR. CLIFFORD'S ACCOUNT

V

One of my visits to the Wapping curio shop of Moris Klaw was made in company with Mr. Halesowen, who, with the others mentioned in the foregoing narrative, I subsequently had met.

Somewhere amid the misty gloom of this place, where loot of a hundred ages, of every spot from pole to pole, veils its identity in the darkness, sits a large gray parrot. Faint perfumes and scuffling sounds tell of hidden animal life near to the visitor; but the parrot proclaims itself stridently:

"Moris Klaw! Moris Klaw! The devil's come for you!"

That signal brings Moris Klaw from his hiding place. He shuffles into the shop, a figure appropriate to its surroundings. Imagine a tall, stooping man, enveloped in a very faded blue dressing gown.

His skin is but a half-shade lighter than that of a Chinaman; his hair, his shaggy brows, his scanty beard, defy one to name their colour. He wears pince-nez.

When upon this particular occasion I introduced my companion, and Moris Klaw acknowledged the introduction in his rumbling voice, I saw Halesowen stare.

Klaw produced a scent spray from somewhere and sprayed verbena upon his high yellow brow.

"It is very stuffy—in this shop!" he explained "Isis! Isis! Bring for my visitors some iced drinks!"

He invoked a goddess, and a goddess appeared: a brilliantly beautiful brunette, with delightfully curved scarlet lips and flashing eyes whose fire the gloom could not dim.

"Good God!" cried Halesowen—and fell back.

"My daughter Isis," rumbled Moris Klaw. "This is Mr. Halesowen, from whom we rescue the Egyptian potsherd!"

"What!"

Halesowen leant forward across the counter.

"You recognize my daughter?" continued Moris Klaw; "but not Doctor Zeda, eh? Or only his poor old voice? You gave us great trouble, Mr. Halesowen. Once, you came in just as Isis, who has climbed on to your balcony, is about to take the potsherd—"

"There was no one in the room!"

"I was in the room!" interrupted the girl, coolly. "I was draped in black from head to foot, and I slipped behind the window hangings, unseen, whilst you fumbled with your lamp!"

"It was indiscreet," continued Moris Klaw, "and made it harder for me; because, afterward, you lock up the treasure and my search is unavailing. Also, I am interrupted. Pah! I am clumsy! I waste time! But, remember, I offered to buy it!"

"Suppose," said Halesowen, slowly, "I give you both in charge?"

"You cannot," was the placid reply; "for you cannot say how you came into possession of the sherd! Professor Sheraton was in a similar forked stick—and that is where *I* come in!"

"What! you were acting for him?"

"Certainly! I happen to be in Egypt at the time, and he is a friend of mine. Your thief, Ali, left a small piece of the pot behind, and I am entrusted to make it complete!"

"You have succeeded!" said Halesowen, grimly, all the time furtively watching the beautiful Isis. "Yes," rumbled Moris Klaw. "I am the instrument of poetic justice. Isis, those cool beverages. Let us drink to poetic justice!"

He sprayed his ample brow with verbena.

In conclusion, you may ask if the value of the potsherd justified the elaborate and costly mode of its recovery.

I reply: Upon what does the present fame of Professor Sheraton rest? His "New Key to the Egyptian Book of the Dead." Upon what is that work founded? Upon the hieroglyphics of the Potsherd of Anubis, which (no questions being asked of so distinguished a savant) was recently acquired from the Professor by the nation at a cost of £15,000!

CASE OF THE CRUSADER'S AX

I

I have heard people speak of Moris Klaw's failures. So far as my information bears me, he never experienced any. "What," I have been asked, "of the Cresping murder case? He certainly failed there."

Respecting this question of his failure or success in the sensational case which first acquainted the entire country with the existence of Crespie Hall, and that brought the old-world village of Cresping into such unwonted prominence, I shall now invite your opinion.

The investigation—the crime having baffled the local men—ultimately was placed in the hands of Detective-Inspector Grimsby; and through Grimsby I was brought into close touch with the matter. I had met Grimsby during the course of the mysterious happenings at the Menzies Museum, and at that time I also had made the acquaintance of Moris Klaw.

Thus, as I sat over my breakfast one morning reading an account of the Cresping murder case, I was no more than moderately surprised to see Inspector Grimsby walk into my rooms.

He declined my offer of a really good Egyptian cigarette.

"Thanks all the same," he said; "but there's only one smoke I can think on."

With that he lighted one of the cheroots of which he smoked an incredible quantity, and got up from his chair, restlessly.

"I've just run up from Cresping by the early train," he began, abruptly. "You've heard all about the murder, of course?"

I pointed to my newspaper, conspicuous upon the front page of which was:

"THE MURDER AT CRESPIE HALL"

"Ah, yes," he said, absently. "Well, I've been sent down and, to tell you the white and unsullied truth, I'm in a knot!"

I passed him a cup of coffee.

"What are the difficulties?" I asked.

"There's only one," he rapped back: "who did it!"

"It looks to me a very clear case against Ryder, the ex-butler."

"So it did to me," he agreed, "until I got down there! I'd got a warrant in my pocket all ready. Then I began to have doubts!"

"What do you propose to do?"

Grimsby hesitated.

"Well," he replied, "it wouldn't do any good to make a mistake in a murder case; so what I should *like* to do would be to get another opinion—not official, of course!"

I glanced across at him.

"Mr. Moris Klaw?"

He nodded.

"Exactly!"

"You've changed your opinion respecting him?"

"Mr. Searles, his investigation of the Menzies Museum outrages completely stood me on my head! I'm not joking. I'd always thought him a crank, and in some ways I think so still; but at seeing through a brick wall I'd put all I've got on Moris Klaw any day!"

"But surely you are wasting time by coming to me?"

"No, I'm not," said Grimsby, confidently. "Moris Klaw, for all his retiring habits, is not a man that wants his light hidden under a bushel! He knows that you are collecting material about his methods, and he's more likely to move for you than for me."

I saw through Grimsby's plan. He wanted me to invite Moris Klaw to look into the Crespie murder case, in order that he

(Grimsby) might reap any official benefit accruing without loss of self-esteem! I laughed.

"All right, Grimsby!" I said. "Since he has made no move, voluntarily, it may be that the case does not interest him; but we can try."

Accordingly, having consulted an A.B.C., we presently entrained for Wapping, and as a laggard sun began to show up the dinginess and the dirtiness of that locality, sought out a certain shop, whose locale I shall no more closely describe than in saying that it is close to Wapping Old Stairs.

One turns down a narrow court, with a blank wall on the right and a nailed-up doorway and boarded-up window on the left. Through the cracks of the latter boarding, the inquiring visitor may catch a glimpse, beyond a cavernous place which once was some kind of warehouse, of Old Thames tiding muddily.

The court is a cul de sac. The shop of Moris Klaw occupies the blind end. Some broken marble pedestals stand upon the footway, among seatless chairs, dilapidated chests, and a litter of books, stuffed birds, cameos, inkstands, swords, lamps, and other unclassifiable rubbish. A black doorway yawns amid the litter.

Imagine Inspector Grimsby and me as entering into this singular Cumaean cave.

Our eyes at first failed to penetrate the gloom. All about moved rustling suggestions of animal activity. The indescribable odour of old furniture assailed our nostrils together with an equally indescribable smell of avian, reptilian, and rodent life.

"Moris Klaw! Moris Klaw! The devil's come for you!"

Thus the scraping voice of the parrot. A door opened, admitting a little more light and Moris Klaw. The latter was fully dressed; whereby I mean that he wore his dilapidated caped black cloak, his black silk muffler and that rarest relic of his unsavoury reliquary, the flat-topped brown bowler.

In that inadequate light his vellum face looked older, his shaggy brows, his meagre beard, more toneless, than ever. Through the gold-rimmed pince-nez he peered for a moment, downward from his great height. He removed the bowler.

"Good morning, Mr. Searles! Good morning, Inspector Grimsby! I am just from Paris. It is so good of you to call so early to tell me all about the poor murdered man of Cresping! Good morning! Good morning!"

II

Moris Klaw's sanctum is certainly one of the most remarkable apartments in London. It is lined with shelves, which contain what I believe to be a unique library of works dealing with criminology—from Moris Klaw's point of view. Strange relics are there, too; and all of them have histories. A neat desk, with flowers in a silver vase, and a revolving chair standing upon a fine tiger skin are the other notable items of furniture.

The contrast on entering was startling. Moris Klaw placed his hat upon the desk, and from it took out the scent spray without which he never travels. He played the contents upon his high, yellow forehead—filling the air with the refreshing odour of verbena.

"That shop!" he said, "it smell very strong this morning. It is not so much the canaries as the rats!"

"I trust," began Grimsby, respectfully, "that Miss Klaw is quite well?

"Isis will presently be here to say for herself," was the reply. "And now—this bad business of Cresping. It seems I am just back in time, but, ah! it is a fortnight old!"

Grimsby cleared his throat. "You will have read—"

"Ah, my friend!" Moris Klaw held up a long, tapering white hand. "As though you do not know that I never confuse my poor brain with those foolish papers. No, I have not read, my friend!"

"Oh!" said Grimsby, something taken aback. "Then I shall have to tell you the family story—" Isis Klaw entered.

From her small hat, with its flamingo-like plume, to her dainty shoes, she was redolent of the Rue de la Paix. She wore an amazingly daring toilette; I can only term it a study in flame tones. A less beautiful woman could never have essayed such a scheme; but this superb brunette, with her great flashing eyes and taunting smile, had the lithe carriage of a Cleopatra, the indescribable diablerie of a *ghaziyeh*.

Inspector Grimsby greeted her with embarrassed admiration. Greetings over—

"We must hurry, Father!" said the girl.

Moris Klaw reclaimed his archaic bowler.

"Mr. Searles and Inspector Grimsby will perhaps be joining us?" he suggested.

"Where?" began Grimsby.

"Where but by the 9:5 train for Uxley!" said Klaw. "Where but from Uxley to Cresping! Do I waste time, then—I?"

"You have been retained?" suggested Grimsby.

"Ah, no!" was the reply. "But I shall receive my fee, nevertheless!"

At the end of the court a cab was waiting. Outside the cavernous door a ramshackle man with a rosy nose bowed respectfully to the proprietor.

"You hear me, William," said Moris Klaw, to this derelict. "You are to sell nothing—unless it is the washstand! Forget not to change the canaries' water. The Indian corn is for the white rats. If there is no mouse in the trap by eight o'clock, give the owl a herring. And keep from the drink; it will be your ruin, William!"

We entered the cab. My last impression of the place was derived from the invisible parrot, who gave us Godspeed with:

"Moris Klaw! Moris Klaw! the devil's come for you!"

As we drove stationward, Grimsby, his eyes rarely leaving the piquant face of Isis Klaw, outlined the history of the Crespie family to the silent Moris. In brief it was this:

The late Sir Richard Crespie, having become involved in serious monetary difficulties, employed such methods of drowning his sorrows as were far from conducive to domestic felicity; and after a certain unusually violent outburst the home was broken up. His son, Roland, was the first to go; and he took little with him but his mother's blessing and his father's curses. Then Lady Crespie went away to her sister in London, only surviving her departure from the Hall by two years. Alone, and deserted, first by son and then by wife, the debauched old baronet continued on his course of heavy drinking for some years longer. The servants left him, one by one, so that in the end, save for faithful old Ryder, the butler, whose family had served the Crespies for time immemorial, he had the huge mansion to himself. Apoplexy closed his unfortunate career; and, since nothing had been heard of him for years, it was generally supposed that the son had met his death in Africa, whither he had gone on leaving home.

With the passing of Sir Richard came Mr. Isaac Heidelberger, and he wasted no time in impressing his noxious personality upon the folks of Cresping. He was a German Jew, large and oily, with huge coarse features and a little black moustache that had been assiduously trained in a futile attempt to hide a mouth that had well befitted Nero. A week after Sir Richard's burial, Mr. Heidelberger took possession of the Hall.

The new occupant brought with him one Heimer, a kind of confidential clerk, and, old Ryder the butler having been sent about his business, the two Jewish gentlemen proceeded to make themselves comfortable. The nature of their business was soon public property; the grand old Hall was to be turned into a "country mansion for paying guests."

Very strained relations existed between the big Jew and the ex-butler, who, having a little money saved, had settled down in Cresping. One night, at the Goblets—the historic village inn—Heidelberger having swaggered into the place, there arose an open quarrel. Said Ryder:

"Sir Richard, with all his faults, was once a good English gentleman, and, but for such as you, a good English gentleman he might have died!"

It was exactly a week later that the tragedy occurred.

"We come to it now, eh?" interrupted Moris Klaw at this point. "So—we also come to the station! I will ask you to reserve us a first-class carriage!"

Grimsby made arrangements to that end. And, as the train moved out of the station, resumed his story.

"What I gather is this," he said.

[I condense his statement and append it in my own words.]

The Goblets was just closing its doors, and the villagers who nightly met there were standing in a group under the swinging sign, when a man came running down the street from the direction of the Hall, and, observing the gathering, ran up. It was Heimer, Isaac Heidelberger's secretary. He was hatless and his flabby face, in the dim light, was ghastly.

"Quick!" he rasped, hoarsely. "Where does the doctor live?"

"Last house but one," somebody said. "What's the matter?"

"Murder!" cried Heimer, as he rushed off down the village street.

Such was the dramatic manner in which the news of the subsequently notorious case was first carried to the outside world. The facts, as soon made known throughout the length and breadth of the land, were, briefly, as follows:

Heidelberger and his secretary, who were engaged in making an inventory of the contents of the Hall and in arranging for such alterations of the rooms and laying out of the neglected grounds as they considered necessary, had practically reached the end of their task. In fact, had nothing intervened, Cresping would, on the following day, have seen the old mansion in the hands of an army of London workmen.

At about half-past seven in the evening, Heidelberger had entered the room occupied by Heimer and had mentioned that he expected a visitor. The secretary, who had more work than he could well accomplish, did not pause to inquire concerning him, believing the other to allude either to the architect or to Heidelberger's man, who was coming down from London. Heidelberger had then gone up to the library, saying that he should not require Heimer again that night.

Between eight and half-past—Heimer was not sure of the time—there was a ring at the bell (that of the tradesmen's entrance). Knowing that Heidelberger could admit the visitor directly to the library, Heimer, hearing nothing more, concluded that the two were closeted there.

The first intimation that he received of anything amiss was a loud and angry cry, apparently proceeding from the old banqueting hall directly overhead, and unmistakably in the voice of Heidelberger. Springing from his chair, he took a step toward the door, and then paused in doubt. There was an angry murmur from above, the tones of the Jew being clearly distinguishable; then a sudden scuffle and an oscillation of the floor as though two heavy men were at hand grips; next, a crash that shook the room, and a high-pitched cry of which he only partially comprehended the last word. This he asserted to be "holy."

That Heimer stood transfixed at the open door throughout all this, suffices to brand him a coward. It was, in fact, only his stories of shadowy figures in the picture gallery and his general disinclination to leave his room after dusk that had prompted Heidelberger—a man of different mettle—to wire to London for the servant.

At this juncture, however, moved as much by a fear of the sudden silence as by any higher motive, he took a revolver from the table drawer, and, holding it cocked in one hand and seizing the lamp in the other, he crept, trembling, up a narrow little stair that led to a door beneath the minstrel's gallery. To open it he had to place the lamp on the floor, and, at the moment of doing so, he heard a sound inside the hall like the grating of a badly oiled lock.

Then, with the lamp held high above his head, he peered inside; and, considering the character of the man, it is worthy of note that he did not faint on the spot, for the feeble light, but serving, as it did, to intensify the gloom of the long and shadowy place, revealed a scene well calculated to shake the nerves of a stouter man than Heimer.

Less than six feet from where he stood, and lying flat on his back with his head toward the light, was Heidelberger in a perfect pool of blood, his skull cleft almost to the chine! Beside him on the floor lay the fearful weapon that had wrought his end—an enormous battle-ax, a relic of the Crusades such as none but a man of Herculean strength could possibly wield.

Sick with terror, and scarcely capable of keeping his feet, Heimer gave one glance around the gloomy place, which showed him that, save for the murdered man, it was empty; then he staggered down the narrow stairs and let himself out into the grounds. Slightly revived by the fresh night air, but fearful of pursuit by the unknown assassin, he ran, as fast as his condition would allow, into the village.

"Here it is—Uxley!" jerked Moris Klaw.

III

"Ah!" cried Moris Klaw, in a species of fanatic rapture, "look at the blood!"

We stood in the ancient banqueting hall of Crespie. By a distant door I could see a policeman on duty. A ghostly silence was the marked feature of the place. Klaw's harsh, rumbling voice echoed eerily about that chamber sacred to the shades of departed Crespies.

Isis Klaw stood beside her father. They were a wildly incongruous couple. The girl looked down at the bloodstained flooring with the calm scrutiny of an experienced criminologist.

"This spot must be alive with odic impressions," she said, softly.

A local officer, who formed one of the group, stared uncomprehendingly. Moris Klaw instinctively turned to him.

"You stare widely, my friend!" he said. "It is clear you know nothing of the psychology of crime! Let me, then, enlighten you. First: all crime"—he waved one long hand characteristically— "operates in cycles. Its history repeats itself, you understand. Second: thoughts are *things*. One who dies the violent death has, at the end, a strong mental emotion—an etheric storm. The air—the atmosphere—retains imprints of that storm."

"Indeed!" said the officer.

"Yes, indeed! I shall not sleep in this place as is my usual custom in such inquiries. Why? Because I am afraid of the shock of experiencing such an emotion as was this late Heidelberger's! Ah!

you are dense as a bull! Once, my bovine friend, I slept upon a spot in desolate Palestine where a poor woman had been stoned to death. In my dreams those merciless stones struck me! Upon the head and the face they crashed! And I was helpless—bound—as was the unhappy one who for her poor little sins had had her life crushed from her tender body!"

He ceased. No one spoke. In such moments, Moris Klaw became a magician; a weaver of spells. The most unimpressionable shuddered as though the strange things which this strangest of men told of, lived, moved, before their eyes. Then—

"Yonder is the ax, sir," said the local man, with a sudden awed respect.

Klaw walked over to where the huge battle-ax stood against a post of the gallery.

"Try to lift it, Mr. Klaw," said Grimsby. "It will give you some idea of what sort of man the murderer must have been! I can't raise it upright by the haft with one hand."

Moris Klaw seized the ax. Whilst Grimsby, the local man and myself stared amazedly, he swung it about his head as one swings an Indian club! He struck with it—to right—to left; he laid it down.

"My father has a wrist of steel!" came the soft voice of Isis. "Did you not know that he was once a famous swordsman?"

Klaw removed his hat, took out the scent spray and bathed his forehead with verbena.

"That is a *man's* ax!" he said. "Isis, what do we know of such an ax? We, who have so complete a catalogue of such relics?"

Isis Klaw produced from her bag a bulky notebook.

"It is the third one," she replied, calmly, passing the open book to her father; "the one we thought!"

"Ah," rumbled Klaw, adjusting his pince-nez, "'Black Geoffrey's' ax!" He turned again to Palmer, the local officer. "All such antiques," he said, "have histories. I collect those histories, you understand. This ax was carried by 'Black Geoffrey,' a very early Crespie, in the first Crusade. It slew many Saracens, I doubt not. But this does not interest me. In the reign of Henry VIII we find it dwelt, this great ax, at Dyke Manor, which is in Norfolk. It was not until

Charles II that it came to Crespie Hall. And what happened at Dyke Manor? One Sir Gilbert Myerly was slain by it! Who wielded it? Patience, my friends! All is clear to me! What a wonderful science is the Science of Cycles!"

Behind the pebbles his eyes gleamed with excitement. It seemed as though his notes (how obtained I was unable to conjecture) had furnished him with a clue; although to me they seemed to have not the slightest bearing upon the case.

"Now, Mr. Grimsby," continued Moris Klaw: "In a few words, what is the evidence against Ryder, the butler?"

"Well," was the reply, "you will note where the ax used to hang, up there before the rail of the minstrels' gallery. The theory is that the murderer rushed up, wrenched the ax from its fastening—"

"Theories, my friend," interrupted Moris Klaw, "are not evidence!"

Isis gazed at Mr. Grimsby with a smile. He looked embarrassed.

"Sorry!" he said, humbly. "Here are the facts, then. In the right hand of the dead man was an open pocket knife. It is assumed— Sorry! Several spots of blood were found on the knife. Do you want to see it?"

Moris Klaw shook his head.

"It has been ascertained," continued Grimsby, "that Ryder went out at eight o'clock on the night of the murder and didn't return until after ten. He was interrogated. Listen to this, Mr. Klaw, and tell me why I haven't arrested him! He admitted that he was the man who rang the bell; he admitted being closeted with Heidelberger in the library; and he admitted that he was in the hall when the Jew met his death!"

"Good!" said Moris Klaw. "And he is still at large?"

"He is! He's made no attempt to run away. I had his room searched, and found a light coat with both sleeves bloodstained! He had a cut on his left hand such as might be caused by the slash of a pocket knife! He said he had caught his hand on a door latch, but blankly declined to say what he was doing here on the night of the murder! Yet, I didn't arrest him! Why?"

"Why?" said Moris Klaw. "Tell me."

"Because I didn't think it feasible that a man of his age could wield that ax—and I hoped to use Ryder as a trap to catch his accomplice!"

"Ah! clever!" rumbled Moris Klaw. "French, Mr. Grimsby! Subtle! But you have just seen what a poor old fool can do with that ax!"

I have never observed a man so suddenly lose faith in himself as did Grimsby at those words. He flushed, he paled; he seemed to become speechless.

"Tell me, Mr. Grimsby," said Klaw, "what does the suspected man do that is suspicious? What letters does he write? What letters does he receive?"

"None!" replied the now angry Grimsby. "But he visits Doctor Madden, in Uxley, every day."

"What for, eh?"

"The doctor says the interviews are of a purely professional nature, and I can't very well suspect a man in his position!"

"You have done two silly things," rumbled Moris Klaw. "You have wasted much time in the matter of Ryder, and you have accepted, unquestioned, the word of a doctor. Mr. Grimsby, I have known doctors who were most inspired liars!"

"Then you are of opinion—"

Klaw raised his hand.

"It is Doctor Madden we shall visit," he said. "This Ryder cannot escape us. Isis, my child, I need not have troubled you. This is so simple a case that we need no 'mental negatives' to point out to us the culprit!"

"Mr. Klaw—" began Grimsby, excitedly.

"My friend," he was answered, "I shall make a few examinations and then we shall be off to Uxley. The assassin returns to London with us by the 3:45 train!"

IV

As we drove through the village Street, in the car which Grimsby had hired, upon the gate of one of the last cottages a tall, white-haired old man was leaning. His clear-cut, handsome features wore an expression of haggard sorrow.

"There he is!" rapped Grimsby. "Hadn't I better make the arrest at once?"

"Ah, no, my friend!" protested Klaw. "But stop—I have something to say to him."

The car stopping, Moris Klaw descended and approached the old man, who perceptibly paled at sight of us.

"Good day, Mr. Ryder!" Klaw courteously saluted the ex-butler.

"Good day to you, sir," replied the old man, civilly.

Whereupon Moris Klaw said a simple thing, which had an astounding effect.

"How is he to-day?" he inquired.

Ryder's face became convulsed. His eyes started forth. He made a choking sound, staring, as one possessed, at his questioner.

"What—what—do you mean?" he gasped.

"Never mind, Mr. Ryder—never mind!" rumbled Klaw. "Isis, my child, remain with this gentleman and tell him all we know about the ax of 'Black Geoffrey.' He will be glad to hear it!"

The beautiful Isis obeyed without question. As the rest of us drove on our way, I could see the flame-coloured figure passing up the garden path beside the tall form of the old butler. Grimsby, a man badly out of his depth, watched until both became lost to view.

"I've got evidence," he suddenly burst out, "that Ryder declared Heidelberger to be the direct cause of Sir Richard's downfall! And I've got witnesses who heard him say, 'Please God! the Jew won't be here much longer!'"

"Good!" rumbled Moris Klaw. "Very good!"

During the remainder of the journey, Grimsby talked on incessantly, smoking cheroots the whole time But Moris Klaw was silent.

Doctor Madden had but recently returned from his morning visits He was a typical country practitioner, fresh-faced and clean-shaven, with iron-gray hair and a good head. He conveyed the impression, in some way, that he knew himself to be in a tight corner.

"What can I do for you, gentlemen?" he said, briskly.

"We have called, Doctor Madden," rumbled Moris Klaw, wagging his finger, impressively, "to tell you that Ryder is in imminent danger—imminent danger of arrest!"

The doctor started.

"And therefore we want a word with one of your patients!"

"I do not understand you. Which of my patients?"

Moris Klaw shook his head.

"Let us be intelligent," he said, "you and I, and not two old fools! You understand so perfectly which of your patients."

Doctor Madden drummed his fingers on the table. "Are you a detective?" he snapped.

"I am not!" replied Moris Klaw. "I am a student of the Science of Cycles—not motor cycles; and a humble explorer of the etheric borderland! You lay yourself open to grave charges, Doctor!"

The doctor began to fidget nervously.

"If indeed I am culpable," he said, "my culpability only dates from last night."

"So!" rumbled Klaw. "He has been insensible?"

Doctor Madden started up.

"Mr. Klaw," he replied, "I do not know who you may be, but your penetration is uncanny. He had lost his memory!"

"What?—lost his memory! How is that?"

"He was thrown from his horse! Come; I see it is useless, now, to waste time. I will take you to him."

As we filed out to the waiting car, I glanced at Grimsby. His stupefaction was almost laughable.

"What in heaven's name is it all about, Mr. Searles?" he whispered to me. "I feel like a man in a strange country. People talk, and it doesn't seem to mean anything!"

En route:

"Tell me, Doctor," said Moris Klaw, "about your patient."

The doctor, without hesitation, now explained that he had been called to attend a Mr. Rogers, an artist, who was staying at Hinxman's farm, off the Uxley Road. On the evening of the tragedy Mr. Rogers went out on Bess, a mare belonging to the farm, and, not having returned by ten, some anxiety was felt concerning him, the mare possessing a very bad reputation. At about a quarter-past ten the animal returned, riderless, and Rogers was brought home later, in an insensible condition, by two farm hands, having been found beside the road some distance from the farm.

For some time Mr. Rogers lay in a critical condition, suffering from concussion. Finally, a change for the better set in, but the patient was found to have lost his memory.

"Last Saturday," added the doctor, "a specialist whom I had invited to come down from London performed a successful operation."

"Ah," rumbled Moris Klaw, "so we can see him?"

"Certainly. He is quite convalescent. His memory returned to him completely last night."

In a state of uncertainty which can well be imagined, we arrived at, and entered, Hinxman's farm. Seated in the shade of the veranda, smoking his pipe, was a bronzed young man who wore a bandage about his head. He was chatting to the farmer when we arrived.

Moris Klaw walked up the steps beside Doctor Madden.

"Good day, Mr. Farmer," he said, amiably. A rosy-cheeked girl face was thrust from an open window. "Good day, Miss Farmer!" He removed the brown bowler. He turned to the bronzed young man. "Good day, *Sir Roland Crespie!*"

V

When Grimsby and I had somewhat recovered from the shock of this dramatic meeting, and Sir Roland, Madden, and Moris Klaw had talked together for a few moments, said Moris Klaw:

"And now Sir Roland will tell us all about the death of Mr. Heidelberger!"

Inspector Grimsby was all eyes when the young baronet began:

"You must know, then, that I, together with three others, have been engaged, since my departure from England, in a mining venture in West Africa. Up to the time when I left, and, for the sake of my health, came to England, our efforts had been attended by only moderate success. Thus, on arriving in Cresping and taking lodgings with Hinxman as 'Mr. Rogers'—for the circumstances under which I left home made me desirous of remaining unknown in the village—I, on learning that my father had just died and that the Hall had fallen into Heidelberger's hands, realized that my slender capital would not allow of my buying him out. The facts of the case came as a great shock to me, and, without revealing my identity—the beard which I had cultivated in Africa, but which the doctors have removed, acting as an effectual disguise—I made inquiries concerning Ryder. I had little difficulty in finding him, and he alone, in Cresping, knew who I really was.

"I now come to the events that immediately preceded Heidelberger's death. There was one object in the old place for which I determined to negotiate, and which, owing to its associations, I particularly desired to retain. This was my mother's portrait. I may mention here that, for certain reasons which I would prefer not to specify, I had rather have burnt the picture than see it fall into the hands of the Jew.

"With this object in view, then, I enlisted the services of Ryder, though from none other than myself would he have accepted the task. This brings me to the day prior to Heidelberger's death, and, on that morning, I received news from Africa which led me to hope that I might, after all, be able to save my old home from an ignominious fate. Herein my hopes have since been realized, for I learnt to-day that the mine has made rich men of us all; and I assume that some ill-advised remark upon the part of Ryder, regarding Heidelberger's possible expulsion, gave rise to the idea that the old man contemplated a violent deed.

"It therefore came about that he made an appointment with Heidelberger, an appointment which he duly kept; and it was solely due to my anxiety on Ryder's behalf, and lest he should meet with some ill treatment from the Jew—whom I knew for a man of most brutal disposition—that I took certain steps which, indirectly, brought about the tragedy.

"In common with most old mansions of the period, the Hall has its hidden entrances and exits—though, in accordance with certain ancient traditions, the secret of their existence is strictly preserved among the family. With a view, therefore, to becoming an unseen witness of the transactions between Ryder and Heidelberger, I made use of a passage that opens into a shrubbery some fifty yards from the west wing. Entering, and mounting the steps at whose foot the tunnel terminates, I found myself at the back of an old painting in the banqueting hall. The frame of this picture forms a door which opens upon pressing a spring, but the apparatus, owing to its great age, works very stiffly. From this position, then, I could hear all that took place in the hall, where, I had anticipated, the negotiations would be conducted, as my mother's picture hangs there.

"This proved to be the case; for I had but just gained the top of the steps when I heard the two enter the hall. Heidelberger spoke first.

"'Think of *you* wanting to buy Lady Crespie's picture, you sentimental old fool!' he said. 'If it had been another I could name who wanted it, the case would have been different!'

"Then I heard Ryder's voice. 'What do you mean, Mr. Heidelberger?' he asked.

"I awaited the Jew's reply with some curiosity. As I had anticipated, it consisted of a foul and unfounded imputation against my poor mother. It was, in fact, more than I could bear in silence, and the tolerance of old Ryder, too, had reached its limit. For, at the moment that I wrenched open the panel and sprang into the room to confront this slanderer, I heard the sound of a blow, followed by an animal-like roar of anger from Heidelberger.

"The next moment, he seized the old man by the throat. Before he had time to proceed further I struck him heavily with my fist, so that he released his grip and turned to face his new assailant.

"One tribute I must pay to Heidelberger. He was, seemingly, incapable of fear; for this sudden attack by a person he had not known to be present seemed only to arouse a new resentment. His face, as he turned and looked me up and down, contained no trace of fear.

"'So it's you that wants the picture, is it?' he sneered. 'I suppose you are—'

"'Stop!' I said. 'I am Roland Crespie, and can listen to no more of your foul slanders!'

"For a second he hesitated, looking from me to Ryder and then toward the picture, dimly discernible in the light of the candle which he had brought with him. Then, before I could divine his intention, he drew a knife from his pocket, and, opening a blade, took a step in the direction of the portrait. 'You shall never have it!' he said.

"He had actually inserted the blade in the canvas—as an examination will show—when I came upon him, and we closed in a desperate struggle.

"In what followed, one can almost trace the finger of destiny. Heidelberger was a more powerful man than myself, but in his fury he endeavoured to stab me with the knife which he held in his hand!

"I seized his wrist, but he wrenched it from my grasp. I leapt back from him—as he struck down with the knife—and to the left of one of the posts supporting the minstrels' gallery.

"In the blindness of his anger, Heidelberger failed to perceive the proximity of this post. Moreover, it was very dark under the gallery. He threw himself forward savagely—and struck his shoulder against the post. The impact was tremendous.

"Gentlemen! I tremble, now, to relate what happened! The ax of 'Black Geoffrey,' which had hung for centuries before the rail above, was shaken from its place by the shock and its time-worn fastenings were torn bodily from their hold. At the instant that Heidelberger's huge body struck the post, the great ax, as though detached by invisible hands, fell, blade downward, cleaving the head of the unfortunate man and remaining, with quivering shaft, upright in the oaken floor!

"The suddenness of the tragedy almost dazed me, and I was awakened to its awful reality by old Ryder's cry— 'Oh, Master Roly!' As Master Roly I had always been known to the old butler, and this name it was which someone stated to be 'holy.'

"Our subsequent action was, perhaps, ill-advised Removing the ax and raising the head of the victim, examination showed him to be dead, and, hearing hesitating footsteps upon the narrow stair beneath the gallery, we seized the candle and retreated through the secret panel, Ryder severely cutting his hand in endeavouring to force the rusty bolt into place. It was not until we stood in a lane bordering the grounds, where I had tethered the mare upon which I had ridden from the farm, that the seemingly guilty nature of our action dawned upon me Now, however, was too late to atone for what I attribute to a momentary panic, and requesting Ryder to keep silence until he received instructions from me, I mounted the mare, intending to return to my lodgings and think the matter quietly over.

"By an unlucky accident, the brute threw me, at some distance from the farm, thereby all but bringing about a second tragedy; and what followed is already known to you.

"Of Ryder I need only say that rather than incriminate me he was prepared to pay the penalty for a deed which was in truth a visitation of God. Doctor Madden recognized me, of course, and to him also I am eternally indebted. I had proposed to make this statement before a magistrate later to-day."

"You see," said Moris Klaw. "I have done nothing! It would all have happened the same if I had been in Peru!"

Grimsby cleared his throat.

"Without casting any doubt upon Sir Roland's word," he began, "there's no evidence to go to a jury that he didn't—"

"Pull down the ax himself?" suggested Klaw.

Grimsby looked uncomfortable.

"Well—*is* there?"

"There is!" rumbled Moris Klaw. "I am he! This case most triumphantly substantiates my theory of Cycles! Almost parallel it occurred hundreds of years ago, at Dyke Manor! The ax has repeated itself!"

"H'um!" said Grimsby. "Your theory of Cycles Wouldn't hold water with twelve good men and true, I'm afraid, Mr. Klaw!"

"Yes?" replied Moris Klaw. "No? You think not, eh? Well, then, there is another little point. I am an old crank-fool, eh? So? But you? You are sublimely mad, my Grimsby! You say he, or Mr. Ryder, may have snatched down the black ax? Yes? Have you tried to reach the spot where it hung before the rail?"

"No," confessed Grimsby, with the light as of the dawning of an unpleasant idea in his eyes.

"No," said Klaw, placidly; "but *I* have. Mr. Grimsby, it is impossible to reach within three feet of the spot, from the stair or from the gallery, and no live thing but a giraffe could reach it from the floor!"

We were seated in the train, homeward bound.

"For this case," grumbled Klaw, "I get no credit. It will be said that it all came out without aid from you or from me. Never mind— I have my fee!"

He patted the haft of the great ax, which ghastly relic in some way he had arranged to appropriate. Grimsby was watching Isis Klaw out of the corner of his eye. From a dainty gold case she offered him a cigarette. Grimsby is no cigarette smoker but he accepted, with alacrity.

The beautiful Isis took one also, and lay back puffing sinuous spirals from between her perfect red lips.

CASE OF THE IVORY STATUE

I

Where a case did not touch his peculiar interests, appeals to Moris Klaw fell upon deaf ears. However dastardly a crime, if its details were of the sordid sort, he shrank within his Wapping curio shop as closely as any tortoise within its shell.

"Of what use," he said to me on one occasion, "are my acute psychic sensibilities to detect who it is with a chopper that has brained some unhappy washerwoman? Shall I bring to bear those delicate perceptions which it has taken me so many years to acquire in order that some ugly old fool shall learn what has become of his pretty young wife? I think not—no!"

Sometimes, however, when Inspector Grimsby of Scotland Yard was at a loss, he would induce me to intercede with the eccentric old dealer, and sometimes Moris Klaw would throw out a hint.

Beyond doubt the cases that really interested him were those that afforded scope for the exploiting of his pet theories: the Cycle of Crime, the criminal history of all valuable relics, the indestructibility of thought. Such a case came under my personal notice on one occasion, and my friend Coram was instrumental in enlisting the services of Moris Klaw. It was, I think, one of the most mysterious affairs with which I ever came in contact, and the better to understand it you must permit me to explain how Roger Paxton, the sculptor, came to have such a valuable thing in his studio as that which we all assumed had inspired the strange business.

It was Sir Melville Fennel, then, who commissioned Paxton to execute a chryselephantine statue. Sir Melville's museum of works of art, ancient and modern, is admittedly the second finest private collection of the kind in the world. The late Mr. Pierpont Morgan's alone took precedence.

The commission came as something of a surprise. The art of chryselephantine sculpture, save for one attempt at revival, in Belgium, has been dead for untold generations. By many modern critics, indeed, it is condemned, as being not art but a parody of art.

Given carte blanche in the matter of cost, Paxton produced a piece of work which induced the critics to talk about a modern Phidias. Based upon designs furnished by the eccentric but wealthy baronet, the statue represented a slim and graceful girl reclining as in exhaustion upon an ebony throne. The ivory face, with its wearily closed eyes, was a veritable triumph, and was surmounted by a headdress of gold intertwined among a mass of dishevelled hair. One ivory arm hung down so that the fingers almost touched the pedestal; the left hand was pressed to the breast as though against a throbbing heart. Gold bracelets and anklets, furnished by Sir Melville, were introduced into the composition; and, despite the artist's protest, a heavy girdle, encrusted with gems and found in the tomb of some favourite of a long dead Pharaoh, encircled the waist. When complete, the thing was, from a merely intrinsic point of view, worth several thousand pounds.

As the baronet had agreed to the exhibition of the statue prior to its removal to Fennel Hall, Paxton's star was seemingly in the ascendant, when the singular event occurred that threatened to bring about his ruin.

The sculptor gave one of the pleasant little dinners for which he had gained a reputation. His task was practically completed, and his friends had all been enjoined to come early, so that the statue could be viewed before the light failed. We were quite a bachelor party, and I shall always remember the circle of admiring faces surrounding the figure of the reclining dancer—warmed in the soft light to an almost uncanny semblance of fair flesh and blood.

"You see," explained Paxton, "this composite work, although it has latterly fallen into disrepute, affords magnificent scope for decorative purposes; such a richness of colour can be obtained. The ornaments are genuine antiques and of great value—a fad of my patron's."

For some minutes we stood silently admiring the beautiful workmanship; then Harman inquired, "Of what is the hair composed?"

Paxton smiled. "A little secret I borrowed from the Greeks!" he replied, with condonable vanity. "Polyclitus and his contemporaries excelled at the work."

"That jewelled girdle looks detachable," I said.

"It is firmly fastened to the waist of the figure," answered the sculptor. "I defy any one to detach it inside an hour."

"From a modern point of view the thing is an innovation," remarked one of the others, thoughtfully.

Coram, curator of the Menzies Museum, who up to the present had stood in silent contemplation of the figure, now spoke for the first time. "The cost of materials is too great for this style of work ever to become popular," he averred. "That girdle, by the way, represents a small fortune, and together with the anklets, armlets, and headdress, might well tempt any burglar. What precautions do you take, Paxton?"

"Sleep out here every night," was the reply; "and there is always someone here in the daytime. Incidentally, a curious thing occurred last week. I had just fixed the girdle, which, I may explain, was once the property of Nicris, a favourite of Ramses III, and my model was alone here for a few minutes. As I was returning from the house I heard her cry out, and when I came to look for her she was crouching in a corner trembling. What do you suppose had frightened her?"

"Give it up," said Harman.

"She swore that Nicris—for the statue is supposed to represent her—had moved!"

"Imagination," replied Coram, "but easily to be understood. I could believe it, myself, if I were here alone long enough."

"I fancy," continued Paxton, "that she must have heard some of the tales that have been circulated concerning the girdle. The thing has a rather peculiar history. It was discovered in the tomb of the dancer by whom it had once been worn; and it is said that an inscription was unearthed at the same time containing an account of Nicris's death under particularly horrible circumstances. Seton—you fellows know Seton—who was present at the opening of the sarcophagus, tells me that the Arabs, on catching sight of the girdle, all prostrated themselves and then took to their heels. Sir Melville Fennel's agent sent it on to England, however, and Sir Melville conceived the idea of this statue."

"Luckily for you," added Coram.

"Quite so," laughed the sculptor, and, carefully locking the studio door, he led the way up the short path to the house.

We were a very merry party, and the night was far advanced ere the gathering broke up. Coram and I were the last to depart; and having listened to the voices of Harman and the others dying away as they neared the end of the street, we also prepared to take our leave.

"Just come with me as far as the studio," said Paxton, "and having seen that all's well I'll let you out by the garden door."

Accordingly, we donned our coats and hats, and followed our host to the end of the garden, where his studio was situated. The door unlocked, we all three stepped inside the place and gazed upon the figure of Nicris—the pallid face and arms seeming almost unearthly in the cold moonlight, wherein each jewel of the girdle and headdress glittered strangely.

"Of course," muttered Coram, "the thing's altogether irregular—a fact which the critics will not fail to impress upon you; but it is unquestionably very fine, Paxton. How uncannily human it is! I don't entirely envy you your bedchamber, old man!"

"Oh, I sleep well enough," laughed Paxton. "No luxury, though; just this corner curtained off and a camp bedstead."

"A truly Spartan couch!" I said. "Well, good-night, Paxton. We shall probably see you to-morrow—I mean later to-day!"

With that we parted, leaving the sculptor to his lonely vigil at the shrine of Nicris, and as my rooms were no great distance away, some half-hour later I was in bed and asleep.

I little suspected that I had actually witnessed the commencement of one of the most amazing mysteries which ever cried out for the presence of Moris Klaw.

II

Some few minutes subsequent to retiring—or so it seemed to me; a longer time actually had elapsed—I was aroused by the ringing of my telephone bell. I scrambled sleepily out of bed and ran to the instrument.

Coram was the caller. And now, fully awake, I listened with an ever-growing wonder to his account of that which had prompted him to ring me up. Briefly, it amounted to this: some mysterious incident, particulars of which he omitted, had aroused Paxton from his sleep. Seeking the cause of the disturbance, the artist had unlocked the studio door and gone out into the garden. He was absent but a moment and never out of earshot of the door; yet, upon his return, *the statue of Nicris had vanished!*

"I have not hesitated to 'phone through to Wapping," concluded Coram, "and get a special messenger sent to Moris Klaw. You see, the matter is urgent. If the statue cannot be recovered, its loss may spell ruin for Paxton. He had heard me speak of Moris Klaw and of the wonders he worked in the Greek Room mysteries, and, accordingly, called me up. I knew, if Klaw came, you would be anxious to be present."

"Certainly," I replied, "I wouldn't miss one of his inquiries for anything. Shall I meet you at Paxton's?"

"Yes."

I lost little time in dressing. From Coram's brief account, the mystery appeared to be truly a dark one. Would Moris Klaw respond to this midnight appeal? There was little chance of a big fee, for Paxton was not a rich man; but in justice to the remarkable person whom it is my privilege to present to you in these papers, I must add that monetary considerations seemingly found no place in Klaw's philosophy. He acted, I believe, from sheer love of the work; and this affair, with its bizarre details—the ancient girdle of the dancing girl—the fear of the model, who had declared that the statue moved—was such, I thought, as must appeal to him.

Ten minutes later I was at Paxton's house. He and Coram were in the hall, and Coram admitted me.

"Do you mean," he asked of Paxton, pursuing a conversation which my advent had interrupted, "that the statue melted into the empty air?"

"The double doors opening on to the street were securely locked and barred; that of the garden was also locked; I was in the garden and not ten yards from the studio," was Paxton's reply. "Nevertheless, Nicris had vanished, leaving no trace behind!"

Incredible though the story appeared, its confirmation was to be found in the speaker's face. I was horrified to see how haggard he looked.

"It will ruin me!" he said, and reiterated the statement again and again.

"But, my dear fellow," I cried, "surely you have not given up hope of recovering the statue? After all, such a robbery as this can scarcely have been perpetrated without leaving some clue behind."

"Robbery!" repeated Paxton, looking at me strangely; "you would be less confident that it is a case of robbery, Searles, if you had heard what I heard!"

I glanced at Coram, but he merely shrugged his shoulders.

"What do you mean?" I said.

"Then Coram has not told you?"

"He has told me that something aroused you in the night and that you left the studio to investigate the matter."

"Correct, so far. Something did arouse me; and the thing was a voice!"

"A voice?"

"It would be, I suppose, about two hours after you had gone, and I was soundly asleep in the studio, when I suddenly awoke and sat up to listen, for it seemed to me that I heard a cry immediately outside the door."

"What kind of cry?"

"Of that I was not, at first, by any means certain; but after a brief interval the cry was repeated. It sounded more like the voice of a boy than that of a man and it uttered but one word: 'Nicris!'"

"And then?"

"I sprang on to the floor and stood for a moment in doubt—the thing seemed so uncanny. The electric light is not, as you know, installed in the studio, or I should have certainly switched it on. For possibly a minute I hesitated, and then, as I pulled the curtains aside and stood by the door to listen, for the third time the cry was repeated and was now coming indisputably from immediately outside."

"You refer to the door that opens on to the garden?"

"Exactly—close to which stands my bed. This, then, decided me. Taking up the small revolver which I have always kept handy since Nicris was completed, I unlocked the door, and stepped out into the garden—"

A vehicle, cab or car, was heard to draw up outside the house. Came the sound of a rumbling voice. Coram sprang to the door.

"Moris Klaw!" I cried.

"Good morning, Mr. Coram!" said the strange voice, from the darkness outside. "Good morning, Mr. Searles!"

Moris Klaw entered.

He wore his flat-topped brown bowler of effete pattern; he wore his long, shabby, caped coat; and from beneath it gleamed the pointed glossy toe-caps of his continental boots. Through his gold-rimmed glasses he peered into the shadows of the hall. His scanty, colourless beard appeared less adequate than ever to clothe the massive chin. The dim light rendered his face more cadaverous and more yellow even than usual.

"And this," he proceeded, as the anxious sculptor came forward, "is Mr. Paxton, who has lost his statue? Good morning, Mr. Paxton!"

He bowed, removing the bowler and revealing his great high brow. Coram was about to reclose the door.

"Ah, no!" Moris Klaw checked him. "My daughter is to come yet with my cushion!"

Paxton stared, not comprehending, but stared yet harder when Isis Klaw appeared, carrying a huge red cushion. She was wrapped in a cloak which effectually concealed her lithe figure, and from the raised hood her darkly beautiful face looked out with bewitching effect. She divided between Coram and myself one of her dazzling smiles.

"It is Mr. Paxton," said her father, indicating the sculptor. Then, indicating the girl, "It is my daughter, Isis. Isis will help us to look for Nicris. Why am I here, an old fool who ought to be asleep? Because of this girdle your statue wore. I so well remember when it was dug up. I cannot know its history, but be sure it is evil. From the beginning, please, Mr. Paxton!"

"I'm awfully indebted to you! Won't you come in and sit down?" said Paxton, glancing at the girl in bewilderment.

"No, no!" replied Klaw, "let us stand. It is good to stand, and stand upright; for it is because he can do this that man is superior to the other animals!"

Coram and I knew Klaw's mannerisms, but I could see that Paxton thought him to be a unique kind of lunatic. Nevertheless, he narrated something of the foregoing up to the point reached at Moris Klaw's arrival.

"Proceed slowly, now," said Klaw. "You left the door open behind you?"

"Yes; but I was never more than ten yards from it. It would have been physically impossible for any one to remove the statue unknown to me. You must remember that it was no light weight."

"One moment," I interrupted. "Are you sure that the statue was in its place before you came out?"

"Certain! There was a bright moon, and the figure was the first thing my eyes fell upon when I pulled the curtain aside."

"Did you *touch* it?" rumbled Moris Klaw.

"No. There was no occasion to do so."

"How much to be regretted, Mr. Paxton! The sense of touch is so exquisite a thing!"

We all wondered at his words.

"Stepping just outside the door," Paxton resumed, "I looked to right and left. There was no one in sight. Then I walked to the wall— a matter of some ten yards—and, pulling myself up by my hands, looked over into the street. It was deserted, save for a constable on the opposite corner. I know him, slightly, and his presence convinced me that no one could either have come into or gone out of the garden by way of the wall. I did not call him, but immediately returned to the studio door."

"In all, you were absent from the studio about how long?" asked Moris Klaw.

"Not a second over half a minute!"

"And on returning once more to the door?"

"A single glance showed me that the statue had gone!"

"Good Heavens!" I said; "it sounds impossible. Was the constable on point duty?"

"He was; there is always an officer there. He stood in sight of the double doors opening on to the street during the whole time, so that 'Nicris' unquestionably came out by way of the garden or melted into thin air. Since the only exit from the garden also opens on to the street, how, but by magic can the statue have been removed from the premises?"

"Ah, my friend," said Moris Klaw, "you talk of magic as one talks of onions! How little you know"—he swept wide his arms, looking upward— "of the phenomena of the two atmospheres! Proceed!"

"The throne," continued Paxton, who was becoming impressed as was evident by the uncanny sense of power which emanated in some way from Moris Klaw, "remains."

"And the statue it was attached to it?"

"As to the figure being attached, I may say that it was only partially so. Materials for completing the work were to have arrived to-day."

"How long would it have taken to detach it?" growled Klaw.

"Granting some knowledge of the nature of the work, not long— for, as I have said, in this respect it was incomplete. Half an hour or so, I should have believed!"

"Then," I said, "the matter, in brief, stands thus: In the course of thirty seconds, during which time a constable was in view of one entrance and you were ten yards from the other, someone detached the statue from the throne—an operation involving half an hour's skilled labour—and, unseen by yourself or the, officer, removed it from the premises."

"Oh, the thing is impossible!" groaned Paxton. "There is something unearthly in the affair. I wish I had never set eyes upon that accursed girdle!"

"Curse not the girdle," rumbled Moris Klaw. "Curse instead its wearer, and inform us, on finding Nicris to be missing, what did you do?"

"I hastily searched the studio. A brief investigation convinced me that neither statue nor thief was concealed there. I then came out, locked the door, and, having examined the garden, hailed the constable. He had been on duty for four hours at that point and had observed absolutely nothing of an unusual nature. He saw you fellows come out by the garden entrance, and from that time until I hailed him, nothing, he declared, had come in or gone out!"

"He heard no cry?"

"No; it was not loud enough to be audible from the corner"

"Lastly," said Klaw, "have you informed Scotland Yard?"

"No," answered the sculptor; "nor will the constable lodge information; moreover, I withheld from him the object of my inquiries. If this business gets into the papers I shall be a ruined man!"

"I have hopes," Klaw assured him, "that it will get in no papers. Let us proceed now to the scene of these wonderful happenings. It is my custom, Mr. Paxton, to lay my old head down upon the scene of a mystery, and from the air I can sometimes recover the key to the labyrinth!"

"So I have heard," said Paxton.

"You have heard so, yes? You shall see! Lead on, Mr. Paxton! No time must be wasted. I am another like Napoleon, and can sleep on an instant. I do not know insomnia! Lead on. Isis, my child, be careful that it brushes against no object in passing—my odically sterilized cushions!"

We proceeded to the studio

"I feel that I am responsible for dragging you here at this un-earthly hour," said Paxton to Isis Klaw. She turned her fine eyes upon him.

"My father is indebted for the opportunity," she replied; "and since he has need of me, I am here. I, too, am indebted."

Her supreme self-possession and tone of finality silenced the artist. So far as I could see, everything in the studio was exactly as before, save that Nicris's throne was vacant. The top of the studio was partially glazed, and Moris Klaw peered up at it earnestly.

"From above," he rumbled, "I should wish to look down into below. How do I reach it?"

"The only stepladder is that in the studio," answered Paxton. "I will bring it out."

He did so. The gray light of dawn was creeping into the sky, and against that sombre background we watched Moris Klaw crawl-ing about the roof like some giant spider.

"Did you find anything?" asked Paxton, anxiously, as the investi-gator descended.

"I find what I look for," was the reply; "and no man is entitled to find more. Isis, my child, place that cushion in the ebony chair."

The girl stepped on to the dais, and disposed the red cushion as directed.

"You see," explained Morris Klaw, "whoever has robbed you, Mr. Paxton, runs some one great danger, however clever his plans There is in every criminal scheme, one little point that only Fate can decide—either to hitch or to smooth out—to bring success and riches or whistling policemen and Brixton Gaol? Upon that so criti-cal point his or her mind will concentrate at the critical moment. The critical moment, here, was that of getting Nicris out of your studio.

"I sleep upon that throne where she reclined—the ivory dancer. This sensitive plate"—he tapped his brow— "will reproduce a nega-tive of that critical moment as it seemed in the mind of the one we look for. Isis, return in the cab that waits and be here again at six o'clock."

He placed his quaint bowler upon a table and laid beside it his black cloak. Then, a ramshackle figure in shabby tweed, reclined upon the big ebony chair, his head against the cushion.

"Place my cloak about me, Isis."

The girl did so.

"Good morning, my child! Good morning, Mr. Searles! Good morning, Mr. Coram and Mr. Paxton!"

He closed his eyes.

"Excuse me," began Paxton.

Isis placed her finger to her lips, and signed to us to withdraw silently.

"Ssh!" she whispered. "He is asleep!"

III

At five minutes to six sounded Isis Klaw's ring upon the door bell. Paxton, Coram, and I had spent the interval in discussing the apparently supernatural happening which threatened to wreak the artist's ruin. Again and again he had asked us, "Should I call in the Scotland Yard people? If Moris Klaw fails, consider the priceless time lost!"

"If Moris Klaw fails," Coram assured him, "no one else will succeed!"

We admitted Isis, who wore now a smart tweed costume and a fashionable hat. Beyond doubt, Isis Klaw was strikingly beautiful.

At the door of the studio stood her father, staring straight up to the morning sky, as though by astrological arts he hoped to solve the mystery.

"What time does your model come?" he asked, ere Paxton could question him.

"Half-past ten. But, Mr. Klaw—" began our anxious friend.

"Where does it lead to," Klaw rumbled on, "that lane behind the studio?"

"Tradesmen's entrance to the next house."

"Whose house?"

"Doctor Gleason."

"M. D.?"

"Yes. But tell me, Mr. Klaw—tell me, have you any clue?"

"My mind, Mr. Paxton, records for me that Nicris was not stolen away, but *walked!* Plainly, I feel her go tiptoe, tiptoe, so silent and cautious! She is concerned, this barbaric dancing girl who escapes from your studio, with two things. One is some very big man. She thinks, as she tiptoes, of one very tall: six feet and three inches at least! So it is not of you she thinks, Mr. Paxton. We shall see of whom it is. Tell me the name of your acquaintance, the point-policeman."

We were all staring at Moris Klaw, spellbound with astonishment. But Paxton managed to mumble: "James—Constable James."

"We shall seek him, this James, at the section house of the police depot," rumbled Klaw. "Be silent, Mr. Paxton; let no one know of your loss. And hope."

"I can see no ground for hope!"

"No? But I? I recognize the clue, Mr. Paxton! What a great science is that of mental photography!"

What did he mean? None of us could surmise, and I could see that poor Paxton reposed no faith whatever in the eccentric methods of the investigator. He would have voiced his doubts, I think, but he met a glance from the dark eyes of Isis Klaw which silenced him.

"My child," said Klaw to his daughter, "take the cushion and return. My negative is a clear one. You understand?"

"Perfectly," replied Isis, with composure.

"Breakfast—" began Paxton, tentatively.

But Moris Klaw waved his hands and enveloped himself in the big cloak.

"There is no time for such gross matters!" he said. "We are busy."

From the brown bowler he took out a scent spray and bedewed his high, bald forehead with verbena.

"It is exhausting, that odic photography!" he explained.

Shortly afterward he and I walked around to the local police depot. Something occurred to me, *en route.*

"By the way," I said, "what was the other thing of which you spoke? The thing that you declared Nicris to be thinking of, though I don't understand in the least how one can refer to the 'thoughts' of an ivory statue!"

"Ah," rumbled my companion, "it is something I shall explain later—that other fear of the missing one."

Arriving at the police depot, "Shall I ask for Constable James?" I said.

"Ah, no," replied Klaw. "It is for the constable that he relieved at twelve o'clock I am looking."

Inquiry showed that the latter officer—his name was Freeman—had just entered the section house. Moris Klaw's questions elicited the following story, although its bearing upon the matter in hand was not evident to me.

Toward twelve o'clock, that is, shortly before Freeman was relieved, a man, supporting a woman, came down the street and entered the gate of Doctor Gleeson's house. The woman was enveloped in a huge fur cloak which entirely concealed her face and figure, but from her feeble step the constable judged her to be very ill. Considering the lateness of the hour, also, he concluded that the case must be a serious one; he further supposed the sick woman to be resident in the neighbourhood, since she came on foot.

He had begun to wonder at the length of the consultation, when, nearly an hour later, the man appeared again from the shadows of the drive, still supporting the woman. Pausing at the gate he waved his hand to the policeman.

Constable Freeman ran across the road immediately.

"Fetch me a taxicab, officer!" said the stranger, supporting his companion and exhibiting much solicitude.

Freeman promptly ran to the corner of Beira Road and returned with a cab from the all-night rank.

"Open the door!" directed the man, who was a person of imposing height—some six-feet-three, Freeman averred.

"Ha, ha!" growled Moris Klaw, "six-feet-three! What a wondrous science!"

He seemed triumphant; but I was merely growing more non-plussed

With that, carefully wrapping the cloak about the woman's figure, the big man took her up in his arms and placed her inside the cab—the only glimpse of her which the constable obtained being that of a small foot clad in a silk stocking She had apparently dropped her shoe.

Tenderly assisting her to a corner of the vehicle, the man, having bent and whispered some word of encouragement in her ear, directed the cabman to drive to the Savoy.

"Did you give him your assistance?" asked Moris Klaw.

"No. He did not seem to require it."

"And the number of the cabman?"

Freeman fetched his notebook and supplied the required information.

"Thank you, Constable Freeman," said Klaw. "You are a very alert constable. Good morning, Constable Freeman!"

Again satisfaction beamed from behind my companion's glasses. But to my eyes the darkness grew momentarily less penetrable. For these inquiries bore upon matters which had occurred prior to twelve o'clock; and, Coram, myself, and Paxton had seen the statue in its usual place considerably after midnight! My brain was in a turmoil.

Said Moris Klaw: "That cab was from the big garage at Brixton. We shall ring up the Brixton garage and learn where the man may be found. Perhaps, if Providence is with us—and Providence is with the right—he has not yet again left home."

From a public call office we rang up the garage, and learned that the man we wanted was not due to report for duty until ten o'clock. We experienced some difficulty in obtaining his private address, but finally it was given to us. Thither we hastened, and aroused the man from his bed.

"A big gentleman and a sick lady," said Moris Klaw, "they hired your cab from Doctor Gleeson's, near Beira Road, at about twelve o'clock last night, and you drove them to the Savoy Hotel."

"No, sir. He changed the address afterward. I've been wondering why. I drove him to Number 6A, Rectory Grove, Old Town, Clapham."

"Was the lady by then recovered—no? Yes?"

"Partly, sir. I heard him talking to her. But he carried her into the house."

"Ah," said Moris Klaw, "there is much genius wasted; but what a great science is the science of the mind!"

IV

Many times Moris Klaw knocked upon the door of the house in Clapham Old Town, a small one, standing well back from the roadway. Within we could hear someone coughing.

Then the door was suddenly thrown open, and a man appeared who must have stood some six feet three inches. He had finely chiselled features, was clean-shaven, and wore pince-nez.

Klaw said a thing that had a surprising effect.

"What!" he rumbled, "has Nina caught cold?"

The other glared, with a sudden savagery coming into his eyes, fell back a step, and clenched his great fists.

"Enough, Jean Colette!" said Morris Klaw, "you do not know me, but I know you. Attempt no tricks, or it is the police and not a meddlesome, harmless old fool who will come. Enter, Jean! We follow."

For a moment longer the big man hesitated, and I saw the shadows of alternate resolves passing across his fine features. Then clearly he saw that surrender was inevitable, shrugged his shoulders, and stared hard at my companion.

"Enter, messieurs," he said, with a marked French accent.

He said no more, but led the way into a long, bare room at the rear of the house. To term the apartment a laboratory would be correct but not inclusive; for it was, in addition, a studio and a workshop.

Glancing rapidly around him, Moris Klaw asked, "Where is it?"

The man's face was a study as he stood before us, looking from one to the other. Then a peculiar smile, indescribably winning, played around his lips. "You are very clever, and I know when I am beaten," he remarked; "but had you come four hours later it would have been one hour too late."

He strode up the room to where a tall screen stood, and, seizing it by the top, hurled it to the ground.

Behind, on a model's dais, reclined the statue of Nicris, in a low chair!

"You have already removed the girdle and one of the anklets," rumbled Klaw.

This was true. Indeed, it now became evident that the man had been interrupted in his task by our arrival. Opening a leather case that stood upon the floor by the dais, he produced the missing ornaments.

"What action is to be taken, messieurs?" he asked, quietly.

"No action, Jean," replied Moris Klaw. "It is impossible, you see. But why did you delay so long?"

The other's reply was unexpected.

"It is a task demanding much time and care, if the statue is not to be ruined; otherwise I should have performed it in Mr. Paxton's studio instead of going to the trouble of removing the figure—and—Nina's condition has caused me grave anxiety, throughout the night." He stared hard at Moris Klaw. We could hear the sound of coughing from some room hard by. "Who are you, m'sieur?" he asked, pointedly.

"An old fool who knew Nina when she posed at Julien's, Jean," was the reply, "and who knew you, also, in Paris."

V

Paxton, Coram, myself, and Moris Klaw sat in the studio, and all of us gazed reflectively at the recovered statue.

"It was so evident," explained Klaw, "that, since you were absent from here but thirty seconds, for any one to have removed the statue during that time was out of the question."

"But someone did—"

"Not during that time," rumbled Moris Klaw. "Nicris was re-moved whilst you all made merry within the house!"

"But, my dear Mr. Klaw, Searles, Coram, and I saw the statue long after that—some time about one o'clock!"

"Wrong, my friend! You saw the *model!*"

"What! Nina?"

"Madame Colette, whom you knew in Paris as Nina—yes! Lis-ten—when I drop off, to sleep here and dream that I am afraid for what may happen to some very large man, I dream, also, that I fear to be *touched!* I look down at myself, and I am beautiful! I am ivory of limb and decked with gold! I creep, so cautiously, out of the studio (in my dream—you would call it a dream), and I know, when I wake, that I must have been Nicris! Ah, you wonder! Listen.

"At about midnight, whilst your party is amiable together, comes one, Jean Colette, a clever scamp from that metropolis of such perverted genius—Paris. Into Doctor Gleeson's he goes, sup-porting Madame—your model. This is seen by Constable Freeman. When the trees hide them they climb over the fence into the lane and over the wall into your garden. Nina has a cast of the studio key. How easy for her to get it!

"Jean, a clever rogue with his hands, and a man who promised to be, once, a great artist, detaches the figure from the throne and arrays it as Madame—in Madame's outer garb! Beneath her cloak, Madame is Nicris—with copies of the jewels and all complete. He is clever, this Jean! He is, too, a man of vast strength—a modern Crotonian Milo. Not only does he carry that great piece of ivory from the studio, he lifts it over the wall—did Madame assist?—and into Doctor Gleeson's drive. He bears it to the gate, wrapped in Nina's furs. He calls a policeman! Ah, genius is here! He gives the wrong address. He is as cool as an orange!

"Do they escape now? Not so! He sees that you, finding Nicris missing, will apply to the point-policeman and get hold upon a thread. He says, 'I will make it to appear that the robbery took place at a later time. I will thus gain hours! Another police man

will be on duty when the discovery is made; he will know nothing.'
He leaves Nina to pretend to be Nicris!

"Ah! she has courage, but her fears are many. Most of all she
dreads that you will *touch* her! You do not. And Jean, the ivory
statue safe at Clapham, returns for Nina. He comes into the doctor's
drive by the farther gate—where the point-policeman cannot see
him. He wears rubber shoes. He mounts to the studio roof. He lies
flat upon the ledge above the door. His voice is falsetto. He calls,
'Nicris!'

"Presently, you come out. You peep over the wall. Ah! out, also,
is Madame! She stretches up her white arms—so like the real
ivory!—he stretches down his steel hands. He raises her beside him!
Name of a dog, he is strong!

"Why to the roof and not over the wall? The path is of gravel
and her feet are bare. On the roof, to prove me correct, upon the
grime are marks of small bare feet; are marks of men's rubber
shoes; are, halfway along, marks of smaller rubber shoes—which
he had brought for Nina. He has forethought. They retire by the
farther gate of your neighbour's drive.

"No doubt he bring her furs as well—no doubt. But she con-
tracts a chill, no wonder! Ah! he is cool, he is daring, he is a great
man—"

A maid entered the studio.

"A gentleman to see you, sir."

"Ask him to come along here."

A short interval—and Jean Colette entered, hat in hand!

"These two wedges, m'sieur"—he bowed to Paxton— "which
help to attach the girdle. I forgot to return them. Adieu!"

He placed the wedges on a table and, amid a dramatic silence,
withdrew.

Moris Klaw took out the cylindrical scent spray from the lining
of the brown bowler.

"A true touch of Paris!" he rumbled. "Did I not say he was a
great man?"

CASE OF THE BLUE RAJAH

I

Inspector Grimsby called upon me one evening, wearing a great glumness of countenance. "Look here," said he, "I'm in a bit of a corner. You'll have heard that a committee of commercial magnates has been formed to buy, and on behalf of the City of London to present to the Crown, the big Indian diamond?"

I nodded and pushed the box of cigarettes toward him.

"Well," he continued, thoughtfully selecting one, "they are meeting in Moorgate Street to-morrow morning to complete the deal and formally take over the stone. Sir Michael Cayley, the Lord Mayor, will be present, and he's received a letter, which has been passed on to me."

He fumbled for his pocket-case. Grimsby is a man who will go far. He is the youngest detective inspector in the service, and he has that priceless gift—the art of using other people for the furtherance of his own ends. I do not intend this criticism unkindly. Grimsby does nothing dishonourable and seeks to rob no man of the credit that may be due. There is nothing underhand about Grimsby, but he is exceedingly diplomatic. He imparts official secrets to me with an ingenuousness entirely disarming—but always for reasons of his own.

"Here you are," he said, and passed a letter to me.

It read as follows:

"*To the Right Hon. the Lord Mayor of London.*

"My Lord:

"Beware that the Blue Rajah is not stolen on Wednesday the 13th inst. Do not lose sight of it for one moment.

"Your Lordship's obedient servant,
"Moris Klaw."

"You see," continued Grimsby, "Wednesday the thirteenth is to-morrow, when the thing is being brought to Moorgate Street. Naturally, Sir Michael communicated with the Yard, and as I'm in the know about Moris Klaw, I got the job of looking into the matter. I was at the Mansion House this morning."

"I suppose Sir Michael regards this note with suspicion?"

"Well, he's not silly enough to suppose that any body who thought of stealing the diamond would drop him a line advising him of the matter! But he'd never heard of Moris Klaw until I explained about him. When I told him that Klaw had a theory about the Cycle of Crime, and his letter probably meant that, according to said theory, on Wednesday the thirteenth the Blue Rajah was due to be lifted, so to speak, he laughed! You'll have noticed that people mostly laugh at first about Moris Klaw?"

"Certainly. You did, yourself!"

"I know it and I'm suffering for it! Klaw won't lift his little finger when I ask him; and as for his daughter, she giggles as though she was looking at a comedian when she looks at me! She thinks I'm properly funny!"

"You've been to Wapping, then?"

"Yes, this afternoon. The Lord Mayor wanted a lot of convincing that Moris Klaw was on the straight after I'd told him that the old gentleman was a dealer in curios in the East End. Finally, he suggested that I should find out what the warning meant exactly. But I couldn't get to see Klaw; his daughter said he was out."

"I suppose every precaution will be taken?"

"To-morrow morning we have arranged that I and two other C.I.D. men are to accompany the party to the safe deposit vaults to fetch the diamond and we shall guard it on the way back afterward."

"Who's going to fetch it?"

"Sir John Carron, representing the India Office, Mr. Mark Anderson—the expert—representing the city, and Mr. Gautami Chinje, representing the Gaekwar of Nizam. I was wondering"—he surveyed the burning end of his cigarette— "if you had time to run down to Wapping yourself and find out from what direction we ought to look for trouble?"

"Sorry, Grimsby," I replied; "I would do it with pleasure, but my evening is fully taken up. Personally, it appears to me that Moris Klaw's warning was a timely one. You seem to be watching the stone pretty closely."

"Like a cat watches a mouse!" he rapped. "If any one steals the Blue Rajah tomorrow, he'll be a clever fellow."

II

Basinghall House, Moorgate Street, is built around a courtyard. You enter under an archway, and find offices before you, offices to right and offices to left. As a matter of fact, Basinghall House was designed for a hotel, but subsequently let off in suites of chambers. The offices of Messrs. Anderson & Brothers are on the left, as you enter, and from the window of the principal's sanctum you may look down into the courtyard.

The room chosen for the meeting on Wednesday morning, however, was one opening off this. In Common with the adjoining office as I have said, that of the principal—it had a second door, opening on a corridor. This latter door, however, was never used and was always kept double-locked. Thus, the doorway from the other office was really its only means of entrance or egress. A large window offered a prospect of the courtyard.

At a quarter to eleven on Wednesday morning, Mr. Anderson (one of the City Aldermen) entered his own private office from the corridor. He was accompanied by Sir John Carron, Mr. Gautami Chinje, and Inspector Grimsby. These three had come with him from the safe deposit vaults. Mr. Anderson had possession of the case containing the diamond.

In the office, already awaiting the party, were Sir Michael Cayley (the Lord Mayor); Mr. Morrison Dell, of the Goldsmiths & Silversmiths Company; Sir Vernon Rankin (ex-Lord Mayor); Mr. Werner, of the great engineering firm; and Mr. Anderson, junior. These constituted the Presentation Committee duly appointed by the City of London (excluding, of course, Sir John Carron, of the India Office; Mr. Chinje, representing the vendor of the jewel; and Mr. Grimsby, representing New Scotland Yard).

"We are all present, gentlemen," said Mr. Anderson. "But before we proceed to the business which brings us here, we will enter the inner room, where we shall be quite private."

Accordingly the party of eight passed through the doorway; and Mr. Anderson, senior, entering last, relocked the door behind him. Inspector Grimsby remained alone in the private office.

Eight oaken chairs and a small oaken table bearing a pewter inkpot, two pens, and a blotting pad represent, with a square of red carpet and a framed photograph bearing the legend: "Jagersfontein Diamond Workings, Orange Free State, 1909," an inventory of the furniture.

The company being seated, Mr. Anderson, by the table, rose and said:

"Gentlemen, our business this morning can be briefly dealt with. I have here"—he produced a leather case, opened it and placed it on the table before him— "the diamond known as the Blue Rajah. Its history may be summarized thus: It appeared in the year 1680 and is supposed to have been found in the Kollur Mine, on the Kostna. It had a weight of 254½ carats in the rough, but was reduced to 132 carats in the cutting. It has been successively owned by Nadir Shah, Princess de Lambelle, the Sultan Abdúl Hámid, Mr. Simon Rabstein of New York, and, finally, the Gaekwar of Nizam. It has no flaws; in fact, two of the original facets were retained when the stone passed through the cutter's hands. It is rose cut and its colour is of the finest water, having the rare blue tint."

He paused, raising the diamond from its receptacle, and holding it in his hand. The sunlight, pouring in through the window, struck flame-spears from the wonderful thing.

"In fact, gentlemen," he concluded, "the Blue Rajah is a fitting offering for the City of London to make to the Crown."

"Hear, hear!" chorused the others; and the diamond was passed from hand to hand. The formal business of making over the stone to the Committee was then transacted. A huge check was placed in the pocket-case of Mr. Gautami Chinje, autographs were affixed to two formidable documents; and the Blue Rajah became the property of the loyal City of London.

"You see," said Sir John Carron, holding the stone daintily between thumb and forefinger, and pointing, lecturer-fashion, "the diamond is perfectly proportioned, being a full three fifths as deep as it is broad."

"Quite so," agreed Mr. Morris Dell, looking over his shoulder.

"It is the most perfectly proportioned stone I have ever handled, Sir John," said the younger Mr. Anderson—and he stood back surveying the gem with the caressing glance of a connoisseur.

Sir John turned and tenderly laid the diamond in its case. At which moment, exactly, arose a blood-curdling scream in the courtyard below,

"Good Lord!" cried Mr. Werner. "What is that?"

There was a crowded rush to the window—those in the second rank peering over the heads and shoulders of those in the first. The horrid cries continued, in a choking yet shrill crescendo.

"Ah! God in Heaven! You are killing me! No! No! Mercy! . . . Mercy! . . . Mercy! . . ."

"It is someone in the archway," said Sir Vernon Rankin, excitedly. "Can any of you see him?"

No one could, though all craned necks vigorously.

"Unfortunately, the window cannot be opened," cried Mr. Anderson. "The catch has jammed in some way. I am having it removed immediately."

The cries ceased. People were running about below, and the blue uniform of a city constable showed among the group in the archway.

"I'll run down and see what has happened," said Mr. Chinje, stepping to the door which opened on the corridor. "Hullo! it is locked!"

Young Mr. Anderson turned to him with a smile.

"Both doors are locked, Mr. Chinje," he said. "For the time being we are virtually prisoners."

"Give me the case," said his father, selecting the key of the door communicating with his private office. "There is no occasion for further delay."

The Lord Mayor turned from the window, through which he had still been vainly peering, and stepped to the table.

"Mr. Anderson!"

"Yes?" said the latter, glancing back, keys in hand.

"Have you the diamond?"

"Certainly not!"

"Then who has it?"

No one had it. But the case was empty!

III

Mr. Anderson replaced the keys in his pocket. His ruddy face suddenly had grown pale. Sir Michael Cayley, the empty case in his hand, stood staring across the room like a man dazed. Then he forced speech to his lips.

"Gentlemen," he said, "since it is physically impossible for the diamond to have left this room, in this room it must be searched for—and found. First, is it by any chance upon the floor?"

A brief examination showed that it was not.

"Then," continued Sir Michael, "the painful conclusion is unavoidable that it is upon someone's person!"

An angry murmur arose. Mr. Anderson raised his hand.

"Gentlemen," he said, "Sir Michael states no more than the fact."

And, his face remaining very pale, he removed his coat and waitscoat and threw them upon the table, emptied his trouser pockets and turned out the linings.

"Be good enough to examine them, gentlemen," he said.

There was a momentary hesitation; but the Lord Mayor stepped forward and in a businesslike way examined the contents of the several pockets. He turned to Mr. Anderson.

"Thank you," he said. "If the others are satisfied, I am."

There was a murmur of assent; and as the owner of the office picked up his property, Sir Michael, in turn, submitted himself to examination. All the others followed suit, without further hesitation. And the result of the inquiry was *nil*.

Eight anxious faces surrounded the little table.

"I suggest,' said Mr. Anderson, quietly, "that we admit the detective who is in my office. His experience may enable him to succeed where we have failed."

All agreeing, the communicating door was opened. Mr. Anderson, without quitting the room, called to Inspector Grimsby. The inspector entered. The door was relocked.

"Inspector," said Mr. Anderson, "the diamond is missing!"

Whereupon Grimsby's eyes opened widely in amazement.

"Are you sure, sir?"

"Unfortunately, I cannot doubt it."

"When did you last see it?"

"At the moment when that uproar broke out below," said Mr. Dell.

"Ah," murmured Grimsby, thoughtfully. "You all rushed to the window, I expect?"

"Exactly."

"Leaving the diamond on the table?"

"Yes."

"That's when it was stolen!"

"Very possibly, Inspector," said the Lord Mayor, a stoutly built man with an imperious manner. "But who took it and where did he conceal it?"

"You must all submit to be searched, gentlemen!"

"We have already done so."

"I am more used to that sort of thing. Do you all agree to being searched by me?"

All did. The previous performance was repeated. Grimsby not only searched the garments but passed his hands all over the persons of the eight, even making them open their mouths and tapping at their teeth with a lead pencil!

"I did some I.D.B. work in South Africa," he explained. "It's wonderful where a clever man can hide a diamond."

But no diamond was found!

The better to bring home to those who read these records the truly amazing nature of this circumstance, I will explain again, here, the construction and furniture of the apartment.

It was a small room, some fourteen feet by eighteen. It contained eight oak chairs and an oak table; a red carpet; its walls were distempered and bare, save for the framed photograph previously mentioned. The one window was closed and fastened. The door opening on the corridor was double-locked. Save when it had been opened to admit Grimsby, the door communicating with the next office had also been locked throughout the course of the meeting. There was no fireplace. Ventilation was provided for by a small, square ventilator above the corridor door.

Having convinced himself that the diamond was not upon the person of any one present, Inspector Grimsby took but two or three minutes to satisfy himself that it was not concealed elsewhere.

"Gentlemen," he said, slowly, "the Blue Rajah is not in this room!"

The Lord Mayor glared. He was a director of the company with which the diamond was insured.

"My good man," he said, "it isn't humanly possible for anything—anything—to have gone out of this room since we entered it!"

"I'm disposed to agree with you, sir," replied Grimsby. "But at the same time I'll stake my reputation that the diamond isn't inside these four walls! Although my search of you gentlemen was a mere formality, I assure you it was thorough. I've searched a few score Kaffirs and I know my business. As to the room itself, it's as bare as a drawing board. A child could find the smallest bead in it inside twenty seconds. You can take it from me as a stone certainty that the diamond has gone!"

"Then we are wasting precious time!" cried Sir Michael. "Commence the pursuit at one; Inspector!"

Grimsby's jaw shot out doggedly.

"If you could give me a hint where to begin, sir," he said, "I shouldn't waste another second!"

"Hang it all, that's your business, my man!"

"I know it is, sir. But I'm only a poor human policeman, after all. We sha'n't gain anything by getting angry, shall we? This room, to all intents and purposes, is a locked box from which something has been abstracted without lifting the lid. That's a conjuring trick, and as puzzling to me as it is to you."

Sir Michael softened. Inspector Grimsby is not a man who can be browbeaten.

"Quite right, Inspector," he said; "I recognize the difficulties. But this loss is horrible. It reflects upon all of us—all of us. If the news of this theft leaks out—if the stone cannot be recovered—a certain stigma—I cannot blind myself to the fact—a certain stigma will attach to our personal integrity. Clean as our records may be, we cannot hope to escape it. For God's sake, Inspector, set your wits to work."

Indeed, those were anxious faces that surrounded the detective. Suddenly—

"Ah!" cried the Lord Mayor, "the man Klaw! On his own showing he knows something of this matter! Mr. Grimsby—"

Grimsby held up his hand and nodded.

"With your permission, gentlemen," he said, "I will try to get into communication with Moris Klaw at once."

"Good," said Mr. Anderson; "and meanwhile, whilst we await the result of your efforts, Inspector, I suggest, in the interests of all, that we lunch in my office. It may be inconvenient for many of you, but for my own part I am anxious to remain on these premises until we have news of the whereabouts of the diamond."

The proposal was carried unanimously. No one of those substantial men of affairs was anxious to lay himself open to the suspicion of having removed the great Blue Rajah from the office! For, as Sir Michael quite justly had pointed out, where a diamond worth an emperor's ransom is concerned, reputations melt like ice beneath a tropical sun.

In this way, then, I found myself concerned in the case; for Grimsby hastened to call me up, begging me to urge the retiring Moris Klaw to quit his Wapping haunt, to which he clung like Diogenes to his wooden cavern, and to journey to Moorgate Street. Fortunately, I was in my rooms, and, willing enough to enjoy an opportunity of studying Klaw at work, I despatched a district messenger to him, trusting that he would be at his shop.

Since evidently he had apprehended that an attempt would be made this morning, I did not doubt that he would be at home. Indeed, he rang me up less than half an hour later and arranged to meet me at Mr. Anderson's office.

"I warned him—that Lord Mayor," came his rumbling continental tones along the wire, "how he must not let it out of his sight. He ignored me. So! Ring him up immediately, and tell him to have ready for me hot black coffee. It stimulates the inner perception when green tea is not obtainable."

Without delay I followed Moris Klaw's instructions, and then hurried out and into a cab. My duties, as Klaw's biographer—self-appointed—forbade my delaying.

We arrived at Basinghall House simultaneously. Our cabs drew up one behind the other. Except for the presence of Inspector Grimsby at the entrance, there was nothing to show that a stupendous robbery had been committed there less than an hour before. As I descended, Grimsby ran and opened the door of the other cab. He offered his hand to the beautiful girl who was within, according her all the nervous deference due to a queen.

And indeed no queen of ancient times could have looked more queenly than Isis Klaw—no Hatshepsu could have carried herself more regally. She wore a dark, close-fitting costume and ermine furs. In contrast to the snowy peltry, her large black eyes and perfect red lips rendered her a study for the brush of a painter, but, like her Oriental grace, defied the pen of the scribe.

Moris Klaw's daughter, her dazzling beauty enhanced by all the feminine arts of Paris, was a rare exotic one would not have sought in the neighbourhood of Wapping Old Stairs. But her father afforded a contrast at least as singular as her residence.

Behind this seductive vision he appeared, enveloped in his caped coat, his yellow bearded face crowned by the brown bowler of Early Victorian pattern—indeed, apparently of Early Victorian manufacture. He peered at the taximeter through his gold-rimmed pince-nez.

"Two and tenpence," he rumbled, hoarsely. "That meter requires inspection, my friend. I have watched it popping up those two pennies, and I have perceived that it does so every time the cab bumps upon a drain-hole. I am to pay, then, for all the drains between Wapping and Moorgate Street. Here it is—three shillings. One and fourpence for the company and one and eightpence for yourself."

He turned aside, raising his hat.

"Good morning, Mr. Searles! Good morning, Mr. Grimsby! I shall charge the City of London one and sixpence for drains. Let us walk on as far as the courtyard I see yonder, and you shall tell me all the facts before I interview those others, who will be, of course, so prejudiced by their misfortune."

We passed on, and many a clerkly glance followed the furry figure of Isis beneath the archway. Hemmed in by offices, a certain quietude prevailed in the courtyard.

"It is a chilly morning," said Moris Klaw; "but here we will stop and talk."

Accordingly Grimsby related the known facts of the case, more often addressing his story to the girl than to her father.

"Yes, yes," growled the latter, when the tale was told; "and this crying out—this screaming of murder—what occasioned it?"

"That's the mystery!" explained the detective. "I wish I had run out at once. I might have learned something. As it is, all I can find out amounts to nothing. The clerks and porters and other people who came flocking to the scene found no one here who knew anything about it!"

"The screamer was missing, eh?"

"Vanished! I can't help thinking it was a ruse; though what anybody profited by it isn't clear."

"It is not clear, you say?" rumbled Moris Klaw. "Ah! you have a fog of the mentality, my friend!" Grimsby flushed.

"Of course," he added, hurriedly, "I can see that it served to divert the attention of the people who ought to have been guarding the diamond. But as both the doors and the window were locked, how did it help to get the stone out of the office?"

Moris Klaw pulled reflectively at his scanty beard.

"We shall see," he rumbled. "Let us ascend."

We entered the lift and went up to the office of Messrs. Anderson & Brothers. The Presentation Committee were awaiting the mysterious Moris Klaw but had not anticipated a visit from a pretty woman. They were prepared to adopt toward the man who would seem to have had some foreknowledge of the robbery a certain attitude of suspicion. It was amusing to note the change of front when Isis entered. Moris Klaw singled out the Lord Mayor and the owner of the office with unerring instinct. He removed his hat.

"Good morning, Mr. Anderson!" he said. "Good morning, Sir Michael! Good morning, gentlemen!"

"This is Mr. Moris Klaw," explained Grimsby, "and Miss Klaw. Mr. Searles."

Mr. Anderson hastened to place chairs. We became seated. Following a short interval, Sir Michael Cayley cleared his throat.

"We are—er—indebted to you, Mr. Klaw," he began, for taking this trouble. "But, in view of your note to me—"

Moris Klaw raised his hand.

"So simple," he said, whilst the Committee watched him, puzzled and surprised—that is, those who were not watching Isis did so. "I have a library, you understand, of records dealing with such historic gems. To show you that I have made some study of these matters I will tell you that the diamond called the Blue Rajah was discovered on the morning of April the thirteenth, 1680, in the Kollur Mine, and stolen the same evening!"

"What is your authority for the exact date, Mr. Klaw?" asked Anderson, with interest; "and for the statement that the diamond was stolen on the day of its discovery?"

"Fact, Mr. Anderson, is my authority," was the rumbling reply, "and I can tell you more. The diamond is the birth stone of the month of April, and this diamond was itself born on the thirteenth of that month. To illustrate how its history is associated with April, I shall only tell you of the beautiful and unhappy Marie de Lamballe. This great diamond was presented to her on the ninth of April, 1790, and taken from her on the twelfth of April, 1792, after her return from England, and only six months before her fair head was stuck upon a pike and held up to the Queen's window!"

He paused impressively, waving his long hands in the air.

"I could recount to you," he resumed, "many such incidents in the history of the Blue Rajah—and all took place within a week of its birthday! What day is to-day?"

"Why, it's the thirteenth of April!" said Sir Michael Cayley, with a start.

"The thirteenth of April," rumbled Moris Klaw. "For many years the diamond has been too closely guarded for any new incident to occur, but when I learn how to-day it is to be brought here, how many hands will touch it, how many eyes will look upon it, I know that there is danger! Its history repeats. These incidents" he waved his hands— "proceed in cycles I warned you. But it was perhaps inevitable. The Cycle of Crime is as inevitable and immutable as the cycle of the ages. Man's will has no power to check it."

Everyone in the room was deeply impressed. Indeed, no one could have failed to recognize in the speaker a man of powerful mind, one of penetrating and unusual intellect.

"Had I had the good fortune to meet you, Mr. Klaw," said the Lord Mayor, "I should have attached a greater, and—er—a different, significance to your note. Your theories are strange ones, but to-day they have received strange and ample substantiation. I can only hope—and I do so with every confidence in your great ability"—Moris Klaw rose and bowed— "that you will be able to recover the diamond whose loss you so truly predicted."

"I will ask you," replied Moris Klaw, "to have sent in to me the black coffee. Myself, my daughter, Mr. Searles, and Mr. Grimsby will view the room from which the robbery took place."

"You would wish us to remain here?" asked Mr. Anderson, glancing at the others.

"I would so wish it, yes."

"I hope, Mr. Klaw," said Sir Michael Cayley, "that you will not hesitate to send me an account of your fee and expenditures."

"I shall not so hesitate," replied Moris Klaw.

IV

We entered the small room from which the Blue Rajah had been spirited away. Grimsby, who was badly puzzled, was evidently glad of Klaw's cooperation. Moris Klaw's letter of warning, leading to the request for Moris Klaw's attendance, had enabled the Scotland Yard man to summon that keen intellect to his aid without compromising his professional reputation. He would lose no credit that might accrue if the gem were recovered and, in short, was congratulating himself upon a diplomatic move.

"It's beyond me," he said, "how the thing was got out of the room. With this door shut, the window fastened, and the other door double-locked, as it always is, practically the place is a box."

Moris Klaw, from its hiding place in the lining of his hat, took out the scent spray and squirted verbena upon his face.

"A box—yes," he rumbled, "and so stuffy. No air."

"There's no ventilation," explained Grimsby. "That square hole over the door is intended for ventilation, but as there's no corresponding aperture over the window or elsewhere it's useless. Anyway, it only opens on the passage."

"Ah. You searched them all quite thoroughly?"

"Certainly; like Kaffirs. But I didn't expect to find it."

"Blessed is he who expecteth little. Isis, my child, there is someone knocking."

Isis opened the door communicating with Mr. Anderson's office, and a boy entered carrying a tray with a coffee pot and cup upon it.

"Good," said Moris Klaw. "I shall not sleep in this room, Mr. Searles. It is difficult to sleep in the morning and I cannot wait for night. I shall sit here at this table for one hour with my mind a perfect blank. I shall think of nothing. That is a great art, Mr. Searles—to think of nothing. Few people but ascetics can do it. Try it for yourself, and you will find that thinking of trying not to think is the nearest you will get to it! I shall expose my mind, a sensitive blank, to the etheric waves created here by mental emotion.

"I shall secure many alien impressions of horror at finding the Blue Rajah to be missing. That is unavoidable. But I hope, amongst all these, to find that other thought-thing—the fear of the robber at the critical moment of his crime! That should be a cogent and forceful thought—keener and therefore stronger to survive, because a thought of danger but of gain, than the thoughts of loss with which this atmosphere is laden."

He stood up, removing his caped coat and revealing the shabby tweed suit which he wore. A big French knot of black silk looked grotesquely out of place beneath his yellow face with its edging of toneless beard.

"Isis," he said, "lay my cloak carefully upon that chair by the window. I will sit there."

Grimsby stepped forward to assist.

"No, no!" said Isis, but smiled enchantingly. "No hand but mine must touch it until my father has secured his impression!"

She laid the coat upon the chair, completely covering it; and Moris Klaw sat down.

"Another cup of coffee," he said; and his daughter poured one out and handed it to him. "This is Java coffee and truly not coffee at all. There is no coffee but *Mocha*—a thing you English will never learn. Return in an hour, gentlemen. Isis, ask that no disturbing sound is allowed within or without. That Committee, it can go home. None of it has the diamond."

"And the other gentlemen?" asked Grimsby. "They'll be anxious to get about their business, too. There's Sir John Carron from the India Office and Mr. Gautami Chinje—the Gaekwar's representative."

"Of course—certainly," mused Moris Klaw. "But, of course, too, they will all be anxious to know immediately the result of my inquiries. Listen—Mr. Anderson will remain; he can represent the city. Mr. Chinje, you will perhaps ask him to remain, to represent the Gaekwar—the vendor; and Sir John Carron, he might be so good. Make those arrangements, Mr. Grimsby, and let nothing again disturb me."

We left him, returning to the outer office.

Sir John Carron expressed himself willing to remain.

"If I may use your telephone for a moment, Mr. Anderson," he said, "I can put off an engagement."

Mr. Chinje had no other engagement, and Mr. Anderson's duties had detained him in any event. There was some general, but subdued, conversation before the rest of the party left; but finally Sir John, Chinje, Grimsby, Isis Klaw, and myself found ourselves in a waiting room on the opposite side of the corridor, provided with refreshments, and the gentlemen of the party with cigars, whilst the hospitable and deeply anxious Messrs. Anderson piled the table with periodical literature for our entertainment.

It was a curious interlude, which I shall always remember.

Sir John Carron, a tall, bronzed military man, middle-aged and perfectly groomed, surveyed Isis Klaw through his monocle with undisguised admiration. She bore this scrutiny with the perfect composure which was hers, and presently engaged the admiring baronet in some conversation about India, in which Mr. Chinje presently joined. Chinje had all the quiet self-possession of a high-caste Hindu, and his dark handsome face exhibited no signs of annoyance when Sir John adopted that tone of breezy patronage characteristic of some Anglo-Indian officers who find themselves in the company of a well-bred native. Grimsby, with recognition of his social inferiority written large upon him, smoked, for the most part, in silence—Isis having given him permission to light up. Seeing his covert glances at this intimate trio, I ultimately succeeded in making the conversation a general one, thereby earning the Scotland Yard man's evident gratitude.

"You know, Inspector Grimsby," said Sir John, "I never was searched before to-day! But, by Jove, you did it very efficiently! I was dreadfully tempted to strike you when you calmly turned out my purse! Your method was far more workmanlike than Sir Michael Cayley's a few minutes earlier. He forgot to look in my watch case, but you didn't!"

Grimsby smiled.

"There's more in a simple thing like searching a man than most people take into consideration," he replied. "I've known a Kaffir in the mines who—excuse me, Miss Klaw—wore no more than Adam, to walk off with stones worth my year's wages."

"I'm prepared to accept your assurance, Inspector," said Sir John, "that none of us had the diamond about our persons."

"My father has accepted it," added Isis Klaw; "and that is conclusive."

Which brought us face to face again with the amazing problem that we were there to solve. How, by any known natural law, had the Blue Rajah been taken out of the room? None of us could conjecture. That the detective was hopelessly mystified, his inaction, awaiting the result of Moris Klaw's séance, was sufficient proof. I wondered if the Commissioner would have approved of his passive attitude and entire dependence upon the efforts of an amateur, yet failed to perceive what other he could adopt. One thing was certain: if the diamond was recovered, its recovery would be recorded among Detective Inspector Grimsby's successful cases! And there he sat placidly smoking one of Mr. Anderson's habanas.

At the expiration of the hour specified, Isis Klaw rose and walked across to Mr. Anderson's office. Mr. Anderson, his ruddy face—typically that of a lowland Scot—a shade paler than was its wont, I fancy, was glancing from his watch to the clock.

Isis knocked on the inner door, opened it, and entered. Sir John Carron was watching with intense interest. Mr. Chinje met my glance and smiled a little sceptically.

Moris Klaw came out with his caped coat on and carrying his bowler in his hand.

"Gentlemen," he said, "I have secured a mental negative, some-what foggy, owing to those other thought forms with which the atmosphere is laden. But I have identified him—the thief!"

A sound like a gasp repressed came from somewhere immedi-ately behind me. I turned. Mr. Anderson and Mr. Anderson, jun-ior, stood at my elbow; close by were Mr. Chinje, Grimsby, and Sir John Carron.

"Who snorts?" rumbled Moris Klaw, peering through his pince-nez.

"Not I," said Sir John, staring about him.

We all, in turn, denied having uttered the sound. "Then there is in this office a ghost," declared Klaw, "or a liar!"

"Excuse me, Mr. Klaw," began Mr. Anderson, with some heat.

Moris Klaw raised his hand. His daughter's magnificent eyes blazed defiance at us all.

"No anger," implored the rumbling voice. "No anger. Anger is a misuse of the emotions. There are present eight persons here. Someone snorted. Eight persons deny the snort. It is a ghost or a liar. Am I evident to you?"

"Your logic is irrefutable," admitted the younger Mr. Ander-son, glancing from face to face. "It pains me to have to admit that you are right!"

In turn, I examined the faces of those present. Grimsby was a man witless with wonder. Both the Andersons were embarrassed and angry. Isis Klaw was scornfully triumphant; her father was, as ever, nonchalant. Sir John Carron looked ill at ease; Mr. Chinje appeared to have changed his opinion of the eccentric investigator and now studied him with the calm interest of the cultured Oriental.

"I shall now make you laugh," said Moris Klaw. "I shall tell you what he was thinking of at the psychological instant—that myste-rious thief. He was thinking of two things. One was a very pretty, fair young lady, and the other was a funny thing. He was thinking of throwing twelve peanuts into a parrot's cage!"

V

There are speeches so entirely unexpected that their effect is unappreciable until some little time after the utterance. This speech of Moris Klaw's was of that description. For some moments no one seemed to grasp exactly what he had said, simple though his words had been. Then, it was borne home to us—that grotesque declaration; and I think I have never seen men more amazed.

Could he be jesting?

"Mr. Klaw—" began Sir John Carron. But—

"One moment, Sir John," interrupted Klaw. "Let all remain here for one moment. I shall return."

Whilst we stared, like so many fools, he shuffled from the office with his awkward gait. During his brief absence no one spoke. We were restrained, undoubtedly, by the presence of Isis Klaw, who, one hand upon her hip and with the other swinging her big ermine muff, smiled at us with a sort of pitying scorn for our stupidity.

Moris Klaw returned.

"Let me see," he rumbled, reflectively, "have you, Sir John Carron or Mr. Chinje, a specimen of the handwriting of the Gaekwar of Nizam?"

Chinje and Sir John stared.

"At the office—possibly," replied Sir John.

"I have my instructions, signed by him," said Mr. Chinje. "But not here."

"At your hotel, yes?"

"Yes," replied Chinje, shortly.

He gave me the impression that he resented Moris Klaw's catechizing as that of a fool and an incompetent meddler with affairs of great importance.

"Then, gentlemen," said Klaw, "we must adjourn to examine that signature."

"Really," the younger Mr. Anderson burst out, "I must protest against this! You will pardon me, Mr. Klaw; I believe you to be sincere in your efforts on our behalf, but such an expedition can be no more than a wild-goose chase! What can the Gaekwar's signature have to do with the theft of the diamond?"

"I will tell you something, my feverish friend," said Moris Klaw, slowly. "The Blue Rajah is not on these premises. It is gone! It went before I came. If it is ever to come back you will put on your hat and accompany me to examine the signature to Mr. Chinje's instructions."

"I must add my protest to Mr. Anderson's," remarked Chinje. "This is mere waste of time."

"Mr. Grimsby," resumed Klaw, placidly, "it is a case to be hushed up, this. There must be no arrests!"

"Eh?" cried Grimsby.

"Sir John Carron will ring up the Commissioner and he will say that Detective-Inspector Grimsby has traced the Blue Rajah, which was stolen, but that, for reasons of state, Detective-Inspector Grimsby will make a confidential report and no arrest!"

"Really—" began Sir John.

"Mr. Klaw," cried Anderson, interrupting excitedly. "You are jesting with men who are faced by a desperate position! I ask you, as man to man, if you know who stole the Blue Rajah and where it is?"

"I reply," rumbled Moris Klaw, "that I suspect who stole it, that I am doubtful how it was stolen, and that when I have examined the Gaekwar's signature I may know where it is!"

His reply had a tone of finality quite unanswerable His attitude was that of a stone wall; and he had, too, something of the rugged strength of such a wall—of a Roman wall, commanding respect.

Sir John got into communication with the Commissioner, as desired by Klaw, and we all left the office and went down in the lift to the hall.

"Two cabs will be needful," said Moris Klaw; and two cabs were summoned.

Sir John Carron, the Andersons, and Moris Klaw entered one; Isis Klaw, Grimsby, Chinje, and I the other.

"The Hotel Astoria," directed Chinje.

Throughout the drive to the Strand, Isis chatted to Grimsby, to his great delight. Mr. Chinje contented himself with monosyllabic replies to my occasional observations. He seemed to be disgusted with the manner in which the inquiry was being conducted. When the two cabs drove into the courtyard of the hotel, the one in which I was seated followed the other. Mr. Chinje, on my left, descended first, and Moris Klaw also descended first from the cab in front. As he did so he stumbled on the step and clutched at Chinje for support. Isis leapt forward to his assistance.

"Ah," growled Klaw, hobbling painfully, and resting one hand upon Chinje's shoulder and the other upon his daughter's. "That foolish ankle of mine! How unfortunate! An accident, Mr. Chinje, which I met with in Egypt. I fell quite twenty feet in the shaft of a tomb and broke my ankle. At the least strain, I suffer yet."

"Allow me, Mr. Chinje," said Grimsby, stepping forward.

"No, no!" rumbled Klaw. "If you will hand me my hat which I have dropped, and see that my verbena has not fallen out—thank you—Mr. Chinje and Isis will be so good as to walk with me to the lift. A few moments' rest in Mr. Chinje's apartments will restore me."

This arrangement accordingly was adopted, and we presently came to the rooms occupied by the Gaekwar's representative, upon the fourth floor of the hotel. At the door, Mr. Chinje asked me to take his place whilst he found his key.

I did so and Chinje opened the door. To my great surprise he entered first. To my greater surprise, Moris Klaw, scorning my assistance and apparently forgetting his injury, rapidly followed him in. The rest of us flocked behind, possessed with a sense of something impending. We little knew *what* impended.

One thing, as I entered the little sitting room, struck my vision with a sensation almost of physical shock. It was a large, empty parrot cage standing on the table!

I had an impression that Chinje dashed forward in a vain attempt to conceal the cage ere Moris Klaw entered. I saw, as one sees figures in a dream, a pretty, fair-haired girl in the room. Then the Hindu had leapt to an inner door—and was gone!

"Quick!" cried Klaw, in a loud voice. "The door! The door!"

He brushed the girl aside with a sweep of his arm and hurled himself against the locked door.

"Mr. Grimsby! Mr. Searles! Someone! Help with this door. Isis! hold her back this foolish girl!"

The inner meaning of the scene was a mystery to us all, but the urgency of Moris Klaw's instructions brooked no denial. With a shrill scream the girl threw herself upon him, but Isis, exhibiting unsuspected strength, drew her away.

Then Sir John Carron joined Klaw at the door and they applied their combined weights to the task of forcing it open.

Once they put their shoulders to it; twice—and there was a sound of tearing woodwork; a third time—and it flew open, almost precipitating them both into the room beyond. Hard on the din of the opening rang the crack of a pistol shot. A wisp of smoke came floating out.

"Ah, just God!" said Moris Klaw, hoarsely, "we are too late!"

And, at his words, with a leap like that of a wild thing, the fair girl broke from Isis, and passing us all, entered the room beyond. Awed and fearful, we followed and looked upon a pitiful scene.

Gautami Chinje lay dead upon the floor, a revolver yet between his nerveless fingers and a red spot in his temple. Beside him knelt the girl, plucking with both hands at her lower lip, her face as white as paper and her eyes glaring insanely at the distorted features.

"Dearest," she kept whispering, in a listless way, "my dearest— what is the matter? I have the diamond—I have it in my bag. What is it, my dearest?"

We got her away at last.

"He had only been in London six months," Moris Klaw rumbled in my ear, "and you see, she adored him—helped him to steal. It is wonderful, snakelike, the power of fascination some Hindus have over women—and always over blondes, Mr. Searles, always blondes. It is a psychological problem."

So ended the case of the Blue Rajah robbery, one of the most brief in the annals of Moris Klaw. The great diamond we found in the girl's handbag, wrapped in a curious little rubber covering, apparently made to fit it.

"You see," explained Moris Klaw, later, to his wondering audience, "this girl—I have yet to find out who she is—was perhaps married to Mr. Chinje. He would, of course, have deserted her directly he returned to India. But here at the Astoria she was known as Mrs. Chinje. Who would have been the losers by the robbery? The insurance company, if I do not mistake the case. For the Gaekwar, through his representative, Chinje, had the diamond insured for all the time it was his property and in England, and the Committee had it insured from the time it became their property. It had become their property. The Gaekwar would have got his check. He gets it now; it is in Chinje's pocket-case. The city would have lost its Blue Rajah, and the insurance company would have paid the city for the loss!

"The next office along the corridor from Mr. Anderson's is the Central London Electric Lighting Company. Many consumers call. Mrs. Chinje was not suspected of any felonious purpose when she was seen in that corridor—and she was seen by a clerk and by an engineer. After my mental negative had told me of a pretty young lady of whom the thief thinks at the moment of his theft, I went to inquire—you recall?—if such a one had been seen near the office.

"From the first my suspicions are with Chinje. The emotions have each a note, distinct, like the notes of a piano, though only audible to the trained mind. Both Isis and myself detect from Chinje the note of *fear*. I arrange, then, that he remains. My talk of examining the Gaekwar's writing is a ruse. It is Chinje's apartment and the fair lady I expect to find there that I am anxious to see.

"Then, in spite that he is the most cool of us all, I see that he suspects me and I have to hold him fast; for, if he could have got first to his room and hidden the parrot cage, where had been our evidence? Indeed, only that I have the power to secure the astral negative, there had been no evidence at all. There is a third accomplice—him who howled in the courtyard; but I fear, as he so cleverly vanished, we shall never know his name.

"And how was it done, and why did this someone howl?"

Moris Klaw paused and looked around. We awaited his next words in tense silence.

"He howled because Chinje had looked out from the window (which, though hidden, the howler was watching) and made him some signal. The signal meant: 'The Blue Rajah has been placed upon the table—*howl!*'

"The one below obeyed, and the Committee, like foolish sheep—yes, gentlemen, like no-headed cattle things!—flocked to the window. But Chinje did not flock with them! Like a deft-handed conjurer he was at the table, the diamond was in the little rubber purse held ready, and Mrs. Chinje, with her large handbag open, was waiting outside the door, in the corridor, like some new kind of wicket-keeper. Chinje tossed the diamond through the little square ventilator!

"He had been practising for weeks—ever since he knew that the Committee would meet in that room—tossing peanuts into the square opening of a parrot cage, placed at the same height from the floor as the ventilator over Mr. Anderson's doorway! He had practised until he could do it twelve times without missing. He had nerves like piano wires, yet he was a deadly anxious man; and he knew that a woman cannot catch!

"But she caught—or, if she dropped it, no one saw her pick it up.

"Gentlemen, these Hindus are very clever, but talking of their cleverness makes one very thirsty. I think I heard Mr. Anderson make some cooling speech about a bottle of wine!"

CASE OF THE WHISPERING POPLARS

I

One afternoon Moris Klaw walked into my office and announced that "owing to alterations" he had temporarily suspended business at the Wapping emporium, and thus had found time to give me a call. I always welcomed a chat with that extraordinary man, and although I could conceive of no really useful "alteration" to his unsavoury establishment other than that of setting fire to it, I made no inquiries, but placed an easy chair for him and offered a cigar.

Moris Klaw removed his caped overcoat and dropped it upon the floor. Upon this sartorial wreckage he disposed his flat-topped brown bowler and from it extracted the inevitable scent spray. He sprayed his dome-like brow and bedewed his toneless beard with verbena.

"So refreshing," he explained; "a custom of the Romans, Mr. Searles. It is a very warm day."

I admitted that this was so.

"My daughter Isis," continued Klaw, "has taken advantage of the alterations and decorations to run over so far as Paris."

I made some commonplace remark, and we drifted into a conversation upon a daring robbery which at that time was flooding the press with copy. We were so engaged when, to my great surprise (for I had thought him at least a thousand miles away), Shan Haufmann was announced. As my old American friend entered, Moris Klaw modestly arose to depart. But I detained him and made the two acquainted.

Haufmann hailed Klaw cordially, exhibiting none of the ill-bred surprise which so often greeted my eccentric acquaintance of singular aspect. Haufmann had all that bonhomie which overlooks the clothes and welcomes the man. He glanced apologetically at his right hand which hung in a sling.

"Can't shake, Mr. Klaw," said the big American, a good-humoured smile on his tanned, clean-shaven face. "I stopped some lead awhile back and my right is still off duty."

Naturally I was anxious at once to know how he had come by the hurt; and he briefly explained that in the discharge of certain official duties he had run foul of a bad gang, two of whom he had been instrumental in convicting of murder, whilst the third had shot him in the arm and escaped.

"Three dagoes," he explained, in his crisply picturesque fashion, "—been wanted for years. Helped themselves to a bunch of my colts this fall; killed one of the boys and left another for dead. So I went after them hot and strong. We rounded them up on the Mexican border and got two—Schwart Sam and one of the Costas; but the younger Costa—we call him Corpus Chris—broke away and found me in the elbow with a lump of lead!"

"So you've come for a holiday?"

"Mostly," replied Haufmann. "Greta hustled me here. She got real ill when I said I wouldn't come. So we came! I'm centring in London for six months. Brought the girls over for a look round. I'm not stopping at a hotel. We've rented a house a bit outside; it's Lal's idea. Settled yesterday. All fixed. Expect you to dinner to-night! You, too, Mr. Klaw! Is it a bet?"

Moris Klaw was commencing some sort of a reply, but what it was never transpired, for Haufmann, waving his sound hand cheerily, quitted the office as rapidly as he had entered, calling back:

"Dine seven-thirty. Girls expecting you!"

That was his way; but so infectious was his real geniality that few could fail to respond to it.

"He is a good fellow, that Mr. Haufmann," rumbled Moris Klaw. "Yes, I love such natures. But he has forgotten to tell us where he lives!"

It was so! Haufmann in his hurry and impetuosity had over-looked that important matter; but I thought it probable that he would recall the oversight and communicate, so prevailed upon Klaw to remains At last, however, I glanced at my watch, and found it to be nearly six o'clock, whereupon I looked blankly at Moris Klaw. That eccentric shrugged his shoulders and took up the caped coat. Then the 'phone bell rang. It was Haufmann.

I was glad to hear his familiar accent as he laughingly apolo-gized for his oversight. Rapidly he acquainted me with the where-abouts of The Grove—for so the house was called.

"Come now," he said. "Don't stop to dress; you've only just got time," and rang off.

I thought Moris Klaw stared oddly through his pince-nez when I told him the address, but concluded, as he made no comment, that I had been mistaken. There was just time to catch our train, and from the station where we alighted it was only a short drive to the house Haufmann's car was waiting for us, and in less than three quarters of an hour from our quitting the Strand, we were driving up to The Grove, through the most magnificent avenue of poplars I had ever seen.

"By Jove!" I cried, "what fine trees!"

Moris Klaw nodded and looked around at the towering trunks with a peculiar expression, which I was wholly at a loss to account for. However, ere I had leisure to think much about the matter, we found ourselves in the hall, where Haufmann and his two fasci-nating daughters were waiting to greet us.

I do not know which of the girls looked the more charming: Lilian with her bright mass of curls and blue eyes dancing with vivacity, or Greta in her dark and rather mystic beauty. At any rate, they were dangerous acquaintances for a susceptible man. Even old Moris Klaw showed unmistakably that his mind was not so wholly filled with obscure sciences as to be incapable of appreci-ating the society of a pretty woman.

Greta I noticed looking thoughtfully at him, and during dinner she suddenly asked him if he had read a book called "Psychic Angles."

Rather unwillingly, as it seemed to me, Klaw admitted that he had, and the girl displayed an immediate and marked interest in psychical matters. Klaw, however, though usually but too willing to discuss this, his pet subject, foiled her attempt to draw him into a technical discussion and rather obviously steered the conversation into a more general channel.

"Don't let her get away on the bogey tack, Mr. Klaw," said Haufmann, approvingly. "She's a perfect demon for haunted chambers and so on."

Laughingly the girl pleaded guilty to an interest in ghostly subjects. "But I'm not frightened about them!" she added, in pretended indignation. "I should just love to see a ghost."

"Oh, Greta!" cried her sister. "What a horrid idea."

"You have perhaps investigated cases yourself, Mr. Klaw?" asked Greta

"Yes," rumbled Klaw, "perhaps so. Who knows?"

Since he thus clearly showed his wish to drop the subject, the girl made a little humorously wry face, whereat her father laughed boisterously; and no more was said during the evening about ghosts. I could not well avoid noticing two things, however, in regard to Moris Klaw: one, his evident interest in Greta; and the other, a certain preoccupation which claimed him every now and again.

We left at about ten o'clock, declining the offer of the car, as we had ample time to walk to the station. Haufmann wanted to come along, but we dissuaded him, with the assurance that we could find the way without any difficulty. Klaw, especially, was very insistent on the point, and when at last we swung sharply down the avenue and, rounding the bend, lost sight of the house, he pulled up and said:

"For this opportunity, Mr. Searles, I have been waiting It may not, of course, matter, but this house where the good Haufmann resides was formerly known as The Park."

"What of that?" I asked, turning on him sharply.

"It is," he replied, "celebrated as what foolish people call a haunted house. No doubt that is the reason why the name has been changed. As The Park it has been dealt with many times in the psychical journals."

"The Park," I mused. "Is it not included in that extraordinary work on the occult— 'Psychic Angles'—of which Miss Haufmann spoke to-night—the place where the monk was supposed to have been murdered, where an old antiquary died, and some young girl, too, if I remember rightly?"

"Yes," replied Moris Klaw, "yes. I will tell you a secret. 'Psychic Angles' is a little book of my own, and so, of course, I know about this place."

His words surprised me greatly, for the book was being generally talked about. He peered around him into the shadows and seemed to sniff the air suspiciously.

"Setting aside the question of any supernatural menace," I said, "directly the servants find out, as they are sure to do from others in the neighbourhood, they will leave *en bloc*. It is a pleasant way servants have in such cases."

"We must certainly tell him, the good Haufmann," agreed Klaw, "and he will perhaps arrange to quit the place without letting the ladies to know of its reputation. That Miss Greta she has the sympathetic mind"—he tapped his forehead— "the plate so sensitive, the photo film so delicate! For her it is dangerous to remain. There is such a thing, Mr. Searles, as sympathetic suicide! That girl she is mediumistic. From The Park she must be removed."

"There is no time to lose," I said. "We must decide what to do to-night. Suppose you come along to my place?"

Moris Klaw agreed, and we resumed our walk through the poplar grove.

Although the night was very still, an eerie whispering went on without pause or cessation along the whole length of the avenue. Against the star-spangled sky the tall trees reared their shapes in a manner curiously suggestive of dead things. Or this fancy may have had birth in the associations of the place. It was a fatally easy matter mentally to fashion one of the poplars into the gaunt form of a monk; and no one, however unimaginative, being acquainted with the history of The Grove, could fail to find, in the soft and ceaseless voices of the trees, something akin to a woman's broken sighs. In short, I was not sorry when the gate was passed, and we came out upon the high road.

Later, seated in my study, we discussed the business thoroughly. From my bookcase I took down "Psychic Angles" and passed it to Moris Klaw.

"There we are," he rumbled, turning over the leaves. I read: "On August 8, 1858, a Fra Giulimo, of a peculiar religious brotherhood who occupied this house from 1851 to 1858, was found strangled at the foot of a poplar close by the entrance gate." "I could never find out much about them, this brotherhood," he added, looking up; "but they were, I believe, decent people. They left the place almost immediately after the crime. No arrest was ever made. Then"—referring to the book— "'about the end of February or early in the March of 1863, a Mr. B— J— took the house. He was an antiquarian of European repute and a man of retired habits. With only two servants—an old soldier and his wife—he occupied The Park'—that is The Grove— 'from the spring of '63 to the autumn of '65.' Then follow verbatim reports by the well known Pepley of interviews with people who had heard Mr. J— declare that a hushed voice sometimes called upon him by name in the night, from the poplar grove. Also, an interview with his man-servant and with wife of latter, corroborating other statements. Mr. B— J— was found one September morning dead in the grove. Cause of death never properly established. The house next enters upon a period of neglect. It is empty; it is shunned. From '65 right up to '88 it stood so empty. It was then taken by a Mr. K—; but he only occupied it for two months, this K—. Three other tenants subsequently rented the place. Only one of them actually occupied it—for a week; the other, hearing, we presume, of its evil repute, never entered into residence. Seventeen years ago the last tragedy connected with the unpleasant Grove took place. An eccentric old bachelor took the house, and, in the summer of '03, had a niece there to stay with him. The evidence clearly indicates to me that this unhappy one was highly neurotic—oh, clearly; so that the tragedy explains itself. She fell, or sprang, from her bedroom window to the drive one night in June, and was picked up quite dead at the foot of the first poplar in the grove. *Sacré!* it is a morgue, that house!"

He returned the book and sat watching me in silence for some moments.

"Did you spend any time in the house, yourself?" I asked.

"On four different occasions, Mr. Searles! It is only from certain of the rooms that the whispering is audible, and then only if the windows are open. You will notice, though, that all the tragedies occurred in the warm months when the windows would be so open."

"Did you note anything supernormal in this whispering?"

"Nothing. You have read my explanation."

II

Haufmann looked rather blank when we told him.

"Just my luck!" he commented. "Greta's read your book, Mr. Klaw, and if she hasn't fixed it yet she's sure to come to it that The Park and The Grove are one and the same. It was largely because of her I arranged this trip," he added. "The trouble I've told you about got on her nerves and she had the idea some guy was tracking her around. The medicos said it was a common enough symptom and ordered a change. Anyhow, I quitted, to give her a chance to tone up. Confound this business!"

He ultimately left quite determined to change his place of residence. But so averse was his practical mind from the idea of inconveniencing oneself on such ghostly grounds, that two weeks slipped by, and still the Haufmanns occupied The Grove. The decoration of Moris Klaw's establishment being presumably still in progress, Klaw accompanied me on more than one other occasion to visit Shan Haufmann and the girls. At last, one afternoon, Greta asked him pointblank if he thought the house to be that dealt with in "Psychic Angles."

Of course, he had to admit that it was so; but far from exhibiting any signs of alarm, the girl appeared to be delighted.

"How dense I have been!" she cried. "I should have known it from the description! As a matter of fact, I might never have found out, but this morning the servants resigned unanimously!"

Klaw looked at me significantly. All was befalling as we had foreseen.

"They told you, then!" he said. "Yes? No?"

"They said the house was haunted," she replied, "but they didn't seem to know much more about it. That simple fact was enough for them!"

Haufmann came in and in answer to our queries declared himself helpless.

"Lal and Greta won't quit," he declared; "so what's to do? I've cabled for servants from home. Meanwhile, we're at the mercy of day girls and charwomen!"

The concern evinced by Moris Klaw was very great. He seized an early opportunity of taking Haufmann aside and questioning him relative to the situation of the rooms occupied by the family.

"My room overlooks the avenue," replied Haufmann, "and so does Greta's. Lal's is on the opposite side. Come up and see them!"

Klaw and I accompanied him. It was a beautiful clear day, and from his window we gazed along the majestic ranks of poplars, motionless as a giant guard, in the still summer air. It was difficult to conjure up a glamour of the uncanny, with the bright sunlight pouring gladness upon trees, flowers, shrubs, and lawn.

"This is the room from which the whisper is the most clearly audible!" said Moris Klaw. "I could tell you—ah! I spent several nights here!"

"The devil you did," rapped Haufmann. "I must sleep pretty soundly. I've never heard a thing. Greta's room is next on the right. She has said nothing."

Klaw looked troubled.

"There is no sound unusual to hear," he answered. "I quite convinced myself of that. But it is the tradition that speaks, Mr. Haufmann! In those silent watches, even so insensible an old fool as I can imagine almost anything, aided by such gruesome memories.

Excepting the monk, who probably fell foul of a prowler thief, the tragedies are easily to be explained. The old antiquarian died of syncope, and the poor girl, in all probability, fell from the balcony in her sleep. She had a tremendously neurotic temperament."

"It's bad, now Greta knows," mused Haufmann. "Her nerves are all unstrung. It's just the thing I wanted to avoid!"

"Can't you induce her at any rate to change her room?" I suggested.

"No! She's as obstinate as a pony! Her poor mother was the same. It's the Irish blood!"

Such was the situation when we left. No development took place for a couple of days or so, then that befell which we had feared and half expected.

Haufmann walked into my office with:

"It's started! Greta says she hears it every night!"

Prepared though I had been for the news, his harshly spoken words sent a cold shudder through me.

"Haufmann!" I said, sternly. "There must be no more of this. Get the girls away at once. On top of her previous nerve trouble this morbid imagining may affect her mind."

"You haven't heard me out," he went on, more slowly than was his wont. "You talk of morbid imagining. What about this: I've heard it!" I stared at him blankly.

"That's one on you!" he said, with a certain grim triumph. "After Greta said there was something came in the night that wasn't trees rustling, I sat up and smoked. First night I read and nothing happened. Next night I sat in the dark. There was no breeze and I heard nothing for my pains. Third night I stayed in the dark again, and about twelve o'clock a breeze came along. All mixed up with the rustling and sighing of the leaves I heard a voice calling as plain as I ever heard anything in my life! And it called *me!*"

"Haufmann!"

"It blame-well called *me!* I'd take my oath before a jury on it!"

"This is almost incredible!" I said. "I wish Moris Klaw were here."

"Where is he?"

"He is in Paris. He will be away over the weekend."

"I met a man curiously enough," continued Haufmann, "just outside the Charing Cross Tube, on my way here, who's coming down to have a look into the business—a hot man on mysteries." He mentioned the name of a celebrated American detective agency. "I'm afraid it's right outside his radius, but he volunteered and I was glad to have him. I'd like Klaw down though."

"What about the girls?"

"I was going to tell you. They're at Brighton for a while. Greta didn't want to quit, but poor Lal was dead scared! Anyway, I got them off."

The uncanny business claimed entire possession of my mind, and further work was out of the question. I accordingly accompanied Haufmann to the hotel where the detective was lodged and made the acquaintance of Mr. J. Shorter Ottley. He was a typical New Yorker, clean-shaven and sallow complexioned with good gray eyes and an inflexible mouth.

"We don't deal in ghosts!" he said, smilingly; "I never met a ghost that couldn't stop a bullet if it came his way!"

"I'll make a confession to you," remarked Haufmann. "When I heard that soft voice calling, I hadn't the sand to go and look out! How's that for funk?"

"Not funk at all," replied Ottley, quietly. "Maybe it was wisdom!"

"How do you mean?"

"I've got an idea about it, that's all. Did Miss Haufmann hear it the same night?"

"Not the same night I did—no. She seems to have dozed off."

"When she did hear it, was it calling you?"

"She couldn't make out what it called!"

"Did she go to the window?"

"Yes, but she only looked out from behind the blind."

"See anything?"

"No."

"I should have very much liked an interview with her," said Ottley, thoughtfully.

"She could tell you no more than I have."

"About that, no! There's something else I would like to ask her."

That evening we all three dined at The Grove, dinner being prepared by a woman who departed directly we were finished. A des-
ultory game of billiards served to pass the time between twilight
and darkness, and the detective and I departed, leaving Haufmann
alone in the house. This was prearranged by Ottley, who had some
scheme in hand. Side by side we tramped down the poplar avenue,
went out by the big gate, and closed it behind us. We then skirted
the grounds to a point on the side opposite the gate, and, scaling
the wall, found ourselves in a wilderness of neglected kitchen
garden. Through this the American cautiously led the way toward
the house, visible through the tangle of bushes and trees in sharp
silhouette against the sky. On all fours we crossed a little yard and
entered a side door which had been left ajar for the purpose, closing it softly behind us. So, passing through the kitchen, we made
our way upstairs and rejoined Haufmann.

A post had been allotted to me in the room next to his and I
was enjoined to sit in the dark and watch for anything moving
among the trees. Haufmann departed to a room on the west front
with similar injunctions, and the detective remained in Haufmann's
room.

As I crept cautiously to the window, avoiding the broad moon-
beam streaming in, I saw a light on my left. Ottley was acting as
Haufmann would have done if he had been retiring for the night.
Three minutes later the light vanished, and the nervous vigil was
begun.

There was very little breeze, but sufficient to send up and down
the poplar ranks waves of that mysterious whispering which Klaw
and I had previously noted. The moon, though invisible from that
point, swam in an absolutely cloudless sky, and the shadow of the
house lay black beneath me, its edge tropically sharp. A broad belt
of moon-bright grass and gravel succeeded, and this merged into
the light-patched gloom of the avenue. On the right of the poplars
lay a shrubbery, and beyond that a garden stretching to the east
call. Just to the left, an outbuilding gleamed whitely. Some former
occupant had built it for a coach house and it now housed

Haufmann's car. The apartments above were at present untenanted.

I cannot say with certainty when I first detected, mingled with
the whistling of the branches, something that was not caused by
the wind. But ultimately I found myself listening for this other
sound. With my eyes fixed straight ahead and peering into the shadows of the poplars I crouched, every nerve at high tension. A slight
sound on my left told of a window softly opened. It was Ottley
creeping out on to the balcony. He, too, had heard it!

Then, with awful suddenness, the inexplicable happened.

A short, shrill cry broke the complete silence, succeeding one
of those spells of whispering. A shot followed hot upon it—then a
second. Somebody fell with a muffled thud upon the drive—and I
leapt to the window, threw it widely open, and stepped out on the
balcony.

"Ottley!" I cried. "Haufmann!"

A door banged somewhere and I heard Haufmann's muffled
voice:

"Downstairs! Come down!"

I ran across the room, out on to the landing, and down into the
hall. Haufmann was unfastening the bolts. His injured arm was
still stiff, and I hastened to assist him.

"My God!" he cried, turning a pale face toward me. "It's Ottley
gone! Did you see anything?" "No! Did you?"

"Curse it! No! I had just slipped away from the window to get
my repeater! You heard the voice?"

"Clearly!"

The door was thrown open and we ran out into the drive.

There was no sign of Ottley, and we stood for a moment, unde-
cided how we should act. Then, just inside the shadow belt we found
the detective lying.

Thinking him dead, we raised and dragged him back to the
house. Having re-fastened the door, we laid him on a sofa in the
morning room. His face was deathly and blood flowed from a terrible wound on his skull. Strangest of all, though, he had a gaping
hole just above the right wrist. The skin about it was discoloured

as if with burning. Neither of us could detect any sign of life, and we stood, two frankly frightened men, looking at each other over the body.

"It's got to be done!" said Haufmann, slowly. "One of us has to stay here and do what he can for him, and one has to go for a doctor! There's no telephone!"

"Where's the nearest doctor?" I asked.

"There's one at the corner of the first road on the right."

"I'll go!" I said.

Without shame I confess that from the moment the door closed behind me, I ran my hardest down the poplar avenue until I had passed the gate! And it was not anxiety that spurred me, for I did not doubt that Ottley was dead, but stark fear!

III

Moris Klaw deposited a large grip and a travelling rug upon the veranda.

"Good day, Mr. Haufmann! Good day, Mr. Searles!" At an open window the white-aproned figure of a nurse appeared. "Good day, Nurse! I am direct from Paris. This is a case which cannot be dealt with under the head of the Cycle of Crime, and I do not think it has any relation with the history of The Park. But thoughts are things, Mr. Haufmann. How helpful that is!"

Forty-eight hours had elapsed since Haufmann and I had picked up Ottley for dead in the poplar avenue. Now he lay in a bed made up in the billiard room hovering between this world and another. I had a shrewd suspicion that the doctor who attended him was mystified by some of the patient's symptoms.

Haufmann stared oddly at Moris Klaw, not altogether comprehending the drift of his words.

"If only Ottley could tell us!" he muttered.

"He will tell us nothing for many a day," I said; "if, indeed, he ever speaks again."

"Ah," interrupted Moris Klaw, "to me he will speak! How? With the mind! Something—we have yet to learn what—struck him down that night. The blow, if it was a blow, made so acute an impression upon his brain that no other has secured admittance yet! Good! That blow, it still resides within his mind. To-night I shall sleep beside his bed. I shall be unable odically to sterilize myself, but we must hope. From amid the phantasms which that sick brain will throw out upon the astral film—upon the surrounding ether—I must trust that I find the thought, the last thought before delirium came!"

Haufmann looked amazed. I had prepared him, to some extent, for Klaw's theories, but, nevertheless, he was tremendously surprised. Klaw, however, paid no attention to this. He looked around at the trees.

"I am glad," he rumbled, impressively, "that you managed to hush up. Distinctly, we have now a chance."

"A chance of what?" I cried. "The thing seems susceptible of no ordinary explanation! How can you account for what happened to Ottley and for his condition? What incredible thing came out from the poplars?"

"No thing!" answered Moris Klaw. "No thing, my good friend!"

"Then what did he fire at?"

"At the coach house!"

I met the gaze of his peculiar eyes, fixed upon me through the pince-nez.

"If you will look at the coach-house chimney," he continued, "you will see it—the hole made by his bullet!"

I turned quickly, and even from that considerable distance the hole was visible; a triangular break on the red-tiled rim.

"What on earth does it mean?" I asked, more hopelessly mystified than ever.

"It means that Ottley is a clever man who knows his business; and it means, Mr. Searles, that we must take up this so extraordinary affair where the poor Ottley dropped it!"

"What do you propose?"

"I propose that you invite yourself to a few days' holiday, as I have done. You stay here. Do not allow even the doctor to know that you are in the house. The nurse you will have to confide in, I

suppose. Mr. Haufmann"—he turned to the latter— "you will
occupy your old room. Do not, I beg of you, go outside after
dusk upon any consideration. If either of you shall hear it again—
the evil whispering—come out by the front door, and keep in the
shadow. Carry no light. Above all, do not come out upon the balcony!"

"Then you," I said, "will be unable to stay?"

"I shall be so unable," was the reply; "for I go to Brighton to
secure the interview with Miss Greta which the poor Ottley so much
required!"

"You don't suggest that she knows—"

"She knows no more than we do, Mr. Searles! But I think she
holds a clue and does not know that she holds a clue! For an hour
I shall slumber—I who, like the tortoise, know that to sleep is to
live—I shall slumber beside the sick man's bed. Then, we shall see!"

IV

It was a quarter to seven when Moris Klaw entered the sick
room. Ottley lay in a trance-like condition, and the eccentric
investigator, of whose proceedings the nurse strongly disap-
proved, settled himself in a split-cane armchair by the bedside,
and waving his hand in dismissal to Haufmann and myself, placed
a large silk handkerchief over his sparsely covered skull and composed himself for slumber.

We left him and tiptoed from the room.

"If you hadn't told me what he's done in the past," whispered
Haufmann, "I should say our old friend was mad a lot!"

The great empty house was eerily silent, and during the time
that we sat smoking and awaiting the end of Moris Klaw's singular
telepathic experiment, neither of us talked very much. At eight
o'clock the man whose proceedings savoured so much of charla-
tanism, but whom I knew for one of the foremost criminologists of
the world, emerged, spraying his face with verbena.

"Ah, gentlemen," he said, coming in to us, "I have recovered
some slight impression"—he tapped his moist forehead— "of that

agonizing thought which preceded the unconsciousness of Ottley.
I depart. Sometime to-night will come Sir Bartram Vane from Half-
Moon Street, the specialist, to confer with the physician who is
attending here. Mr. Searles, remain concealed. Not even he must
know of your being here; no one outside the house must know.
Remember my warnings. I depart."

Behind the thick pebbles his eyes gleamed with some excitement repressed. By singular means, he would seem to have come
upon a clue.

"Good-night, Mr. Haufmann," he said. "Good-night, Mr.
Searles. To the nurse I have said good-night and she only glared.
She thinks I am the mad old fool!"

He departed, curtly declining company, and carrying his huge
plaid rug and heavy grip. As his slouching footsteps died away along
the avenue, Haufmann and I looked grimly at each other.

"Seems we're left!" said my friend. "You won't desert me,
Searles?"

"Most certainly I shall not! You are tied here by the presence
of poor Ottley, in any event, and you can rely upon me to keep you
company."

At about ten o'clock Sir Bartram Vane drove up, bringing with
him the local physician who was attending upon Ottley. I kept well
out of sight, but learnt, when the medical men had left, that the
course of treatment had been entirely changed.

Thus commenced our strange ordeal; how it terminated you
presently shall learn.

Moris Klaw, in pursuit of whatever plan he had formed, never
appeared on the scene, but evidence of his active interest reached
us in the form of telegraphic instructions. Once it was a wire telling Haufmann to detain the American servants in London should
they arrive and to go on living as we were. Again it was a warning
not to go out on the balcony after dusk; and, again, that we should
not desert our posts for one single evening. On the fourth day the
doctor pronounced a slight improvement in Ottley's condition, and
Haufmann determined to run down to Brighton on the following
morning, returning in the afternoon.

That night we again heard the voice.

The house was very still, and Haufmann and I had retired to our rooms, when I discerned, above the subdued rustling whisper of the leaves, that other sound that no leaf ever made. In an instant I was crouching by the open window. A lull followed. Then, again, I heard the soft voice calling. I could not detect the words, but in obedience to the instructions of Klaw, I picked up the pistol which I had brought for the purpose, and ran to the door. The idea that the whispering menace was something that could be successfully shot at robbed it of much of its eerie horror, and I relished the prospect of action after the dreary secret sojourn in the upper rooms of the house.

I groped my way down to the hall. As we had carefully oiled the bolts, I experienced no difficulty in silently opening the door. Inch by inch I opened it, listening intently.

Again I heard the queer call

Now, by craning my neck, I could see the moon-bright front of the house; and looking upward, I was horrified to see Shan Haufmann, a conspicuous figure in his light pajama suit, crouching on the balcony! The moonlight played vividly on the nickelled barrel of the pistol he carried as he rose slowly to his feet.

Though I did not know what danger threatened, nor from whence it would proceed, I knew well that Klaw's was no idle warning. I could not imagine what madness had prompted Haufmann to neglect it, and was about to throw wide the door and call to him, when a series of strange things happened in bewildering succession

An odd *strumming* sound came from somewhere in the outer darkness. Haufmann dropped to his knees (I learnt, afterward, that the loose slippers he wore had tripped him). The glass of the window behind him was shattered with a great deal of noise.

A shot! . . . a spurt of flame in the black darkness of the poplar avenue! . . . a shriek from somewhere on the west front . . . and I ran out on to the drive.

With a tremendous crash a bulky form rolled down the sloping roof of the coach house, to fall with a sickening thud to the ground!

Then, out into the moonlight, Moris Klaw came running, his yet smoking pistol in his hand!

"Haufmann!" he cried, and again, "Haufmann!"

The big American peered down from the balcony, hauling in something which seemed to be a line, but which I was unable to distinguish in the darkness.

"Good boy!" he panted. "I was a fool to do it! But I saw him lying behind the chimney and thought I could drop him!"

Moris Klaw ran, ungainly, across to the coach house and I followed him. The figure of a tall, lithe man, wearing a blue serge suit, lay face downward on the gravel. As we turned him over, Haufmann, breathing heavily, joined us. The moonlight fell on a dark saturnine face.

"Gee!" came the cry. "It's *Corpus Chris!*"

V

"Where did I get hold upon the clue?" asked Moris Klaw, when he, Haufmann, and I sat, in the gray dawn, waiting for the police to come and take away the body of Costa. "It was from the brain of Ottley! His poor mind"—he waved long hands circularly in the air—"goes round and round about the thing that happened to him on the balcony."

"And what was that?" demanded Haufmann, eagerly. "Same as happened to me?"

"It was something—something that his knowledge of strange things tells him is venomous—which struck his wrist as he raised his revolver! What did he do? I can tell you; because he is doing it over and over again in his poor feverish mind. He clapped to the injured wrist the barrel of his revolver and fired! Then, swooning, he toppled over and fell among the bushes. The wound that so had puzzled all becomes explained. It was self-inflicted—a precaution—a cauterizing; and it saved his life. For I saw Sir Bartram Vane today and he had spoken with the other doctor on the telephone. The new treatment succeeds."

"I am still in the dark!" confessed Haufmann.

"Yes?" rumbled Moris Klaw. "So? Why do I go to Brighton? I go to ask Miss Greta what Ottley would have asked her."

"And that is?"

"What she feared that made her so very anxious to get you away from your home. To me she admitted that she had received from the man Costa impassioned appeals, such as, foolish girl, she had been afraid to show to you—her father!"

"Good heavens! the scamp!"

"The *canaille!* But no matter, he is dead *canaille!* After you got the brother hanged, this Corpus Chris (it was Fate that named him!) sent to your daughter a mad letter, swearing that if she does not fly with him, he will kill you if he has to follow you around the world! Yes, he was insane, I fancy; I think so. But he was a man of very great culture. He held a Cambridge degree! You did not know? I thought not. He tracked you to Europe and right to this house. Its history he learned in some way and used for his own ends. Probably, too, he had no opportunity of getting at you otherwise, without leaving behind a clue or being seen and pursued."

Moris Klaw picked up an Indian bow which lay upon the floor beside him.

"A bow of the Sioux pattern," he rumbled, impressively.

He stooped again, picking up a small arrow to which a length of thin black twine was attached.

"One standing on the balcony in the moonlight," he continued, "what a certain mark if the wind be not too high! And you will remember that on gently blowing nights the whispering came!"

He raised the point of the arrow. It was encrusted in some black, shining substance. Moris Klaw lowered his voice.

"*Curari!*" he said, hoarsely, "the ancient arrow poison of the South American tribes! This small arrow would make only a tiny wound, and it could be drawn back again by means of the twine attached. Costa, of course, mistook Ottley for you, Mr. Haufmann. Ah, a clever fellow! I spent three evenings up the second tree in the avenue waiting for him. I need not have shot him if you had followed my instructions and not come out on the balcony. We could have captured him alive!"

"I'm not crying about it!" said Haufmann.

"Neither do I weep," rumbled Moris Klaw, and bathed his face with perfume. "But I loathe it, this *curari*—it smells of death. Ah! the *canaille!*"

CASE OF THE CHORD IN G

I

It has been suggested to me more than once that the extraordinary crime which became known throughout the press as the Chelsea studio murder was the Waterloo of my eccentric friend, Moris Klaw, to which I reply that, on the contrary, it was his Austerlitz. This prince of criminologists, some of whose triumphs it has been my privilege to chronicle, never more dramatically established his theory of what he termed "Odic negatives" than in his solution of the mystery of the death of Pyke Webley, the portrait painter.

His singular power, which I can only term post-telepathy, of recovering thought-forms from the atmosphere, earned him the derision of the ignorant, as I have shown, but the grateful appreciation of the better informed—not least among these, Detective Inspector Grimsby, of New Scotland Yard.

I cannot doubt that the recent experiments of Professor Gilbert Murray were based upon that law of "psychic angles" laid down by the strange genius of Wapping Old Stairs.

During lunch, I had been reading an account of the Chelsea tragedy in an early edition of the *Evening Standard*, and on returning to my chambers I found Inspector Grimsby waiting for me. A preamble was unnecessary. Simple deduction told me why he had come.

He was in charge of the Chelsea mystery—and out of his depth.

By several years the youngest detective inspector in the Service, Grimsby is a man earmarked by nature for constant promotion. He possesses a gift more precious than genius—the art of *using* genius, allied to which he has that knack indispensable to any man who would succeed—the knack of finding the limelight. Although he may have done no more than stand in the wings throughout the performance, Detective-Inspector Grimsby invariably takes the last curtain.

This is as it should be, and I accord him my respectful admiration. Therefore, on seeing him:

"The murder of Pyke Webley?" I said, interrogatively.

"Well, that's wonderful!" he declared, trying to look surprised. "I shall begin to think you are Moris Klaw's only rival if you spring things like this on me."

"I see," said I, tossing my paper on the table. "The case is not so simple as it appears."

"Simple," cried Grimsby. He threw the stump of a vicious-looking cheroot into my hearth. "Simple? It's too simple. By which I mean that there is nothing to work upon—nothing *I* can see."

He stood, his back to the hearth, looking at me appealingly; and:

"Have you 'phoned to Wapping?" I asked.

Grimsby nodded.

"I could get no reply," he answered gloomily.

"Then what do you suggest?"

"Well"—he hesitated— "I know your time is of value, Mr. Searles, but I was wondering—I have a taxi outside if you had time to run down to Moris Klaw's place with me for a chat?"

"Why not go alone?"

"Ah!" He selected a fresh cheroot and made it crackle between finger and thumb. "His daughter is the snag. She thinks I waste his time. I doubt if she'd let me see him."

"Your own fault," I said. "She's a charming girl. You don't handle her properly."

"Ah!" he repeated, and became silent, fumbling for matches. Finally, taking pity upon him:

"Very well," I agreed, "I have a couple of hours to spare, and if Klaw takes up the case my time will not be wasted."

II

"You see," said Grimsby, plaintively, as the cab threaded dingy highways, "there is absolutely no motive. Pyke Webley seems to have been a decent, clean-living man, with absolutely no vices as far as I can gather. Of course, I have tried to find a woman in the case, but the only women I've found are heartbroken about his death. A most popular chap. Revenge is out of the question; robbery is out of the question; and I'd take my oath that jealousy is out of the question. So what am I to make of it?"

"He was strangled?"

"Yes." Grimsby nodded. "By a very powerful man. His face is horrible to see, and there are blue weals on his neck where the strangler's fingers bit into the flesh."

"Who saw him last, alive?"

"The door-keeper of the Ham Bone Club," came the answer, promptly. "He dined there, stayed an hour talking to friends and then went out, saying that he had work to do at his studio. The studio is separated from the house by a small garden and can be entered direct from a side entrance. There are only two servants—he was a bachelor—a cook general and a man who has been with him for years. Neither of them heard him come into the house, so that we presume he went straight into the studios. Early this morning a charwoman, who comes daily, finding the studio door locked (I mean the one that opens on the garden) reported this to Parker (that's the man's name) and he came down with the key."

"But," I interrupted, "Parker must surely have known before this that his master was not in the house?"

"No!" Grimsby shook his head emphatically. "Mr. Webley often worked late and Parker had orders never to disturb him until his bell rang."

"I see," said I. "So they unlocked the studio—"

"Yes," Grimsby went on, "and found him there—lying strangled on the floor."

"How long had he been dead?"

"Well, the police surgeon says several hours. Everything points to the fact that it happened shortly after he entered the place."

"Someone may have been concealed there," I suggested.

"God knows!" Grimsby muttered. "I can't find a thing to work upon. And in a case like this the first twelve hours are important. But here we are," he added, nervously.

At the head of that blind alley which shelters the all-but-indescribable establishment of Moris Klaw, we directed the taxi man to wait. This was a foggy afternoon and only dimly could we discern the lights in front of the shop. A chill in the atmosphere told of the nearness of old Father Thames, and as we approached that stacked-up lumber which represented the visible stock-in-trade of the proprietor, a singular piece of human flotsam was revealed propped against the door-post, a fragment of cigarette adhering to the corner of his mouth and threatening at any moment to ignite the stained and walrus-like moustache which distinguished William, Moris Klaw's salesman.

"Good afternoon," I said; "will you tell Mr. Moris Klaw that I have called?"

"Certainly, sir," wheezed the inebriate. "Great pleasure, sir, I'm sure, sir."

William paused, turned, and looked back.

"Do you mind a-waitin' outside?" he added. "There's a boy with red 'air 'angin' about somewhere as 'as got 'is eye on this 'ere golf club"—indicating a dilapidated niblick. "If we all goes in 'e'll nip orf with it."

Accordingly we lingered, and:

"Moris Klaw! Moris Klaw! The devil's come for you!" screeched the parrot who mounted guard within.

Presently came Klaw's unmistakable deep, rumbling voice from the interior gloom:

"Ah! Good afternoon, Mr. Searles! Is it Detective-Inspector Grimsby you have with you? Good afternoon, Mr. Grimsby."

He advanced through the odorous shadows, a strange, a striking figure and—

"Behold!" he said, "*I* have my hat and *you* have your cab. It is
to Chelsea you take me? Yes?"

From the lining of the flat-topped hat he took out his cylindrical scent spray and played its contents upon his high, bald crown.

"Verbena," he rumbled. "My guinea-pigs, they detest it, but I
find it so refreshing." He replaced the spray in the hat, the hat on
his crown. "I have recently bought a fine pair of armadillos," he
explained, "and they have an odour peculiar which, to me, is
objectionable."

He regarded William, who was glancing suspiciously up and
down the narrow alley.

"William," he admonished, "cease to dwell upon the youth with
red hair. He becomes with you an obsession. Give the sheldrake
some fresh seaweed, and if the hedgehogs continue to refuse apples,
they may have each a small piece of raw steak."

He approached the waiting taxi cab, and on the step he paused.

"Mr. Searles, I shall buy no more hedgehogs. They are not only
delicate in captivity but one was in my bed last night."

We all entered the cab; and:

"Now, Mr. Grimsby," Moris Klaw continued, "tell me all about
this poor fellow who is murdered. I am expecting you. I see it is
not simple. I say, 'The old fool from Wapping is wanted here.'"

III

"You are squeamish, Mr. Searles," said Moris Klaw, wagging a
long finger at me. "You squeam. You are not yet recovered from
the blue face of the murdered. Ah, well! it is horrible."

The body had been removed and we had been to view it. Now
we stood in the studio where the crime had taken place, and although some time had elapsed since we had left the mortuary, I
confess that I was not entirely myself. Dusk was come and we had
turned up the studio lights. A faint mist hung in the place, for the
fog had grown denser.

I looked about me at half-completed pictures: groups; studies for magazine jackets; portraits of children and of women—and the ghastly face seemed to rise up before me, the distorted face of the man whose hand would never touch again the brushes of his craft.

"It isn't the first time I've seen a strangling case," said Grimsby, "but it's the first time I've seen marks like that."

"Ah! really!" Moris Klaw rumbled, turning to him. "Never before, eh, like that? You interest me, my friend; you begin to notice. Your intellect it expands like a sunflower in the sun. What is it that you see different in those marks?"

Grimsby stared hard, painfully uncertain whether to regard the words as a compliment or a joke, but finally:

"The pressure was greater," he replied. "The murderer must have had amazing strength."

"Ah, yes!" Moris Klaw removed his hat and stared reflectively into the crown thereof. "Amazing strength? And the surgeon, what does he think?"

"He thinks the same."

"Ah! but no more, eh? Amazing strength only?"

Grimsby figuratively pricked up his ears.

"I don't quite follow you, Mr. Klaw," he said. "Did you notice something else?"

Moris Klaw placed his hat upon a little table.

"I did take notice of some other thing, Mr. Grimsby," he replied, "and for a moment I had dreams that you synchronize with me. It is a complimentary mistake which I make. Please forgive me. This ashtray"—he took up an ashtray from the table beside his hat— "is of great interest. You are agreeable, Mr. Searles"—turning to me— "that it is of great interest?"

I stared rather helplessly. It was a common brass ashtray containing match sticks and cigarette ends. I could see nothing unusual about it, and so presently I shook my head.

"Ah!"

Moris Klaw inserted two long yellow fingers gingerly and plucked out a cigarette stump. He replaced the tray and held up the stump.

"Behold!" he said, "what I find!"

Grimsby now was frankly amazed and not a little angry. As for myself, familiar though I was with Klaw's peculiar methods, I could not divine at what he was driving.

"My friends," he continued, looking from one to the other of us, and holding up the cigarette stump as a lecturer holds up a specimen, "the cigarette, a vice which has killed many men. I have known a woman to hang because of a hairpin, but men and women, too, many of them, because of a cigarette."

He opened a bulging pocket-case and tenderly deposited the stump inside. As he was about to close the case:

"One moment, Mr. Klaw!" said Grimsby. "If that is evidence—though I can't for the life of me see how it can be . . ."

"But *I* see!" cried Moris Klaw— "I, the old foolish from Wapping, behold in this the hangman's rope!"

He closed the case.

"But—" Grimsby began again.

"But me no buts!" Moris Klaw implored. "In *my* hands it is the evidence, in *your* hands it is the cigarette stump. But listen!" A bell rang "It is Isis. I had arranged with her to meet me here. Perhaps, Mr. Grimsby, you would be so good as to open the door?"

Grimsby obeying with alacrity, the beautiful Isis presently entered, exquisitely gowned. She gave me smiling greeting, this lovely daughter of a singular father, and whilst Grimsby deferentially held the door wide open, managed to introduce into the studio, without brushing it against the sides of the door, a large brown paper bag.

"Ah!" Moris Klaw exclaimed, "it is my odically sterilized cushion. Place it here, my child." He indicated a spot upon the floor. "My other engagements do not allow of my sleeping here for more than two hours, but, in that time, I shall hope to recapture the etheric storm in the mind of the slayer or the last great emotion in the brain of the slain. Something, certainly, I shall get, for this was no common crime."

From its paper wrappings Isis Klaw took a red silk cushion and placed it upon the spot where the dead man had been found.

I turned aside, shuddering. That any human being, having seen what we had seen that day, could lie down and, above all, could sleep upon that haunted spot, was almost more than I could believe. Yet such was Moris Klaw's intention, and that he would carry it out I did not doubt.

"Isis, my child," he said, "awake me in two hours."

Removing his caped coat and revealing the shabby tweed suit which he wore beneath it, he spread the garment on the carpet, stretched his gaunt shape upon it, and rested his head on the red cushion.

"Gentlemen," he said in his queer, rumbling tones, "leave me to my slumber. When I awake, I perhaps shall know something more about the man who smoked"—he tapped long fingers upon his breast pocket— "this cigarette."

We went out of the studio through the door leading to the garden. Isis was last to leave and I heard her father's voice:

"Isis, my child, be pleased to extinguish the lights."

So, leaving the eccentric investigator to his dark and ghastly vigil, we went up to the house; and, taking pity upon Grimsby, whose anxiety to talk to Isis was almost pathetic, I sought out Parker, the dead artist's manservant, and endeavoured to obtain from him some useful information. In this, however, I was wholly unsuccessful.

"He hadn't an enemy in the world, sir," the man declared emotionally. "He was the best employer I've ever had or am ever likely to have. I don't deny that he had his little affairs, sir, but there was nothing that left a nasty taste behind. Believe me, there was no woman in it, like the Scotland Yard men tried to make out."

And indeed, the more I considered the facts of the case, the more inexplicable these became.

For instance, there were no signs of a struggle. If one had taken place the murderer had removed all traces of it before leaving. Upon the fingerprint evidence which Scotland Yard hoped to obtain, I based little hope of result. But the astute perceptions of Moris Klaw had undoubtedly enabled him to pick up a clue where no one else had found one; and strange though his behaviour appeared to be, I had good reason to know that his subconscious mind, termed by him "the astral negative," rarely failed to obtain some record under conditions such as those which, he maintained, prevail upon the scene of a crime of violence.

When at the appointed time we returned to the studio, we found it to be brightly lighted, and entering, discovered Moris Klaw engaged in squirting verbena upon his high, bald forehead. He stooped and picked up the caped coat.

"Ah, my friends," he said, "there are many laws governing the functions of mind which have yet to be classified. I think so; yes. Why is it that some emotions register"—he waved his long hands in the air— "indelibly; others, impermanently, and some, not at all? I ask myself the question, and no one replies. We are, then, ignorant, and stupid. To-night"—he lowered his voice— "I do murder with my bare hands! Yes! I am the assassin! My motive—"

"Yes, yes!" cried Grimsby, eagerly.

"No, no!" Moris Klaw frowned at him. "My motive beats in my brain, my second brain, my subconscious brain. Myself I do not see, nor my victim; but I hear, I *hear*. I hear a *sound!*"

"A sound," Isis whispered. "Do you mean a horrible sound—his death cry?"

"No, no!" her father assured her. "I hear a *beautiful* sound."

IV

Time passed and no arrest was made. Other matters engaged public attention, and the Chelsea studio murder gradually dropped out of sight, occupying less and less space in the press and presently disappearing altogether.

Between Inspector Grimsby and Moris Klaw a definite breach occurred.

"He's either bluffing or else hiding something," the Inspector declared to me. "Why did he keep that cigarette? What the devil was the sound he heard, or thought he heard, or pretended he heard? All I know is that I've made a fool of myself. There's not a ghost of a clue."

I was not without sympathy for Grimsby. He had grown so used to finding his difficulties resolved by the genius of Wapping Old Stairs that beyond doubt in the Chelsea case he had promised more than he had been able to perform, optimistically trusting Klaw to provide light in the darkness, and the great man had proved to be fallible

It was a dreadful blow to Detective-Inspector Grimsby, and, I must confess, a surprise to me. Although I had no definite evidence, I nevertheless had certain reasons to suppose that Moris Klaw was not entirely inactive during this time. Twice I met him, accompanied by the dazzling Isis, in the neighbourhood of Queen's Hall, and on the second occasion as he entered a car which was waiting for him:

"Mr. Searles," he said, "tell him, that Detective Inspector, that all work and no play makes of Jean a dull fellow. Recommend to him music. Tell him he should sometimes steal an afternoon and at a concert relax himself."

I reported the conversation to Grimsby in due course and had never seen him more angry.

"He's pulling my leg!" he said. "It'll be a long time before I ask him to help me again. Concerts! What time have *I* got for concerts?"

Such, then, was the state of affairs at the time that Len Hassett, a black-and-white artist of my acquaintance whose work was beginning to attract attention, leased the house and studio of ill-fame where poor Pyke Webley had met his death.

Hassett was ultra-modern and very morbid, but although he professed to have taken the place because its murderous atmosphere appealed to him, I had more than a suspicion that the low rental, consequent upon its evil reputation, had done much more to influence his decision. However, in due course I received an invitation to the house-warming, and on the same day a telephone message from Moris Klaw.

"Good morning, Mr. Searles," came his rumbling greeting over the wires; "it is very wet again. This appalling English climate becomes disastrous. I have lost in one week two marmosets and a Peruvian squirrel. They see the fog and rain, they sneeze, they cough, they die. I have to make to you a request, Mr. Searles: it is that you secure for myself and Isis the invitation to Mr. Len Hassett's party at his new studio."

"Certainly, Mr. Klaw," I replied, trying to keep a note of surprise from my voice; "Hassett and I are old friends. I have only to mention your name and you will be heartily welcomed."

That Isis would be welcome I did not doubt, but, mentally picturing the eccentric figure of Moris Klaw at such a gathering, I could not deny that it seemed out of place. However, I doubted not that some purpose deeper than amusement underlay the request, and the matter was arranged accordingly.

Moris Klaw called for me in a Daimler, wherein, queenly, Isis reclined in an ermine cloak. I think I had never before become so fully conscious of the mystery enshrouding the life of this oddly assorted pair as I did during that drive to Chelsea.

Who, I asked myself, was Moris Klaw, the inscrutable genius who so gladly offered his services to the guardians of law and order?—who dealt in beasts and birds and reptiles, old furniture and fusty books?—who lived in one of the most unsavoury quarters of London?—whose daughter was an unchallenged beauty, possessed of clothes and jewels which never were purchased out of the profits of the Wapping business? My reflections, however, availed me nothing.

Arrived at Chelsea, we met our host in the lounge hall of the house, and, introductions being over and the beauty of Isis having annoyed every other pretty woman in the place, I presently found myself escorting Morris Klaw's daughter through the garden to the studio, whither some of the party had preceded us. We paused for a moment and looked in at the window.

A group of a dozen people or so gathered around the piano at the farther end of the place; but, nearer to us, seated in a high armchair before the blazing fire and caressing a black cat which rested upon his knee, was a strange-looking, gaunt-faced man. Upon his harsh features the dancing firelight painted odd shadows, so that at one moment it was a smiling, benevolent face, and, in the next, the face of a devil.

It was a mere illusion, of course, but when I turned again to Isis and we proceeded toward the door, I saw her biting her lip in sudden agitation, and:

"What is the matter?" I asked.

"Nothing," she replied— "but what a queer-looking man that was sitting before the fire."

Presently we met him, however, as well as the black cat (which proved to belong to Len Hassett). He was Serg Skobolov, a Russian pianist whose reputation was growing by leaps and bounds. Upon Isis his curious small eyes rested greedily; and that she was repelled, the girl was unable to disguise. In due course, when the merriment was in full swing, there were songs, and a certain amount of dancing took place; and then melting at the right moment to the entreaties of Hassett, Skobolov agreed to play.

"You know," said a lady journalist who was sitting on the floor near me, "Skobolov has composed numerous works but not one of them is published."

"Ah!" came a hoarse whisper. I glanced over my shoulder and saw Moris Klaw standing in the shadow behind us. "How strange! Does he refuse then to publish his compositions?"

"Absolutely," the lady declared earnestly. "He maintains that no one else could play them."

"Is that so?" wheezed Moris Klaw. "Perhaps he is right. Presently we shall hear and judge for ourselves."

He became silent, as the pianist, seating himself, began to speak:

"Ladies and gentlemen," he said in his broken English, "you know that the friend of us all, our good Hassett, takes this studio because it is haunted. Here, murder is done, yes, and so I shall play to you a prelude newly composed in which—it is appropriate—I try to express in music the lust of slaying."

He paused amid an uncomfortable silence, and then:

"Some of you must know," he resumed, "that all my compositions are emotions, attempts to paint in chords things experienced. Some experiences one cannot have and so can never paint—for atmosphere, atmosphere, is everything! Now I shall paint for you the story of this studio."

With that, he began to play; and although I had never heard him before, I realized from the outset that he was a master of his instrument. Indeed, I thought, a genius. His theme and its treatment alike were unusual, grotesque. There was some quality in the man's technique which I found myself unable to define. He possessed uncanny power. When, at last, the prelude ended, it was greeted by a silence more eloquent than any applause.

It was only momentary, of course. Then came a wild outburst of enthusiasm. Yet it had been long enough, that moment of stillness, for me to hear the squirting of Moris Klaw's scent spray immediately behind me. And when at last the clapping and shouting died down:

"That prelude," came his voice, almost in my ear, "it has a bad smell. Soon, Isis my child, we must go. It grows late. But perhaps Mr. Bassett will permit me to telephone to my chauffeur, as I allow him to go away? It is all right? Very well. How wonderful is that prelude."

V

Skobolov's attentions to Isis Klaw became very marked. Presently, following some whispered words from her father, I noticed with surprise that she had ceased to avoid the Russian pianist, indeed was consenting to smile upon him. Hence, when presently Moris Klaw's car arrived, I was prepared for Skobolov's acceptance of an offer of a lift as far as his hotel.

For my own part I confess quite frankly that I disliked the man. I had disliked him on sight, and nearer acquaintance did nothing to dispel that first impression. That Isis disliked him, also, I could not doubt. Therefore I divined that she was playing a part, although its purpose defeated my imagination.

Throughout the drive from Chelsea to the hotel Moris Klaw discussed music, a subject with which I had not hitherto believed him to be acquainted. Perhaps his intention was to exhibit Skobolov's intense egotism, for indeed the man was a monument to his own colossal vanity. His genius I could not dispute, but his personality was detestable.

I had foreseen that he would try to detain the party at his hotel, or, rather, that he would try to detain Isis. (I had no doubt whatever that he would gladly have excused both Moris Klaw and myself.) But I had not been prepared for Klaw's acceptance of the offer. However, as we descended from the car and I hesitated whether to accept Skobolov's grudging inclusion of myself in the party, or to walk home, I detected an unmistakable expression in Moris Klaw's queer eyes, twinkling behind the pebbles of his pince-nez.

Suddenly the fact came home to me that I was a minor actor in some mysterious comedy directed by the genius of Wapping Old Stairs.

The Russian occupied a luxurious suite, and Moris Klaw, with reluctance which I could see to be feigned, agreed at Skobolov's pressing invitation to drink one glass of wine and then to depart for home.

Skobolov did his best to make himself agreeable, proffering cigars and cigarettes, and opening a bottle of Bollinger. Moris Klaw and I declined to smoke, but Isis accepted a cigarette and lay back in a deep lounge chair blowing smoke rings and watching the vainglorious Russian musician through half-lowered lashes.

There was a grand piano in the room, and Moris Klaw, who had not touched his wine, prevailed upon Skobolov to play for us once more the prelude which we had heard at Hassett's studio.

The pianist shrugged, glanced at Isis, and then seated himself at the instrument. Placing his cigarette in a little ashtray, he laid his fingers caressingly on the keyboard, and once more my soul was harrowed by those indescribable strains.

As the sound of the last chord died away:

"Good," said Moris Klaw, "excellent, most excellent. And now, please"—he stood up— "I am an old nuisance, an absent old foolish. Do you object that I telephone to my chauffeur? I just remember that Isis leaves her ermine cloak in the car. Is it not so, my child?"

"Good heavens, yes!" Isis exclaimed.

He crossed the room to the telephone, circling ungainly around the piano, raised the instrument, and:

"Will you be pleased to ask Mr. Moris Klaw's chauffeur to bring in from the car the cloak," he said, distinctly. "Yes, all right, very well." He hung up the receiver and turned to face us again, shrugging his shoulders. "So greatly tempting," he explained, "to some prowler thief."

I now became aware that Isis had suddenly grown very pale. She had stood up and was watching Skobolov intently. He seemed rather to be enjoying the scrutiny of her fine dark eyes—when there came a peremptory rap upon the door.

"Come in!" said the Russian sharply.

The door opened—and Detective-Inspector Grimsby stood on the threshold!

Moris Klaw nodded in Skobolov's direction, and, literally stupefied with astonishment, I heard Grimsby say:

"Serg Skobolov, I arrest you on a charge of having murdered Mr. Pyke Webley at his studio on the night of November the fourteenth. I must warn you—" But he got no further.

Uttering a sound which I can only describe as the roar of a wild beast, Skobolov leapt upon him, clasped his hands about the speaker's throat, and hurled him to the floor!

To Moris Klaw, Grimsby owed his life. The Russian was kneeling on the detective's chest and literally squeezing life out of him, when Klaw, surprisingly agile, sprang forward. He stooped over the would-be murderer and performed some simple operation which threw Skobolov upon his back.

In two seconds the madman was up again; and, even now, I sometimes see in my dreams that devil face, transfigured by such evil as I could not have supposed to reside in any human being. He opened and closed his hands in a horrible, writhing, suggestive movement, looked at Grimsby who was trying slowly, painfully to struggle to his feet, looked at Isis, looked at Moris Klaw, looked at myself. Then, bursting into peals of laughter, he ran to the French windows, threw one open, sprang on to the parapet outside, and uttering one final frenzied shriek, leapt into the courtyard sixty feet below!

VI

"Everyone will say," Moris Klaw declared, "'he was a failure, that old fool from Wapping'—for how can a dead man confess, and what use for the newspapers to tell the public why this poor Russian leaps from his window?" He shrugged his shoulders, looking around my study. "You say to me," he continued, addressing Grimsby: "'What is the sound you hear when you sleep in the studio?' and I do not tell you because you would not understand. But now I shall tell you. I hear, my friend, a chord in G Minor!

"Ah! you wag your head. I knew you would wag your head! But beware that your brains do not rattle. This is what I hear, and this is the thing in the mind of the murderer at the moment that he does the murder—a chord in G Minor, Mr. Grimsby! I, the old fool, have the music sense, and this chord it intrigues me. Why? because it is not playable—yet it is a chord upon a piano."

"Not playable!" Grimsby exclaimed.

"Not playable, my friend, except by a man having enormous hands! And also, my good Grimsby, the poor Webley could not have been strangled as he was except by one having enormous hands.

"This is what I first perceive when I see his body, and what for one absurd moment I dream that you have perceived also. I, myself, have large hands, but although I try I cannot span within inches of the marks made upon his throat by the monster who kills him. And so, when I hear this chord, and I question and I try and I find that it cannot be played by any normal hand, I say, 'Yes! it is a musician with abnormal hands!' And I look for him and I listen for him. And to him I have one other clue—a *hashish* cigarette."

"*What* kind of cigarette?" Grimsby muttered.

"I said *hashish*, my friend—a cigarette containing the drug Indian hemp; a kind of cigarette very rarely met in England. In that ashtray, among a dozen others, I detect it immediately. Is it not strange"—he turned to me— "how the murderer is drawn to the place of the murder? It is why, when I hear of the house-warming, I plan to go. Perhaps it is accident—perhaps something else.

"He was a mad genius, that Skobolov. He tries to know supreme emotion that he may write supreme music. Perhaps he succeeds. Who can say? But his compositions cannot live—for no other man can play them, on the piano at any rate. Where did he meet the poor Webley? Who can say? Perhaps they were acquainted, perhaps they met in the street. Webley was Bohemian. He invites Skobolov into the lonely studio. Good! There could be no evidence. It was his opportunity—to know the emotion of *murder* and to get safe away!

"To-night I hear it again—the dream chord: I see his great hands. But he smokes no cigarette in the studio, not until he has returned to his own rooms. For this I waited, this last piece of evidence. Behold!"

From his pocket-case he took out *two* cigarette stumps.

"To-night, in the studio, at last I hear again my dream chord—the chord in G, in G Minor; yet when I telephone to you, my good Grimsby, you think I am the old fool. I say, 'Hurry to Chelsea. I await.' You obey, but you reluct. I say, 'When at the place we go I send a message, "the cloak is in the car." Enter.' You enter and you permit the strangler to escape the law."

He shrugged, stooped to where his brown bowler rested upon the floor beside him, took out the scent spray and squirted verbena upon his forehead.

"I have the hot brain," he explained; "it is the activity. But yours, my friend"—turning to Grimsby— "is as cool as a lemon."

CASE OF THE HEADLESS MUMMIES

I

The mysteries which my eccentric friend, Moris Klaw, was most successful in handling undoubtedly were those which had their origin in kinks of the human brain or in the mysterious history of some relic of ancient times.

I have seen his theory of the Cycle of Crime proved triumphantly time and time again; I have known him successfully to demonstrate how the history of a valuable gem or curio automatically repeats itself, subject, it would seem, to that obscure law of chance into which he had made particular inquiry. Then his peculiar power—assiduously cultivated by a course of obscure study—of recovering from the atmosphere, the ether, call it what you will, the thought-forms—the ideas thrown out by the scheming mind of the criminal he sought for—enabled him to succeed where any ordinary investigator must inevitably have failed.

"They destroy," he would say in his odd, rumbling voice, "the clumsy tools of their crime; they hide away the knife, the bludgeon; they sop up the blood, they throw it, the jemmy, the dead man, the suffocated poor infant, into the ditch, the pool—and they leave intact the odic negative, the photograph of their sin, the thought thing in the air!" He would tap his high yellow brow significantly. "Here upon this sensitive plate I reproduce it, the hanging evidence! The headless child is buried in the garden, but the thought of the beheader is left to lie about. I pick it up. Poof! he swings—that child-slayer! I triumph. He is a dead man. What an art is the art of the odic photograph."

But I propose to relate here an instance of Moris Klaw's amazing knowledge in matters of archaeology—of the history of relics. In his singular emporium at Wapping, where dwelt the white rats, the singing canary, the cursing parrot, and the other stock-in-trade of this supposed dealer in oddities, was furthermore a library probably unique. It contained obscure works on criminology; it contained catalogues of every relic known to European collectors with elaborate histories of the same. What else it contained I am unable to say, for the dazzling Isis Klaw was a jealous librarian.

You who have followed these records will have made the acquaintance of Coram, the curator of the Menzies Museum; and it was through Coram that I first came to hear of the inexplicable beheading of mummies, which, commencing with that of Mr. Pettigrew's valuable mummy of the priestess Hor-ankhu, developed into a perfect epidemic. No more useless outrage could well be imagined than the decapitation of an ancient Egyptian corpse; and if I was surprised when I heard of the first case, my surprise became stark amazement when yet other mummies began mysteriously to lose their heads. But I will deal with the first instance, now, as it was brought under my notice by Coram.

He rang me up early one morning.

"I say, Searles," he said; "a very odd thing has happened. You've heard me speak of Pettigrew the collector; he lives out Wandsworth way; he's one of our trustees. Well, some demented burglar broke into his house last night, took nothing, but cut off the head of a valuable mummy!"

"Good Heavens!" I cried. "What an original idea!"

"Highly so," agreed Coram. "The police are hopelessly mystified, and as I know you are keen on this class of copy I thought you might like to run down and have a chat with Pettigrew. Shall I tell him you are coming?"

"By all means," I said, and made an arrangement forthwith.

Accordingly, about eleven o'clock, I presented myself at a gloomy Georgian house standing well back from the high road and screened by an unkempt shrubbery. Mr. Mark Pettigrew, a familiar figure at Sotheby auctions, was a little shrivelled man, clean-shaven, and with the complexion of a dried apricot. His big spectacles seemed to occupy a great proportion of his face, but his eyes twinkled merrily and his humour was as dry as his appearance.

"Glad to see you, Mr. Searles," he said. "You've had some experience of the outré, I believe, and where two constables, an imposing inspector, and a plain-clothes gentleman who looked like a horse have merely upset my domestic arrangements, you may be able to make some intelligent suggestion."

He conducted me to a large gloomy room in which relics, principally Egyptian, were arranged and ticketed with museum-like precision. Before a wooden sarcophagus containing the swathed figure of a mummy he stopped, pointing. He looked as though he had come out of a sarcophagus himself.

"Hor-ankhu," he said, "a priestess of Sekhet; a very fine specimen, Mr. Searles. I was present when it was found. See—here is her head!"

Stooping, he picked up the head of the mummy. Very cleanly and scientifically it had been unwrapped and severed from the trunk. It smelt strongly of bitumen, and the shrivelled features reminded me of nothing so much as of Mr. Mark Pettigrew.

"Did you ever hear of a more senseless thing?" he asked. "Come over and look at the window where he got in."

We crossed the dark apartment, and the collector drew my attention to a round hole which had been drilled in the glass of one of the French windows opening on a kind of miniature prairie which once had been a lawn.

"I am having shutters fitted," he went on. "It is so easy to cut a hole in the glass and open the catch of these windows."

"Very easy," I agreed. "Was anyone disturbed?"

"No one," he replied, excitedly; "that's the insane part of the thing. The burglar, with all the night before him and with cases containing portable and really priceless objects about him, contented himself with decapitating the priestess. What on earth did he want her head for? Whatever he wanted it for, why the devil didn't he *take* it?"

We stared at each other blankly.

"I fear," said Pettigrew, "I have been guilty of injustice to my horsey visitor, the centaur. You look as stupid as the worst of us!"

"I feel stupid," I said.

"You are!" Pettigrew assured me with cheerful impertinence. "So am I, so are the police; but the biggest fool of the lot is the fool who came here last night and cut off the head of my mummy."

That, then, is all which I have occasion to relate regarding the first of these mysterious outrages. I was quite unable to propound any theory covering the facts, to Pettigrew's evident annoyance; he assured me that I was very stupid, and insisted upon opening a magnum of champagne. I then returned to my rooms, and since reflection upon the subject promised to be unprofitable, had dismissed it from my mind, when some time during the evening Inspector Grimsby rang me up from the Yard.

"Hullo, Mr. Searles," he said; "I hear you called on Mr. Pettigrew this morning?"

I replied in the affirmative.

"Did anything strike you?"

"No; were you on the case?"

"I wasn't on the case then, but I'm on it now."

"How's that?"

"Well, there's been another mummy beheaded in Sotheby's auction rooms!"

II

I knew quite well what was expected of me.

"Where are you speaking from?" I asked.

"The auction rooms."

"I will meet you there in an hour," I said, "and bring Moris Klaw if I can find him."

"Good," replied Grimsby, with much satisfaction in his voice; "this case ought to be right in his line."

I chartered a taxi and proceeded without delay to the insalubrious neighbourhood of Wapping Old Stairs. At the head of the blind alley which harbours the Klaw emporium I directed the man to wait. The gloom was very feebly dispelled by a wavering gaslight in the shed-like front of the shop. River noises were about me. Somewhere a drunken man was singing. An old lady who looked like a pantomime dame was critically examining a mahogany chair with only half a back, which formed one of the exhibits displayed before the establishment.

A dilapidated person whose nose chronically blushed for the excesses of its owner hovered about the prospective purchaser. This was William, whose exact position in the Klaw establishment I had never learned, but who apparently acted during his intervals of sobriety as a salesman.

"Good evening," I said. "Is Mr. Moris Klaw at home?"

"He is, sir," husked the derelict; "but he's very busy, sir, I believe, sir."

"Tell him Mr. Searles has called."

"Yes, sir," said William; and, turning to the dame: "Was you thinking of buyin' that chair, mum, after you've quite done muckin' it about?"

He retired into the cavernous depths of the shop, and I followed him as far as the dimly seen counter.

"Moris Klaw, Moris Klaw! The devil's come for you!"

Thus the invisible parrot hailed my entrance. Indescribable smells, zoo-like, with the fusty odour of old books and the unclassifiable perfume of half-rotten furniture, assailed my nostrils; and mingling with it was the distinct scent of reptile life. Scufflings and scratchings sounded continuously about me, punctuated with squeals. Then came the rumbling voice of Moris Klaw.

"Ah, Mr. Searles—good evening, Mr. Searles! It is the Pettigrew mummy, is it not?"

He advanced through the shadows, his massive figure arrayed for travelling, in the caped coat, his toneless beard untidy as ever, his pince-nez glittering, his high bald brow yellow as that of a Chinaman.

"There has been a second outrage," I said, "at Sotheby's."

"So?" said Moris Klaw, with interest; "another mummy is exe-
cuted!"

"Yes, Inspector Grimsby has asked us to join him there."

Moris Klaw stooped and from beneath the counter took out his
flat-topped brown bowler. From its lining he extracted a cylindrical scent spray and mingled with the less pleasing perfumes that
of verbena.

"A cooling Roman custom, Mr. Searles," he rumbled, "so refreshing when one lives with rats. So it is Mr. Grimsby who is
puzzled again? It is Mr. Grimsby who needs the poor old fool to
hold the lantern for him, so that he, the clever Grimsby, can pick
up the credit out of the darkness! And why not, Mr. Searles, and
why not? It is his business; it is my pleasure."

He raised his voice. "Isis! Isis!"

Out into the light of the fluttering gas lamp, out from that nightmare abode, stepped Isis Klaw—looking more grotesque than a
French fashion plate in an ironmonger's catalogue. She wore a costume of lettuce-green silk, absolutely plain and unrelieved by any
ornament, which rendered it the more remarkable. It was cut low
at the neck, and at the point of the V, suspended upon a thin gold
chain, hung a big emerald. Her darkly beautiful face was one to
inspire a painter seeking a model for the Queen of Sheba, but an
ultra-modern note was struck by a hat of some black, gauzy material which loudly proclaimed its Paris origin. She greeted me with
her wonderful smile.

"What, then," I said. "Were you about to go out?"

"When I hear who it is," rumbled Moris Klaw, "I know that we
are about to go out; and behold we are ready!"

He placed the quaint bowler on his head and passed through
to the front of the shop.

"William," he admonished the ripe-nosed salesman, "there is
here a smell of fourpenny ale. It will be your ruin, William. You
will close at half-past nine, and be sure you do not let the cat in
the cupboard with the white mice. See that the goat does not get at

the Dutch bulbs. They will kill him, that goat—those bulbs; he has for them a passion."

The three of us entered the waiting cab; and within half an hour we arrived at the famous auction rooms. The doors were closed and barred, but a constable who was on duty there evidently had orders to admit us.

The thing we had come to see lay upon the table with an electric lamp burning directly over it. The effect was indescribably weird. All about in the shadows fantastic "lots" seemed to leer at us. A famous private collection was to be sold in the morning and a rank of mummies lined one wall, whilst, from another, stony Pharaohs, gods and goddesses scorned us through the gloom. We were a living group in a place of long-dead things. And yellow on the table beneath the white light, with partially unwrapped coils of discoloured linen hanging gruesomely from it, lay a headless mummy!

I heard the spurt of Moris Klaw's scent spray behind me, and a faint breath of verbena stole to my nostrils.

"Pah!" came the rumbling voice; "this air is full of deadness!"

"Good evening, Mr. Klaw," said Grimsby, appearing from somewhere out of the gloom. "I am so glad you have come." He bowed to Isis. "How do you do, Miss Klaw?"

The bright green figure moved forward into the pool of light. I think I had never seen a more singular picture than that of Isis Klaw bending over the decapitated mummy. Indeed, the whole scene would have delighted Rembrandt.

"I am pleased to meet you, Mr. Klaw," said a middle-aged gentleman, stepping up to the curio dealer; "the Inspector has been telling me about you."

Moris Klaw bowed, and his daughter turned to him with a little nod of the head.

"It is the same period," she said, "as Mr. Pettigrew's mummy. Possibly this was a priest of the same temple. Certainly both are of the same dynasty."

"It is instructive," rumbled Moris Klaw, "but so confusing."

"It's amazing, Mr. Klaw," said Grimsby. "If I understand Miss Klaw rightly, this is the mummy of someone who lived at the same period as the priestess whose mummy is in Mr. Pettigrew's possession?"

"I do not trouble to look," rumbled Moris Klaw, who, in fact, was staring all about the room. "If Isis has said so, it is so."

"If I happened to be superstitious," said Grimsby, "I should think this was a sort of curse being fulfilled, or some fantastic thing of that sort."

"You should call a curse fantastic, eh, my friend?" said Moris Klaw. "Yet here in your own country you have seen a whole family that was cursed to be wiped out mysteriously. Am I with you?"

Grimsby looked very perplexed.

"There's nothing very mysterious about how the thing was done," he said. "Some madman got in here with a knife early in the evening. It's always pretty dark, even during the daytime. But the mystery is his object."

"His object is a mystery, yes," agreed Klaw. "I would sleep here in order to procure a mental negative of what he hoped or what he feared, this lunatic headsman, only that I know he is a man possessed."

"Possessed!" I cried; and even Isis looked surprised.

"I said possessed," continued Klaw, impressively. "He is some madman with a one idea. His mad brain will have charged the ether"—he waved his long arms right and left— "with mad thoughts. The room of Mr. Pettigrew also will be filled with these grotesque thought-forms. Certainly he is insane, this butcher of mummies. In this case I shall rely, not upon the odic photography, not upon that great science the Cycle of Crime, but upon my library."

None of us, I am sure, entirely understood his meaning; and following a brief silence, during which, in a curiously muffled way, the sounds of the traffic in Wellington Street came to us as we stood there around that modern bier with its 4000-year-old burden, Grimsby asked, with hesitancy:

"Don't you want to make any investigations, Mr. Klaw?"

Then Moris Klaw startled us all.

"I have a thought!" he cried, loudly. "Name of a dog! I have a thought!"

Grabbing his brown bowler, which he had laid on the table beside the headless mummy, "Come, Isis!" he cried, and grasped the girl by the arm. "I have yet another thought, most disturbing! Mr. Searles, would you be so good as also to come?"

Wondering greatly whence we were bound and upon what errand, I hastened down the room after them, leaving Inspector Grimsby staring blankly. I think he was rather disappointed with the result of Moris Klaw's inquiry—if inquiry this hasty visit may be termed. He was disappointed, too, at having spent so short a time in the company of the charming Isis.

The middle-aged gentleman came running to let us out.

"Good-night, Inspector Grimsby!" called Moris Klaw.

"Good-night! good-night, Miss Klaw!"

"Good-night, Mr. Someone who has not been introduced!" said Klaw.

"My name is Welby," smiled the other.

"Good-night, Mr. Welby!" said Moris Klaw.

III

During the whole of the journey back to Wapping, Moris Klaw regaled me with anecdotes of travels in the Yucatan Peninsula. I had never met a man before who had ventured fully to explore those deadly swamps; but Moris Klaw chatted about the Izamal temples as unconcernedly as another man might chat about the Paris boulevards. Isis took no part in the conversation, from which I gathered that although she seemed to accompany her father everywhere, she had not accompanied him into the jungles of Yucatan.

"In the heart of those forests, Mr. Searles," he whispered, "are stranger things than these headless mummies. Do you know that the secret of those great temples buried in the swamps and the jungles and guarded only by serpents and slimy, crawling things, is a door which science has yet to unlock? What people built them, and what god was worshipped in them? Suppose"—he bent to my ear— "I hold the key to that riddle; am I assured to be immortal? Yes? No?"

His conversation, although it often seemed to be studiously eccentric, was always that of a man of powerful and unusual mind, a man of vast and unique experience. I was rather sorry when we arrived at our destination.

As the cab drew up at the head of the court, I saw that the shop of Moris Klaw was in darkness; but again telling the man to wait, we walked down past the warehouse, beyond whose bulk tided muddy Thames, and my eccentric companion producing a key from one of the bulging pockets of his caped coat inserted it into the lock of a door which looked less like a door than a section of a dilapidated hoarding.

The door swung open.

"Ah!" he hissed. "It was not locked!"

Klaw struck a match and peered into the odorous darkness.

"William!" he rumbled. "William!"

But there was no reply. Isis suddenly laid her hand upon my arm, and it occurred to me that for once her wonderful composure was shaken.

"Something has happened!" she whispered.

Her father lighted a gas-burner, and the yellow light flared up, reclaiming from the gloom furniture, pictures, cages, glass cases, statuettes, heaps of cheap jewellery and false teeth, books, and a hundred-and-one other items of that weird stock-in-trade.

Then, under the littered counter we found William lying flat on his back with his arms spread widely.

"Ah! *cochon!*" muttered Klaw; "beer-swilling pig!"

He stooped to raise the head of the prostrate man, and then to my surprise dropped upon his knees beside him, stooped yet lower, and sniffed suspiciously. Again Isis Klaw seized my arm, and her dark eyes were opened very widely as she leaned forward watching her father. He stood up, holding a glass in his hand which yet contained some drops of what was apparently beer. At this, too, he sniffed. He walked over to the gaslight and examined the fluid closely, whilst Isis and I watched him, together. Finally Moris Klaw inserted a long white forefinger into the dirty glass and applied the tip to his tongue.

"Opium!" he said. "Many drops of pure opium were put in this beer."

He turned to me with a curious expression upon his parchment-coloured face.

"Mr. Searles," he said, "my second idea was a good idea. I shall now surprise you."

He led the way through that neat and business-like office which opened out of the unutterably dirty and untidy shop. Although within the shop and in front of it only gaslight was used, in the office he switched on an electric lamp. But we did not delay long in Moris Klaw's sanctum, lined with its hundreds of books, its obscure works of criminology, its records of strange things: we proceeded through another door and up a thickly carpeted stair.

I had never before penetrated thus far into the habitable portion of Moris Klaw's establishment; the book-lined office hitherto had marked the limit of my explorations. But now, as more electric lights were switched on, I saw that we stood upon a wide landing panelled in massive black oak. Armoured figures stood sentinel-like against the walls, and several magnificent specimens of Chinese porcelain met my gaze. I might have thought myself in some old English baronial hall. Next we entered a big, rectangular room, which I wholly despair of describing. Apparently it was used as a study, a library, a laboratory, and a warehouse for all sorts of things, from marble Buddhas to innumerable pairs of boots. Also, there was in it a French stove; and upon a Persian coffee table stood a frying pan containing a cooked sausage solidified in its own fat. There was clear evidence, moreover, in the form of a rolled-up hammock, that the place served as a bedroom.

Altogether there were four mummies in the apartment. One of these, partly unwrapped, lay amongst the litter on the floor—headless!

"Mon Dieu!" cried Isis, clasping her hands; "it is uncanny, this!"

She was evidently excited, for her French accent suddenly asserted itself to a marked degree. Moris Klaw, from somewhere amongst the rubbish at his feet, picked up the severed head of the mummy and stared at it intently. In the stillness I could hear the river noises very distinctly, and a sort of subterranean lapping and creaking which suggested that at high tide the cellars of the establishment became flooded. Moris Klaw dropped the head from his hands. It fell with a dull thud to the floor.

From the lining of his hat he took out the inevitable scent spray and moistened his brow with verbena.

"I need the cool brain, Mr. Searles," he said. "I, the old cunning, the fox, the wily, am threatened with defeat. This slaughter of mummies it surpasses my experience. I am nonplussed; I am a stupid old fool. Let me think!"

Isis was looking about her in a startled way.

"It is horribly uncanny, Miss Klaw," I said. "But the drugging of the man downstairs points to very human agency. Perhaps if we could revive him—"

"He will not revive," interrupted Moris Klaw "for twelve hours at least. In his beer was enough opium to render unconscious the rhinoceros!"

"Is there anything missing?" I asked.

"Nothing," rumbled Klaw. "He came for the mummy. Isis, will you prepare for us those cooling drinks that help the fevered mind, and from downstairs bring me the seventh volume of the 'Books of the Temples.'"

Isis Klaw immediately walked forward to the door.

"And Isis, my child," added her father, "remove the tall cage to the top end of the shop. Presently that William's snores will awake the Borneo squirrel."

As the girl departed, Klaw opened an inner door and ushered me into a dainty white room, an amazing apartment indeed, a true Parisian boudoir. The air was heavy with the scent of roses, for bowls of white and pink roses were everywhere. Klaw lighted a silver table lamp with a unique silver gauze shade apparently lined with pale rose-coloured silk. Evidently this apartment belonged to Isis, and was as appropriate for her, exquisite Parisian that she seemed to be, as the weird barn through which we had come was an appropriate abode for her father.

When presently Isis returned I saw her for the first time in her proper setting, a dainty green figure in a white frame. Moris Klaw opened the bulky leather-bound volume which she had handed to him, and whilst I sat sipping my wine and watching him, he busily turned over the pages (apparently French MS.) in quest of the reference he sought.

"Ah!" he cried, in sudden triumph; "vaguely I had it in my memory, but here it is, the clue. I will translate for you, Mr. Searles, what is written here: 'The "Book of the Lamps," which was revealed to the priest, Pankhaur, and by, him revealed only to the Queen'— it was the ancient Egyptian Queen, Hatshepsu, Mr. Searles— 'was kept locked in the secret place beneath the altar, and each high priest of the temple—all of whom were of the family of Pankhaur— held the key and alone might consult the magic writing. In the 14th dynasty, Seteb was high priest, and was the last of the family of Pankhaur. At his death the newly appointed priest, receiving the key of the secret place, complained to Pharaoh that the "Book of the Lamps" was missing.'"

He closed the volume and placed it on a little table beside him.

"Isis," he rumbled, looking across at his daughter, "does the mystery become clear to you? Am I not an old fool? Mr. Searles, there is only one other copy of this work"—he laid a long white hand upon the book— "known to European collectors. Do I know where that copy is? Yes? No? I think so!"

There was triumph in his hoarse voice. Personally I was quite unable to see in what way the history of the "Book of the Lamps" bore upon the case of the headless mummies; but Moris Klaw evidently considered that it afforded a clue. He stood up.

"Isis," he said, "bring me my catalogue of the mummies of the Bubastite priests."

That imperious beauty departed in meek obedience.

"Mr. Searles," said Moris Klaw, "this will be for Inspector Grimsby another triumph; but without these records of a poor old fool, who shall say if the one that beheads mummies had ever been detected? I neglected to secure the odic negative because I thought I had to deal with a madman; but I was more stupid than an owl. This decapitating of mummies is no madman's work, but is done with a purpose, my friend—with a wonderful purpose."

IV

The Menzies Museum (scene of my first meeting with Moris Klaw) was not yet opened to the public when Coram (the curator), Moris Klaw, Grimsby, and I stood in the Egyptian Room before a case containing mummies. The room adjoining—the Greek Room— had been the scene of the dreadful tragedies which first had acquainted me with the wonderful methods of the eccentric investigator.

"Whoever broke into Sotheby's last night, Mr. Maw," said Grimsby, "knew the ins and outs of the place; knew it backward. It's my idea that he was known to the people there. After having cut off the head of the mummy he probably walked out openly. Then, again, it must have been somebody who knew the habits of Mr. Pettigrew's household that got at his mummy. Of course"—his eyes twinkled with a satisfaction which he could not conceal— "I'm very sorry to hear that our man has proved too clever for *you!* Think of a burglar breaking into Mr. Moris Klaw's house!"

"Think of it, my friend," rumbled the other; "if it makes you laugh go on thinking of it, and you will grow fat!"

Grimsby openly winked at me. He was out of his depth himself, and was not displeased to find the omniscient Moris Klaw apparently in a similar position.

"I am not resentful," continued Klaw, "and I will capture for you the mummy man."

"What?" cried Grimsby. "Are you on the track?"

"I will tell you something, my laughing friend. You will secretly watch this Egyptian Room like the cat at the mouse-hole, and presently—I expect it will be at night—he will come here, this hunter of mummies!"

Grimsby stared incredulously.

"I don't doubt your word, Mr. Klaw," he said; "but I don't see how you can possibly know that. Why should he go for the mummies here rather than for those in one of the other museums or in private collections?"

"Why do you order a bottle of Bass," rasped Klaw, "in a saloon, rather than a bottle of water or a bottle of vinegar? It is because what you want is a bottle of Bass. Am I a damn fool? There are others. I am not alone in my foolishness!"

The group broke up: Grimsby, very puzzled, going off to make arrangements to have the Egyptian Room watched night and day, and Coram, Klaw, and I walking along in the direction of the Greek Room.

"I have no occasion to remind you, Mr. Klaw," said Coram, "that the Menzies Museum is a hard nut for any burglar to crack. We have a night watchman, you will remember, who hourly patrols every apartment. For any one to break into the Egyptian Room, force one of the cases and take out a mummy, would be a task extremely difficult to perform undetected."

"This mummy hunter," replied Klaw, "can perform it with ease; but because we shall all be waiting for him he cannot perform it undetected."

"I shouldn't think there is much likelihood of any attempt during the day?" I said.

"There is no likelihood," agreed Klaw; "but I like to see that Grimsby busy! The man with the knife to decapitate mummies will come to-night. Without fear he will come, for how is he to know that an old fool from Wapping anticipates his arrival!"

We quitted the Museum together. The affair brought back to my mind the gruesome business of the Greek Room murders, and for the second time in my life I made arrangements to watch in the Menzies Museum at night.

On several occasions during the day I found myself thinking of this most singular affair and wondering in what way the "Book of the Lamps," mentioned by Moris Klaw, could be associated with it. I was quite unable to surmise, too, how Klaw had divined that the Menzies Museum would become the scene of the next outrage.

We had arranged to dine with Coram in his apartments, which adjoined the Museum buildings, and an oddly mixed party we were, comprising Coram, his daughter, Moris Klaw, Isis Klaw, Grimsby, and myself.

A man had gone on duty in the Egyptian Room directly the doors were closed to the public, and we had secretly arranged to watch the place from nightfall onward. The construction of the room greatly facilitated our plan; for there was a long glass skylight in the centre of its roof, and by having the blinds drawn back we could look down into the room from a landing window of a higher floor—a portion of the curator's house.

Dinner over, Isis Klaw departed

"You will not remain, Isis," said her father. "It is so unnecessary. Good-night, my child!"

Accordingly, the deferential and very admiring Grimsby descended with Coram to see Isis off in a taxi. I marvelled to think of her returning to that tumble-down, water-logged ruin in Wapping

"Now, Mr. Grimsby," said Moris Klaw, when we four investigators had gathered together again, "you will hide in the case with the mummies!"

"But I may find myself helpless! How do we know that any particular case is going to be opened? Besides, I don't know what to expect!"

"Blessed is he that expecteth little, my friend. It is quite possible that no attempt will be made to-night. In that event you will have to be locked in again to-morrow night!"

Grimsby accordingly set out He held a key to the curator's private door, which opened upon the Greek Room, and also the key of a wall case. Moris Klaw had especially warned him against making the slightest noise. In fact, he had us all agog with curiosity and expectation. As he and Coram and I, having opened, very carefully, the landing window, looked down through the skylight into the Egyptian Room, Grimsby appeared beneath us. He was carrying an electric pocket torch.

Opening the wall case nearest to the lower end of the room, he glanced up rapidly, then stepped within, reclosing the glass door. As Klaw had pointed out earlier in the evening, an ideal hiding place existed between the side of the last sarcophagus and the angle of the wall.

"I hope he has refastened the catch," said our eccentric companion; "but not with noisiness."

"Why do you fear his making a noise?" asked Coram, curiously.

"Outside, upon the landing," replied Moris Klaw, "is a tall piece of a bas-relief; it leans back against the wall. You know it?"

"Certainly."

"To-night, you did not look behind it, in the triangular space so formed."

"There's no occasion. A man could not get in there."

"He could not, you say? No? That exploits to me, Mr. Coram, that you have no eye for capacity! But if you are wrong, what then?"

"Any one hiding there would have to remain in hiding until the morning. He could not gain access to any of the rooms; all are locked, and he could not go downstairs, because of the night attendant in the hallway."

"No? Yes? You are two times wrong! First— someone is concealed there!"

"Mr. Klaw!" began Coram, excitedly.

"Ssh!" Moris Klaw raised his hand. "No excitement. It is noisy and a tax upon the nerves. Second—you are wrong, because presently that hidden one will come into the Egyptian Room!"

"How? How in Heaven's name is he going to *get* in?"

"We shall see."

Utterly mystified, Coram and I stared at Moris Klaw, for we stood one on either side of him; but he merely wagged his finger enjoining us to silence, and silent perforce we became.

The view was a cramped one, and standing there looking out at the clear summer night, I for one grew very weary of the business. But I was sustained by the anticipation that the mystery of the headless mummies was about to come to a climax. I felt very sorry for poor Grimsby, cramped in the corner of the Egyptian Room,

SAX ROHMER

for I knew him to be even more hopelessly in the dark respecting the purpose of these manoeuvres than I was myself. In vain I racked my brain in quest of the link which united the ancient "Book of the Lamps" with the singular case which had brought us there that night.

Coram began to fidget, and I knew intuitively that he was about to speak.

"*Ssh!*" whispered Moris Klaw.

A beam of light shone out beneath us, across the Egyptian Room!

I concluded that something had attracted the attention of Grimsby. I leaned forward in tense expectancy, and Coram was keenly excited.

The beam of light moved; it shone upon the door of the very case in the corner of which Grimsby was hiding, but upon the nearer end, fully upon the face of a mummy.

A small figure was dimly discernible, now, the figure of the man who carried the light. Cautiously he crossed the room. Evidently he held the key of the wall case, for in an instant he had swung the door back and was hauling the mummy on to the floor.

Then out upon the midnight visitor leapt Grimsby. The light was extinguished—and Moris Klaw, drawing back from the window, seized Coram by the arm, crying, "The key of the door! The key of the door!"

We were down and into the Egyptian Room in less than half a minute. Coram switched on all the lights; and there with his back to the open door of the wall case, handcuffed and wild-eyed, was—Mr. Mark Pettigrew!

Coram's face was a study—for the famous archaeologist whom we now saw manacled before us was a trustee of the Menzies Museum!

"Mr. Pettigrew!" he said, hoarsely. "Mr. Pettigrew! there must be some mistake—"

"There is no mistake, my good sir," rumbled Moris Klaw. "Look, he has with him a sharp knife to cut off the head of the priest!"

It was true. An open knife lay upon the floor beside the fallen mummy!

Grimsby was breathing very heavily and looking in rather a startled way at his captive, who seemed unable to realize what had happened. Coram cleared his throat nervously. It was one of the strangest scenes in which I had ever participated.

"Mr. Pettigrew," he began, "it is incomprehensible to me—"

"I will make you to comprehend," interrupted Moris Klaw. "You ask"—he raised a long finger— "why should Mr. Pettigrew cut off the head of his own mummy? I answer for the same reason that he cut off the head of the one at Sotheby's. You ask why did he cut off the head of the one at Sotheby's? I answer for the same reason that he cut off the head of the one at my house, and for the same reason that he came to cut off the head of this one! What is he looking for? He is looking for the 'Book of the Lamps'!" He paused, gazing around upon us. Probably, excepting the prisoner, I alone amongst his listeners understood what he meant.

"I have related to Mr. Searles," he continued, "some of the history of that book. It contained the ritual of the ancient Egyptian ceremonial magic. It was priceless; it gave its possessors a power above the power of kings! And when the line of Pankhaur became extinct it vanished. Where did it go? According to a very rare record—of which there are only two copies in existence—one of them in my possession and one in Mr. Pettigrew's!—it was hidden *in the skull of the mummy of a priest or priestess of the temple!*"

Pettigrew was staring at him like a man fascinated.

"Mr. Pettigrew had only recently acquired that valuable manuscript work in which the fact is recorded; and being an enthusiast, gentlemen"—he spread wide his hands continentally— "all we poor collectors are enthusiasts—he set to work upon the first available mummy of a priest of that temple. It was his own. The skull did not contain the priceless papyrus! But all these mummies are historic; there are only five in Europe."

"*Five?*" blurted Pettigrew.

"Five," replied Klaw; "you thought there were only four, eh? But as a blind you called in the police and showed them how your mummy had been mutilated. It was good. It was clever. No one suspected you of the outrages after that—no one but the old fool who knew that you had secured the second copy of that valuable work of guidance!

"So you did not hesitate to use the keys you had procured in your capacity as trustee to gain access to this fourth mummy here." He turned to Grimsby and Coram. "Gentlemen," he said, "there will be no prosecution. The fever of research is a disease; never a crime."

"I agree," said Coram, "most certainly there must be no prosecution; no scandal. Mr. Pettigrew, I am very, very sorry for this."

Grimsby, with a rather wry face, removed the handcuffs. A singular expression proclaimed itself upon Pettigrew's shrivelled countenance.

"The thing I'm most sorry for," he said, dryly, but with the true fever of research burning in his eyes, "if you will excuse me saying it, Coram, for I'm very deeply indebted to you—is that I can't cut off the head of this fourth mummy!"

Mr. Mark Pettigrew was a singularly purposeful and rudely truculent man.

"It would be useless," rumbled Moris Klaw. "I found the fifth mummy in Egypt two years ago! And behold"—he swept his hand picturesquely through the air— "I beheaded him!"

"What!" screamed Pettigrew, and leapt upon Klaw with blazing eyes.

"Ah," rumbled Klaw, massive and unruffled, "that is the question—*what?* And I shall not tell you!"

From his pocket he took out the scent spray and squirted verbena into the face of Mr. Pettigrew.

CASE OF THE HAUNTING OF GRANGE

I

A large lamp burned in the centre of the table; a red-shaded candle stood close by each diner; and the soft light made a brave enough show upon the snowy napery and spotless silver, but dispersed nothing of the gloom about us. The table was a lighted oasis in the desert of the huge apartment. One could barely pick out the suits of armour and trophies which hung from distant panelled walls, and I started repeatedly when the butler appeared, silent, at my elbow.

Of the party of five, four were men—three of them (for I venture to include myself) neatly groomed and dressed with care in conventional dinner fashion. The fourth was a heavy figure in a dress coat with broad satin lapels such as I have seen, I think, in pictures of Victorian celebrities. I have no doubt, judging from its shiny appearance, that it was the workmanship of a Victorian tailor. The vest was cut high and also boasted lapels; the trousers, though at present they were concealed beneath the table, belonged to a different suit, possibly a mourning suit, and to a different sartorial epoch.

The woman, young, dark, and exceedingly pretty, wore a gown of shimmering amber, cut with Parisian daring. Her beautiful eyes were more often lowered than raised, for Sir James Leyland, our host, was unable to conceal his admiration; his face, tanned by his life in the Bush, was often turned to her. Clement Leyland, the baronet's cousin, bore a striking resemblance to Sir James, but entirely lacked the latter's breezy manner. I set him down for a man who thought much and said little.

However, conversation could not well flag at a board boasting the presence of such a genial colonial as Sir James and such a storehouse of anecdotal oddities as Moris Klaw. Mr. Leyland and myself, then, for the most part practised the difficult art of listening; for Isis Klaw, I learned, could talk almost as entertainingly as her father.

"I am so glad," said Moris Klaw, and his voice rumbled thunderously about the room, "that I have this opportunity to visit Grange."

"It certainly has great historic interest," agreed Sir James. "I had never anticipated inheriting the grand old place, much less the title. My uncle's early death, unmarried, very considerably altered my prospects; I became a landed proprietor who might otherwise have become a 'Murrumbidgee whaler'!"

He laughed, light-heartedly, glancing at Isis Klaw, and from her to his cousin.

"Clem had everything in apple-pie order for me," he added, "including the family goblin!"

"Ah! that family goblin!" rumbled Moris Klaw. "It is him I am after, that goblin!"

The history of Grange, in fact, was directly responsible for Moris Klaw's presence that night. An odd little book, "Psychic Angles," had recently attracted considerable attention among students of the occult, and had proved equally interesting to the general public. It dealt with the subject of ghosts from quite a new standpoint, and incidentally revealed its anonymous author as one conversant apparently with the history of every haunted house in Europe. Few knew that the curio-dealer of Wapping was the author, but as Grange was dealt with in "Psychic Angles," amongst a number of other haunted homes of England, a letter from Sir James Leyland, forwarded by the publisher, had invited the author to investigate the latest developments of the Leyland family ghost.

I had had the privilege to be associated with Moris Klaw in another case of apparent haunting—that which I have dealt with in an earlier paper: the haunting of The Grove. He had courteously invited me, then, to assist him (his own expression) in the inquiry at Grange. I welcomed the opportunity, for I was anxious to include in my annals at least one other case of the apparent occult.

"We shall without delay," continued the eccentric investigator, "endeavour to meet him face to face—this disturber of the peace. Sir James, it is with the phenomena you call ghosts the same as with valuable relics, with jewels, with mummies—ah, those mummies!—with beautiful women!"

"To liken a beautiful woman to a relic," said Sir James, "would be—well"—he glanced at Isis— "hardly complimentary!"

"It would be true!" Moris Klaw assured him, impressively. "Nature, that mystic process of reproduction, wastes not its models. Sir James, all beauty is duplicated. Look at my daughter, Isis." Sir James readily obeyed. "You see her, yes? And what do you see?"

Isis lowered her eyes, but, frankly, I was unable to perceive any evidence of embarrassment in this singularly self-possessed girl.

"Perhaps," resumed her father, "I could tell you what you see; but I will only tell you what it is you *may* see. You may see a beauty of your Regency or a favourite of your Charles; the daughter of a Viking, an ancient British princess; the slave of a Caesar, the dancer of a Pharaoh!"

"You believe in reincarnation?" suggested Clement Leyland, quietly.

"Yes, certainly, why not, of course!" rumbled Moris Klaw. "But I do not speak of it now, not I; I speak of Nature's reproduction; I tell you how Nature wastes nothing which is beautiful. What has the soul to do with the body? I tell you how the reproduction goes on and on until the mould, the plate, the die, has perished! So is it with ghosts. You write me that your goblin has learned some new tricks. I answer, your goblin can never learn new tricks; I answer, this is not he, it is another goblin! Nature is conservative with her goblins as with her beautiful women; she does not disfigure the old model with alterations. What! Chop them about? Never! she makes new ones."

Clement Leyland smiled discreetly, but Sir James was evidently interested.

"Of course I've read 'Psychic Angles,' Mr. Klaw," he said; "consequently, your novel theories do not altogether surprise me. I gather your meaning to be this: a haunted house is haunted in exactly the same way generation after generation? Any new development points to the presence of a new force or intelligence?"

"It is exactly quite so," Moris Klaw nodded, sympathetically. "You have the receptive mind, Sir James; you should take up ghosts; they would like you. There is a scientific future for the sympathetic ghost-hunter, for—I will whisper it—these poor ghosts are sometimes so glad to be hunted! It is a lonely life, that of a ghost!"

"The Grange ghost," Sir James assured him, "is a most gregarious animal. He doesn't go in for lonely groanings in the chapel or anything of that kind; he drops into the billiard room frequently, he's often to be met with right here in the dining room, and of late he's been sleeping with me regularly!"

"So I hear," rumbled Moris Klaw; "so I hear. It is quaint, yes; proceed, my friend."

Isis Klaw sat with her big eyes fixed upon Sir James, as he continued:

"The traditional ghost of Grange was a gray monk who, on certain nights—I forget the exact dates—came out from the chapel beyond the orchard carrying a long staff, walked up to a buttress of the west wall, and disappeared at the point where formerly there was a private entrance. In fact, there used to be a secret stair opening at that point and communicating with a room built by a remote Leyland of the eighth Henry's time—a notorious roué. The last Leyland to use the room was Sir Francis, an intimate of Charles II. The next heir had the wing rebuilt, and the ancient door walled up."

"Yes, yes," said Moris Klaw. "I know it all, but you tell it well. This is a most interesting house, this Grange. I have recorded him, the gray monk, and I learn with surprise how another spook comes poaching on his preserves! Tell us now of these new developments, Sir James."

Sir James cleared his throat and glanced about the table.

"Please smoke," said Isis; "because I should like to smoke, too!"

"Yes, yes," agreed Moris Klaw. "Remain, my child, we will all remain, do not let us move an inch. This banqueting hall is loaded with psychic impressions. Let us smoke and concentrate our minds upon the problem."

Coffee and liqueurs were placed upon the table and cigarettes lighted. In deference to the presence of Isis, I suppose, no cigars were smoked, but the girl lighted an Egyptian cigarette proffered by Sir James with the insouciance of an old devotee of my Lady Nicotine. The butler having made his final departure, we were left— a lonely company in our lighted oasis—amid the shadow desert of that huge and ghostly apartment.

"All sorts of singular things have happened," began Sir James, "since my return from Australia. Of course, I cannot say if these are recent developments, because my uncle, for seven or eight years before his death, resided entirely in London, and Grange was in charge of the housekeeper. It is notorious, is it not, that house-keepers and such worthy ladies never by any chance detect any-thing unseemly in family establishments with which they are associ-ated? Anyway, when I was dug up out of the Bush, and all the for-malities were through, good old Clement here set about putting things to rights for me, and I arrived to find Grange a perfect pic-ture from floor to roof. New servants engaged, too, though the housekeeper and the butler, who have been in the family for years, remained, of course, with some other old servants. As I have said, everything was in apple-pie order."

"Including the ghost!" interpolated his cousin, laughing.

"That's the trouble," said Sir James, banging his fist upon the table; "the very first night I dined in this room there was a most uncanny manifestation. Clement and I were sitting here at this very table; we had dined—not unwisely, don't think that—and were just smoking and chatting, when—"

He ceased abruptly; in fact, the effect was similar to that which would have resulted had a solid door, suddenly been closed upon the speaker. But the stark silence which ensued was instantly interrupted. My blood seemed to freeze in my veins, a horrid, supernatural dread held me fast in my chair. For, echoing hollowly around and about the huge, ancient apartment, rolled, booming, a peal of demoniacal laughter! From whence it proceeded I was wholly unable to imagine. It seemed to be all about, above us, and beneath us. It was mad, devilish, a hell-sound, impossible to describe. It rose, it fell, it rose again—and ceased abruptly.

"My God!" I whispered. "What was it?"

II

In the silence that followed the ghostly disturbance we sat around the table listening. Sir James was the first to speak.

"A demonstration, Mr. Klaw!" he said. "This sort of thing happens every night!"

"Ah!" rumbled Moris Klaw, "every night, eh? That laughing? You have investigated—yes—no?"

"I tried to investigate," explained the baronet, "but quite frankly I didn't know where to begin."

We were all recovering our composure somewhat, I think.

"You hear that laughter nowhere but in this room?" asked Klaw.

"I have always heard it when we have been seated at this table," was the reply, "at no other time, but it can be heard clearly beyond the room. The servants have heard it. Excepting the housekeeper and the butler, they are leaving almost immediately."

"Ah! *canaille!*" grunted Moris Klaw; "fear-pigs! It is always so, these servants. So you have not located the one that laughs, no?"

"No," answered Sir James; "and he doesn't stop at laughing—does he, Clem?"

Clement Leyland shook his head. He looked even paler than usual, I thought, and the uncanny incident seemed to have disturbed him greatly.

"What else?" rumbled Moris Klaw. "The gray monk is forgetting his manners. He becomes rude, eh—that gray monk?"

"The house has practically become uninhabitable," said the baronet, bitterly. "None of the usual phenomena are missing. We have slamming doors, phantom footsteps, and, if the servants are to be believed, half the forces of hell loose here at night!"

"But your *own* experiences?" interrupted Klaw.

"My own experiences in brief amount to this: I rarely sit at this table at night without hearing that beastly laughter, at least once. I never go into the billiard room, which opens out under the gallery yonder, without feeling a cold wind blowing upon my face or head, even in perfectly still weather, or with all the windows closed. To the left of the billiard room, and opening out of it, is a third centre of these disturbances. It's the gun room, and guns have been fired there in the night, with the door locked, on no fewer than five occasions!"

Moris Klaw, from a tail pocket of his coat, produced a cylindrical scent spray and squirted verbena upon his high yellow forehead.

"It grows exciting, this," he said. "I require the cool brain."

"Finally," added Sir James, "the only other point worth mentioning is the ghostly voice which regularly wakes me from my sleep at night."

"A voice," rumbled Klaw; "what voice, and what does it say, that voice?"

"I won't repeat what it says!" replied the baronet, glancing at Isis; "but it offers obscene suggestions or that is the impression I have of it—a low, filthy mumbling; if you can follow me, the voice of something dead and infinitely evil."

Moris Klaw stood up.

"This intelligence," he rumbled, "a living or a dead one, has thoughts then, and thoughts, Sir James, are things. I shall sleep in one of the centres of its activity to-night, perhaps here, perhaps in the billiard room or the gun room. Isis, my child, bring for me my odically sterilized pillows. This is a charming case and worthy of the subtle method."

He placed his hands upon the shoulders of Sir James Leyland, who stood facing him.

"Evil thoughts live, Sir James," he said. "I cannot explain to you how hard it is to slay them. Few good thoughts survive; but such an ancient abode as this"—he waved his long hands characteristically about him— "is peopled with thought-forms surviving from the dark ages. I have opened the inner eye, my friend. Mercifully, perhaps, the inner eye is closed in most of us; in some it is blind. But I have opened that eye and trained it. As I sleep"—he lowered his voice oddly— "those thought things come to me. It is an uncomfortable gift, yes; for here in Grange I shall find myself to-night an evil company. Murders long forgotten will be accomplished again before that inner eye of mine! I shall swim in blood! Assassins will come stealing to me, murdered ones will scream in my ears, the secret knife will flash, the honest ax do its deadly work, for in the moment of such deeds two imperishable thought-forms are created: the thought-form of the slayer, strong to survive, because a blood-lustful thought, a revengeful thought; and the thought of the slain, likewise a long-surviving thought because a thought of wildest despair, a final massing of the mental forces greater than any generally possible in life, upon that last awful grievance."

He paused, looking around him.

"From the phantom company," he said, "I must pick out that one whose thought is of laughter, of firing guns, and of evil whisperings. What a task! Wondrous is the science of the mental negative!"

The meeting broke up, then, and Isis Klaw, having brought from a large case, which formed part of her father's luggage, two huge red cushions, bade us good-night and retired to her own room. Moris Klaw, with a cushion swinging in each hand, went shuffling ungainly from room to room like some strange animal seeking a lair.

"Do I understand," Clement Leyland whispered to me, "that your friend proposes to sleep down here?"

"Yes," I replied, smiling at his evident wonderment; "such is his method of investigation, eccentric, but effective."

"It is really effective, then? The experiences given in 'Psychic Angles' are not fabulous?"

"In no way. Moris Klaw is a very remarkable man. I have yet to meet the mystery which is beyond him."

Moris Klaw's rumbling voice, which frequently reminded me of the rolling of casks in a distant cellar, broke in upon our conversation:

"Here is the ideal spot; here upon this settee by the door of the gun room I am in the centre of these psychic storms which nightly arise in Grange."

"If you are determined to remain here, Mr. Klaw," said Sir James, "I shall not endeavour to dissuade you, of course; but I should prefer to see you turn into more comfortable quarters."

"No, no," was the reply; "it is here I shall lay down my old head, it is here I shall lie and wait for him, the one who laughs."

Accordingly, since the hour grew late, we left this novel ghost-hunter stretched out upon the settee in the billiard room; and as I knew his objection to any disturbance, I suggested to Sir James that we should retire out of earshot for a final smoke ere seeking our separate apartments.

We sat chatting for close upon an hour, I suppose. Then Clement Leyland left us, saying that he had had a heavy day.

"Clement's been working real hard," the baronet confided to me. "In the circumstances, as I think I told you, I have decided to abandon Grange, and we are having the old Friars House, a mile from here, but on part of the estate, restored. It hasn't been inhabited for about three generations, and it's very much older than Grange; part of it dates back to King John. Perhaps I can get servants to stop there, though, and it's quite impossible to keep up Grange without a staff. Clement has been superintending the work over there all day; he's one of the best."

A few moments later we parted for the night. I left Sir James at the door of his room, which had formerly opened off the balcony overlooking the banqueting hall. That door was now walled up, however, and the entrance was from the corridor beyond. The room allotted to me was upon the opposite side of the same corridor and farther to the north.

I felt particularly unlike sleep. The extremely modern furniture of my room could not rob the walls, with their small square panelling, of the air of hoary antiquity which was theirs. The one window, deep set and overlooking an extensive orchard, was such as might have formed the focus for cavalierly glance, was such as might have framed the head of a romantic maid of Stuart days.

And with it all was that gloomy air that had a more remote antiquity, that harked back to darker times than those of the Merry Monarch: the air of ghostly evil, the cloud from which proceeded the devilish laughter, the obscene whisperings.

Where the shadows of the trees lay beneath me on the turf, I could fancy a gray cowled figure flitting across the lighted patches and lurking, evilly watching, amid the pools of darkness. Sleep was impossible. Moris Klaw, to whom such fears as mine were utterly unknown, might repose, nay, was actually reposing, in the very vortex of this psychical storm; but I was otherwise constituted. I had been with him in many cases of dark enough evil-doing, but this purely ghostly menace was something that sapped my courage.

Grange stood upon rather high ground, and in a northeasterly direction, peeping out from the trees of a wooded slope, showed a gray tower almost like a giant monkish figure under the moon. I watched it with a vague interest. It was Friars House, to which the baronet projected retreat from the haunted Grange. Lighting my pipe, I leaned from the window, idly watching that ancient tower and wondering if more evil deeds had taken place within it—long as it had stood there amid the trees—than those which had left their ghostly mark upon Grange.

The night was very beautiful and very still. Not the slightest sound could I detect within or without the house. How long I had lounged there in this half-dreamy, but vaguely fearful, mood I cannot say, but I was aroused by a tremendous outcry. Loud it broke in upon the silence of the night, broke in on my mood with nerve-racking effect. My pipe dropped to the floor, and taking one step across the room I stood there, rooted to the spot with indefinable horror.

"Father!" it came in a piercing scream, and again: "Father! O God! save him! save him!"

III

The voice was that of Isis Klaw!

Whenever I accompanied her father upon any of his inquiries I came armed, and now, with a magazine pistol held in my hand, I leapt out into the corridor and turned toward the stair. A door slammed open in front of me and Sir James Leyland also came running out, pulling on his dressing gown as he ran. One quick glance he gave me; his face was very pale; and together we went racing down the stairs into the hall patched with ghostly moonlight.

"You heard it?" he breathed, hoarsely. "It was Miss Klaw! What in God's name has happened? Where is she?"

But even as he asked the question, and as we pressed on into the billiard room, it was answered. For Isis Klaw, with a dressing gown thrown over her night apparel, was kneeling beside the settee upon which her father lay.

"What has happened? What has happened?" groaned Sir James. Then, as we approached together: "Mr. Klaw! Mr. Klaw!" he cried.

"All right, my friend!" came the rumbling voice, and to my inestimable relief Moris Klaw sat up and looked around upon us, adjusting his pince-nez to the bridge of his massive nose: "I live! It has saved me, the Science of the Mind!"

Isis Klaw bowed her head upon the red cushion, and I saw that she was trembling violently. It was the first time I had known her to lose her regal composure, and, utterly mystified, I wondered what awful danger had threatened Moris Klaw.

"Thank Heaven for that!" said the baronet, earnestly.

Approaching footsteps sounded now, and a group of frightened servants, headed by the butler, appeared at the door of the billiard room. Through them came pressing Mr. Clement Leyland. His face was ghastly, showing a startling white against the dull red of the dressing gown he wore.

"James!" he said, huskily. "James! that awful screaming! What was it? What has occurred?"

I knew that he slept in the west wing and that he must have been unable to distinguish the words which Isis had cried. Thus heard, the shrill scream must have sounded even more terrifying.

Moris Klaw raised his hand protestingly.

"No fuss, dear friends," he implored, in rumbling accents, "no wonderings and botherings. They so disturb the nerves. Let us be calm, let us be peaceful." Be laid his hand upon the head of the girl who knelt beside him. "Isis, my child, what a delicate instrument is the psychic perception! You knew it, the danger to your poor old father, to the poor old fool who lies here waiting to be slaughtered! Almost you knew it before I knew it myself!"

"For God's sake, Mr. Klaw," said Clement Leyland, shakily, "what has happened? Who, or what, came to you here? What occasioned Miss Klaw's terror?"

"My friend," replied Klaw, "you ask me conundrum-riddles. Some dreadful thing haunts this Grange, some deadly thing. The man has not lived who has not tasted fear, and I, the old foolish, have lived indeed to-night! I fail, my friend. There is some evil intelligence ruling this Grange, which I cannot capture upon my negative"—he tapped his brow characteristically— "to attempt it would be to die. It is too powerful for me. Grange is unclean, Sir James. You will leave Grange without delay; it is I, the old experienced who knows, that warns you. Fly from Grange. Take up your residence to-morrow at Friars House!"

No further explanation would he vouchsafe.

"I am defeated, my friends!" he declared, shrugging, resignedly.

Accordingly, Isis, her beautiful face deathly pale and her great eyes feverishly bright, returned to her room. She covered her face with her hands as she passed to the door. Moris Klaw accepted the use of an apartment next to mine, and we all sought our couches again in states of varying perturbation.

That there was some profound mystery underlying these happenings of the night was evident to me. Moris Klaw and Isis Klaw were keeping something back. They shared some dark secret and guarded it jealously; but with what motive they acted in this fashion was a problem that defied my efforts at solution.

The morning came and brought a haggard company to the breakfast table. Few, if any, beneath the roof of Grange, had known sleep that night, although, so far as I could gather, there had been no manifestations of any kind.

Moris Klaw talked incessantly about the fauna of the Sahara Desert, and so monopolized the conversation with his queer anecdotes of snakes and scorpions that no other topic found entrance.

After breakfast the whole party, in Sir James's car, drove over to Friars House; and despite the up-to-date furniture and upholstery, I found it a very gloomy residence. Stripped of its ghostly atmosphere, Grange had been quite a charming seat for any man; but this dungeonesque place, with its lichened tower that had dominated the valley when John signed Magna Charta, with its massive walls and arrow-slit windows, its eccentrically designed apartments and crypt-like smell, was altogether too archaic to be comfortable.

Moris Klaw, standing in the room which had been fitted up as a library, removed his flat-topped brown bowler and fumbled for his scent spray.

"This place," he said, "smells abominably of dead abbots!"

He squirted verbena upon himself and upon Isis. He replaced the scent spray in the lining of the hat, and was about to replace the hat on his head, when he paused, staring straight up at the ceiling reflectively.

"My notes!" he said, abruptly; "I have left those notes in my valise. I must have them. Curse me, for an old foolish! Sir James, you will show Isis this charming old tower in my absence? Do I intrude? But I would borrow the car and return to Grange for my notes!"

"Not a bit!" replied the baronet, readily. "Clement can go with you!"

"No, no! Certainly no! I could not think of it! My old friend, Mr. Searles, may come if he so likes; if not, I go alone."

Naturally, I agreed to accompany him; and, leaving the others at the ancient gateway, we set off in Sir James's car back to Grange. Down into the valley we swept and up the slope to Grange, Moris Klaw sitting muttering in his beard, but offering no remark and patently desirous to avoid conversation.

"Come, my friend," he said, as the car drew up before the house, "and I will show you what my mental negative recorded to me last night, just before the great danger came."

He led the way into the billiard room, curtly directing the butler to leave us. When we were alone—

"You will note something," he rumbled, swinging his arm vaguely around in the direction of the banqueting hall. "What you will note is this: the laughter—where is it heard? It is heard here, in the gun room on my right, in the banquet room before me. Great is the Science of the Mind! I will now test my negative."

I followed him with wondering gaze as he stepped into the deep old-fashioned fireplace which formed one of the quaintest features of the room. He bent his tall figure to avoid striking his head upon the stonework, and placed the historic brown bowler upon one of the settles.

"Perhaps I cannot find it," came his rumbling voice; "my negative was fogged by assassinations, murderous sieges, candle-light duels, and other thought-forms of the troubled past; but I may triumph—I may triumph!"

He was standing on a settle with his head far up the chimney, and presently a faint grating sound proceeded from that sooty darkness.

"I have it!" he rumbled, triumphantly. "And in my pocket reposes the electric lamp. I ascend; you, my good friend, will follow."

True enough he scrambled upward and, to my unspeakable amazement, disappeared in the chimney. Filled with great wonder I followed and saw him standing in a recess high above my head, a recess which he must have opened in some way unknown to me. He extended a long arm and grasped my hand in his.

"Up!" he cried, exerted his surprising strength, and jerked me up beside him with as little effort as though I had been a child.

He pressed the button of a torch which he held and I saw that we stood upon an exceedingly steep and narrow wooden stair.

"It is in the thickness of the wall between the panellings," he whispered, solemnly; "a Jacobite hiding place. Sir James knows nothing of it, for has he not spent his life in the Bush?"

He mounted the stair.

"On the right," his voice came back to me, "the gun room, the billiard room! On the left, the banquet room. From here comes the laughter—from here comes the danger."

Still he ascended and I followed. The narrow stair terminated in a dusty box-like apartment no more than six feet high by six feet square. Moris Klaw, ducking his head grotesquely, stood there shining the light about him. From the floor he took up a square wooden case and waved to me to descend again.

"No exit," he said; "no exit. Sir James's bedroom is upon the farther side, but, as I had anticipated, there is no exit."

We returned the way we had come; clearly there was no other. Beneath his caped coat Moris Klaw jealously concealed the case which he had discovered in the secret chamber. I was filled with intense curiosity; but Moris Klaw, having gone to his room, asking me to await him outside in the drive, returned, ultimately, without the case, but carrying a huge notebook, and intimated that he was prepared to reenter the waiting car.

Behind the pebbles of his pince-nez his strange eyes gleamed triumphantly.

"We triumph," he said. "The haunting of Grange succumbs to the Science of the Mind!"

IV

We all had lunch at Friars House, but were by no means a jovial party. Sir James seemed worried and preoccupied, and Clement Leyland even more reticent than usual. Moris Klaw talked, certainly, but his conversation turned entirely upon the subject of the Borgias, concerning which notorious family he was possessed of a stock of most unsavoury anecdote. So realistic were his gruesome stories, delivered in that rumbling whisper, wholly impossible to describe or imitate, that every mouthful of food which I swallowed threatened to choke me.

Afterward we wandered idly about the beautiful old grounds, which bore ineffaceable marks of monkish cultivation. Sir James, who was walking ahead with Moris Klaw and Isis, suddenly turned and waited for me. I had been examining a sundial with much interest, but I now walked on and joined our host.

"Mr. Searles," he said, "may I press you to remain here over the week-end?"

"That's very good of you," I replied. "I think I could manage it, and I should enjoy the stay immensely."

I concluded that Moris Klaw also was remaining, and consequently was surprised when a short time later he drew me aside
into a rose-covered arbour and announced that he was leaving by
the four-o'clock train.

"But I shall be back in the morning, Mr. Searles," he assured
me, wagging his finger mysteriously; "I shall be back in the morning!"

"And Miss Klaw?"

"She, too, goes by the four-o'clock train and will not be returning—for the present."

"I understand that Sir James is taking up his residence here at
Friars House from now onward?"

"It is so, my friend; he deserts Grange. The servants come over
here to-day. Is he not well advised? Mr. Clement has all along rec-
ommended that this shall be his residence. He was against it, the
idea of inhabiting Grange, from the first. He is wise, that Mr. Clement. He has lived in these parts so long. He knows that Grange is
haunted, is uninhabitable."

Later, then, Moris Klaw and Isis took their departure, and just as
the car was about to drive off my eccentric friend removed his brown
bowler and sprayed his bald brow with verbena. He bent to me:

"Day and night," he whispered, huskily, "do not lose sight of
him, Sir James! Above all, allow him not to *explore!*"

With that the car drove off, and I stood looking after it, wondering, utterly mystified. On the steps behind me stood Clement
Leyland and his cousin. The latter's gaze followed the course of
the car along the picturesque winding road until it became lost from
view. I thought I heard him sigh.

Ensued an uneventful day and night. Life was pleasant enough
at Friars House, if a trifle dull; and Sir James seemed unsettled,
whilst his disquietude was reflected in his cousin. The latter, now
that his active labours in preparing this new residence for the baronet were checked, seemed a man at a loss what to do with himself. His was one of those quietly ardent temperaments, I divined,
and idleness palled upon him. Apparently he had no profession,
and although I presumed that he had some residence of his own in
the neighbourhood, he, apparently, was prepared indefinitely to

prolong his stay at Friars House. I think his companionship was welcome to Sir James, for the latter was yet strange to the new duties of a landed gentleman.

The next morning brought Moris Klaw, and I learned with ever-growing surprise that he had made arrangements to spend the following week beneath the hospitable roof of Friars House.

I have nothing to record of interest up to the time I left; but often during the ensuing six days the problem of the haunting of Grange, and the mystery of Moris Klaw's protracted visit to Friars House came between me and my work. Then on the Saturday morning arrived a telegram:

> "Can you join us for week-end—car will meet
> 2:30. Wire reply. Best wishes.—Leyland."

I determined to accept the invitation; for respecting the nature of Moris Klaw's business at Friars House—and that he had some other motive than ordinary in sojourning there I was persuaded—my curiosity knew no bounds. Accordingly, I packed my grip, and at about five o'clock on a delightful afternoon found myself taking tea in a cloister-like apartment of the former Friary.

"Grange," said Sir James, in answer to a question of mine, "is shut up."

"It is shut, yes," rumbled Moris Klaw. "What a pity! What a pity!"

In the course of the day occurred incidents which I have since perceived to have been significant. I will pass over them, however, and hasten to what I may term the catastrophe of this very singular case.

Four of us sat down to dinner in an apartment which clearly had been the ancient refectory of the monks. Clement Leyland, who had arrived barely in time to dress, looked haggard and worried. I determined that he had some private troubles of his own, and beneath his quiet geniality I thought I could detect a sort of brooding gloom. His pale, clean-shaven face, so like yet so unlike that of his cousin, was a mask that ill repaid study; yet I knew that the real Clement Leyland was a stranger to me, perhaps to all of us.

I was most anxious to learn if Moris Klaw had divulged the secret of the hidden chamber at Grange to Sir James; and I was unspeakably curious concerning the box of which I had had but a glimpse—the box that he had found there. But he baffled my curiosity at every point.

Have you experienced that sense of impending calamity which sometimes heralds tragic things? It was with me that night, throughout dinner; and afterward, when we entered the library and sat over our cigars, it grew portentously. I felt that I stood upon the brink of a precipice. And literally I was not in great error. Moris Klaw, to the evident discomfort of Sir James, brought the conversation around to the subject of the haunting. I observed him to glance at his watch, with a rather odd expression upon his vellum-hued face.

"Is it not singular," he said, "how poor spectres are confined, like linnets, to their cages? They seem, these spooks, never to roam. That laughing demon of Grange—look at him. He remains in that empty, desolate house; he—"

There was a dreadful interruption.

Commencing with a sort of guttural rattle, out upon the cloisteresque stillness burst a peal of wicked laughter.

It rang throughout the room; it poured fear into my every fibre. It died away—and was gone.

Sir James, clutching the leather-covered chair arms, looked like a man of stone. I was frankly terrorized. Moris Klaw stood behind me, by a bookcase, him I could not see. But Clement Leyland's face I can never forget. It was positively deathlike. His eyes seemed starting from their sockets, and his teeth chattered horribly.

"God in Heaven!" he whispered, brokenly. "What is it? O God! What is it! Take it away—take it away!"

Then Moris Klaw spoke, slowly:

"It is for *you* to take it away, Mr. Leyland!"

Clement Leyland rose from his seat; he swayed like a drunken man, and there was madness in the glaring eyes that he turned in Klaw's direction.

"You—you—" he gasped.

"I—I—" rumbled Moris Klaw, sternly, and took a step forward; "I have entered the Jacobite hiding place at Grange, and there I found a box! Ah! you glare! glare on, my friend! I returned that box to where I found it; but first I examined its contents! What! that demon laughter frightens you! Then descend, Mr. Leyland, descend and bring him out—the one who laughs!"

Rigidly, Sir James sat in his chair; I, too, seemed to be palsied. But at sight of the next happening we both stood up. Moris Klaw stamped heavily upon the oaken floor in a deep recess; then applied his weight to a section of the seemingly solid stone wall.

It turned, as on a pivot, revealing a dark cavity. He stood there, a bizarre figure, pointing down into the blackness.

"Descend, my friend!" he cried. "The one who laughs is upon the seventh step!"

"The seventh step!"

In a whisper the words came from Clement Leyland. A draft of damp, cavernous air blew into the library out of the opening.

"Descend, my friend!"

Remorselessly, Moris Klaw repeated the words. In the centre of the room, Clement Leyland, a pitiable sight, stood staring—and hesitating. Suddenly his cousin spoke.

"Don't go, Clement!" he whispered.

The other turned to him, dazedly.

"Don't go—down that place. But—O God! I understand at last, or partly. . . . *Quit!* I give you half an hour!"

Sir James sank back into his chair and buried his face in his hands; Moris Klaw never moved from where he stood by the cavity. But Clement Leyland, with bowed head, walked from the room.

In the silence that followed his going—

"Await me, gentlemen," rumbled Klaw; "I descend for the laughter!" He stepped into the opening.

"One," he counted, "two—three—four—five—" his voice came up to us from the depths— *"six!"*

We heard him ascending. Walking into the library he placed upon the table beside Sir James a very large and up-to-date gramophone!

"The laughter!" he explained, simply. "That night, my friends, when first I slept at Grange, I secured, among a host of other dreadful negatives, the negative of one who lurked in a secret hiding place. I saw him come creeping from the chimney corner, bearing a great mace which I recognized for one that had hung in the hall! Almost, the Science of the Mind betrayed me; for I mistook him for a thought-form! But the mind of Isis is *en rapport* with the mind of her poor old father. In her dreams she saw my peril, and she it was who, screaming, saved me!—saved me from the murderer with the mace!"

Sir James made no sign. Moris Klaw continued:

"I gathered, then, that the one who sometimes lurked in the Jacobite hiding place and who, somehow, made the demon laughter, and the other phenomena, sought *one* end. It was to cause you to leave Grange and to live in Friars House! Beyond so far, my science could not show me. I assisted, therefore, the project of the lurker; and came myself, too, in order to watch, my friend, to guard and to spy!

"His gramophone I found, examined, and replaced. It had a clockwork attachment, very ingenious, which both started and stopped it; there was little or no scraping. To-night, from his room, unknown to him, I removed the instrument from its case, which lay hidden at the bottom of his trunk. Yes! I stole his key! I am the old fox! Why did he bring it here? I cannot reply. Perhaps he meant again to use it; his future projects are dark to me, but their object is all too light."

Sir James groaned.

"Old Clem!" he whispered, "and how I trusted him!"

"He did not quite believe in my science," resumed Moris Klaw, "but he did not know that, hidden, I slept almost beside him as he sat, planning, in this very room! From his own bad mind I secured my second negative; and it showed me the death trap of some bad old son of Mother Church! At Grange there was but the Jacobite hiding place, but here was the devilry of feudal times! I returned to London. Why? To learn if my suspicions were well founded. Yes!

You may or may not be aware; but if you die childless, the wicked Clement inherits Grange!"

"I knew that," whispered Sir James.

"Ah! you knew? So. I returned to here, for, even at that time, I suspected that your accidental death was the object of removal! Then I secured it, my second negative. Biding my time, I explored that death-smelling place. Its wicked machinery had been *freshly oiled!* Ah! he knew its secrets well, the old house that he hoped to inherit!

"One night, all innocent, as you sat here, with other guests, he would have blundered upon that doorway! And you, the host, would have led the search party! But I saw that he feared to move whilst I remained, and so I played the ghost upon him with his own spook!"

Sir James Leyland looked up. His bronzed face was transformed with emotion.

"Mr. Klaw," he said, huskily, "why did you lay so much emphasis upon the words, 'the seventh step'?"

Moris Klaw shrugged, replying simply:

"Because *there is no seventh step—only the mouth of a well!*"

CASE OF THE VEIL OF ISIS

I

I have made no attempt, in these chronicles, to arrange the cases of my remarkable friend, Moris Klaw, in sections. Yet, as has recently been pointed out to me, they seem naturally to fall into two orders. There were those in which he appeared in the role of criminal investigator, and in which he was usually associated with Inspector Grimsby. There was another class of inquiry in which the criminal element was lacking: mysteries which never came under the notice of New Scotland Yard.

Since Moris Klaw's methods were, if not supernatural, at any rate supernormal, I have been asked if he ever, to my knowledge, inquired into a case which proved insusceptible of a natural explanation—which fell strictly within the province of the occult.

To that I answer that I am aware of several; but I have refrained from including them because readers of these papers would be unlikely to appreciate the nature of Klaw's investigations outside the sphere of ordinary natural laws. Those who are curious upon the point cannot do better than consult the remarkable work by Moris Klaw entitled, "Psychic Angles."

But there was one case with which I found myself concerned that I am disposed to include, for it fell between the provinces of the natural and super natural in such a way that it might, with equal legitimacy, be included under either head. On the whole, I am disposed to bracket it with the case of the headless mummies.

I will take leave to introduce you, then, to the company which met at Otter Brearley's house one night in August.

"This is most truly amazing," Moris Klaw was saying; "and I am indebted to my good friend Searles"—he inclined his sparsely covered head in my direction— "for the opportunity to be one of you. It is a séance? Yes and no. But there is a mummy in it—and those mummies are so instructive!"

He extracted the scent spray from his pocket and refreshed his yellow brow with verbena.

"How to be regretted that my daughter is in Paris," he continued, his rumbling voice echoing queerly about the room. "She loves them like a mother—those mummies! Ah, Mr. Brearley, this will cement your great reputation!"

Otter Brearley shook his head.

"I am not yet prepared to make it public property," he declared, slowly. "No one, outside the present circle, knows of my discovery. I do not wish it to go farther—at present."

He glanced around the table, his prominent blue eyes passing from myself to Moris Klaw and from Klaw to the clean-cut dark face of Doctor Fairbank. The latter, scarce heeding his host's last words, sat watching how the shaded light played, tenderly, amid the soft billows of Ailsa Brearley's wonderful hair.

"Shall you make it the subject of a paper?" he asked suddenly.

"My dear Doctor Fairbank!" rumbled Moris Klaw, solemnly, "if you had been paying attention to our good friend you would have heard him say, that he was not prepared, at present, to make public his wonderful discovery."

"Sorry!" said Fairbank, turning to Brearley. "But if it is not to be made public I don't altogether follow the idea. What *do* you intend, Brearley?"

"I intend to experiment," answered Brearley.

"In what way?" I asked.

"In every way possible!"

Doctor Fairbank sat back in his chair and looked thoughtful.

"Rather a comprehensive scheme?"

Brearley toyed with the bundle of notes under his hand.

"I have already," he said, "exhaustively examined seven of the possibilities; the eighth, and—I believe, the last—remains to be considered."

"Listen now to me, Mr. Brearley," said Moris Klaw, wagging a long finger. "I am here, the old curious, and find myself in delightful company. But until this evening I know nothing of your work except that I have read all your books. For me you will be so good as to outline all the points—yes?"

Otter Brearley mutely sought permission of the company, and turned the leaves of his manuscript. All men have an innate love of "talking shop," but few can make such talk of general interest. Brearley was an exception in this respect. He loved to talk of Egypt, of the Pharaohs, of the temples of the priesthood and its mysteries; but others loved to hear him. That made all the difference.

"The discovery," he now began, "upon which I have blundered—for pure accident, alone, led me to it—assumes its great importance by reason of the absolute mystery surrounding certain phases of Egyptian worship. In the old days, Fairbank, you will recall that it was my supreme ambition to learn the secrets of Isis-worship as practised in early Egyptian times. Save for impostors, and legitimate imaginative writers, no one has yet lifted the veil of Isis. That mystical ceremony by which a priest was consecrated to the goddess, or made an arch adept, was thought to be hopelessly lost, or, by others, to be a myth devised by the priesthood to awe the ignorant masses. In fact, we know little of the entire religion but its outward form. Of that occult lore so widely attributed to its votaries we know nothing—absolutely nothing! By we, I mean students in general. I, individually, have made a step, if not a stride, into that holy of holies!"

"Mind you don't lose yourself!" said Fairbank, lightly.

But, professionally, he was displeased with Brearley's drawn face and with the feverish brightness of his eyes. So much was plain for all to see. In the eyes of Ailsa Brearley, so like, yet so unlike, her brother's, he read understanding of his displeasure, I think, together with a pathetic appeal.

Brearley waved his long white hand carelessly.

"Rest assured of that, Doctor!" he replied. "The labyrinth in which I find myself is intricate, I readily admit; but all my steps have been well considered. To return, Mr. Klaw"—addressing the latter— "I have secured the mummy of one of those arch adepts! That he was one is proved by the papyrus, presumably in his own writing, which lay upon his breast! I unwrapped the mummy in Egypt, where it now reposes; but the writing I brought back with me and have recently deciphered. A glance had showed me that it was not the usual excerpts from the 'Book of the Dead.' Six months' labour has proved it to be a detailed account of his initiation into the inner mysteries!"

"Is such a papyrus unique?" I asked.

"Unique!" cried Moris Klaw. "Name of a little blue man! It is priceless!"

"But why," I pursued, "should this priest, alone among the many who must have been so initiated, have left an account of the ceremony?"

"It was forbidden to divulge any part, any word, of it, Searles!" said Brearley. "Departure from this law was visited with fearful punishments in this world and dire penalties in the next. Khamus, for so this priest was named, well knew this. But some reason which, I fear, can never be known, prompted him to write the papyrus. It is probable, if not certain, that no eye but his, and mine, has read what is written there."

A silence of a few seconds followed his words.

"Yes," rumbled Klaw, presently; "it is undoubtedly a discovery of extraordinary importance, this. You agree, my friend?"

I nodded.

"That's evident," I replied. "But I cannot altogether get the hang of the ceremony itself, Brearley. That is the point upon which I am particularly hazy."

"To read you the entire account in detail," Brearley resumed, "would occupy too long, and would almost certainly confuse you. But the singular, thing is this: Khamus distinctly asserts that the

goddess appeared to him. His writing is eminently sane and reserved, and his account of the ceremony, up to that point, highly
interesting. Now, I have tested the papyrus itself—though no possibility of fraud is really admissible, and I have been able to con-
firm many of the statements made therein. There is only one point,
it seems to me, remaining to be settled."

"What is that?" I asked.

"Whether, as a result of the ceremony described, Khamus did
see Isis, or whether he merely imagined he did!"

No one spoke for a moment. Then—

"My friend," said Moris Klaw, "I have a daughter whom I have
named Isis. Why did I name her Isis? Mr. Brearley, you must know
that that name has a mystic and beautiful significance. But I will
say something—I am glad that my daughter is not here! Mr.
Brearley—beware! Beware, I say: you play with burning fires; my
friend—beware!"

His words impressed us all immensely; for there was something
underlying them more portentous than appeared upon the surface.

Fairbank stared at Brearley, hard.

"Do I understand," he began, quietly, "that you admit the first
possibility?"

"Certainly!" replied Brearley, with conviction. "You are prepared to admit the existence, as an entity, of Isis?"

"I am prepared to admit the existence of anything until it can
be proved not to exist!"

"Then, admitting the existence of Isis, what should you assume
it, or her, to be?"

"That is not a matter for presumption; it is a matter for inquiry!"

The doctor glanced quickly toward Ailsa Brearley, and her beautiful face was troubled.

"And this inquiry—how should you propose to conduct it?"

"In surroundings as nearly as possible identical with those described in the papyrus," replied Brearley, with growing excitement.
"I should follow the ceremony, word by word, as Khamus did!"

His eyes gleamed with pent-up enthusiasm. We four listeners,
again stricken silent, watched him; and again it was the doctor who
broke the silence.

"Is the ceremony spoken?"

"In the first half there is a long prayer, which is chanted."

"But Egyptian, as a *spoken* language, is lost, surely."

"The exact pronunciation, or accent, is lost, of course; but there are many who can speak it. I can, for instance."

"And I," rumbled Moris Klaw, gloomily. "But these special surroundings? Eh, my friend?"

"I have spent a year in searching for the necessary things, as specified in the writing. At last my collection is complete. Some of the things I have had made, in the proper materials mentioned. These materials, in some cases, have been exceedingly difficult to procure. But now I have a complete shrine of Isis fitted up! Khamus's initiation took place in a small chamber of which he gives a concise and detailed account. It is because my duplicate of this chamber is ready that I have asked you to meet me here to-night"

"How long have you been at work upon this inquiry?" said Fairbank

He put the question as he might have put one relating to a patient's symptoms, and this Brearley detected in his tone, with sudden resentment.

"Fairbank," he said, huskily, "I believe you think me insane!"

With his pale, drawn face and long, fair hair, he certainly looked anything but normal, as he sat with bright, staring eyes fixed upon the other across the table.

"My dear chap," replied the doctor, soothingly, "what a strange idea! My question was prompted by a professional spirit, I will admit, for I thought you had been sticking to this business too closely. You are the last man in the world I should expect to go mad, Brearley, but I should not care to answer for your nerves if you don't give this Isis affair a rest."

Brearley smiled, and waved his hand characteristically. "Excuse me, Fairbank," he said, "but to the average person my ideas do seem fantastic, I know. That is what makes me so touchy on the point, I suppose."

"You are hoping for too much from what is at most only a wild conjecture, Brearley. Your translation of the manuscript, alone, is a sufficiently notable achievement. If I were in your place, I should leave the occult business to the psychical societies. 'Let the cobbler,' you know."

"It has gone too far for that," returned Brearley, "and I must see it through, now."

"You are putting too much into it," said the doctor, severely. "I want you to promise me that if nothing results from your final experiment, you will drop the whole inquiry."

Brearley frowned thoughtfully.

"Do you really think I am overdoing it?" he asked.

"Sure," was the answer. "Drop the whole thing for a month or two."

"That is impossible."

"Why?"

"Because the ceremony must take place upon the first night of *Panoi*, the tenth month of the Sacred Sothic year. This we take to correspond to the April of the Julian year."

"Yes," rumbled Moris Klaw, "it is to-night!"

"Why!" I cried, "of course it is! Do you mean, Brearley, that you are going to conduct your experiment *now*?"

"Exactly," was the calm reply; "and I have asked you all—Mr. Moris Klaw in particular—in order that it may take place in the presence of competent witnesses!"

Moris Klaw shook his massive head and pulled at his scanty, toneless beard in a very significant manner. All of us were vaguely startled, I think, and through my mind the idea flashed that the first of April was a date pathetically appropriate for such an undertaking. Frankly, I was beginning to entertain serious doubts regarding Brearley's sanity.

"I have given the servants a holiday," said the latter. "They are at a theatre in town; so there is no possibility of the experiment being interrupted."

Something of his enthusiasm, unnatural though it seemed, strangely enough began to communicate itself to me.

"Come upstairs," he continued, "and I will explain what we all have to do."

Moris Klaw squirted verbena upon his brow.

II

"Doctor Fairbank!"

Fairbank, startled by the touch on his arm, stopped. It was Ailsa Brearley who had dropped behind her brother and now stood confronting us. In the dense shadows of the corridor one could barely distinguish her figure, but a stray beam of light touched one side of her pure oval face and burnished her fair hair.

She wanted help, guidance. I had read it in her eyes before. I was sorry that her sweet lips should have that pathetic little droop.

"Doctor Fairbank! I have wanted to ask you all night—do you think he—"

She could not speak the words, and stood biting her lips, with eyes averted.

"Miss Brearley," he replied, "I do, certainly, fear that your brother is liable to a nervous breakdown at any moment. He has applied his mind too closely to this inquiry, and has studiously surrounded himself with a morbid atmosphere."

Ailsa Brearley was now watching him, anxiously. "Should we allow him to go on with it?"

"I fear any attempt to prevent him would prove most detrimental, in his present condition."

"But—" There was clearly something else which she wanted to say. "But, apart from that"—the suddenly turned to Moris Klaw, instinctively it almost seemed— "Mr. Klaw—is this—ceremony *right*?"

He peered at her through his pince-nez.

"In what way, my dear Miss Brearley—how right?"

"Well—what I mean is—it amounts to idolatry, does it not?"

I started. It was a point of view which had not, hitherto, occurred to me.

"You probably understand the nature of the thing better than we do, Miss Brearley," said Fairbank. "Do you mean that it involves worship of Isis?"

"He has always avoided a direct answer when I have asked him that," she said. "But it is only reasonable to suppose that it does. His translation of the writing I have never seen. But he has been

dieting in a most extraordinary manner for nearly a year! Since
the workmen completed it, no one but himself has been inside the
chamber which he has had constructed at the end of his study; and
he spends hours and hours there every day—and every night!"

Her anxiety became more evident with each word.

"You saw that he ate nothing at dinner," she continued, "and
taxed him with faddism. But it is something more than that. Why
has he sent the servants away to-night? Oh, Doctor Fairbank! I
have a dreadful foreboding! I am so afraid!"

The light in her eyes, suddenly upturned to him in the vague
half-light, the tone in her voice, the appeal in her attitude—were
unmistakable. Fairbank had been abroad for three years, and I
could see that between these two was an undeclared love, and almost I felt that I intruded. Moris Klaw looked away for a moment,
too. Then—

"My dear young lady," he rumbled, paternally, "do not be afraid.
I, the old know-all, so fortunately am here! Perhaps there is danger—yes, I admit it; there may be danger. But it is such danger as
dwells here"—he tapped his yellow brow— "it is a danger of the
mind. For thoughts are things, Miss Brearley—that is where it lies,
the peril—and thought things can kill!"

"Ailsa! Fairbank! Mr. Klaw!" came Brearley's voice. "We have
none too much time!"

"Proceed, my friends," rumbled Moris Klaw; "I am with you."
And, oddly enough, I was comforted by his presence; so, it was
evident, were the girl and the doctor; for Moris Klaw, beneath that
shabby, ramshackle exterior, Moris Klaw, the Wapping curio
dealer, was a man of power—an intellectual ark of refuge.

In the Egyptologist's study all appeared much the same as when
last I had set foot there. The cases filled with vases, scarabs, tab-
lets, weapons, and the hundred-and-one relics of the great dead
age with which the student had surrounded himself; the sar-
cophagi; the frames of papyri—all seemed familiar.

Brearley sat at the huge writing table, littered, as of yore, and
in picturesque confusion.

"We must begin almost immediately!" he said, as we entered.

A danger spot burned lividly upon either pale cheek. His eyes gleamed brilliantly. The prolonged excitement of his strange experiment was burning the man up. His nerve centres must be taxed abnormally, I knew.

Brearley glanced at his watch

"I must be very brief," he explained, hurriedly, "as it is vitally important that I commence in time. Beyond the bookcase, there, you will see that a part of the room has been walled off."

We looked in the direction indicated. Although it was not noticeable at first glance I now saw that the apartment was, indeed, smaller than formerly. The usual books covered the new wall, giving it much the same aspect as the old; but, where hitherto there had been nothing but shelves, a small, narrow door of black wood now broke the imposing expanse of faded volumes.

"In there," Brearley resumed, "is the Secret Place described by Khamus!"

He placed his long, thin hand upon a yellow roll that lay partly opened on the table.

"No one but myself may enter there until after to-night, at any rate!" with a glance at Moris Klaw. "To the most minute particular"—patting the papyrus— "it is equipped as Khamus describes. For many months I have prepared myself, by fasting and meditation, as *he* prepared! There was, as no doubt you know, a widespread belief in ancient times that for any but the chosen to look upon the goddess was death. As I admit the possibility of Isis existing, I must also admit the possibility of this belief being true the more so as it is confirmed by Khamus! Therefore none may enter with me."

"One moment, Mr. Brearley," interrupted Klaw; "in what form does Khamus relate that the goddess appeared?"

A cloud crossed Brearley's face.

"It is the one point upon which he is not clear," was the reply. "I do not know, in the least, *what* to expect!"

"Go on!" I said, quickly. Although I seriously doubted my poor friend's sanity, I began to find the affair weirdly, uncannily fascinating.

Brearley continued:

"The ritual opens with a chant, which I may, broadly translate as 'The Hymn of Dedication." Its exact purport is not very clear to me. This hymn, is the only part of the ceremony in which I am assisted. It is to be 'sung by a virgin beyond the door.' That is, directly I have entered yonder it must be sung out here. Ailsa has composed a sort of chant to the words, which, I think, is the proper kind of setting. Have you not, Ailsa?"

She bowed her graceful head, glancing, under her lashes, toward Fairbank.

"She has learned the words—for, of course, it must be sung in Egyptian—"

"But have no idea of their meaning," said his sister, softly.

"That is unnecessary," he went on, quickly. "After this, I want you all just to remain here in this room. I am afraid you will have to sit in the dark! Any sounds which you detect, please note. I will not tell you what to expect, then imagination cannot deceive you. I will be back in a moment."

With another hasty glance at his watch, he went out in high excitement.

"Please," began Ailsa Brearley, the moment he was gone, "do not think that because I assist him I approve of this attempt! I think it is horrible! But what am I to do? He is wrapped up in it! I *dare* not try to check him!"

"We understand that," said Fairbank; "all of us. Do as he desires. When he has made the attempt, and failed—as, of course, he must do—the folly of the whole thing will become apparent to him. Do not let it worry you, Miss Brearley. Your brother is not the first man to succumb, temporarily, to the glamour of the Unknown."

She shook her head sadly.

"It is an unpleasant farce," she said. "But there is something more in it than that."

Her blue eyes were full of trouble.

"What do you mean, Miss Brearley?" asked Moris Klaw.

"I hardly know, myself!" was the reply; "but for the past two months an indefinable horror of some kind has been growing upon me."

With a deep sigh, she turned to a tall case and took from it a kind of slender harp. The instrument, of which the frame, at any rate, was evidently ancient Egyptian work, rested upon a claw-shaped pedestal.

"Do you play this? Yes? No?" inquired Moris Klaw, with interest.

"Yes," she said, wearily. "It comes from the tomb of a priestess of Isis and was played by her in the temple. It is scaled differently from the modern harp, but any one with a slight knowledge of the ordinary harp, or even of the piano, can perform upon it with ease. It is sweet toned, but—creepy!"

She smiled slightly at her own expression, and I was glad to see it.

Brearley returned.

He wore a single loose garment of white linen, and thin sandals were upon his feet. Save for his long, fair hair, he looked a true pagan priest, his eyes bright with the fire of research that consumed him, his features gaunt, ascetic.

Some ghost of his old humorous expression played, momentarily, about his lips as he observed the astonishment depicted upon our faces. But it was gone almost in the moment of its coming.

"You wonder at me, no doubt," he said; "and at times I have wondered at myself! Do not think me fanatic. I scarcely hope for any result. But remembering that the writing is authentic and that there prevails, to this day, a widespread belief in the occult wisdom of the Egyptians, *why* should not this problem in psychics receive the same attention from me that one in physics would receive from you, Fairbank?"

There was reason in his argument and in his manner of advancing it. Fairbank glanced from Brearley to the girl sitting with her white hands listlessly caressing the harp strings. The silence of the great empty house grew oppressive. Suppose the ancients indeed possessed the strange lore attributed to them? Suppose in those Dark Continents, the Past and the Future, somewhere in the vast unknown, there existed a power, a being, a spirit, named by the Egyptians, Isis?

Those were my thoughts, when Moris Klaw said suddenly:

"Mr. Brearley, it is not yet too late to turn back! This sensitive plate" he tapped his forehead— "warns me that some evil thought thing hovers about us! You are about to give form to that thought being. Be wise, Mr. Brearley—abandon your experiment!"

His tone surprised everyone. Otter Brearley looked at him with an odd expression and then glanced at the watch upon the writing table.

"Mr. Klaw," he said, quietly, "I had hoped for a different attitude in you; but if you really disapprove of what I am about to attempt, I can only ask you to withdraw; it is too late for further arguments."

"I remain, my friend! I spoke not for myself—my life has been passed in this coping with evil things; I spoke for others."

None of us entirely understood his words, but Brearley went on, impatiently:

"Listen, please. I rely upon your cooperation. From now onward I require absolute silence. Whatever happens make no noise."

"I shall not be noisy, I, my friend!" rumbled Moris Klaw. "I am the old silent; I watch and wait—until I am wanted."

He shrugged his shoulders and nodded, significantly.

"Good!" said Brearley, and his voice quivered with excitement; "then the experiment, the final experiment, has begun!"

III

He suddenly extinguished the light.

Passing to a window, he looked up to the moon, and, a moment later, lowered the blind. Dimly visible in his white garment, he crossed the room. He might be heard unfastening the door of the inner chamber, and a faint, church-like smell crept to our nostrils. The door closed.

Immediately the harp sounded.

Its tone was peculiar—uncomfortable. The strain which Ailsa played was a mere repetition of three notes. Then she began to sing.

Our eyes becoming more accustomed to the gloom, we could vaguely discern her now; the soft outlines of her figure; the white, ghost-like fingers straying over the strings of the instrument. The music of the chant was very monotonous, and weird to a marked degree. The sound of that ancient tongue, dead for many ages, chanted softly by Ailsa Brearley's beautiful voice, was almost incredibly eerie. I found myself gripped hard by a powerful sense of the uncanny.

No other sound was audible. Throughout the rambling old house intense silence prevailed. A slight breeze stirred the cedars outside. Every now and again it came—like a series of broken sighs.

How long the chant lasted I cannot pretend to state. It seemed interminable. I became aware of a curious sense of physical loss. I found myself drawn to high tension, as though the continuance of the chant demanded a vast effort on my part. Though I told myself that imagination was tricking me, the music seemed to be draining my nerve force!

Ailsa's voice grew louder and clearer, until the queer words, of unknown purport, rang out passionately, imperatively.

She ceased.

In the ensuing silence I could hear distinctly Moris Klaw's heavy breathing. A compelling atmosphere of mystery had grown up about us. Repel it how we might, it was there—commanding acknowledgment.

Fairbank, who sat nearest, was the first to see Ailsa Brearley rise, unsteadily, and move in the direction of the study door.

Something in her manner alarmed us all, and the doctor quietly left his seat and followed her. As she quitted the room, he came out behind her; and in the better light on the landing, as he told us later, saw that she was deathly pale.

"Miss Brearley!" he said.

She turned.

"*Ssh!*" she whispered, anxiously, "it is nothing—Doctor Fairbank. The excitement has made me rather faint, that is all. I shall go to my room and lie down. Believe me, I am quite well!"

"But there is no servant in the house," he whispered, "if you should become worse—"

"If I need anything I shall not hesitate to ring," she answered. "It is so still, you will hear the bell, Please go back! He has hoped for so much from this."

Fairbank was nonplussed. But the appeal was so obviously sincere, and the situation so difficult, that he saw no alternative. Ailsa Brearley passed along the corridor. Fairbank slipped back into the study, where Moris Klaw and I anxiously awaited him.

From the inner room came Brearley's voice, muffled.

The long vigil began.

I found myself claimed by the all-pervading spirit of mystery. For some little time I listened in expectation of hearing Ailsa Brearley returning. But soon the strange business of the night claimed my mind, to the exclusion of every other idea. I found myself listening only for Brearley's muffled voice. Although the half-audible words were meaningless, their sound assumed, as time wore on, a curious significance. They seemed potent with a strange power proceeding not *from* them, but *to* them.

Then I heard a new sound.

Fairbank heard it—for I saw him start, and Moris Klaw muttered something.

It did not come from the trees outside, nor from the inner room. It was somewhere in the house.

A faint rattling it was, bell-like but toneless.

Brearley's voice had ceased.

Again the sound rose—nearer.

I turned my head toward Fairbank, and seemed to perceive him more clearly. I had less difficulty in distinguishing the objects about.

Again it came—the shivering, bell-like sound.

Even the strings of the harp were visible now.

"Curse me!" came Moris Klaw's hoarse whisper; "it seems to grow light! That is a delusion of the mind, my friends—repel it—repel it!"

Fairbank drew a quick, sibilant breath. A half-suppressed exclamation from Klaw followed; for the high-pitched rattle came from close at hand! The sense of the supernormal had grown unbearable.

Fairbank's science and my own semi-scepticism were but weapons of sand against it.

The door opened silently, admitting a flood of the soft moon-like radiance. And Ailsa Brearley entered!

Her slim figure was bathed in light; her fair hair, unbound, swept like a gleaming torrent about her shoulders. She looked magnificently, unnaturally beautiful. A diaphanous veil was draped over her face. From her radiant figure I turned away my head in sudden, stark *fear!*

Fairbank, clutching the arms of his chair, seemed to strive to look away, too.

Her widely opened eyes, visible even through the veil, were awful in their supernormal, significant beauty. *Was* it Ailsa Brearley? I clenched my fists convulsively; I felt my reason tottering. As the luminous figure, so terrible in its perfect loveliness, moved slowly toward the inner door, with set gaze that was not for any about her, Doctor Fairbank wrenched himself from his chair and leapt forward.

"Ailsa!"

His voice came in a hoarse shriek. But it was drowned by a rumbling roar from Moris Klaw.

"Look away! Look away!" he shouted. "The good God! Do not look at her! *Look away!*"

The warning came too late. Fairbank had all but reached her side, when she turned her eyes upon him—looking fully in his face.

With no sound or cry he went down as though felled with a mighty blow!

She passed to the door of the inner room. It swung open noiselessly. A stifling cloud of some pungent perfume swept into the study; and the door reclosed.

"Fairbank!" I whispered, huskily. "My God! he's dead!"

Moris Klaw sprang forward to where Fairbank, clearly visible in the soft light, lay huddled upon the floor.

"Lift him!" he hissed. "We must get him out—before she returns—you understand?—before she returns!"

Bending together, we raised the doctor's inanimate body and half dragged, half carried him from the room. On the landing we laid him down and stood panting. A voice, clear and sweet, was speaking. I recognized neither the language nor the voice. But each liquid syllable thrilled me like an icy shock. I met Moris Klaw's gaze, set upon me through the pince-nez.

"Do not listen, my friend!" he said.

Raising Fairbank, we dragged him into the first room we came to—and Klaw locked the door.

"Here we remain," he rumbled, "until something has gone back where it came from!"

Fairbank lay motionless at our feet.

Presently came the rattling.

"It is the sistrum," whispered Moris Klaw, "the sacred instrument of the Isis temples."

The sound passed—and faded.

"Searles! Fairbank!"—it was Brearley's voice, sobbingly intense— "do not *touch* her! Do not *look* at her!"

The study door crashed open and I heard his sandals pattering on the landing.

"Fairbank! Mr. Klaw! Good God! Answer me! Tell me you are safe!"

Moris Klaw unlocked the door.

Brearley, his face white as death and bathed in perspiration, stood outside. As Klaw appeared, he leapt forward, wild eyed.

"Quick! Did any one—

"Fairbank!" I said, huskily.

Brearley pushed into the room and turned on the light. Fairbank, very pale, lay propped against an armchair. Moris Klaw immediately dropped on his knee beside him and felt his heart.

"Ah, the good God! He is alive!" he whispered. "Get some water— no brandy, my friend—water. Then look to your sister!"

Brearley plunged his trembling hands into his hair and tugged at it distractedly.

"How was I to know!" he moaned, "how was I to know! There is water in the bottle, Mr. Klaw. Searles will come with me. I must look for Ailsa!"

A bizarre figure, in his linen robe, he ran off. Moris Klaw waved me to follow him.

The door of his sister's room was closed.

He knocked, but there was no reply. He turned the knob and went in, whilst I waited in the corridor.

"Ailsa!" I heard him call, and again, "Ailsa!" then, following an interval, "Are you all right, dear?" he whispered.

"Oh, thank Heaven it is finished!" came a murmur in Ailsa Brearley's soft voice. "It *is* finished, is it not?"

"Quite finished," he answered.

"Just look at my hair!" she went on, with returning animation. "My head was so bad—I think that was why I took it down. Then I must have dropped off to sleep."

"All right, dear," said Brearley. "I want you to come downstairs; be as quick as you can."

He rejoined me in the corridor.

"She was lying with her hair strewn all over the pillow!" he whispered, "and she had been burning something—ashes in the hearth—"

Ailsa came out. She seemed suddenly to observe her brother's haggard face.

"Is there anything the matter?" she said, quickly. "Oh! has something dreadful happened?"

"No, dear," he answered, reassuringly. "Only Doctor Fairbank was overcome—"

She turned very pale.

"He is not ill?"

"No. He became faint. You can come and see for yourself."

Very quickly we all hurried downstairs. Moris Klaw, on his knees beside the doctor, was trying to force something between his clenched teeth. Ailsa, with a little cry, ran forward and knelt upon the other side of him.

"Ralph!" she whispered; "Ralph!"—and smoothed the hair back from his forehead.

He sighed deeply, and with an effort swallowed the draught which Klaw held to his lips. A moment later he opened his eyes, glaring wildly into Ailsa's face.

"Ralph!" she said, brokenly.

Then, realizing how tenderly she had spoken—using his Christian name—she hung her graceful head in hot confusion. But he had heard her. And the wild light died from his eyes. He took both her hands in his own and held them fast; then, rather unsteadily, he stood up.

As his features came more fully into the light, we all saw that a small bruise discoloured his forehead, squarely between the brows.

Then Brearley, who had been back into the study, came running, crying:

"The papyrus! And my translation! Gone!"

I thought of the ashes in Ailsa Brearley's room.

IV

"My friends," rumbled Moris Klaw, impressively, "we are fortunate. We have passed through scorching fires unscathed!"

He applied himself with vigour to the operating of the scent spray.

"God forgive me!" said Brearley. "What did I do?"

"I will tell you, my friend," replied Klaw; "you clothed a thought in the beautiful form which you knew as your sister! Ah! You stare! Ritual, my friends, is the soul of what the ignorant call magic. With the sacred incense, *kyphi* (yes, I detected it!), you invoked secret powers. Those powers, Mr. Brearley, were but *thoughts*. All such forces are thoughts.

"Thoughts are things—and you gathered together in this house, by that ancient formula, a thought thing created by generations of worshippers who have worshipped the moon!

"The light that we saw was only the moonlight, the sounds that we heard were thought-sounds. But so powerful was this mighty thought-force, this centuries-old power which you loosed upon us, that it drove out Miss Ailsa's own thoughts from her mind, bringing what she mistook for sleep; and it implanted itself there!

"She was transformed by that mighty power which for a time dwelled within her. She was as powerful, as awful, as a goddess!

None might look upon her and be sane. Hypnotism has similarities with the ancient science of thought—yes! *Suggestion* is the secret of all so-called occult phenomena!"

With his eyes gleaming oddly, he stepped forward, resting his long white hands upon Fairbank's shoulders.

"Doctor," he rumbled, "you have a bruise on your forehead."

"Have I?" said Fairbank, in surprise. "I hadn't noticed it."

"Because it is not a physical bruise; it is a mental bruise, physically reflected! Nearly were you slain, my friend—oh, so nearly! But another force—as great as the force of ancient thought—weakened the blow. Doctor Fairbank, it is fortunate that Miss Ailsa loves you!"

His frank words startled us all.

"Look well at the shape of this little bruise, my friends," continued Moris Klaw. "Mr. Brearley—it is a shape that will be familiar to you. See! it is thus." He drew an imaginary outline with his long forefinger—

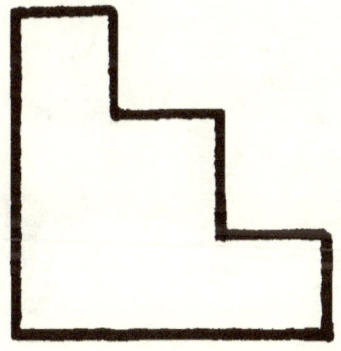

"And that is the sign of Isis!"

COACHWHIP PUBLICATIONS

COACHWHIPBOOKS.COM

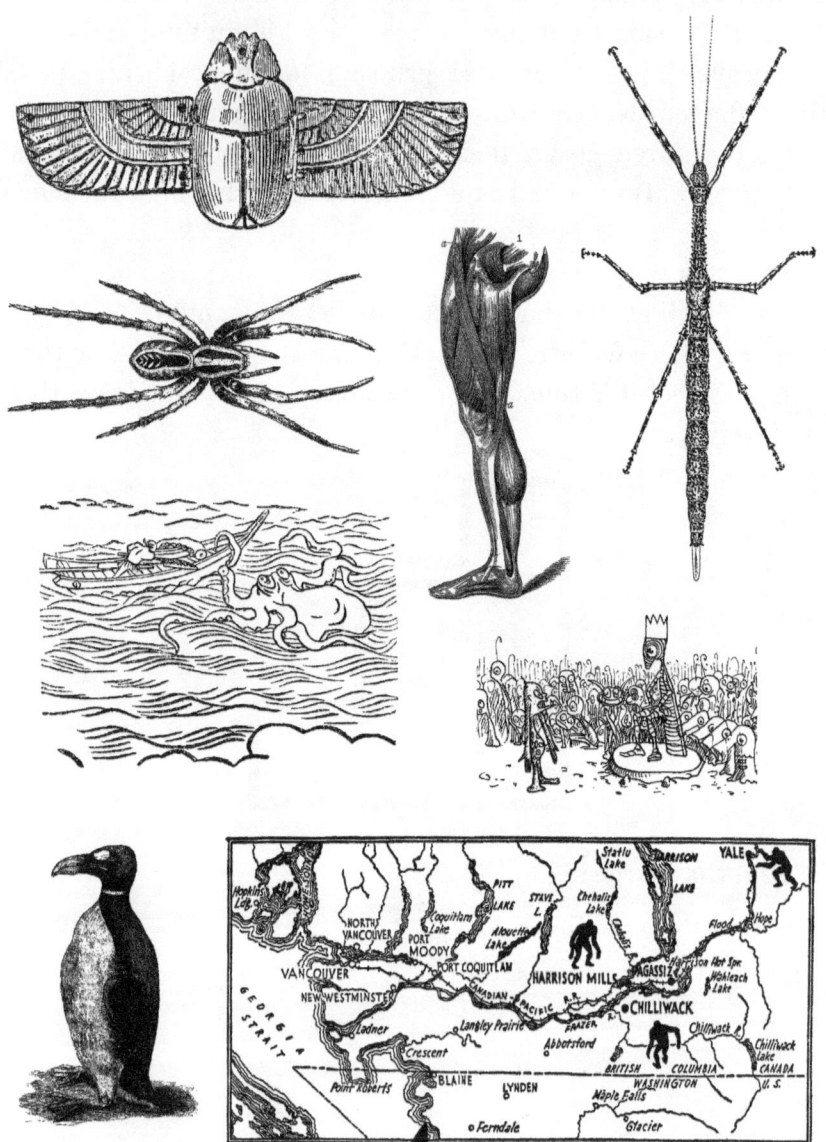

COACHWHIP PUBLICATIONS

ALSO AVAILABLE

CARNACKI: GHOST FINDER
WILLIAM HOPE HODGSON

JOHN BELL: GHOST EXPOSER
L. T. MEADE AND ROBERT EUSTACE

SUPERNATURAL DETECTIVES

Supernatural Detectives 1:
Carnacki / John Bell
ISBN 1-61646-086-5

The Gold Point and Other Strange Stories
ISBN 1-61646-085-7

Ancient Haunts
ISBN 1-61646-005-9

COACHWHIP PUBLICATIONS

ALSO AVAILABLE

BLACK SPIRITS
AND WHITE
RALPH ADAMS CRAM

TALES OF THE
SUPERNATURAL
JAMES PLATT

SHADOWS GOTHIC
AND GROTESQUE

Shadows Gothic and Grotesque
ISBN 1-61646-059-8

THE SUPERNATURAL
STORIES OF MONSIGNOR
ROBERT H. BENSON

THE LIGHT INVISIBLE
A MIRROR OF SHALOTT

*The Supernatural Stories of
Monsignor Robert H. Benson*
ISBN 1-61646-004-0

THE
SPECULATIVE
CONAN DOYLE

TALES OF TERROR, FANTASY,
AND SCIENCE FICTION BY
SIR ARTHUR CONAN DOYLE

The Speculative Conan Doyle
ISBN 1-61646-024-5

John Silence: The Complete Adventures
ISBN 1-930585-90-X